LET'S BE FRIENDS

(THE NURSE NATE SERIES, BOOK 3)

BREA BROWN

WAYZGOOSE PRESS

Edited by Maggie Sokolik

Cover design by Keri Knutson at alchemybookcovers.com

(Note: An earlier, slightly modified edition of this novel, with the same title, was originally published in 2016, ISBN 9781530400232 .)

CONTENTS

For the world's nurses.
I'm proud to say I know a few of you in real life, and you astound me
with your tireless, selfless dedication. You're not in it for glory or
money; you're in it for others.
Thank you!

NEW STATE OF BEING

"LEFT CLICK. NO, LEFT. *LEFT*. DOUBLE CLICK."

Velma, the practice receptionist, calmly continues to look over her bifocals and repeatedly single click the right mouse button, which does nothing on the empty appointment slot in the scheduling program.

"I'm clickin', but it's not workin', sugar!"

"Your other left. This one." I gently grab her knobby index finger and push it down twice onto the left mouse button. The appointment window opens. "There."

"Well, I declare!"

I let go of her hand and wipe the sweat from my forehead with the shoulder of my dinosaur scrubs. "Okay, now. All you have to do is type the patient's name, click the type of appointment it is—which will tell the program the duration—and add any notes in the comments section."

I watch impatiently as she writes each of my words down in her steno pad with her spidery cursive, her tongue poking from the side of her mouth.

"You don't have to write all this down, Velma. After you do it a few times, it'll be second nature. Just try it." I pull the leather-bound, handwritten appointment book closer to us. "Enter Drew Taylor's appointment for tomorrow morning."

She begins typing.

"Not here. This isn't the right appointment time."

"Well, why'd you tell me to open this one then, you goober?"

In spite of my frustration, I laugh. "I was showing you the gist. You have to exit out of here and go back to the calendar, click on the day you want, then open the correct time slot."

She sighs and throws up her hands, backing away from the counter. "Lands, this is complicated!"

"It's really not. C'mon. You can do it."

"That's easy for you to say! You've worked with these things your whole life." She gestures to the computer like it's an unsavory person who's walked in off the street. "I don't see why we can't keep using the appointment book. How is this going to make things easier around here?"

I grit my teeth, grasping for the disappearing ends of my patience. *Because Dr. Reitman and I can't read your handwriting half the time.*

Biting back that response, I simply say, "Because this is how modern practices stay organized. We all have access to this system, from our computers and our phones, 24/7. The appointment book can only be in one place. And the electronic schedule holds much more useful information. Plus it has some built-in fail-safes. I've changed the settings so you get an error message if you try to double-book a slot." I stop, realizing I sound like a salesperson for the software. "Just trust me, V, okay?"

She flutters her lashes at me from behind her large glasses. With a coy blush and a stroke of my forearm, she says, "Oh, Nate. You know I can't say no when you call me V."

Noted. Never calling her that again, no matter how convenient it would be to get my way.

I clear my throat and move my arm out from under her hand. "Right. Well." I nod back at the screen. "Let's practice entering some appointments, okay?"

She sighs, turns back to the book, and studies the entry for Drew Taylor, who's coming in tomorrow for a sports physical. Tongue poking from the corner of her mouth, she runs her finger over the cursive pencil scratchings until she gets to the date and time, then tilts up her head to look at the monitor through her bifocals as she grabs hold of the mouse.

"Now, what do I do with this dillybopper? Left click? How do I do that? I'm right-handed."

"You use the index finger of your right hand, but you click the button on the left side of the mouse. Two times, fast."

"If you say so."

"Click that little 'x' up there in the corner to get out of this appointment. One click will do it."

Miraculously, she does what I've described without any problems.

"Great! Good! That's..." I tone down my exuberance over something my two-year-old daughter could do. "There you go. Now, find the right appointment time for Drew Taylor and click on that."

She does. Once.

"Double-click."

She tries, but her clicks are too slow.

"Faster."

"This is as fast as my finger goes! I have arthur-itis, you know!" Finally, she manages to open an appointment window. Unfortunately, it's the wrong one.

"Wait. That's for this afternoon."

"So?"

"Drew's appointment is *tomorrow* afternoon."

She drops the mouse and pushes it away. "Well, shoot a monkey! See? This isn't gonna work!"

I run my hand through my hair. "It's not a biggie. Close this window, like you did the other one."

"How'd I do that, again?"

"The 'x' in the upper right corner."

She tries to right click it.

"Left click."

She does. Twice.

"Just once."

"Sometimes it's 'click once'; sometimes it's 'click twice'... How the heck am I supposed to remember which is which?"

"You just will."

"What a hassle! Dr. Jacobson never made me do all this. He liked my system." She removes her glasses and lets them dangle from the chain around her neck. "I'll tell you what. I'll keep the book, and you can enter the appointments at the end of each day into the computer, since that's the system you prefer —and you're so much better at it than I am, anyway. It'll be more efficient. Now, I have some cookies in the oven that are about to come out. Let me grab a nice hot one for you."

As she pushes away from the desk and speed-walks toward the kitchen, I call after her, "I don't want a cookie! I want you to learn how to do this!"

Without a backward glance, she waves. "Be right back!"

Dr. Reitman sticks her head, then the rest of her body, through her office door. "Everything all right out here?"

I swallow my disappointment and smile at my boss. "No. But we'll try again tomorrow. Or something." I circumnavigate the counter and walk into my office, careful not to slam the door behind me.

After completing a few paces in front of the window, I

collapse in my chair and open the manila file in the center of my desk, flipping through the pages but not reading a single word.

Several minutes later, a knock on my door startles me from a doze. I clear my throat, then call, "Come in!" and look down at the papers on my desk, like I've been studying them all along.

The door pushes inward an inch or two, and through the crack I see a familiar gray eye and a sliver of thick, blonde bangs, plus the tip of a nose. "Is it safe to come in?" Dr. Reitman asks. The crevice widens. Her hand slips through, holding my steaming "Murses Do It Better" mug in one hand and a cookie in the other. "I come bearing sugar and caffeine. And if it's too late in the day for that, I can brew some herbal tea. Or make a smoothie. Or anything you want. I'll drive to *North* Carolina, if I have to."

I laugh at her theatrics and wave her in. "Get in here. Why should you be scared?"

She heeds my invitation, and when I extend my arms to accept the hot coffee and cookie, she carefully transfers the items to my hands, then sprawls on the couch against the wall, across from my desk. Starting a new practice together hundreds of miles from our hometown has naturally led to a different relationship than the one we had in Green Bay. We're definitely more like friends and business partners here in Jasper, South Carolina, than we ever were up North.

"Because," she answers, "I dragged you to a strange land with the promise of a better life only to bog you down in the business of running a medical practice, where you work longer hours than you ever did in Green Bay. Which is saying something."

I dunk the cookie in my mug and take a huge bite of the dripping snack before it falls apart. After a few more sweet nibbles and restorative sips, I say, "You have a point. And you forgot to mention how freaking hot and steamy it is down here. But this town and this clinic also have their advantages."

The papers on my desk receive a hand wave from her. "Please, tell me. Because the fact that you're looking at invoices for toilet paper and paper towels can't possibly go in the 'plus' column."

Is that what I've supposedly been reading? I close the folder and push it to a corner of my messy desk. Resting my mug on top of it, I brush cookie crumbs from my fingertips. "Yeah, well... I don't work weekends at Urgent Care anymore. No more Dr. Chancellor. Or snowstorms. We're only a couple of hours from several beautiful beaches and the relaxing ocean. *And* I have my own office. With air conditioning." I wiggle my eyebrows and gesture to the sunny room around us, which served as this house's dining room once upon a time, when it was a private residence. "I'd say it's worth having to sift through invoices for butt wipes once in a while."

She pinches her eyes and laughs. "Oh, man. We need an office manager."

"We can't afford one."

"That'll be our first big 'purchase,' then. Priority number one. And until then, we should add supplies ordering to Velma's responsibilities."

I glance nervously at the open door leading to reception.

Dr. Reitman says, "She's gone for the day. Left the rest of the cookies on the front desk for you to take home to Betty. Said 'there's no calories in chocolate chip cookies for mamas-to-be.'"

I groan, because nobody's supposed to know about that yet. I spilled the beans in the clinic kitchen one morning when a bout of Betty's morning sickness made me late for my first appointment. Then I swore the doctor and receptionist to secrecy, but I might as well have said, "Tell everyone, and talk about it all the time," because they won't shut up about it. My only salvation is that Betty never comes to the office, and she and I don't do more than wave to our neighbors or smile at people in parks and grocery stores, so nobody's revealed my bone-headedness to my wife. Yet. It's only a matter of time, for sure.

Now I whine about our receptionist. "She's so nice!"

"I know."

"But so clueless!"

"I know."

Plunking my elbow onto my desk and my cheek into my hand, I ask, "When is she retiring, again? Ever? Do you think we could throw her a retirement party, and she'd go along with it and not show up to work the next day?"

Another laugh-groan bubbles from the doctor. "I don't know. At this point, it may be worth a shot." She holds her thumb and forefinger apart by a half-inch, squinting at the space, as if it holds all her hopes and dreams. "Rob told me she was *this* close to retiring when I took over, so I promised to keep her on." She drops her hand with a slap against her thigh. "But since we've re-opened for business, she hasn't mentioned it to me once. When she does, I'll jump all over it."

"The kids and parents love her; she's great at greeting people when they walk through the door and seeing them out after their appointments—or after they're told they have to come back, because she wrote down their appointment in the wrong place."

Dr. Reitman heaves a huge sigh and sits up, resting her elbows on her knees. "And it's hard enough trying to get to know new-to-us patients; then she scrawls their names so illegibly that I can't even hazard a guess. I suspect she does it on purpose so I have to ask her, and she can show off that she knows everyone in this town."

My face slips against my hand, pulling my mouth sideways when I say, "I called a kid 'Boris' the other day as I walked into an exam room. Then I looked up and saw he was a she. And I was informed her name is Maria. Fortunately, the girl and her mom had a sense of humor about it, but it was pretty embarrassing."

"She's going to have to learn the electronic system. I invested too much money on the software license for us not to use it."

Scooting back a few inches, I kick my feet onto the corner of my desk and lace my fingers behind my head. "I'm trying! But she doesn't even understand the difference between right- and left-clicking. And she calls the mouse a 'dillybopper.'"

A giggle flutters from my companion.

"If we fire her, we'll look like the evil Northerners who deprived the beloved Velma of her livelihood." I drop my head back and stare at the ceiling. "This is a nightmare."

"It's not *that* bad. We need to keep things in perspective."

I level an incredulous stare at her. "Not that bad? How long will this practice survive if we continue to be the dumb Yankees who can't keep their appointments straight? Or get patients' names right? Or we're so exhausted from doing our jobs plus half the things a competent receptionist and office manager would do that we sleepwalk through exams? It's not fair to our patients that I'm sometimes thinking about the cotton swabs inventory when I should be focused on them."

Too late, I remember I'm talking to my boss. Her rapid blinks tell me she's both surprised and dismayed by this information, and maybe I shouldn't have admitted it at all. Sure, things are a lot more casual here, but every once in a while, she reminds me who owns this practice, and it isn't me. I'm just the guy who orders the toilet paper.

Before I can backtrack, she stands and says, "I'll take care of Velma, I promise. I'll talk to Rob and see if he has any ideas. Coping mechanisms."

I stifle a yawn. "M'kay."

"You look tired." She states it like an unfortunate diagnosis.

"So do you."

"My name's on the sign out front, so I'm supposed to look tired."

"It'll get better. At least we have patients. I was afraid nobody would want to bring their kids to the Yankees."

"Lookie-loos, most of them," she says, playing with the tail of her French braid.

"Hey, who cares how we get them in the door? As long as we provide the best care—"

"And don't call little girls 'Boris'..."

I laugh. "And that." Relocating the optimism that brought me here in the first place takes a level of energy I don't think I have, but I manage to muster it. "It'll be okay. I'd say we're doing well, considering we only opened three months ago."

She nods distractedly then claps her hands together once and stands. "Two things for tomorrow, then."

Returning my feet to the floor, I grab a pen and scramble for the cube of sticky notes next to my computer monitor. "I'm ready."

"No need to write it down."

She underestimates my exhaustion.

Instead of saying as much and deepening her apparent guilt, I simply tap the pen against my cheek (partly to keep myself awake) while she continues, "I'll speak to Velma about...

things. Wearing her reading glasses while setting appointments and *printing* the names will be a good start. And you..."

I wait.

She smiles. "Take tomorrow off and enjoy a long weekend."

The pen falls from my hand and skitters across the paper-strewn desk. "But—"

Shaking her head, she interrupts, "Nope. Not negotiable. We don't have anything close to a full load between the two of us, so I can handle it."

"Are you sure?"

"Would I be saying this if I wasn't sure?"

"You seem sure."

"Then get out of here."

I glance at the clock on my computer, which confirms it's only three o'clock.

As if reading my mind, she narrows her eyes at me. "I'm perfectly aware what time it is. And if I remember parenting a toddler well enough, a certain chubby-cheeked cherub will probably be waking up from her afternoon nap and would love to spend some extra time with her daddy."

I shut down my PC, straighten the chaos on my desk into somewhat less messy piles, and grab my coffee mug to take to the kitchen.

She smiles smugly after me and calls, "I knew that would seal the deal! See you Monday!"

2

FAMILY MAN

Juicy air slams into me as soon as I slide open the glass door to exit the clinic's kitchen and step onto the wooden deck off the back of the structure. Technically, we're too far away from the coast to smell the ocean—or so I've been told—but I swear the breeze carries the scent of salt and fish. I like it. Every whiff stirs excitement and elation, akin to that first-day-of-summer-vacation sensation. It reminds me we're not in Wisconsin anymore. We're strangers in a strange land, far away from everything and nearly everyone familiar to us. That means we're also far away from our past problems.

Still. The weight of the air is something I haven't yet grown accustomed to. Even now, in early October, it feels more like an early summer day back home. I exhale audibly and mutter, "Gross," while trotting down the stairs that lead to the gravel parking area. As I round the bottom of the steps, movement from across the sun-bleached rocks grabs my attention. Plate of cookies in one hand, I shield my eyes with the other and, squinting, spy the advancing figure of Dr. Rob Jacobson, the practice's former owner... and Dr. Reitman's current boyfriend.

It's not as awkward or weird as it sounds.

Well, sometimes it is.

"Bustin' out early?" he asks me lightly in his slow drawl, punctuating it with a friendly smile and propping one foot on the bottom step.

"Doctor's orders," I reply, blotting my upper lip. "I thought it was out of concern for her overworked employee, but now I see she may have had an ulterior motive for getting rid of me."

Rob's laugh rumbles deep and loud. Instead of outright denying an afternoon rendezvous with my boss, he simply says, "I wish," which makes *me* wish I hadn't joked about it, since his tone elicits psyche-damaging flashbacks of walking in on my parents last year.

He either doesn't notice my gag/shiver or chooses not to ask about it. "Pat has no idea I'm here. She called me about five minutes ago and asked if we could go to supper tonight so she could discuss something about the practice with me—any idea what that could be?"

"Uh, possibly."

Fortunately, he doesn't ask for me to elaborate. "I was in the neighborhood when she called, so I figured, why the heck not swing by and talk about it now? That way, we can skip the shop talk over supper. It's bad for digestion."

I shift the plate to my other arm and edge into the shade. "Good luck with that, then."

"Should I be worried?"

With a faint chuckle, I shake my head and hit the button on my key fob to unlock my car. "I'm not saying anything. That's on *her* to-do list."

He shrugs. "All right. I suppose I'll find out soon enough."

"That you will. Have a nice evening."

"You too, now."

His shoes swoosh and thump against the wood overhead as he finishes the climb and arrives at the top of the stairs.

"Knock, knock," I hear him both say and do, tapping his knuckle against the glass door. "Did somebody call for a doctor?" A gleeful giggle accompanies the swish of the sliding door.

Dr. Reitman's reply is inaudible as I sit behind the wheel of my stifling car, close the door, and push the power button to start the vehicle.

I breathe through my mouth to try to draw enough oxygen from the stale air blowing through the vents into my face. I'll be home before the air conditioning truly kicks in, so I lower all four windows for the five-minute commute.

I'm not surprised when I arrive home to a quiet house. Depositing the melting cookies in the refrigerator to recover from their sweltering transport, I tiptoe up the stairs to the bedrooms. Georgia's door's still closed, and Betty's sacked out in the middle of our bed, limbs spread like Da Vinci's Vitruvian Man.

As quietly as possible, I shower off the day's germs. When I emerge from the bathroom, clad only in a towel, and see Betty hasn't moved an inch, I tiptoe toward her, grinning in anticipation. Slowly, I lower myself onto the bed, one of my knees between her legs, my hands on either side of her shoulders. The equal weight distribution results in minimal mattress movement. Still, I hold my breath and look down into her peaceful face, hoping she's not going to suddenly wake up and do something like knee me in the crotch.

I gently press my lips to her forehead, then trail kisses down the side of her face, until I arrive at her slightly parted lips. Eyes still closed, she returns my kiss, bringing her arms up to my shoulders and joining her hands behind my neck.

"Mmm," she half-moans, half-murmurs when I pull back a few seconds later. "Hi there, Nathaniel."

"How'd you know it was me?" I whisper playfully next to her ear.

"Who says I did? I was actually hoping it was the guy I was dreaming about."

"Nice."

"Kidding! I know how you taste." Dropping one of her hands, she reaches down and grabs me between my legs. I gasp but hold my position. "I'm extremely familiar with the contours of this guy, too."

"You think you're so clever, don't you?"

"Yes."

"You're right; you are." I grind against her hand.

She exposes her neck to my kisses but tenses. "What time is it? Did I oversleep? We'll never get Georgia to bed at a decent time if—"

"Shh, don't worry about it. I'm home early. And I've been ordered to take a long weekend." I slide my hand up her shirt and cup her warm, rounded tummy against my palm.

Rubbing her hands against my chest, she murmurs, "Mmm... A long weekend, huh? Why? What's the matter?"

"Nothing." My kisses trail lower, until her pesky shirt gets in the way. I tug at it to give her the hint to take it off, then look down into her eyes.

Not moving, she holds my eye contact. "If nothing was wrong, you'd be too busy to take a long weekend."

"Everything's fine. Just go with it."

"Not my forte."

"But good things tend to happen when you do. Remember Atlanta?"

She squints, as if trying to recall. "Vaguely."

"That turned out nice, right?"

"Eventually. I suppose."

Sick of waiting for her, I push up her tank and see she's not wearing a bra underneath. Delighted, I take in the sight of her while she finishes undressing and tosses her clothes to the floor.

"This long weekend thing works out nicely," she says while my fingers roam her naked curves. "I've been promising Georgia we'll go to story time at the library, but I'm too tired to tackle it on my own."

I kiss a line from her belly to her breasts.

"And I hear there's a farmer's market downtown—or what passes for downtown in this place—on Friday evenings and Saturday mornings."

My lips trace higher while she babbles about a dog bakery and popping into the local hardware store for new drawer and cabinet pulls to replace the outdated ones in the kitchen. Mouth against her neck, I say, "Betts."

"Huh?"

"Shut up."

Her throat vibrates with something like a laugh but much sexier. "Well, what are you waiting for, Nathaniel? Take off your towel and take me."

* * *

AFTER A POWER NAP, I practically skip downstairs to find our usual Friday night meal spread out on a large plate on the coffee table. The olives, meat, cheese, hummus, crackers, bruschetta, and fruit beckon, and my stomach yowls its approval.

Betty releases Georgia from her booster seat at the dining table. Our daughter's face, still damp and rosy from its after-dinner washing, lights up when she sees me. "Daddy!"

"Hey, George! Did you eat without me?" On my way to the fridge to grab a beer for me and some water for the pregnant lady, I snag the divided plastic plate from the table and inspect what's left of its contents, smeared across the cast of *Inside Out*. "Green beans and...?" That's all I can ascertain. The girl is a loyal member of the Clean Plate Club.

"Chicken, applesauce, and red potatoes," Betty says, lowering herself to the floor next to the coffee table and loading her own plate while protecting the serving platter from the toddler's curious hands.

I set Georgia's dirty dish in the sink to deal with later. "A real feast."

Georgia waddles over and hugs my legs. Before my heart can melt too much, she demands, "Cookie!"

I coax a "Pwease" from her, then hand her a bite-sized ginger snap from the jar on the counter. She sits on the floor to devour it while I retrieve what I originally came in here for and join Betty in the living room, handing down her water and setting my beer out of her eye line.

"I can still smell it," she states around a mouthful of prosciutto.

"Sorry," I say half-heartedly while fixing my plate and settling on the floor across the narrow table from her.

"Most annoying craving ever."

"You want a tiny sip?"

"No!"

"A tiny sip isn't going to hurt anything, but it might satisfy your taste for it."

"I want to guzzle the whole thing."

"Okay."

She slaps my hand hard enough for me to almost drop my food.

"Hey! I'm just saying. As long as you don't guzzle one a day..."

"Alcohol shall not pass these lips."

"Then stop whining, and let me enjoy my beer." To prove I'm half-kidding, I rise on my knees, lean over the table, and kiss her lips. "Mmm. You taste delicious."

"You've already said that a few times today."

"Can't say it enough."

Without warning, something hard hits me in the temple. "Ow!" I flinch away from the assault and glare at Georgia, who bangs her weapon of choice—a sippy cup—on the floor.

"*My* mommy!" she says sweetly but firmly, cuddling up to Betty's arm.

"Georgia Louise! It's not nice to hit," Betty scolds, nevertheless rewarding my abuser by pulling her into her lap and planting a kiss on her cheek. "Tell your daddy you're sorry."

"Sawee!" The two-year-old sounds about as sincere as I did responding to Betty's complaints about my fragrant beer. Sometimes karma is swift.

I roll my eyes but accept her lame apology as she toddles to the corner where we try to contain most of her toys.

Betty leans back and fans herself while trying not to laugh.

"Real funny," I grumble, palpating the lump on my head.

"Oh, don't be such a wuss."

"I'm not being a wuss! It hurt! And you're not going to laugh if she does that when she thinks her younger brother or sister is getting too much attention. We need to nip that behavior in the bud."

Betty covers her full mouth with her hand and says, "Fine, fine. You're right."

"Darn right I'm right."

"You do realize you sound like Barney Fife right now, don't you?"

I pop an olive into my mouth and chew, deciding not to respond to such a ridiculous—yet accurate—observation.

Instead, after a few bites of meat and cheese and a drink to wash them down, I blow a beer-scented burp her way.

She laughs. "You're such a..."

Smirking, I ask, "What? What am I?"

"I can't say it because there's a child in the room. But it rhymes with 'lick.'"

I wiggle my eyebrows at her. "I'll lick you later."

"You wish."

Ensuring the daddy-beater is still preoccupied, I scoot around the end of the table, closer to Betty, and brush my lips against her smile. "Here. The taste of beer with no guilt," I murmur before kissing her deeply.

She holds onto my shoulders and returns the kiss, then pulls her head back suddenly. "Oh, gosh." Scrambling to her feet, she says, "I'm going to throw up," and runs to the nearest bathroom, where, with no time to close the door, she retches loudly.

I try not to take it personally.

Georgia looks up from her toys and toward the horrible noise. She tilts her head at me. "Mommy?" When she tries to run that way, I intercept her with an arm around the waist.

"She'll be okay. Her tummy hurts. Stay here with me."

For once, she doesn't object—even a toddler knows it's best to keep her distance in this situation—but resumes playing when I set her on her feet.

Nauseated myself now, I wipe my mouth and pack up the food, which I quickly wrap and store in the refrigerator before Betty returns.

When she does, however, she says, "Hey! Where'd my dinner go?"

I blink at her. "In the fridge."

"Why? I wasn't finished."

"I... I thought... You were..."

She stomps past me. "So? I do that about three times a day. If anything, I'm hungrier now that my stomach's empty." Opening the fridge, she slides out the platter, unwraps it, and starts eating right there, standing up, eyes closed with rapture after she pops a piece of smoky Gouda into her mouth.

I'm not sure whether to be turned on or disgusted. Turned on is winning. But barely. And only because there may be something seriously wrong with me.

She holds the plate out to me and says after swallowing, "You want more of this?"

Yes. Yes, I do. Right here on the kitchen floor. But the kid's still around. And I'm worried you'll puke again.

I kiss her temple on the way to the sink. "Nah. I'm finished." When I pour out the rest of my beer, Betty whimpers.

Ignoring her Homer Simpsonesque noises, I say, "Velma made us some cookies."

"Cookies!" Georgia comes running at one of her favorite words.

I laugh and set my bottle in the glass recycling bin, then swoop the toddler into my arms. "You need a bath, George."

Betty continues eating, alternating olive, meat, cheese, and bread dipped in hummus. About the receptionist, she says, "She's so sweet!" After re-wrapping the platter and putting it into the refrigerator for good this time, she leans with her back against the appliance to wait for my agreement.

"Yeah. She's... great." I exit the kitchen with Georgia, hoping to end the conversation there.

Betty follows me down the hallway and leans in the doorway as I turn on the taps, adjust the water temperature, and deposit the toddler on the floor to strip off her clothes while the tub fills.

"So, there *is* something wrong."

"Huh? Who says that?"

"The way you said, 'She's [pause, pause, pause] great,' like you considered about a hundred other words first, none of which are nice."

"I don't have anything more to add. She *is* great."

"But?"

I glance at her over my shoulder. "But nothing. Can you hand me a towel and a wash cloth?" With a final test of the water against my wrist, I turn off the faucet and plunk Georgia onto her slip-free bath mat, where she splashes gleefully. A few bath toys join her, to keep things interesting.

Betty delivers the linens I requested, along with a pointed glare. "Mm-hm. Something's up, but you're not telling me, and that worries me more."

"You shouldn't worry. That shit's not good for the baby."

"Shit!" Georgia parrots.

Betty and I freeze and stare at one another, horrified. Before either one of us scolds the toddler, I shake my head tersely at my wife and mouth, *"Sorry!"* then clear my throat and tap my forefinger against Georgia's rosebud lips. "Oopsie! That's not a nice word, George."

"Shit, shit, shit, shit, shit!" she replies, punctuating each syllable with a splashy slap against the water's surface.

"No, no!" I'm a bit more animated now when I cover the whole lower half of her face with my wet palm to stem the flow of verbal excrement.

She shakes her head and struggles against me. To prevent injury, I let go and hang my head while we wait for the profane concert to end.

When it finally does, Betty sighs and mutters, "Way to go. Let's hope she gets sick of that word before we go out in public."

I'm about as optimistic of that as I am that Betty's going to stop trying to figure out what my problem is.

* * *

JUST AS I THOUGHT, that wasn't even close to the end of that topic. My wife tried to lead me to believe it was, though. She's tricky like that.

After we settled Georgia in bed, Betty turned on one of her ghastly British detective shows; I crammed my earbuds in and watched an assortment of TED Talks on my phone. We sat side-by-side on the couch like that for a couple of hours, hips grazing, feet rubbing against each other from their propped-up positions on the coffee table in front of us, Reba snoring softly on top of the nearby air conditioning vent.

Bedtime rolled around, and without a word, Betty clicked off the TV, I pocketed my phone, and we performed out nightly routine. She put out the dog. I loaded the straggling cups and dishes into the dishwasher and started it. She let the dog back in. I checked the door locks and set the alarm. We peeked in on Georgia together, quietly chuckling at her ridiculous pose and drooling mouth before pulling her blanket more fully over her Buddha body, bursting from her pajama tee and diaper-bulging boy shorts.

Now, in the bathroom, with both of our toothbrushes working furiously, I sneak sly glances at Betty in the mirror, marveling that someone like her would commit to someone like me for eternity. Not only that, but that she would want to produce children with me as an open acknowledgment of our commitment.

My eyes fill, but I pretend it's the minty toothpaste stinging my sinuses, and I lower my head to spit out the foam, blinking away my emotions.

Male PMS. It's a thing. The letters may stand for something different (I propose, Passionate Man Sappiness), but it definitely exists. Don't let macho guys tell you otherwise.

Betty interrupts my composure-gathering by nudging me slightly aside so she can spit, too. While rinsing her brush, she asks, "What's the deal at work?"

I keep my eyes down, like what I'm doing requires all my concentration. She drops her toothbrush into the holder, steps back, and crosses her arms over her chest, waiting for me to answer.

With the utmost care, I slide my brush into its usual slot and answer diplomatically, "It's an adjustment, that's all."

"How so?"

I rest my hip against the edge of the sink, prop my elbow in my hand, and rub my chin. When I can't think of a way to elaborate without segueing into a full-blown rant, I lift my left shoulder slightly. "I don't know. My role isn't exactly what I imagined it would be."

"How so?"

I sigh and drop my arms, edging past her to get to the door. "Please stop asking that."

"I'm trying to understand!"

"There's nothing you can do about it, so what's the point in me complaining about it?"

Following close behind me, she asks, "How many times do we have to have this conversation, Nathaniel? It doesn't matter if I can or can't do anything; I still want to know. I need to know. I *deserve* to know." She throws back the covers on the bed and slides in.

I plug in my cell phone for overnight charging and check the alarm on it one more time. "There's nothing to know."

Legs straight out in front of her, she remains sitting, worrying the edge of the blankets pulled tightly across her abdomen. "You're shutting me out, and it's freaking me out. I have nobody here but you and Georgia."

"You have Dr. Reitman."

"No, *you* have Dr. Reitman. Do I know her? Yes. Are we friendly? Sure, when we see each other, which is rare. Are we best buddies? No. She's my husband's boss. And right now, I have a hunch she's part of the problem."

Shaking my head, I get into my side of the bed and turn off the lamp on my bedside table, then lie on my back, staring at the ceiling. "Dr. Reitman and I are getting along better than ever."

"Mmm-hmm."

"We are! As a matter of fact, a couple of weeks ago, she offered to babysit Georgia for us so the two of us could go out every once in a while. I told her I'd talk to you and get back to her, but I keep forgetting. Would this Saturday work?"

She flicks my head through my hair. "Stop trying to change the subject!"

I laugh. "How is that changing the subject? You brought up Dr. Reitman and hypothesized that she was upsetting me; I provided proof that everything is, in fact, dandy on that front."

She flounces onto her side, facing away from me, reaching up to turn off her lamp and plunging us into darkness. "You're hopeless."

I scoot behind her and curl myself around her, cupping her breast. "C'mon, Betts."

She lifts my hand by one finger and flings it away. "Get your grubby mitts off me."

"You didn't seem to mind what my grubby mitts were doing a couple of hours ago."

"That's not going to work this time. You get nothing until you tell me what's going on at work."

"Fine!" I flop onto my back and run my hand through my hair. Taking a second to organize my thoughts, I finally say, "We're having some issues with Velma."

She rolls and stares at my profile. "I knew it! Like, what kind of issues? She seems so nice every time I talk to her or see her."

I swallow my guilt. "She *is* nice. She's like everyone's favorite grandma."

"So?"

"It's not a personality thing, necessarily. It's... I don't want to work with my grandma."

Releasing a tiny gasp, she whispers, mock-horrified, "That's ageist! And anyway, aren't your grandmas all dead?"

"It has nothing to do with her age. She's not much older than Beulah." I groan wistfully. "Oh, Beulah. What I wouldn't give to have that woman running the office here."

"In what ways is Velma falling short?"

"In what ways *isn't* she? My grandmothers *are* all dead. And probably still more willing to learn how to use a computer. Velma refuses."

"So she's a little technophobic."

"The coffeemaker, Betts?"

She giggles and flips fully on her side, cuddling up to my shoulder.

This is an improvement. Keep talking, Bingham.

As inconspicuously as possible, I drop my arm and press my hand against her lower back, drawing her more tightly to me. "We can't read her handwriting, which is an issue, considering she won't use the computer. And if she were any good at keeping track of the appointments in the book, that might be a different story, but she consistently puts people down on the wrong day or at the wrong time. Then they show up at the agreed-upon time, but according to the book, they're not supposed to be there until the next day or sometimes the next week. And in many cases, someone else is scheduled at the time they thought was theirs."

Betty snorts.

"It's not funny. It's unprofessional!"

She pats my chest. "Okay, okay. Shhh..."

"It's frustrating, that's all."

"Have you sat down with her and shown her the software, step by step?"

"Yes. Disastrous."

"But you're such a good, patient teacher. I'm surprised she didn't get it in a snap."

I pause, trying to detect sarcasm in her tone.

"I'm serious," she says, petting me. "You taught me how to drive your crazy spaceship car without killing us, remember?"

"Velma's not interested. Her answer to learning anything new is, 'You're so much better at it; *you* should do it.'"

"Yikes."

I sigh. "And I'll admit there are other things at work that may be rubbing my nerves the wrong way. I don't particularly like being in charge of ordering supplies, and it's frustrating that I don't have as much authority in this state as I did in Wisconsin. So I may not be as easygoing as usual."

"Since when have you been easygoing?"

"Uh... compared to you, I'm chill."

"Shut up. Back to Velma..."

Relieved I don't have to go into the things at *home* that are putting me on edge, I say, "We can't fire her."

"Nooooo. You can't do that."

"She seems to have no plans whatsoever to retire, though."

"Bummer."

"And we don't want to do or say anything to make her want

to quit, either. That's not us." I kiss the top of Betty's head and say into her hair, "So we're stuck."

She traces her finger absentmindedly along the underside of my pec through my t-shirt and says sleepily, "That sucks, hon. I'm sorry." Her hand stills and falls to rest over my heart.

"I thought moving here would solve all our problems. I've simply exchanged young ones for old ones. Exit Dr. Douche; enter Grandma Moses." When my (admittedly lame) joke doesn't get so much as a titter, I tilt my chin down. All I see of Betty's eyes are her lids, her lashes resting against her cheeks. Her deep, measured breathing, coupled with her departure from the conversation, tell me she's asleep.

It's just as well. I don't want to talk or think about this anymore. And having sex twice in one night would be pushing it (no pun intended) for this guy. I'm not in my twenties anymore. That much is painfully obvious on a daily basis.

3

FIRST IMPRESSIONS

FOR THE FIRST TIME—EVER—I'VE FAILED TO FIND THE perfect pastel-covered book at the library for my next read. Nothing appeals. The new trend in covers appears to be glossy photos of half-dressed, almost-kissing couples. Or worse, merely word art. Blech. I hate to be so shallow, but neither of those appeals.

Anyway, we all do it. Whether it's literally judging a book by its cover or, more figuratively, assuming things about *people* based on their clothes, accent, hair, hometown, or the car they drive, we rely on stereotypes to give our lazy brains a shortcut to figuring out the world around us.

With books, I need vector art to lure me to a story. And with people, I've always gotten the impression—however wrong—that anyone with a Southern accent sounds less than educated. There's something about the consistent dropping of *g*'s from the end of words that sounds apathetic. And apathetic equals stupid, right? No. Obviously not. I'm simply trying to explain (not justify) my Yankee prejudices.

The people here are equally as ignorant of me, although I don't imagine any of them make unflattering judgments about my intelligence based on what Velma calls my "Dutchy" accent. That *is* an incorrect assumption about my ancestry, however. My family hails from Norway, England, Sweden (and eventually Canada), thank you very much, not Holland. Big difference. I think. Anyway.

The point is, I moved here with a dangerous set of stereotypes rattling around in my head about my new neighbors, thanks to pop culture. What I thought I knew about this area of the country was mostly cobbled together from books like *To Kill a Mockingbird* (not even the same region, much less state, but when you're from Wisconsin, the South is all the South, right?); movies like *Steel Magnolias*, *The Help*, and *A Time to Kill*; TV characters like Frank Underwood on *House of Cards*; and reality shows like *Honey Boo-Boo*.

Awful, right? But it's not my fault this region has a serious PR problem. I'm as much a victim of this misleading characterization as the people I prematurely judge based on it. This area has somehow become the whipping boy of the United States. And the people who live here seem to take weird pride in that.

I can't figure it out. So I've stopped trying. And I've made a more conscious effort to approach each new encounter and experience with as few preconceptions as possible. It's not easy, and I often fail, but it's helped with patients and their parents, so I'm counting on it to help in my personal life, too.

It's a no-go with reading material, though. I can't seem to get excited about a book that screams its title at me and nothing else, like a socially inept toddler. I already live with one of those. So I walk away from the shelves empty-handed to join the rest of my family at story time in the children's section.

On the floor, I pull Georgia into my lap and focus on the animated performance of the librarian at the front of the room. I've never heard *Where the Wild Things Are* recited quite like this ("Lyeet the wahld rumpus stahrt!"), but it's entertaining. And Georgia doesn't care. She loves it. In fact, she'll probably learn to talk with a drawl befitting of her name.

Oh, geez.

No, that's okay. My brother will have a field day with that, but screw him. I'd much rather my daughter have a bit of a twang to her speech patterns than have her eat, sleep, and breathe football. That is, if I had to choose.

I look down at her, settled in the nest made by my crossed legs as we sit on the shaggy rug with a dozen other kids and their parents. She's enthralled, her jaw slack as she listens to the hypnotic cadence of the storyteller. Taking her cues from the older kids around us, she occasionally claps her hands or kicks her feet when the other children react to a particularly exciting part of the story.

At the end of the book, she joins the chant of "More, more!" and "Again, again!" but the librarian, whose name tag declares her to be Gwendolyn, simply laughs and says, "Now, y'all! It's time to pick your own books to take home and read!"

This launches the junior attendees into motion. They tug impatiently on the hands of parents who don't have the agility to hop from the floor to their feet in one easy motion, and they implore, "Hurry up! We gotta find the good books before they're all gone!" They spout the characters' strange names like they're best friends. "Let's find Caillou!"

Betty lifts Georgia from my lap, then kindly averts her eyes as I less-than-gracefully stand after sitting in the same position for too long. I tap the circulation into my sleeping right foot and say, "Well, George, what's it gonna be?"

"*Cord'roy!*" she immediately replies with a toothy grin up at me.

"We have *Corduroy* at home, though. Let's find something

new."

"*Cord'roy!*"

Betty tilts her head and smiles. "This oughta be fun."

Not ready to give up yet, I grab a display book from one of the low shelves nearby. "How about this one? It's about a bear, too. But we've never read it."

"*Cord'roy!*"

Her volume is decidedly louder than the typical "library" range, so I kneel down and say quietly, close to her face, "Okay, okay. Shhh. We'll find *Corduroy*. And some new friends, too."

"Hi, there!" comes from above us.

"Hello," Betty replies with an embarrassed smile.

I stand at my full height, coming face-to-face with the perky Gwendolyn. "Oh, hey."

"Did I hear that someone wants to take home a copy of *Corduroy?*"

"Pretty sure they heard that a hundred miles away in Charleston," I mumble, rubbing the back of my neck.

Betty laughs. "Yeah. Sorry about the noise."

"What? Oh, heavens no!" the librarian says with a gentle swat to Betty's arm. "We're not bothered by happy voices, especially in this part of the building. We love 'em! Means someone's excited about readin'!" She lowers herself to Georgia's level. "Hi, I'm Gwen. What's your name?"

Georgia buries her face in my knees.

"Georgia," Betty and I supply at the same time, then chuckle nervously. To give myself something to do, I lift our daughter into my arms and hold her against my side. She transfers her face to my neck.

Gwen rises. "Well, Georgia, that's a pretty name. And I have some great news for you. I saw *Corduroy* this morning, when I was puttin' him back on the shelf. Let's go grab him for you."

This prompts Georgia to look up and kick her feet, almost tagging me in my beanbag. "Down, pwease!"

I gladly set her on her feet and watch her run to keep up with her literary guide. Betty and I follow closely behind, linking hands and smiling proudly at our budding bibliophile.

Could we be any cuter? We're like the perfect family in a literacy ad.

When we catch up to the two G's, the librarian is peering at the spines on the shelf and rubbing her lower lip, her forehead crinkled. "Hmm... It was right here. I shelved it myself."

"Cord'roy!"

Distracted, Gwen smiles. "That's right, Sugar. Your buddy is..." She trails off and frowns. "Oh, dear. It looks like..." Turning to us, she winces and mouths, "It's checked out again."

Dread spreads through my abdomen and climbs my ribcage to my breastbone. Foreseeing an ugly scene, I pick up Georgia, who wriggles in my arms and yells, "*Cord'roy!*"

My tone remains light. "He's playing hide and seek today, but I have an idea where he might be." Close to her ear, I whisper, "He's at home, waiting for you."

She pulls her head away from my lips and gives me the clearest, *Bitch, please*, look I've ever seen from a kid her age— but one that I've received from her mother more times than I care to count. And always before some major unpleasantness. This time is no different.

"I. Yaunt. *Cord'roy!*"

"Yep. I get it, baby girl, but—"

"Not baby guhl! *Cord'roy!*"

Gwen edges away from us. "I'll, uh, leave you guys to..." Obviously at a loss for how to finish that, she points to the circulation desk. "I'll be right over there if you need anything else."

I need flippin' Corduroy, *lady. What kind of library only has one copy of that classic? Huh? HUH?*

Instead of yelling that, I smile tightly and blink against the baby blows falling on my shoulders. Betty takes charge, pulling Georgia away from me and saying, "Georgia Lou, that's enough. Now, let's pick some other books, or we'll leave now, and you'll go straight down for a nap when we get home."

"*Cord'roy!*" she wails.

I blow a sigh through my lips and try to pretend I don't care that everyone is staring at us. Like their kids have never had public meltdowns over a book about a teddy bear. I chance a peek at another dad openly gaping at us and shoot him a sheepish half-smile. He turns away from me to say something to his perfectly behaved sundress-clad princess. Probably telling her, "If you evuh act like that, Little Miss, I'll cut you out of the will. With God as my witness." (Or something. For some reason, he talks like Scarlett O'Hara in my head. So much for abandoning those stereotypes.)

"Okay, let's go," I say to Betty.

"We can't carry her through the whole library like this," she hisses back at me. "She's hysterical."

"Well, take her into the bathroom, then."

"They're by the doors. We might as well leave, at that point."

"Let's do it, then."

"This is humiliating."

"She'll calm down in a second."

"I YAUNT *CORD'ROY!* I YAUNT *CORD'ROY!*"

Desperate to end the nightmare, I snatch Georgia from her mother, toss her over my shoulder like a sack of fertilizer, and, red-faced and sweating, haul ass for the exit.

Just as I think we're home free, pushing through the doors to the parking lot, Georgia bellows a parting "*Shiiiiiiiiiiiiiiit!*" behind us.

There goes the neighborhood.

* * *

AFTER SEVERAL MINUTES OF HOWLING, our demanding diva has finally exhausted herself and is sleeping the comatose slumber of the tear-drained indignant. Last I checked, Betty was face down on our bed with a pillow clamped over her head. Too suffocating for me, so I adjourned to the back yard.

Now, it's probably safe to go back inside, but I'm rather enjoying myself in a masochistic way, out here on the stamped patio, cooking in the late-morning sun... with a beer. It's beer o'clock somewhere. Hell, when you're the parent of a two-year-old, it's always beer o'clock.

Nobody informed my next-door neighbor of that. He keeps sneaking not-so-sly glances my way while he skims bugs from his pool. But that's okay. If he doesn't object to me drinking before noon, I won't ask him to stop tossing the stuff he lifts from the surface of his swimming pool over the fence into my yard, as if I'm not right here. Maybe he thinks I'm too drunk to care.

Eventually, he sets down his skimming pole and calls over to me, "You're makin' me mighty jealous over there, Bubba."

I glance over my shoulder to ensure he's talking to me, then reply, "That's only because you don't know the whole story."

He chuckles and draws closer, hooking his arm over the top of the wooden fence. "I may have heard a little somethin' about your excitin' visit to the library."

I freeze, mid-drink.

Squinting one eye into the sun, he explains, "It's a small town. You'll get used to it. My wife has book club at the library every other Saturday morning. Thinkin' she only goes to get out of the house and away from me and the kids for a couple of hours. I doubt she's ever read the book selection. 'Course, none of 'em do. Seems pointless to me, but I guess she likes it. I'm Winn, by the way. We met once, when you first moved in, but it was just a quick wave."

I lower my beer. "Hey. Yeah. I'm Nate. You're welcome to come over and join me. I'm about to re-beer."

He grins. "Why the heck not?" Unlatching the gate that separates our two yards, he crosses the grass and takes one of the other three chairs at the patio table. I open the umbrella to give us some shade. "Hang on. I'll be right back."

When I return with two more bottles from the beer fridge in the garage, I say, "So. Your wife..."

"Laurel," he fills in the blank.

"Laurel witnessed my humiliation this morning, eh?"

"Yep. Said it was pretty epic."

"Fantastic." I settle into my chair and slouch down far enough that I can rest my head on the low, padded back. "We're the morning-drinking Yankees with the profanity-spewing toddler, I suppose."

"Appears that way, Yank."

"Bottoms up, then." I clink bottles with him.

"Ah, don't worry too much about what people think. We've all been there."

"Your kids yell obscenities in public?" It's hard for me to imagine the well-groomed children I see loading the bus each morning as I'm backing from my driveway doing anything of the sort.

"Nah. But I had one who liked to strip naked every chance he got. And another who was a biter. We've been black-listed from so many playgroups... In fact, that's when Laurel started going to Book Club."

In spite of my humiliation and downheartedness, I laugh.

"I guess every normal kid embarrasses their parents now and then."

"We'll get 'em back when they're teenagers."

"Hell, yes. I'll drink to that."

After a few minutes of companionable silence, I say, "You have two boys and a girl, right? In elementary school?"

He nods. "Yep. Kirby's in fifth grade, Titus is in fourth, and Rumer's in second. She was the biter, by the by, and still pretty feisty when cornered, so... watch yourself."

"Good intel."

"Chances are you'll cross paths with all of them, at some point. We took them to Dr. Jacobson and plan to keep them at the practice on Woodcliff, with the new doctor."

Of course, he knows I work there, despite my never having told him. I'm starting to feel like someone ran a background check on both Betty and me when we moved here and published it in the local paper. Maybe we should get a subscription, for no other reason than to keep informed about what people are saying. Will today's disaster be in Monday's edition? *Pre-Potty-Trained Potty Mouth Terrorizes Tranquil Story Time*.

"I'm sure your kids will like Dr. Reitman as much as they liked Dr. Jacobson."

"Dr. Jacobson seems to like her just fine."

I study him in my peripheral vision and determine there's no malice in his statement; he's merely letting me know he knows. Everything.

I clear my throat. "Yes. Well, yeah. They're... friends."

"More than that, I heard."

"You heard correctly."

Winn peels the label from his bottle. "Ah, well. Good for them. The doc deserves happiness. His wife and only daughter were killed in a car accident on the way home from Hilton

Head Island, oh, a long time ago. Back when I was in high school. He never remarried. Not for lack of tryin' on the part of lots of people in this town. Then your Dr. Reitman shows up, and he goes and falls for a Yankee. That hasn't gone over too terribly well 'round these parts, let me tell you. Fortunately for her, all the people who have their noses out of joint are too old to have kids who need a pediatrician. And *their* kids don't give a crap. For the most part."

"For the most part?"

"There's always gonna be a few snobs and busybodies who hold grudges and don't take to outsiders, just like their mamas and daddies. Y'all don't want their business anyway. Buncha helicopter parents with nothin' better to do than walk behind their kids, wipin' their asses all the way to college... and then some."

I snort at the mental image.

"I guess what I'm tryin' to say is, people around here like to talk, because they don't have anything better to do. Most of 'em are still good folks, though. And they'll always be polite to your face. Southern hospitality demands it." He wiggles his eyebrows at me.

"What do you do for a living, then? I feel a bit underinformed in this conversation."

Swatting at a fly, he stomps his flip-flop-clad foot. "Aw, I help my daddy with the family business."

"Which is?"

"We own the hardware store and lumber yard in town."

I almost ask, "Which one?" out of habit, but his use of the word "the" tells me there's only one, so I inquire instead, "And business is good?"

"Business is always good. People in this area have money, and people with money like to build houses. Or build onto and restore the houses they already have, many of which are dinosaurs that have been in their families for generations. We're never hurtin' for business. My great-grandfather was a real bastard, but he set us up for life when he opened that store."

"You can't choose your family, but you can hope they find some way to redeem themselves, I suppose."

"Amen, bruthuh." He sets down his now-empty beer on the table and wads up the shredded label in his hand, then stuffs it in his shorts pocket. "Anyway, I don't have as large a share in the company as my dad, uncles, and cousins..."

That explains the modest house in the modest neighborhood next door to modest moi.

"...but that means I don't have to do as large a share of the work, if you get my drift. And I don't have to make heavy decisions, like who to hire, who to fire, and what brands of caulk we keep on the shelves."

"What *do* you do, then?"

"I go to work and play. I'm the resident do-it-yourself expert. Every once in a while, I run kids' workshops on the weekend. And I host a video blog—a 'vlog' if you're down with the lingo—for simple fixes around the house. Best of all, when I'm not at work, I try not to think about work."

"Sounds great."

"It is. Zero responsibility. But it pays for my house, my cars, my boat, and my pool, with plenty left over for a couple of family vacations every year... and then some."

"And your other relatives don't resent you or gripe that you don't pull your weight?"

He laughs. "That's none of my business. And if they do feel that way, it's because they're jealous they didn't think up such a sweet gig for themselves."

Betty comes to the back door and stands in its frame. "Hello," she says shyly to Winn, who rises. "Oh, don't get up because of me. I was just checking with Nate to see if he had any ideas about lunch. Besides liquid."

I could murder a radish and mayo sandwich right now, but saying that will only invite ridicule—or vomit—from my wife, who doesn't understand my affinity for the admittedly strange food combination I've loved since my paternal grandfather introduced me to it when I was little. Something tells me a meat-and-potatoes guy like Winn wouldn't get it either.

I turn my head slightly to look at her and answer, "I'm not picky, hon. You're the one who's always hungry."

She shoots me a warning glare when Winn laughs at my statement.

"Dang, Yank. You better watch it," he says from the side of his mouth.

Before I can defend myself, Betty laughs at his reaction. "It's okay. He's right. And I *am* hungry right now, so..."

Winn claps his hands. "How's this, y'all? Let me fire up the grill, and we'll have us an impromptu poolside bar-bee-cue. Whatd'ya say?"

Betty and I exchange looks that convey we're both okay with that, but Winn continues as if we need further convincing. "C'mon. You'll be doin' me a favor. It'll get my kids out of the house, and the missus will think I'm a real swell guy for doin' the cookin' today."

I haul myself to my feet. "Sounds great. What can we bring?"

"Yourselves. Oh, and maybe some more of that beer. I've never had anything like it, but it's excellent!"

I nod while mentally taking stock of the Titletown beer I brought with me from Wisconsin. Since drinking before noon —and drinking alone, in general—isn't a habit of mine, I still have plenty, more than I can drink before it goes skunky. "You got it. Give us a few minutes, and we'll be right over."

BETTY TO THE RESCUE

A FEW DAYS LATER, I PULL BACK FROM THE SIDE OF PAISLEY Martin's head, turn off my otoscope, and declare, "Swimmer's ear."

Her mom tuts from her chair as if I've diagnosed her ten-year-old with an STD.

"Not a biggie." I smile reassuringly. "Although, I must say, being from Wisconsin, it's crazy to be diagnosing swimmer's ear in October. They're practically ice fishing back home by now." I wink at Paisley, who giggles and then winces, cupping her hand over her ear.

Mrs. Martin says, "If I've told her once, I've told her a thousand times, do *not* go underwater at that fishin' hole at your granddaddy's. Who knows what's lurkin' in there? Sewage, probably. She had pink eye twice last summer, because she insisted on openin' her eyes underwater. And now this! We have a pageant next week, and if you think a cotton ball in your ear is the hot new accessory, think again."

I clear my throat and keep my eyes down on the prescription for ear drops, one of the few 'scripts I'm qualified to write in this state. "Next week? You should be good to go by then,

Paisley, if you and your mom remember to put the drops in your ears when you're supposed to." I sign and hand over the piece of paper to Mrs. Martin. "Two to three drops, three to four times a day, every day for five days." To the patient, I say, "And stay out of the water for the next week or so, all right? Give that ear time to heal."

"Oh, don't you worry about that," Mrs. Martin says. "I'll be watchin' her like a hawk." She stands, and Paisley hops down from the examination table.

Before opening the door to the room, I say to Mrs. Martin, "And if things don't get better in a few days—or if they get worse, or she starts complaining of a sore throat or runs a fever —bring her back in, and we'll start her on a course of oral antibiotics, too."

For the first time, the mother looks more worried about her kid's health than annoyed or embarrassed (or fretful about the impact on a beauty pageant). "Is that common?"

I shrug. "Not overly. Depends on how hearty that bacteria is in the ear canal and how well the drops reach it and kill it. Keep an eye on things and follow the directions on the drops to the letter. And even after she's feeling better, keep using them for the full course."

She nods solemnly.

Clipping my pen to the V in my scrubs collar, I turn to Paisley. "Hey, good luck with that pageant."

She shrugs morosely. "Thanks. I guess."

I laugh. "You don't sound very excited."

Her mom steps forward and beams down at her. "Oh, she *loves* it! What little girl wouldn't? She's just feelin' under the weather today, isn't that right, Princess?"

With a shaky smile and another "I guess," the fifth grader allows herself to be led from the room and down the hall to the waiting area and out the front door. I watch after them for a while, contemplating how most "princesses" don't like swimming in muddy fishing holes and wearing cut-off denim shorts and dirty canvas shoes. Makes me wonder how out of touch Mrs. Martin is with her daughter.

Fortunately, I'm only in charge of assisting parents with the physical side of child rearing, but the psychiatrists' kid inside me can't help but shake his head at the tough truths some people—Mrs. Martin included, it seems—eventually have to face when their dreams for their kids don't mesh with their children's personalities.

My own parents did, for sure. Maybe not to the extent of a beauty queen with a tomboy daughter, but they still had expectations that I fell short of. When I fell in love with pediatric nursing and my brother, Nick, decided he wanted to cut people up and sew them back together, we abandoned the original plan of becoming general practitioners in private practice and never looked back. Given our personalities, our diverging career paths were definitely for the best.

Mom and Dad recognize that. Now. At the time, it wasn't that simple. Nick and I would have made a complementary team (jerk doctor/nice doctor), but I blinked first, so I was perceived to be the killer of the dream. Never mind that Nick admitted he no longer shared the same dream either; he was still going to be a doctor. In fact, he was going to do one better and become a thoracic *surgeon*. Meanwhile, I was *just* going to be a nurse.

And now, years later, I can't imagine working with my brother every single day. I'd suffer from "bro" overload—in more ways than one—and wind up in a mental institution. Or prison.

In the wake of Paisley Martin's visit, I wonder what expectations I have for Georgia's future that won't match up with what she wants. It's not like I have any preconceptions for her, career-wise, but every parent has *some* hopes and dreams that can easily be derailed by life. Even if those hopes merely entail her being happy and healthy, a multitude of things can get in the way. Bad habits, gross boyfriends, teenage angst, and piercings and tattoos come to mind immediately. How am I going to react to the less-than-ideal situations when they arise? I have a sneaking suspicion I won't be very relaxed about it.

I'm so deep in my thoughts that I start to imagine hearing my little girl's voice. I blink and shake my head, then mobilize, sanitizing the exam room for its next patient.

That's when I hear it again.

"Daddy!"

Only this time, Betty's voice floats down the hall after it. "In a second, sweetie. Daddy's busy. Come here and look at these— Georgia Louise, you better get your diapered butt back here right now!"

I stride to the door and place one leg into the hall in time to see my daughter run for it, her chubby legs moving much faster than she can control for long, her blue eyes wide and her mouth pursed in a tiny "Oh" as she careens toward me.

"George! What are you doing?"

"Disobeying her mother," Betty says, trotting behind and snatching her right as the toddler loses her balance for good but before she faceplants on the hardwood floor.

While Georgia flails and screeches, Betty holds tight, blowing a strand of hair from her own eyes and tightening her lips in a straight line.

"What's up? Is everything okay? Oh, no, what's wrong?" Because immediately, I go there, assuming my wife and child are here to see the doctor. I step forward and press my hand to Georgia's forehead, which isn't easy, considering it's a moving target.

"She's fine," Betty replies. "If you call 'ornery' and 'rebellious' fine."

"I call it typical toddler behavior." Since I haven't dealt with any patients exhibiting symptoms of communicable diseases today, I bend my usual "no contact" in my scrubs rule and take Georgia from her mother before she causes one or both of them bodily harm. "Hey," I say to calm her down, "chill." After she heeds my gentle command, I kiss her round, rubbery cheek. "What are you guys doing here?"

Betty places her hands on her hips and pauses to catch her breath, then answers, "Helping you guys out."

I tilt my head at her.

She glances over her shoulder to check we're still alone in the hallway. The coast is clear, but she bobs her head toward my office door closer to the front of the building. "Let's go in there, and I'll explain."

* * *

IN MY OFFICE, it looks like a mega toy outlet blew up. As soon as I set her down, Georgia runs to the middle of the mess and grabs two stuffed animals, who commence beating the crap out of each other. A doll, a dump truck, and a few board books lay scattered around her, too.

"What the heck?" I wonder, tossing the damp paper towel from my hands into the wastepaper basket next to my desk.

Betty smiles sheepishly at me while closing the door. "Sorry for the invasion, but I wasn't sure how long we'd be here, and I didn't want her to get bored, so... I may have brought a few too many things with us."

"You planning to live here for the rest of the week?"

"No, but I called Dr. Reitman this morning and volunteered to lend a hand with some things."

"Like?"

"Training Velma on the computer."

I toss my head back to laugh, banging it on the door. Rubbing the tender spot on my scalp, I walk farther into the office and, still laughing, sputter, "Good one."

"No, seriously."

My laughter trails off like a trombone whose player has run out of air. "Now... what, now?"

She shrugs and perches on the arm of the couch, her hands hanging between her knees, which bounce as she taps her toes, alternating between her left and right foot. "I figured, why not? You guys are in a bind; I have the time and the skills."

"And hopefully the patience."

"It'll be fine. And you'll have one less thing to worry about."

"Except now I can add to the list you or George picking up some random bug from this place."

"Don't be such a germaphobe, Nathaniel."

"And did you say you *volunteered* to do this? Meaning, no pay?"

With a long-suffering sigh, she replies, "I hardly felt right asking to be paid, since it was my idea. Plus it'll be my only focus, so I can't imagine it'll take *that* long."

I'm about to disabuse her of her misconception, but the determined look in her eye tells me it's no use. She's going to have to see for herself what a massive task she's undertaken.

After sucking my lips against my teeth, I say, "Alrighty then. Good luck with that. In the meantime, George is just going to hang out here, in the oversized playpen that is my office?"

"She can play in the waiting room, if you'd rather."

"No!"

With a smirk, she stands. "That's what I thought. As long

as you keep your door open, I can keep an eye on her from the check-in desk while you're with patients."

We meet in front of the door. "You've thought of everything, huh?"

Gripping the handle, she grins and kisses me in a way that conjures fantasies a pediatric nurse should never imagine at work. "We'll try not to be a distraction," she says in that husky way that gives me InstaBoner®.

Behind us, Georgia bangs one of her books against the side of the plastic dump truck and chants, "Daddy, Daddy, Daddy!"

"Too late," I reply, holding the door closed while I steal one more kiss... right before I receive a karate chop to the back of the knee.

5

ON THE SPOT

EVERY FRIDAY NIGHT AND SATURDAY MORNING, THE GOOD folks of Jasper sacrifice three "downtown" blocks and divert traffic so that vendors can set up tents and booths and sell their wares at the Farmer's Market. Unlike the one we frequented in Green Bay during the spring and summer months, though, most of the participants here are actually farmers. Much like the one in our hometown, however, most attendees aren't here to do their produce shopping. They're like Betty and me—on an overdue date, walking the floodlit promenade hand-in-hand, people-watching, sampling jams, jellies, fruits, veggies, cheeses, and dips. They're here to see and be seen, to break up the monotony of isolating small-town life without sitting in a pew or pushing a grocery cart.

Betty and I walk shoulder-to-shoulder with strangers who aren't strangers to each other. And they seem to know us, which is weird... but expected. Actually, not all of them are strangers to me, either. I've recognized quite a few people from the clinic. It's nice to be able to nod and smile, then say hi and not talk about green mucus or pus-filled wounds. It's good to get out and be seen in something besides scrubs.

Walking beside my beautiful wife also goes a long way to proving I'm a semi-normal guy. *"See? She married me. Right? I can't believe it, either."* Having Georgia with us would have been a nice touch (or maybe not, after the whole story time thing), but there will be other chances for that. Tonight is about catching up with each other, without catching flying sippy cups on the side of the head. Taking Dr. Reitman up on her offer to babysit was the best decision we've made all week.

"This is nice," Betty says, squeezing my hand and resting her head against my upper arm in a modified hug that doesn't require stopping and impeding the flow of foot traffic.

"Yeah. It is."

"Reminds me of home."

"Not 'home' anymore, though, right?"

She smiles up at me. "Always will be, I'm afraid. Moving here has only reinforced that. You can take the Yankee out of the North, but you can't take the North out of the Yankee. Or something like that."

"Don't say that too loud out here," I warn, smiling at a couple of harried parents trying to navigate through the throng without losing their two running and weaving children.

Glancing over her shoulder at them as they pass, yelling their kids' names, Betty says, "Oh, gosh. That's us in a year. Maybe."

"We can get leashes."

She snorts at me, then glares. "Wait. You *are* kidding, right?"

"Of course. Duh. Although I might recommend them for that family."

Without warning, Betty steps out of the stream of market-goers to further explore a booth that's caught her eye: a hodge-podge of handmade purses hanging from wooden racks and soaps and lotions stacked neatly in boxes on tables and stands.

Still attached to her hand, I have no choice but to follow, ducking to avoid hitting my head on the entrance to the tent. I smile uncertainly at the sweaty, heat-flushed husband and wife duo sitting behind the table. They look less amused by this activity than the people free to roam up and down the street. Judging by their full table, they haven't had much business so far this evening. They might sell more stuff if they'd wipe those sour looks from their faces.

"Hey," I say, when my smile gets me nowhere. I get a reluctant, "Ev'nin'," for my trouble.

Fortunately, Betty moves from the table to the racks, so our backs are turned to the happy couple. "Tough crowd in here," I mutter near Betty's ear.

She inspects the seams on a purse, then fingers the price tag. "They probably get sick of window shoppers. Or maybe they had a fight while they were setting up. What do you think of this one?" She holds up a large quilted bag adorned with beads and fringe and featuring an animal print of sorts, although the most experienced zoologist would be hard-pressed to identify which beasts had mated to result in *that*.

"Hideous," I answer immediately. "And huge."

Undeterred by my disgust, she lifts it higher and turns it to and fro, then loops it on her shoulder to check its fit. "It would be a cute diaper bag."

"I'm not carrying that thing," I mumble from the side of my mouth, glancing anxiously toward Ma and Pa, who are watching us like they're expecting us to steal their ugly creation. Again, I smile and nod, but I quickly turn back to Betty and lean closer to her to say, "If you feel sorry for them, buy some soap."

"I don't feel sorry for them. I legitimately like this bag. It's out of my price range, though." She loops its strap over the wooden peg where she found it.

Thank God.

Some more customers enter the tent, drawing our hosts' attention away from us. Apparently, the vendors are acquainted with the newcomers and like them a heck of a lot more than they like us. I should have never spoken. It immediately branded me as "not from around these parts" and garnered suspicion.

As did my clothing. Everyone else, including Betty, is wearing some form of long pants while I stubbornly hold to my shorts and t-shirt, because I don't care what the calendar says, it's still too freaking warm for fall clothes. For some reason, my choice of attire annoys people down here. It earns more stares than my accent, even. And that's saying something.

While Farmer and Mrs. Dour yuk it up with their more welcome customers, Betty transfers her attention to the goat milk soaps in the wooden divided boxes on the side tables. Starting at the top and working her way down, she picks up each bar and sniffs, then pulls a face to signify, "Ew," "Interesting," "Meh," or "Mmm!" Since there are approximately six thousand scents on this table alone, we're going to be here a while. I watch her reactions for a while but eventually decide I might as well entertain myself during her evaluations.

"How's it going with Velma? You've been tight-lipped about all that."

She lifts her shoulder toward her ear and gags—presumably at the cilantro and hibiscus cube she quickly re-shelves.

I laugh. "That great, huh?"

"She's not that bad."

"Liar."

"She's super-nice."

When all I can do is laugh more intensely, she says over the noise, "She seems to be trying, so I don't want to badmouth her. That would be mean."

"It's not badmouthing to tell the truth and admit she's a lost cause when it comes to technology. That's a simple fact."

"Your appointments are in the computer now. And you didn't have to do any of your own insurance coding this week."

"Because you did it. Am I right?"

Her jaw tightens, confirming my suspicions. "I'm not giving up. Plus she bakes the most amazing chocolate chip cookies I've ever had. Ever." She inhales a huge whiff of Blueberry Cream, her eyes closing in rapture.

"Someday, you won't be pregnant, and food won't hold as much sway. But you'll still be trying to teach her the difference between left- and right-clicking."

Her eyes reopen. She keeps the blueberry soap in hand and picks up another sniff candidate. "Shut up. She'll be good to go long before I have this baby."

I edge down the table, out of smacking range. "Doubt it. But you keep telling yourself that."

"Okay, it's more challenging than I thought it was going to be," she admits, following me. She leans over to examine the labels on the next row of bars.

"Mm-hm. You thought I was exaggerating."

"You tend to do that, Nathaniel." She brings a cake up to her nose, then holds it out for me. Apparently, this one requires my approval before becoming a serious candidate for adoption.

"But in this case, I was downplaying her cluelessness." I sniff experimentally, then harder when I like the initial whiff of spearmint and rosemary. "Nice."

Suddenly abandoning the rest of the as-yet-unsniffed soaps, she pays for the two in her hands.

When we're alone again, standing to the side in the now-crowded tent as Betty sorts through her change and tucks her wallet back into her purse, she says, "For once, your assessment was accurate. She's... resistant to change and learning new things."

"That's putting it mildly."

"That's sticking to the facts."

"The fact is, she calls anything more modern than the electric typewriter a 'newfangled contraption,' and everything she doesn't want to learn to use is a 'complicated doohickey.'"

Betty laughs and hands me the bag with her purchases. "Not everyone embraces technology, Nathaniel. Don't be a jerk about it."

I duck from the tent and follow her down the promenade. "I wouldn't, if it didn't prevent her from performing her *job*. She could be the biggest Luddite on the planet if all she had to do all day was bake cookies and crochet blankets."

"Speaking of, is that blanket she's working on for us?"

Aw, snap.

I pull the corners of my mouth down in an innocent frown, pretending to consider it for the first time. "Is it?"

"I don't know why it would be, since we haven't told anyone our news yet. Right?"

Swallowing, I move to the next booth, wishing there were something more interesting here than mums and hay bales. As if the topic bores me, I say, "Right. Maybe she's knitting it for Georgia."

"It's green and yellow."

"So?"

"If it's for Georgia, don't you think she'd go with more feminine colors?"

"What the heck are 'feminine colors'? Could you be more sexist?"

"Green and yellow are gender neutral. Like something

you'd use if you didn't know the sex of a baby. Because it was too early for you to know *anything*."

"Our... situation... is still private." *Oh, sheesh. Forgive me for lying, but I want to live!* "It must be for someone at her church. Or maybe for herself. She might like those colors. And what's with the third degree here, anyway? Hey, aren't these mums... mumm-y?"

She slaps my shoulder. "You are such a dumb-ass."

"What? They'd look nice on our front porch. I like these maroon ones."

"You care about flowers almost as much as you care about football. Look at me."

Reluctantly, I do. But I pretend it's all I've ever wanted to do. Gazing down into her face, I say, "I love you."

"You totally told them, didn't you?"

"Betts, I hate to break it to you, but the minute you walked into the clinic last Wednesday, they knew." *Technically the truth.*

"I'm not showing yet, with clothes on."

"Not because of that." *Let's try...* "You're glowing."

"That's called sweat."

"Also, it was a dead giveaway when you had to run to the bathroom in the middle of helping Velma transfer the appointments from the book to the scheduling program. The whole waiting room heard 'The Revenge of the Curds.'"

She groans. "Oh, gosh. I'll never eat cottage cheese again. Or any cheese curds, for that matter."

I overlook her blasphemy in order to drive home my point. "So don't blame me." *Even though you most definitely could and should.* "I don't understand why it has to be such a big secret, anyway. Nobody around here knows us well enough to care, and nobody who would care is here to annoy the crap out of you with their well-meaning advice, gross anecdotes, and over-protective coddling."

Grabbing my hand, she pulls me away from the mums—I guess we're not getting any of those. Pity. They *would* look nice on our porch—and leads me through the crowd, walking as close as she can to me without stepping on my feet. At the first unoccupied bench we encounter, she sits and, squinting up at me, says, "I'm afraid something will happen. Then people will have to be sad for us. I don't want that again, especially from strangers. It was awful last time."

I sit next to her so I'm no longer backlit by the floodlights lining the street behind me. Wrapping my arm around her shoulders, I pull her to me in a side hug. "I get it, but we're almost to the second trimester. We can relax a little."

"'Almost' doesn't cut it. And even after that... things happen."

I know she knows she doesn't have to tell me, of all people. I also know she's saying it so I'll contradict her. But I can't. Things *do* happen. However, I have to pretend like this is routine, and I'm not worried at all, because she's obviously worried enough for both of us, so I need to be strong. And upbeat.

I'm seriously under-qualified for the job.

The problem is, my pep talks sound insincere and over-the-top, but if I keep my mouth shut, it comes off like I'm silently fretting. Because I am. But not all the time. I truly believe what's meant to happen will happen. How trite does that sound, though? Really trite. And passive, like we have no control or stake in the outcome. Betty has little patience for "trite" and zero tolerance for "passive." The one time I made the mistake of saying the baby we lost "wasn't meant to be" was nearly the end of me. I was only trying to make some sense of it. Turns out, I was being clueless and insensitive.

Since "what's meant to happen will happen" is merely a variation of that taboo sentiment, I'm determined not to say it out loud. That doesn't mean I don't believe it, though. I have to believe it.

But Betty can't. I get that. She's a take-charge woman, which is incredibly admirable (and hot). That means this current situation is difficult for her, though. So as futile as her efforts with Velma are, they're good. Leaving the house every day to focus on something outside of being a wife and mom gives her a much-needed reprieve from her relentless *what if*s.

My silence could be misconstrued as apathy, like I'm not at all worried, but I do worry. Plenty. I close my eyes and see that toilet bowl and wonder how we made it through that the first time. The thought of going through it again brings on panic attacks. My way of coping has been to deny the possibility. On my best days, I pretend the first time never happened. Not to us. That was some other couple. Some other baby.

Now, I say, "Hey, let's keep moving. I promised George I'd bring home some little pumpkins for us to paint."

"That'll be fun," Betty replies, sniffing, blinking, and smiling. "I saw a booth with smaller gourds and stuff on the other side. We can catch it on our way back."

I stand and offer her a hand up. "Sounds great."

"First, though, I need to find something to eat. I'm so hungry, I could puke."

Lovely.

6

BUDDING BROMANCE

THE PIERCING WHINE OF A POWER SAW WAKES ME FROM A deep sleep the next morning. I squint at the time projected onto the ceiling from the clock on my nightstand, but the numbers don't compute. Why is that sound happening when the first digit in the time is a three? How? What? Who?

I sit on the side of the bed and glance over my shoulder at Betty, whose ears sport a pair of hot pink foam earplugs. The only thing she's hearing right now is her own breathing—and occasional snoring (although she'll deny that until her dying day). Crossing to the window that overlooks our backyard, I separate two white wooden blinds at eye level and peer down. A single suspect emerges when I glimpse the light spilling from the open double doors of Winn's shed.

And I thought we could be friends.

"What the hell?" I grumble, grabbing the first pair of scrubs bottoms to meet my hand in the closet. From a standing position, I hop into the pants and tie the drawstring, then flap the bottom of my t-shirt over the waistband.

When I open the bedroom door, Reba decides whatever I'm doing warrants her attention and follows me down the hallway, pausing when I do to check on Georgia. The toddler's obviously inherited her mother's talent for deep sleep, although she uses a sound machine, not earplugs. I turn up the volume a notch on the whooshing ocean coming from the plastic box on her dresser and back from the room, silently shutting the door behind me.

At the back door, I slip on the flip-flops I keep there for convenience and exit the house, the dog so close, her cold, wet nose presses against my ankles. At the gate, I say, "Stay. I'll be right back. Go pee on some things. But don't eat any grass." Cleaning up her barf later is the last thing I need.

I cross my neighbor's yard and stand in the open doors of his shed, inhaling the sharp tang of freshly cut treated lumber. For a few seconds, I watch undetected while my neighbor marks slabs of wood with a flat pencil he then tucks under the band of the industrial hearing protection he's wearing. He cuts along the markings and tosses the smaller pieces onto a pile of similar-sized and -shaped wood, letting up on the arm of the saw, which comes to a stop, leaving a sound vacuum.

When I transfer my hands to my hips, the movement grabs his attention, and he flinches, then yanks off the bright orange headphones. "Shootfire! You scared the stuffin' out of me, Yank!"

"Did I? Wow. Sorry."

"Coulda cut off my dadburned finger."

Seeing for myself that wasn't a threat, I blink, unimpressed. "Let's call it even, since you woke me before sunrise on a Saturday."

He smiles sheepishly. "Didn't realize you could hear this in your house. You might want to consider replacin' those windows and beefin' up your insulation. It'll save you money on your energy costs, too."

"Save the sales pitch. What the heck are you doing?" I

gesture at the pile of sawdust at his feet and the mound of smallish squares and rectangles behind him.

"I have a kids' workshop at the store later this morning, and I sorta chose to spend time out on the boat yesterday—it was a gorgeous day, wasn't it?—rather than preppin' my materials. We're makin' birdhouses."

"Oh, of course. Birdhouses. Critical. I was thinking maybe your roof caved in and you were out here, performing some emergency repairs, but birdhouses... Totally worth waking up the neighborhood."

He laughs as he bends over to retrieve the pencil that fell into the sawdust when he removed his headphones. "You don't have to be all sarcastic. Plus, it *is* a worthy cause. Before you know it, we'll be overrun by your feathered Yankee refugees, escapin' the cold, stoppin' through on their way to warmer places south of here. Gotta get these little motels up so they have restin' spots." He spins the pencil across his knuckles.

"Do you do this often, work with loud power tools when every other normal person is trying to sleep?"

Shoving the pencil behind his ear, he shrugs. "Occasionally."

"And nobody's ever complained before?"

"Naw. I always figured nobody could hear. But maybe they just accepted it as another one of my eccentricities."

I sigh and scratch my noggin, feeling for the first time how epic my bedhead is. Too tired to care.

I wave and half-turn away from him to leave, but he stops me. "Yank. Man. I'm sorry. For real. Did I wake up your baby girl, too?"

I swivel at the waist to face him and answer, "No. Apparently, I'm the only one in my family with normal hearing."

"Let me make it up to you. Come by the store later on. The

workshop starts at ten. I'll help you and Georgia build a birdhouse."

I snort. "We both fall outside your target demographic."

"It's never too soon to show a kid how to build. C'mon. It's a real simple project, and I bet she'll love the paintin' part."

That detail reminds me of the pumpkins we have waiting for us to paint later, when I'll no doubt be tired and short on patience, thanks to this lovely interruption in my sleep cycle. I scrape my hand along my stubbly jaw. "Uh, pass. But thanks anyway."

"You drive a hard bargain. How 'bout this, then: I'll take you out on the lake later. Just you, me, and the boat. Some guy time."

"That's much more appealing."

"Let's do it, then. I should be ready to go by about two o'clock. You bring the beer?"

"I'll bring the beer," I agree, shuffling away.

"Awesome. And Yank?"

I stop at the gate but keep my back to him. "What?"

"I, uh, really need to get this wood cut, so..."

I raise my hand in a resigned wave. "Whatever. I'll deal."

"You're the best! See you later!"

Before Reba and I even clear the back door, the saw starts up again.

* * *

WHEN I MEET up with Winn in front of his garage nearly twelve hours later, I hoist the cooler of beers into the back of his pickup and say, "We ready?"

He looks over the side of the truck bed at the small container. "Is that all we're bringin'?" Adjusting the position of his rods and reels and a large, beat-up tackle box, he waits for my answer.

"I figure sailing and driving fall under roughly the same categories when it comes to drinking. In any case, I don't know how to operate a boat, so I can't be your DD."

"You underestimate my alcohol tolerance, my friend."

"You, like most people, probably overestimate it. And while we're at it, I wouldn't want to drive this beast home, towing your boat, either."

He shrugs and checks the hitch one more time, then proudly pats the tailgate. "*This* is a man's vehicle. Runs on American pride."

"And the souls of future generations."

Tossing back his head, he laughs at the sky. "Good one, Yank. Fair 'nough. Let's hit the road, then." He rounds the side of the truck and opens the driver's door. "Betty's okay with you cuttin' out for the afternoon?"

I hide my pause in the act of climbing into the high beast. Once inside the cab, I answer while putting on my seatbelt, "Yeah. It's good to spend some time apart. We get a *lot* of together time."

He smirks. "I do believe there's a story there, and I'll be gettin' to the bottom of that when we're out on the water. Meantime, let's crank up the country music and pretend for the next twenty minutes that we're a coupla young, single guys with nothin' more pressing on our minds than meetin' our catch limit. You got your license on ya? I don't want any trouble from water patrol."

Having just purchased it a couple of hours ago, I have the documentation tucked neatly in my back pocket. "Ready to go. Let's be wild, crazy manly-men."

Indulging in Winn's fantasy is fine by me. Honestly, I'm hoping we can continue it well into our afternoon on the water and skip anything deeper than idle chit-chat about the weather.

Not that I want to be single again. No, no, no. That wasn't the life for me. And I haven't had this life long enough to harbor any nostalgia for those lonely, empty days. But if the single-guy act makes Winn happy, I'll go along with it for an afternoon, safe in the knowledge that I'll return to a happy house occupied by the two (and a half-ish) people I love most.

It *is* good to get away for a few hours. And judging by Betty's grin and hug when I told her about my plans, she was equally glad for the solitude. Confused that I'd be up for such a stereotypical male bonding experience, but glad nonetheless. Anyway, brand new experiences with new friends are good. Otherwise, it would feel like I was merely replacing my old friends, like worn-out, oft-washed scrubs too threadbare and stained for further service.

I do miss my old friends, but Winn and Laurel are a fun-loving couple who remind me of Betty and me. They tease each other, yet I've never heard either of them cross the line into mean-spirited jabs. They're not afraid to show affection, either, while also avoiding those sickening-sweet interactions that unsettle any witnesses to it.

It appears we've hit the neighbor jackpot—if you don't count the middle-of-the-night power saw sessions.

Now, parked in the center of the lake and settled in the boat with our first beers, our rods propped in their holders, lines trailing over the side, and bobbers bouncing on the surface of the water, it appears quiet-time is over.

Winn stretches out his legs and crosses his ankles. "Ahhh, yes."

I swat a fly away from my sunscreen-coated knee.

"Aren't you freezing?" he asks me.

I look down at my shorts, t-shirt, and flip-flops. "Um, no. It's in the seventies, and the sun's shining."

He shivers. "Low seventies. And there's a breeze out here on the water."

I laugh. "This is tropical weather where I'm from."

"Your blood will thin out eventually."

"So by December, I'll be wearing jeans? But still short sleeves?"

His lips against his tilted-up bottle, he smiles. "Somethin' like that."

"Seriously. Do you guys ever get winter temperatures?"

"Yes, sir! Last February, we had a stretch of forty-degree days that liked to kill us."

I nearly do a spit-take of my beer. After swallowing, I wipe my lips on my forearm and say, "Weenies. What about snow?"

"Only when we've been real bad and God wants to punish us."

I grin. "That's exactly what I like to hear. I'm not going to miss my snowblower."

"What's the most you've ever seen on the ground?"

"I don't know... It's typical to have gotten forty to fifty inches by the end of the spring."

"*Forty to fifty inches?*" He pauses to do the math. "More than four feet?"

I shrug. "Yeah. A few years ago, though, we had close to ninety."

"NINETY?"

"Well, not all at once. It falls and melts a bit, then falls some more. But yeah. If you add up all the precipitation for the whole snow season..."

"I couldn't do it. I couldn't live there."

"If you don't know any different, though..."

"Nope. Shootfire! Do y'all just hunker down and stay inside all winter?"

I pull a face. "No. Who does that?"

"We do! If there's snow on the roads, we don't go anywhere. Everything's closed. Everything. Schools, churches, businesses..."

"I've heard of this mythical creature called the 'snow day.' But I've never experienced one. They're equipped to deal with it where I'm from. Now, ice... that's another story. But we didn't get that too often, and when we did, we weren't down for long. Sometimes they close schools because the temperatures are too low to start the buses. That's usually the rub: the temps."

"What's the coldest it's ever gotten up there, that you can remember?"

I snort. "What do I look like, *The Farmer's Almanac*? It gets cold, man. We bundled up, put the snow tires on the cars—"

"You had special tires to put on your vehicles?"

"Uh, yeah."

"Like every time it snowed, or...?"

"No! Dude. Around this time of year, before the first big snowfall, you put the snow tires on—not gonna miss that, either—and they stay on until May-ish. Sometimes June."

"You're still gettin' snow in June?!"

"No. Well, only once that I can remember. But after particularly bad winters, there are still snow piles melting then. Plus, like anything, switching out the tires is one of those chores you tend to put off. It's a pain."

He leans back on the steering wheel behind him and shakes his head. "Well, I guess you've helped me decide where Hell on Earth is. Your hometown."

"It's not *that* bad. And Hell is hot, remember? That would qualify *this* place more than Green Bay. When the temperature was over a hundred with about three thousand percent humidity in July and August for weeks at a time, I started to wonder if I had died and was being punished for all those horrible things I've thought about my brother."

Winn puffs out his chest as if he's personally responsible for—and proud of—this area's beastly summer weather. "Yep. We get some hot ones."

"You do realize it's not normal to still have your pool open when Halloween decorations are up in stores, right?"

"The pool's heated. I keep it open year-round. Pain in the ass, closin' it, only to have the kids whining about openin' it again in a couple of months."

"It doesn't even need to be heated yet, though."

"I guess not, if you're Nate 'Eskimo' Bingham. Give it a couple more weeks."

I set my beer on the deck near my feet and lean back with my hands behind my head, staring out at the sparkling water. "That's okay. I may not like the sauna effect, but the weather right now... I could go for twelve months of this." I close my eyes and inhale through my nose. "Heaven. And it'll be nice to see kids going door-to-door for Halloween without snowsuits under their costumes."

"See, that's crazy." He jiggles his line, reels it closer a few feet, then pops open another beer and offers it to me. I shake my head, so he says, "Suit yourself," and keeps it for himself.

I return to my sun worship, figuring I have about fifteen more minutes before I need to put on a hat and reapply my sunscreen. There's a fine line between a healthy dose of Vitamin D and skin cancer.

"You got a bite."

"Huh?" I open my eyes and drop my arms, then blink toward the end of my line.

Sure enough, the bobber has disappeared under the

surface, and my line is pulling out. I don't want to look like too much of an novice, so I grab the rod and wind the reel toward me, instead of going with my instinct and saying, "You do it!" or "What do I do?"

Unfortunately, that gives Winn the impression I have this under control, so he doesn't offer any advice or guidance.

"Uhh... What now?"

He laughs. "I knew it! This your first time fishin', Yank?"

"Not my *first* time. Maybe second or third. But I was a kid those other times, so I didn't have to know how to do anything."

"I could tell by the look on your face when you had to worm your hook."

"Worms are dirty and nasty."

"Says the guy who regularly handles blood, poop, and barf."

"Just tell me what to do!"

"Keep reelin'. And calm down." He leans over the side and watches as I pull my catch closer to the surface. "That's it. Nice and slow, so you don't jerk it off the hoo—" He cuts off abruptly, his shoulders shaking.

"What?" I strain to see over him. At first, only air wheezes from him, but soon coughing laughter joins the symphony. "Oh, geez. Did I catch a boot, or something?"

"N-n-noo," he finally manages to splutter, grabbing at the line. "Reel up, and you'll see." He gives up pulling it for me and staggers to his feet, waiting for the big reveal.

Finally, the hook clears the water, and I feel a slight increase in weight against my hands as gravity exerts a stronger pull without the water to support the fish's weight. I stare at the puny creature dripping and flipping and dangling from my line, then swing it closer for inspection.

"What the heck *is* that thing?"

"A pumpkinseed. Or a really lame redear sunfish. They look a lot alike, only a pumpkinseed is smaller."

Upon examination of the orange, green, and gold fish, I decide, "It's pretty."

He coughs harder. "Pretty useless."

"Hey, I'm not here to put food on my family's table or win any trophies."

"Good thing."

"And what have you caught so far?"

"I'd rather catch nothin' than somethin' that embarrassin'." He grabs the acrylic line. "Reel in a bit more and lock it, so I can take it off the hook and throw it back."

"Be gentle. I don't want to kill it."

He rolls his eyes. "Yeah. It would be a shame to deprive another angler of such a thrilling catch."

I do as he says but ignore his teasing. This is what I hate about male bonding activities. They turn usually civilized, cordial people into competitive assholes. And it's not that I can't laugh at myself; the fish *is* small, but I'm not debating that, am I? I'm not standing next to a professional angler, claiming this is an epic catch. I'm merely hanging out on a motorboat with my friend, drinking a couple of beers. Whatever bites our hooks is secondary. To me. But it seems like no matter who I'm with on these outings—whether it be fishing, golf, tennis, batting cages, or whatever—my male companions feel the need to use it as an opportunity to display their masculine superiority... as if I ever put that up for debate.

Winn honors my request, at least, by leaning over the edge of the boat and submerging his fish-filled hand in the water, then gently releasing it, rather than pitching it, as he might like to.

"Bye, fishy!" I say with a silly wave. "Nice to meet you! Just say 'no' to worms from now on."

I retake my seat and reevaluate my desire for a second beer. As I'm cracking it open, Winn asks, "Don't you want to recast?"

"Nope."

"Seriously? You're going to let that stand as your catch of the day?"

"Yep."

He studies me for a few seconds, shakes his head, and shrugs. "Okay. Fine."

He reels in his own line to check his hook, and sure enough, it's been picked clean. Muttering about ninja fish (which may or may not be a real species, as far as I know), he skewers another night crawler and casts his line with a flick of his wrist and a high-pitched whine from the reel. Retaking his seat and his beer, he settles in for another round of waiting for possibly nothing to happen. Even a newb like me can recognize we're out here at a horrible time to catch anything of substance. The lack of other boats confirms it.

Despite his trash-talking, though, something tells me Winn doesn't care about catching keepers, either.

After a few minutes of easy silence, my companion clears his throat and says, "So, uh... There's this thing, this... this... Thanksgivin' dinner my parents put on for the whole town, practically—had a ding-danged community center built for it —and anyway... Seein' that you and Betty don't have any family 'round these parts, I thought... I mean... You don't have to, 'course, but if you wanted to... Comin' to that would save you some cookin', anyway."

I look out over the water to give him a chance to recover from his self-conscious invitation. "That would be nice, thanks."

I was actually looking forward to a nice, quiet holiday. One of the advantages of moving more than a thousand miles from home, after all, is no longer having to spend Thanksgiving with your crazy family members. And now to commit to spending it with someone else's crazy family members... That's hardly an improvement.

Personally, I'd be okay with staying home, cooking a small turkey for the three of us, mashing some potatoes, and calling it good. Or finding somewhere that caters to lonely—or lazy—people and serves a full traditional Thanksgiving feast for a nominal fee. Or better yet, volunteering at a shelter that provides the meal to less fortunate folks. But I'm no dummy; I fully comprehend what little say I have in the matter. Betty would jump on this offer.

Plus, I know I've made the right choice by immediately accepting when Winn chuckles with relief, drains his beer, and says, "It'll be nice to have a friend at my table."

7

WORLDS COLLIDING

"I'm retirin'."

I can't believe what I'm hearing, what I'm seeing, what I'm experiencing. If only I could get Betty to stop smiling at the floor and look up at me. I slide my hand in my pocket and pinch my leg through the cotton material, then wince when it actually hurts. Still... this can't be happening. Any minute now, Velma's going to say, "Just kidding!" Then I'm going to cry.

But she seems earnest as she passes around a plate of cookies in the clinic's kitchen, where she's called us for this tribunal before leaving for the day. "And I feel bad that Betty here's gone to all this trouble to teach me about computers— she's done a great job, by the by—but that's part of why I'm so sure this is the right thing. I'm not worried about leavin' y'all now. You'd be in capable hands. That is, if Betty would be willing to take over for me." She looks at Dr. Reitman and me over her glasses. "That *is* the only condition to my retirement: that you hire Betty as my replacement."

Now Betty's head *does* snap up.

I'd laugh if I weren't as blown away by this proviso as she is.

The heir apparent is the first to find her words. "Velma,

that's sweet, but I'm not an administrative assistant. I was only—"

"Well, bless your heart! You'll do fine. More than fine!"

I snort into my hand and pretend it was a sneeze.

Betty, not fooled, sends me a look that's both a warning and a rescue plea.

Dr. Reitman ignores our exchange and addresses Velma after swallowing another bite of cookie. "Let me get this straight. You want to retire, but only if we offer your job to Betty, and she agrees to take it?"

"Yep!"

Now it's my turn to direct pleading eyes at Betty. *Oh, Betts. Say yes. It doesn't have to be for real. Let's just get Velma out of here!*

Betty's jaw slides slightly forward as she strains to keep the smile plastered to her face.

Into the awkward silence, Velma launches her "Betty for Receptionist" campaign. "It's perfect, y'all! Well, almost. You'll be missin' out on havin' someone from around here who could give you the scoop on patients and their families before they come in—you know, like I do—but you can always call me if you need to. I could serve as a consultant."

"That's too kind," Dr. Reitman mutters.

"In every other way, though, this job is perfect for a busy mama and mama-to-be!"

Eff me. Shut up, Velma!

Shuffling my feet, I studiously avoid eye contact with my beloved while Velma rattles on, "This'll be an easy way for you to earn some mad money, sugar. Buy yourself somethin' nice now and again and experience some independence."

Oh, gosh. I'm going to laugh. Desperately, I hold back the giggles while Velma gives Betty her nineteen-fifties' women's lib speech.

"And you two are such a sweet couple. *Family.*" She gestures toward my office, where Georgia's sleeping on a nest of quilts on the floor. "Wouldn't it be wunnerful to spend more time together? Now you can!" She pulls each of our hands so Betty and I are standing with her in the middle, then wraps her arms around us and squeezes until we're side-by-side, our shoulders jammed together as she steps out from between us.

I snake my arm around Betty's waist and pull her more tightly against me with my hand against her hip. When she stiffens, I stifle more laughter and can't resist playing along, if for no other reason than to get *her* to laugh about this... eventually.

"She's right, Betts."

"'Course I am!"

"It'll be good for you to get out of the house a few hours a day. And I can never get enough of you. You know that."

"Aww! See?"

"And you are *so good* with all that computer stuff. Plus, you make the best coffee..."

"It's settled, then?" Velma checks.

Dr. Reitman cuts in before Betty can reply. "We'll, uh, take it under advisement. But Velma, you know... nobody can replace *you*. No offense," she tosses toward Betty, who clenches her teeth.

"None taken."

Velma grabs her purse from a cabinet and opens the back door. "I see. You have to at least pretend to open the job to the public, right? Isn't that some sorta law?"

"Yes!" Betty seizes that not-so-accurate technicality.

"That's fine, y'all. But if anyone else tries to bully their way in here, don't worry; I'll hear about it, and I'll be back before you can say, 'Velma to the rescue!'"

Dr. Reitman smiles. "We appreciate your dedication."

"We can talk about the details tomorrow. I figure it'll take about two weeks for me to show Betty the ropes... and for y'all to plan a sweet retirement party for me." She winks.

I lift my free hand in a wave. "You're the best, V. See you tomorrow!"

As soon as she's gone, Betty shoves me away and slaps my shoulder. "'You're the best, V,'" she mocks.

I laugh and fake-flinch, then grab her wrists and pull her closer to my chest as I affect an exaggerated twang. "Aw! Now, darlin'... Won't it be nice to have your own job, a little project to keep you busy when you're not fixin' my meals, and takin' care of my babies?"

Through her own laughter, she says, "Screw you, Nathaniel."

"That's part of your *real* job, sugar-booger."

She struggles against me, trying to get enough leverage to land a blow or two, but I'm stronger than she is (barely), so she raises her knee in a threat that has me letting go of her and backing off. "Hey, hey. Not the boys."

"You're not going to need them anymore, anyway."

Dr. Reitman watches in amusement, then hops onto the nearest counter, her feet swinging off the floor. "You two! All joking aside, we do have a serious issue to discuss here."

Betty and I turn to her, our mouths slack. Finally, I say, "You're kidding."

Always more diplomatic than I am, Betty clears her throat. "This is flattering and everything, but..."

"I realize it's only part-time, and it may seem like it wouldn't pose enough of a challenge for you, given your background, but you'd really be helping us out here."

"Hang on," I butt in. "We're not considering this, are we?"

Betty's shoulders straighten. "Why is that so crazy? You think I can't do it?"

"No! Definitely not that, but—"

"You don't want me around? Worry you'll get sick of me?"

Uhhhh...

"Absolutely not! Betts, I'm only considering *you*. This"—I wave toward the doorway leading to the front office—"isn't you. You're... you're creative and funny and smart. One week of insurance coding and appointment setting and office supplies inventory and ordering and coffee-making and, 'Please fill out this form,' and you'll be bored out of your skull."

"Who says? I can work on some advertising strategies for you guys between all that other stuff, drum up some new patients for you... or at least convince the ones you inherited from Dr. Jacobson to stay with you."

"Okay, but what about Georgia? And the new baby?"

"What about 'em? Georgia can go to pre-school, and the new one—which, thanks for telling all God's creation about that before our agreed-upon date—"

I glance guiltily at Dr. Reitman. "I didn't!"

"Whatever. The point is, we used to be a two-income household. And I used to leave the house to work every day. And it was fine. Why would this be different? If anything, it would be better, because I could bring the baby here—"

"Whoa, whoa, whoa... Here? Around sick kids all day? No way."

"We'd work something out."

"Five minutes ago, you wanted nothing to do with this job."

"Five minutes ago, you weren't telling me you didn't want me to take it."

I rub the back of my neck. "Geez, Betts, I don't know..."

"You heard Velma. It's me or her. Which one do you prefer?"

"You!" Dr. Reitman and I practically shout in unison.

"Hands down," I say. "No contest. Obviously. But..."

"Then there's your answer."

I shoot an entreating look at the doctor, but she merely shrugs and dismounts, performing a perfect two-footed landing. "Betty would make a great addition to our team. Think of all the fun we'll have."

"And when she has the baby?"

"I'll go on maternity leave, like any other working woman in this country. And we'll go from there," she replies, refusing to be talked about like she's not in the room. "There's only one thing left to negotiate..."

I watch as she slinks nearer and wraps her arms around the back of my neck. She plays with my hair, her hooded eyes creating a pleasant-but-unwelcome tingle between my legs.

Oh, geez. See? This is already a problem. This can't be happening to me at work!

Her husky voice doesn't help when she asks, "Can I borrow some of your scrubs until I can order my own?"

Aw, hell no!

* * *

To celebrate (ahem) Betty's new job two weeks later, we leave Georgia with Dr. Reitman for the evening and head out for a night on the town with Winn and Laurel. Technically, that meant we had to drive several miles, to a *different* town, to find the nearest movie theater. But it was worth it.

As we pile back into the car, I see it's still early and say, "Anyone interested in going somewhere to hang out for a while?"

Betty wrinkles her nose. "You mean, like a club? Aren't we a little old for that?"

"I was thinking more along the lines of the lounge at that Ramada near the highway."

Winn leans forward from the back seat. "A bar? First you

put me in this electric car of yours, then you take me to a chick flick—"

"It wasn't a chick flick," I patiently explain for the hundredth time. "It was a quirky comedy featuring mostly women. And it was hilarious. And you liked it. I heard you laughing louder than anyone."

"Now you expect me to go to a bar? Yank, I can't go to a bar."

"Why not?"

"I'm a Southern Baptist!"

"So what? I'm a Lutheran. Sort of. Was. At one time. Still am, I guess. That doesn't expire, does it?" I look to Betty for confirmation.

She shrugs. "Expiration or not, you're a crappy Lutheran. No offense."

"Uh, some taken!"

"Just sayin'... You never go to church!"

Winn coughs before I can defend myself (we'd be here all night, anyway, since I have no defense). "Yeah, well your people—"

"*My* people?"

"—have embraced the alky-hall. Southern Baptists don't drink at bars. Or anywhere public, come to think of it."

Laurel pipes up, "Haven't you heard that old joke? 'What's the best way to make sure your Baptist fishin' buddy doesn't drink all your beer?'" Before I can guess, she finishes, "'Bring another Baptist along.'"

I laugh. "That punchline would be lost on most people where we're from. Not many teetotalers up there. Or Southern Baptists."

"This area's crawlin' with 'em," Winn says. "And I'm a pillar of the community."

"Not this community. Nobody knows who you are here. Or

cares." I step on the brake, push the power button on my "electric car" to start it and, ask into the rear view mirror, "What's it going to be? Are you in or out?"

Winn returns to the back seat. "My vote is 'in,'" he says, as if there was never a doubt.

Laurel leans forward and rests her hand on Betty's shoulder. "Are you okay with this? Doesn't sound like much fun, sittin' around while everyone else drinks."

Betty tosses a surprised glance toward her new friend then narrows her eyes at me while answering, "I don't mind being the designated driver. Now that I can drive this thing."

To distract from yet another instance of Betty finding out our secret's not so secret, I put the car in reverse and back from the spot. "Well, nobody's going to get wasted. We're just going to have a drink or two, talk a bit"—*hopefully not about what a big-mouth I am*—"and head home. No biggie."

At the hotel lounge, we pack into a booth, leaving the bar and sofas to suited business travelers, flirting with each other and looking for the kind of anonymous "fun" out-of-town travel provides for some. Without discussion, Winn and I sit on one side while Betty and Laurel slide in on the other, facing us.

"This is cozy," Winn says, pretending to snuggle up to my arm, then quickly dropping it when the server comes by to get our drink orders.

I stick with my usual beer, Winn orders a Jack and Coke, and Laurel chooses a white wine spritzer. Betty nonchalantly says, "Water," but as soon as we're alone again, she turns to Laurel. "Tell me the truth. Did you figure it out on your own, or did Nate blab to you guys?"

It seems like a non sequitur, but everyone at the table understands exactly what she's talking about. I wish I had a drink to spill and cause a diversion. Not that I'd ever waste good beer like that.

Before Laurel can reply, Winn smoothly answers, "If Yank wasn't supposed to tell anyone, then we definitely heard it from him."

"Thanks, pal."

He winks. "No problem. Anything to help."

It does help, since it makes everyone—including Betty— laugh, especially when Winn goes on a half-serious rant about "women's secrets," finally ending with, "Guys aren't like that. We share our knowledge. 'Cause it's so rare that we know anything."

Our drinks arrive, and as soon as we lower our glasses to the table after our first swallows, Laurel nods at Betty's tall, sweaty water glass. "Actually, I figured it out by myself. You never drink alcohol."

"A lot of people don't drink," Betty says. "You and Winn supposedly don't."

Laurel shrugs. "Well, that was only one clue of many. I can spot an expectin' mama from miles away. I recognize that glazed look."

"Oh." Betty seems disappointed she can't blame me... this time.

If she only knew...

"And... Nate told Winn at the cookout, when you left 'to get sunscreen,' but it was obvious you were about to throw up every single bite of the two hamburgers you'd scarfed."

Aw, hell.

Betty touches her tongue to her upper lip and smirks across the table at me.

I drain the last of my beer and set down the glass. Wiggling my eyebrows at her, I say, "What're you gonna do? I'm happy. I'm excited. I want to tell the whole world."

"It's adorable," Laurel says, nudging Betty. "You should be proud of how sweet your husband is."

"I'd be prouder if he could be sweet *and* keep his big yap shut for twelve lousy weeks."

My hand swallows her on the table between us, "Twelve weeks is a long time!"

Winn snorts. "You're about to find out just how long it is. It'll probably be at least that before you get back your conjugal privileges."

"Winston, don't be uncouth!"

"Oh, boy, I'm in trouble when Laurel starts talkin' like her mama," he mutters to me. "Joke's on her, though, because her mama was a MILF before that was even a thing."

Laurel rolls her eyes at her husband but has to work hard to suppress her laughter. "You, mister, are hopeless."

"Yes, ma'am. And proud of it."

* * *

AFTER WE'VE FULLY DISSECTED the movie—and strong-armed a confession from Winn that he enjoyed it—talk turns to the reason for our celebrations.

Betty shrugs. "It's not exactly what I had in mind, but it's a paycheck and it *does* get me out of the house, which is a must. I've quickly figured out I'm not stay-at-home mom material."

"Oh, sugar, you must be doin' it wrong, then. I'm perfectly content to sit at home, eatin' bon-bons, watchin' soap operas, and perfectin' my scrapbookin' skills," Laurel says, pushing away her half-full second spritzer.

Winn scoffs. "You don't do any of that stuff."

"That's what everyone assumes I do."

Gazing into her icy water, Betty says, "I'm sure you keep plenty busy."

"Apologizin' for Winn's antics is a full-time job. See, you have a husband who knows how to behave in polite society."

"Usually."

"I save my worst behavior for at home or around family," I say. "Compartmentalizing is key."

Betty ignores my joke and directs at Laurel, "Well, if you can recommend any good daycares or preschools, we'd appreciate it. Georgia can't come with me to the clinic forever, and I definitely won't be able to keep up with two of them and get any work done."

Laurel's eyes brighten. "Hey, bring 'em over to me."

Betty and I laugh at what we perceive to be our neighbor's jesting, but Laurel says, "I'm serious! My kids are gone most of the day at school, and I'd love to have babies around the house again."

"Babies you send home at the end of the day are the best," Winn agrees.

"We'd pay you," I quickly add, before the offer expires.

Winn high fives me. "Even better."

Laurel nods. "It's perfect; they'll be right next door, so when you come home from work, you can just pop over and get 'em."

"You're sure it won't be too much trouble?"

"I'm sure."

"And if it does become a pain, you'll be honest and tell us, so we can find somewhere else before it becomes a strain on our friendship?"

"That's not gonna happen," Laurel says with a laugh, "but yes. I'll agree to those terms."

Winn winks at her. "Atta girl, babycakes. Seal the deal before they weigh the possibility of their kids turnin' out like ours."

Since their three children are impeccably mannered, call

adults "sir" and "ma'am" in their cute little Southern drawls, and play well together—with the occasional sibling spat thrown in there now and again to prove they're not cyborg children Winn built in his shed—I'm not worried at all. They love Georgia, too (the feeling is mutual), and always entertain her when we're all together.

"Your kids are angels," I say, cracking up both of the Bakers.

"They are!" Betty agrees. "I've never seen them put a toe out of line."

Winn raises an eyebrow and leans across the table as if about to share a trade secret. "Years of shock therapy have taught them how to behave for company. When nobody's around, it's a free-for-all."

Laurel sobers slightly. "We're kidding, of course. And thank you for the compliment. They're turning out okay, finally. It was touch-and-go for a while there. The twos and threes..." She shudders.

"So what do you say? Do we have a deal?" Winn presses.

"If you'd rather they go to an accredited, licensed daycare, I understand," Laurel says when Betty hesitates. "I can certainly recommend the most popular ones in town."

Blushing, Betty replies, "Oh, gosh. It's not that at all. I really am worried about putting you out."

"It was my idea!"

"Yeah, but I get how easy it is to extend an offer, trying to help, without thinking it through." She looks pointedly across the table at me. "Then you find yourself the receptionist at your husband's pediatric practice."

"It's not *my* practice."

"Mm-hm."

"And you're free to change your mind at any time, as long as Velma doesn't find out."

She waves off my potential conversational tangent and returns her attention to Laurel. "It would be a major relief for Georgia to be with someone we trust. My stomach's been in knots for weeks, wondering where we're going to take her."

It has?

I squeeze one of her hands while Laurel grips the other one. Betty rolls her filling eyes, jarring some tears loose onto her cheeks. "Oh, gosh. I'm sorry. I'm just..."

"Hormones," Laurel says, handing her an extra cocktail napkin from the end of the table.

"Yes. They're awful. I'm such a mess."

Winn lifts what's left of his watered-down drink. "Oh, c'mon, y'all. Let's drink to friends, and get the heck out of here before we all end up blubberin' like babies."

"Hear, hear!" I say, clinking my glass with his.

The ladies join in, with Betty nodding and saying softly, "To friends."

8

BRAINSTORM BETTY

EVERYONE—INCLUDING FAMILY FAR AND WIDE—IS AWARE OF the new Bingham on the way, and everyone's thrilled. Well, Kitty and Witt don't know the meaning of that word, but they did say, "Congratulations," on Skype, and the pixelation of the video gave the illusion of smiles. Good enough.

In addition to the gag order being lifted, there's less gagging in general and more eating without repercussions in our house. One Saturday morning, Betty woke up and decided that food was back in style.

With the arrival of her second trimester and the return of her appetite, her energy level has soared, too. Enter Brainstorm Betty. Sometimes I simply stare at her in awe (mixed with a bit of horror, I'm not going to lie). *Who is this person? And what is she going to do (or make me do) next?*

"You know what we should do?" she asks now as she barges into my office.

"Learn to knock?" I grumble, setting my feet on the floor and sliding my phone onto my desk. Kicking Nick's ass at trivia is apparently going to have to wait.

"We should host a Christmas party at the clinic," she answers herself, ignoring my wisecrack.

"Yeah, we did that at Greenbrier, too. I'm sure Dr. Reitman will do something similar here."

"Not only for current patients, though. I mean, yes, they'd be invited, obviously, but this would be a great chance to network and advertise, get some *new* patients."

"Okay…"

She paces in front of the couch. "I'm thinking little stocking goody bags stuffed with personal healthcare items—"

"Fun."

"—sitting on Santa's lap, a photo booth with funny elves' hats and other Christmas-y costume items, a bounce house, fruit and veggie trays, instead of the usual candy and baked goods, games with prizes—of course…"

"Of course."

"And for the parents, some helpful handouts with information about typical seasonal complaints, plus the clinic's contact information, including yours and Dr. Reitman's pictures, so they can put faces to names and see how friendly you both look."

It's all I can do not to chirp, "Goody!" But the last thing I want is to piss on Betty's parade. The poor woman has finally emerged from three months of feeling like something that dropped from Reba's posterior. She deserves to enjoy her rediscovered energy. So I keep my sarcastic asides to myself.

"That means we need to update your head shots. We can't legally use the one from Greenbrier, and even if we could, we wouldn't. It's too outdated; you look about twelve."

"This all sounds… awesome. Of course. But money is—"

"You have to spend money to make money. And since advertising isn't easy to come by in 'these here parts,' we have to advertise creatively. Hence this party."

"We'll have to itemize the entire thing and present it to Dr. Reitman, so—"

"Already done. Pat loves it."

Pat?

"I didn't have definite prices for some things—I have no idea how much it would cost to hire a Santa. I would have *you* do it, but it's important you're *you* that day so people can see you and get to know you. Maybe Rob would be willing."

I blink. "Wait. You've already run all this by Dr. Reitman?"

"Yeah. She owns the place."

Replaying the conversation in my head, I look toward my forehead. "Okay, but when you came in here, you acted like you just got this idea and were bouncing ideas off me."

"I did?" She considers that, then waves me off. "I didn't mean to. Whatever. Who cares?"

Glancing at my phone, I note with disappointment that I still have a ton of time until my next patient arrives. Which bolsters Betty's argument that we need this blowout event to drum up new business. Pretending I *don't* care I was the last to hear about this big bash, I move on. "How do you plan to get the word out?"

"Maybe at the Bakers' Thanksgiving dinner, we can hand out little postcards."

I've found out a bit more about the Bakers' Thanksgiving dinner, and I'm not sure it's the right venue for shameless self-promotion. Winn's parents invite the entire staff of the hardware store and lumber yard, plus their families, *plus* anyone who's anyone in town. It's a big, fancy, catered affair that requires RSVPs and formal attire.

So while I'm not willing to do any parade-pissing, in general, I do feel beholden in this case to rein her in just a tad.

"Postcards on people's plates? That seems a bit tacky. I get the impression the Bakers' Thanksgiving is *the* social event of the year around here."

She taps her lips with her fingertips. "I bet Winn would be willing to make an announcement for us; after the meal and everything, of course. Or we could get his kids to help us put the cards under people's windshield wipers."

I wince at the thought.

She narrows her eyes at me. "Do *you* have any better ideas?"

"Yeah. Leave people alone to enjoy their meal."

Hands on her hips, she flares her nostrils and waits for me to give her a real answer.

I scramble for one. "Uh, let's see. Um, how about we ask, instead, if we can put up fliers on church bulletin boards? Or in newsletters?"

She grins. "Great idea! And oh! I just thought of something!" She points to her midriff. "Tap the market for the newest of new patients!"

"I'm not sure what the best medium is for unborn children. Definitely not print. Radio? They can hear, but the message will have to be crazy-subliminal."

She sticks out her tongue at my smart-assery, then rolls right over it. "Soon-to-be-parents, especially first-timers, want to have their pediatrician lined up before the birth, right?"

"Usually."

"Then we need to get postcards or fliers into prenatal classes. Expectant parents can drop by during the party and see how you and Pat interact with kids, and it's a nice time for them to do some informal interviewing. You need to have good answers for more controversial things like co-sleeping and bottle versus breastfeeding."

"We do. And they're hardly controversial."

"To you. To new parents, these are big issues."

"Yeah. I know. I've been doing this a while."

The light fades from her eyes, and her face slackens. Then her jaw tightens as she approaches my desk, places both palms flat on it, and leans toward me on straight arms. "What the heck is your problem, Nathaniel?"

"What? I don't have a problem."

She comes around the side of the furniture so it's no longer between us. I sit straighter in my chair, then regret it when she plops into my open lap hard enough for it to be considered a preview of Tchaikovsky's holiday classic.

"Oof!"

"You're being a sarcastic a-hole about this whole thing. Is this because I talked about it with Pat first?"

"No! That would be childish and stupid."

"Because she writes the checks. There'd be no point in planning anything without her go-ahead."

"Fine. I get that."

She brushes my hair to the side on my forehead while I subtly try to readjust my man parts under her. "Then what's your deal?"

Pressing my nose to her shoulder, I say, "Nothing. I'm glad you're feeling better and have the energy for all this stuff."

She laughs. "No, you're not. At least not the last part. Am I getting on your nerves? Because I have ideas? And I'm making you implement them? And that means a little more work?"

Danger, danger, danger! Do not answer any of those questions. Distract. Divert.

Truth is I *am* somewhat annoyed. I've grown accustomed to having some downtime between appointments. I never had that at Greenbrier. Ever. I ran my ass off from opening to closing every single day, sometimes not even having time to choke down lunch.

Here, things move more slowly. And I like it. I enjoy having an office with a door, which affords me some privacy. I like that I can sit down behind my desk, put my feet up, and putz around on my phone for fifteen minutes at a time (or a half hour, depending on how slow the day is). When there's work to do, and I'm with a patient, I still give it my all. But it's nice that I'm no longer being asked to give one hundred percent, non-stop, for twelve straight hours.

Admitting that to myself and saying it out loud to Betty are two different things, though. The former is self-aware; the latter is suicide.

I lift my head and kiss her chin. "You're amazing."

"But?"

"No buts."

"You're such a liar."

"I'm at your service, as usual. You tell me what to do and where to be, when, and I'm there."

She relaxes against me. "In that case, I need to find a photographer and schedule a session with you and Pat."

I barely suppress my inward groan at the thought—and her repeated use of the doctor's first name.

"If I can't find one to come here on short notice, you two might have to go to a studio. Like at a department store in Columbia. On a Saturday, or something. In your scrubs. With your stethoscopes. You can use Georgia as a prop kid." As I'm imagining this prospective spectacle, she laughs and rises from my lap. "Just kidding. I'll find a way to make it happen here."

The main phone line rings.

I chuckle weakly at her back as she returns to the front desk to answer it. "I knew you were joking!"

* * *

A FEW HOURS LATER, after my last patient of the day departs, I dump the folder in the "Filing" tray on Betty's desk and peer over her shoulder at the first draft of the open house flier. "Wow. That looks like a bit more than goody bags, fruit trays, and a Santa imposter."

"I had a few more ideas."

I clear my throat. "Hm. I see. Cool. And Dr. Reitman's okay with all this?"

"I'll talk to her about it on Monday. I'm sure it'll be fine, though." She saves her work and closes the publishing program, then eyes the stack of patient files in her inbox. "Right now, I have a date with the file room."

Holding to the edge of her desk for balance, I block her chair from swiveling with my foot. "Hang out with me for a few minutes. You've been going non-stop all day. Did you eat lunch?"

She sighs at my nagging. "Of course I ate lunch. I finished *second* lunch a few minutes ago."

When she leans back, I move my leg, satisfied she's not going anywhere right this second. "I'm so ready for a long weekend." *Even if I have to spend part of it at the world's largest Thanksgiving dinner.*

"Right? It's going to be nice." She arches and rubs her back. "I figured we could hit Charleston or Columbia and do some Christmas shopping. Maybe look for some baby stuff. Nothing gender-specific, obviously, but..."

Like internal stitches, my lazy weekend dissolves. "Shopping? The weekend after Thanksgiving?"

"Laurel says there will be some massive sales. We could save a ton of money."

"Or we could pay more, shop online, and save on gas. And other kinds of energy."

"It's more fun to see that stuff in person, though, don't you think?"

No. I don't. I think it's more fun to be a complete slug and not step

foot outside of my house for three days. It's bad enough we have to be
social and eat Thanksgiving dinner with strangers. Plus, buying baby
stuff leads to assembling baby stuff, which leads to painting and other
DIY projects that I can't face right now.

"Can't we be one with the couch this weekend?"

"I'm nesting, Nathaniel."

"It's too early for that."

"What would you know about it?"

"Plenty." At her withering glare, I backtrack, "Okay, not firsthand, but through study and observation. And anyway, I thought we agreed we'd take stock of Georgia's stuff and reuse as many things as possible. It'll take a while to sort all that out."

She pulls up a document on her computer. "Done."

I squint at the two-column list. The "Want/Need" side is much longer than the "Have" side. Alarmingly so. "Does this take into account the things that Heidi and Laurel have already offered us?"

"Yes. I made this list with Laurel last time you and Winn abandoned us to spend all afternoon fostering your budding bromance."

"I'd hardly call installing a dog-waste septic system in our backyard 'male bonding.'"

"Whatever."

"And you're welcome, by the way, for everything I do to keep our property free of land mines."

She tilts her head and smiles. "Aw, honey! I *do* appreciate it."

"Then give me this weekend off. Please. I'm begging you."

"Well, you don't have to beg." She closes the want/have/need list and stands, hoisting the stack of patient files and resting them against the rise under her breasts.

"Never mind. I thought maybe you were as excited about everything as I am, but apparently not."

I suppress a sigh but snag her by the elbow. "Hey. I *am* as pumped as you are to meet this person and figure out who he or she is going to be. But breaking the bank and fighting through hordes of Christmas shoppers for stuff we don't need when both of us desperately require some rest isn't my idea of fun. I'd much rather spend that time with you and Georgia, while she's still the only one we have to worry about." As a peace offering, I wiggle my fingers toward the files. "Hand 'em over."

She swivels at the waist, pulling the folders out of my reach. "What? No. That's my job."

"I have a firm grip of the alphabet, so I'm fully qualified."

Her jaw tightens. "The fact that a kindergartner can do my job isn't the point." Sidestepping, she tries to go around me, but I'm faster and block her way.

"That's not what I—"

"I'm perfectly capable and don't need any favors."

"You can make it up to me some other time by..."

"...cleaning an exam room"? No, too germy.

"...sitting on my face"? No, too sexual harass-y.

"...having my baby"? Gonna happen anyway—hopefully—and not here at work.

"...ordering those latex-free gloves I like."

"Don't patronize me, Nathaniel!"

When I suspect she's about to push me out of the way (or worse), Dr. Reitman emerges from the hallway with her last patient and his mother.

The scowl falls from Betty's face, replaced by a warm smile. "Hey, Jackson. Did the doctor fix you up?" she asks innocently.

I snatch the folders from Betty while she's distracted and

hold up my free hand for a high five from one of the few kids we've seen multiple times since opening our doors.

Jackson slaps my hand and rolls his eyes. "I already felt fine."

"It never hurts to check," the boy's mom, Maeve, says in her own defense. "Rashes make me nervous. They can be symptoms of so many things."

"That they can," I agree magnanimously with the maternal hypochondriac.

Dr. Reitman shoots me a look as if to tell me not to encourage the woman, but I merely grin. Hey, if Maeve Andretti wants to spend hundreds of dollars a year in co-pays to have us look at every scrape, bruise, and pimple on her only child, that's her business. Actually, it keeps *us* in business. Do I reinforce her fears when she drags the poor guy in here every other week? No. But I'm perfectly content to have her pay me to tell her not to worry. She's the customer, and if that's what she wants...

Then again, another glance at her miserable kid provides a quick reminder that she's negatively affecting someone else with these unnecessary visits. I can relate all too well.

When I was his age, both of my parents were constantly psychoanalyzing my brother and me and sometimes jumping to some crazy (literally) conclusions. There's nothing like being told you *may* be a sociopath to warp your fragile self-perception at an impressionable age. But being able to sing doesn't make one a bird; being a liar doesn't make one a sociopath, either. Turns out most teenagers lie to their parents on a regular basis, even when it doesn't make any sense to do so. They tend to do it more when those parents diagnose them with psychoses based on everything they say and do. Mom and Dad may have been on the right track with Nick, though. At the very least, he's a raging narcissist.

To Betty, Dr. Reitman hands over a scrawled-on square of prescription paper and says, "Do you mind calling that in? Joe's Pharmacy, right?" she verifies with Mrs. Andretti, who nods eagerly.

"That salve'll fix you right up," I say to Jackson, who again rolls his eyes.

"I hope it doesn't stink like that one stuff."

I glance at the prescription again while Betty types the information into the local pharmacy's online request form. "Nah. Colorless and odorless. A little sticky, but..."

"Great."

"Hey, no more itch. That's a good thing."

"Whatever," he grumbles under his breath.

His mom nudges his shoulder. "Jackson! Don't be so disrespectful, young man."

He raises his eyes to mine. "Sorry. Whatever, *sir*."

Unable to hold back, I laugh at his disgust and ruffle his hair. "Aw, life's not so bad, buddy. Nothing some ointment can't cure."

Of course, no prescription in the world is going to help him in the Mom department. But nobody can say she doesn't care.

After they've gone, Dr. Reitman rounds the counter and peers at the schedule on the monitor. "That's it, right? We're free for the weekend?"

I flap my arm away from my body to draw attention to the folders in my grasp, but at the same time, I step away from Betty's reach, through the archway that leads to the walk-in file room. "As soon as I'm finished with this filing."

9

FAMILY DRAMA

It figures that the first day I wear long pants and a long-sleeved shirt (plus a tie) down here, I have to jump in a pool to rescue my new best friend.

Hang on. Let me back up.

Betty, Georgia, and I went to the Bakers' Thanksgiving dinner, and it was every bit as crowded and loud as I expected it to be. Held in the Baker Community Center, the dinner seemed to be attended by nearly everyone in Jasper, dressed in their Sunday best. Each table featured a Baker family representative whose job was to make their guests feel welcome and important.

As promised, we were seated at Winn and Laurel's table, so we weren't completely surrounded by strangers, but it soon became clear it was no sacrifice to place Winn with the newcomers. He's the kind of family black sheep who puts my experience with that role to shame. Within five minutes of meeting his parents—and his smarmy cousin, Burke, the obvious golden boy of the Baker clan—it all made sense. And I seriously wanted to give Winn a hug right there.

But you know, it's a small town, and rumors start so easily, so I stifled the urge and embraced the stuffing of my face with turkey, mashed potatoes, and dressing, instead.

Burke Baker. What a nightmare. He's Winn's older cousin by about a week, so he's the true heir to the Baker empire. It sounds like something on a miniseries, but it's real life. Winn's mom and aunt were probably trying every wives' tale in the book at the end of their pregnancies, in an effort to be the first to give birth so they'd have the oldest grandson. And it looks like Winn's parents still haven't forgiven him for gestating longer.

They introduced me to Burke like they were introducing me to Jesus. "Oh, and this is *Burke*, the brains behind the Baker empire." When he held out his hand for me to shake, I was surprised it was sideways and not knuckles-up, so I could kiss it while bowing.

The worst part was how Winn shrank in his cousin's presence. Only moments before, he was joking and laughing, telling us about the time he nearly got dragged off his boat by a largemouth bass, the one he has mounted on the wall in his den. I'm much more jealous of the mostly dormant bar in said den, but I *was* impressed when he told me the fish on the wall behind it was one of his catches. I'd crap my pants if I had to reel in something like that.

The story of how he came to catch it is a modern-day, Southern redneck *Moby Dick*. And he tells it fabulously. At least, he *was* regaling our entire twelve-person table with the tale before his parents and Burke interrupted him to say hello and thank all of us for coming.

After Burke pulled up an empty chair next to me and proceeded to monopolize the conversation for the rest of the evening, I didn't hear another word from my friend. It's like Burke was specifically told to sit with us and quiet us down, like the bossy older-brother figure he obviously is. And since most of his questions and statements were directed at me and about Dr. Reitman buying out Dr. Jacobson's practice, I felt obligated to answer as completely and transparently as possible. People were hanging on my every word. Betty was squeezing my knee under the table, as if to remind me it was the perfect networking opportunity, and I'd better not screw it up by saying something dumb or coming across as too humble.

By the time I had revealed everything I possibly could about the practice and had answered every question about Planet Wisconsin that people could throw at me, everyone had forgotten Winn's story.

I tried to get us back there by saying, "So, Winn, what happened with you and that fish?" but he merely mumbled, "You've seen it. I caught it and had it mounted. The end." Then he smiled weakly at the table, pushed away, and announced, "I'm gonna go see what's holdin' up the pumpkin pie."

After he'd gone, Burke chuckled and said, "Priorities, right?" and the whole table—including Laurel—thought that was hilarious. I wanted to punch that smug a-hole.

Instead, I grabbed Georgia and the diaper bag and used her as the perfect excuse to go after my friend. But I never did find him before Georgia eventually did need some attention in the stinky pants department. By the time I finished with that task, the combination of baby poop and Burke's bullcrap had killed any appetite I might have had for dessert. Therefore, when Betty leaned over and said she was tired and nauseated from eating too much, I was happy to say our goodbyes and thank yous and take our leave.

It's only after we've been home for a few minutes, and I'm in the backyard with Reba enjoying some fresh air and looking up at the stars that I find out why Winn was nowhere to be found at the community center. Movement from the corner of my eye draws my attention to my neighbor's side of the fence. I glance, then do a double-take, when I see my friend, fully clothed, lying on his back on a raft in the middle of the lit-up pool, a bottle of Jim Beam between his sprawled legs. His head's tilted back, his eyes covered by the bill of a ball cap, his mouth gaping open.

"Oh, boy," I mutter. With a quick check of Reba's location, I slip through the gate separating our neighboring yards and approach the pool. Winn doesn't move. Searching the patio area, I spy a pile of pool noodles and grab a hot pink one, sliding it through my hand as far as I can while still holding onto the end of it. Experimentally, I nudge Winn's knee. He doesn't move.

"Yo. Buddy!" I say quietly, so as not to startle him.

Nothing.

I clear my throat and try a little louder. "Winn."

He snores, proving he's alive. For now. If that was a full bottle of liquor before he thought it was a good idea to get in the pool in his dress clothes, shoes included, he's going to wish he was dead in a few hours. And Laurel might kill him for stranding her at the Thanksgiving dinner and coming home without her and the kids.

But first things first. It was a relatively warm, sunny day, but now that the sun's gone down, there's a nip in the air. Regardless of how warm that water is, lying only a quarter of the way submerged leaves the parts of him that are wet but above the pool's surface exposed to the ambient air temperature and at risk of exposure.

I slap him harder in the face with the foam noodle. He swats at the annoyance, which throws off his balance—and there he goes, into the chlorinated drink. His alcoholic one sinks to the bottom of the pool, its brown liquid seeping and mingling with the aquamarine water around it. Winn sinks just as quickly. When his feet touch bottom, I expect him to push off and spring to the surface, but he merely rests there, bubbles escaping from his mouth, nose... and rear end. I laugh at the sight, still waiting for him to stop screwing around and swim to the top. But he remains face down, his arms and legs relaxed and still.

The laughter dies in my throat while the seconds tick by like hours. I cup my hands around my mouth and shout, "Winn!" as I lean closer to the water.

No reaction.

"Sonofa..." I mutter, wishing I felt more put out than panicked. But I'm starting to freak out. The guy's not moving. If it's up to him, he might never.

I pry my shoes off with the toes of each opposite foot and nudge them aside on the patio. There's no time to peel off my socks or unbutton the cuffs or collar of my dress shirt or undo the button and zipper on my chinos to remove them, but I do yank off my tie and toss it in the general direction of my shoes before diving into the pool and swimming frantically toward my friend. On the cement bottom, I grab his elbow and pull him up with me, kicking furiously and straining against his dead weight, which threatens to keep me submerged.

Oh, shit. That second helping at dinner was a huge mistake!

When I break through the water's surface, I take a colossal breath and heave one more time to bring Winn's head into the night air. I push on his shoulder to flip him onto his back. Eyes wide open and lashes beaded with moisture, he grins, then spouts water into my face like a drunken whale. His legs and arms begin to move as he treads water. Before I can do anything more than wipe the saliva-filled water from my face, he shrugs me off and doggy paddles to the stairs in the shallow end, where he sits on the third one from the bottom and reclines with his head on the lip of the patio. He has plenty of breath to laugh.

I float on my back, trying to recover from the oxygen deprivation and adrenaline rush. "Son of a bitch!" I yell at the stars, which makes Winn laugh harder behind me. "It's not funny, you stupid asshole!"

"Yeah, it is. You shoulda seen your face when you turned me over."

"I thought you were drowning!" Now that I can feel my limbs again, I flip to my stomach and freestyle to the stairs, taking up a similar position to Winn's, on the other side of the metal handle. "I hate you so much right now."

"Actually, you must really love me to do what you did."

"It was instinct."

"I woulda kept up the act, but I was afraid you'd give me mouth-to-mouth, and—no offense—I'm just not that into you, Yank."

"Shut up. Just shut up before I come over there and hold your head underwater for real, you drunk dumbshit."

"I'm not drunk. Not even close."

"Right. Whatever."

"I'm not!"

I turn my head to look at him, and sure enough, he seems sober.

"I've been workin' on that bottle of Jim Beam for years. Got it three counties over on a whim one night when Rumer was teethin'. Heard it would help if I rubbed it on her gums. I just wanted her to shut up. Laurel wouldn't let me. I pull out that bottle every few months and try to drink some of it, because it seems like the manly thing to drink when you're feelin' low, but... it tastes awful."

"Bourbon's not my thing, either," I admit.

"I like beer. And occasionally, if I'm channelin' my inner tough guy, tequila."

I gag at the sense memory that dates back to college and a Cancun spring break that involved "eating the worm." "I'll stick with beer, thanks. I try scotch every once in a while, supposing I'll eventually learn to like it, but it tastes like medicine."

After a few minutes of silence, Winn says, "I'm sorry I scared you, Yank."

"No, you're not."

"Yeah, I am. I thought you'd think it was funny. I didn't realize how terrified you'd be."

Ruffling my hair so it'll dry faster, I say, "I take human life seriously. Silly me."

He sighs. "Yeah. And I'll do anything for a laugh. I guess those two things don't mix."

Remembering the events of the day and what must have brought him to the pool with his Jim Beam, I soften. "Don't worry about it. I *did* laugh, before I thought you were dying. The underwater farts were a nice touch." I lean back on my elbows and try not to think about how uncomfortable I'm going to be when I finally get out of the water and walk my soggy ass to my own house.

"Farts are always funny."

"Speaking of funny, I'm sorry your story got interrupted at dinner."

"Ah. Whatever."

"I only answered your cousin's questions because I would have looked like a major jerk if I hadn't."

Winn kicks his submerged feet, sending ripples toward the deep end. "You were just bein' polite. You're too nice for your own good, Yank."

"But it *is* for my own good, in this case. I can't afford to look like a dick to potential patients' parents. That sounds mercenary, but..."

"Nah. Not everyone can have it made from birth. I get that most people have to work for everything they have."

"You're included in that group."

"Not according to Burke."

"Burke. What kind of name is that, anyway?" Hey, if I can't manufacture a legitimate reason to dislike the guy, outside of intuition, I might as well resort to middle-school tactics, right? "Burke Baker. Sounds like a soap opera character."

"He's a character, all right."

"He's a douche canoe."

"You don't have to tell me. But he's a smart douche canoe."

"Ruthless and intelligent are two different things. He strikes me as more of the former." When Winn doesn't support or deny that statement, I press, "What makes him such a genius, anyway?"

"He's come up with this plan to franchise the business, so there'll be a Baker's Hardware in nearly every town within a fifty-mile radius of here. We can't compete with the big box stores' prices, but he's countin' on convenience to win out."

"Sounds like Business One oh One to me. Big deal."

"Well, nobody else in our family's history has had the balls to try it, so he's gonna get credit for bein' a trailblazer."

I slide lower on the steps to submerge my body from the shoulders down, so the cool night breeze no longer has access to my rock-hard nipples through my shirts. "From where I'm sitting, *you're* the smart one. You have your priorities in order. You chose a role in the company that would allow you to spend time with your family, not sit in an office for fourteen hours a day, just so you could have a huge house that you never get to enjoy."

"Yeah, well... According to my extended family, that makes me selfish and lazy, not smart. I have no ambition."

"Did you have a choice about going into the family business?"

He snorts. "Oh, sure. I coulda done whatever I wanted—if I'd wanted to be written off completely."

"What would you have done if you'd been allowed to do anything?"

He rubs his neck. "Thinkin' about it would be a waste of time."

"Bullshit."

While I wait for a real answer, he peels off his socks, wrings the water from them, and lobs them toward the house. I'm about to give up hope that he's going to say anything more when he states, "I wanted to be a professional angler. Like go on the circuit and enter tournaments and stuff. But Dad woulda never gone for it, and without his support, I wouldn't have had the money to invest in the stuff I'd need, plus the tournament fees... so I tell people how to replace their toilets and show kids how to build birdhouses. And I fish whenever I get the free time."

"Surely you have enough of your own money saved now to do it, right?"

He shrugs. "Savin' up to send three kids to college doesn't leave room to fund silly fantasies. And I've given up that dream, to tell you the truth. Anyway, maybe it wouldn't be as fun if I had all this pressure to do it and win enough money to support my family."

"You could go semi-pro."

"Nah. Most of the tournaments are on the weekends, and that's when we're busiest at the store." He grabs the metal handrail between us and heaves himself to his feet, quite a bit more unsteadily than someone who's "not drunk."

I remain seated, looking up at him as he stares wistfully across the pool at the raft bobbing aimlessly back and forth above the sunken bottle of bourbon and sodden baseball cap. A familiar buzzing from the garage door breaks his trance. "Aw, hell. Laurel and the kids are home."

I crawl the rest of the way up the steps and stagger to my feet, ten pounds of water dragging my pants down so I'm walking on the bottom hems. "How much trouble are you in?"

"Laurel knows the drill. I rarely last through a full family get-together. She always plans to have someone bring her home after I disappear."

"You're lucky to have such an understanding wife."

"Oh, I'm thankful, trust me." He turns toward the house and lifts his hand in a halfhearted wave. "Thanks for playing lifeguard with me."

I retrieve my shoes and tie, holding them away from my body to avoid dripping on them. "Any time, neighbor. But next time, how about you let me know it's a game?"

"You're no fun, Yank."

* * *

BACK AT MY own house and still dripping, I can't help laughing at the mental picture of Winn and me in the pool in all our clothes. Despite his cruel drowning trick, Winn's like the brother I *wish* I had. Fun, funny, and willing to tell it like it is, without the mean streak Nick has.

Don't get me wrong; I miss my family too, in their own way, but I don't miss the grief they've all seemed to cause me in recent years. Once those memories have faded, sentimentality will kick in, and I'll wish we could spend more time together. For now, I'm okay with them being up there and me being down here and all of us Skyping or talking on the phone a few times a month.

By Christmas, I'll be ready to share a beach house with them for a week. No, I won't. I'll never be ready for that. But I'll be readier than I am now. Here's hoping, anyway. Because to atone for escaping to Jamaica with Betty last year for the holiday, I've agreed to a Bingham family reunion at a beach house in Myrtle Beach this year. Blame temporary insanity—or guilt—but at the time, it seemed like no big deal. A few months closer to the actual event, and I break out in hives every time I imagine it.

I strip to nakedness in the laundry room and grab two of the beach towels from the wire shelving above the washer and dryer. One I wrap around my waist, the other I scrub against my hair.

Betty's voice, swollen with tears, halts my furiously rubbing hand. "Oh, my gosh. What happened to *you*?"

I shove the towel aside and lift my head to turn it toward her. That's when I see her red eyes and nose, her cheeks bisected by wet, salty tracks.

My arms fall limp, and my fingers barely keep hold of the towel. "What happened to *you*?" I echo stupidly.

Dear Lord, please tell me this is about an emotional viewing of Extreme Makeover: Home Edition. *Or Frankenberry cereal. Or one of those "Save the Children" commercials that always upset her so much.*

When she steps forward and almost tackles me with her fierce hug, the towel slips from my grip to the floor. I stand with my arms at my sides, not fully in control of any muscles required for activities other than remaining upright. My heart thunders in my ears, competing for attention as Betty cries with her hot face against my chest.

Déjà vu hits me so hard, I may as well be back in Green

Bay, kneeling on the bedroom floor with her, surrounded by sneakers and slides and strappy sandals. I swallow the terror that's pitched a tent in my throat. "What happened? What's happening?"

All she's capable of doing is shaking her head, her nose rubbing back and forth through my chlorine-scented chest hair.

"I was only gone for a few minutes. And Winn fell in the pool. But not really. He was joking around. But I thought he truly was drunk and drowning. So I dove in after him. Then we talked. About... stuff. And... and... I... I had no idea you were over here, upset. About... whatever. *Why* are you crying?" Deciding I can't wait for her dreaded answer, I murmur into her hair, "Is it happening again? Damn it. It's happening again, isn't it? The baby... We're losing it. Oh, Betts, I'm sorry. Shh... It's okay."

She pushes away from me. "No!" Grabbing my face in her hands, she says, "No, no. That's not— I'm *not*. Oh, Nate. I'm so sorry."

My cheeks pressed between her palms, I squeak through smashed lips, "Why are you sorry? What's to be sorry about?"

She releases my head and catches my trembling fingers, dragging them to her belly. "I'm sorry you came home—again—to me crying and thought *that*. It's not that. I'm fine. We're fine."

My relief is so intense, I have to yank one hand away and brace it against the dryer to prevent sinking to the floor. But that only lasts a second, because there's still *some* reason for the tears. Something's not right. I do a mental inventory of household members. Betty and baby: okay; Georgia: passed out early thanks to holiday excitement and turkey overload; Reba: still outside.

That means someone else must be dead. Or hurt. Or dying.

Mom? Dad? Nick? Heidi? One of their kids? Oh, sweet Jesus, no. Sweat pours from me like drunks from Lambeau Field on a late Sunday afternoon. Again, my dinner threatens to revolt. Breathing deeply in my nose and through my mouth, I struggle to prevent hyperventilation and to keep all digestive byproducts inside my body.

Suddenly, dreading the upcoming holiday with my family all those times seems petty and ungrateful. If anything happened to one of them...

Gathering my wet clothes at my feet, Betty throws them in the washer. I stand idly by, not sure I could move if I tried. When the clothes are out of the way, she turns and rests her forehead against my shoulder.

"I... I've been trying to stop crying, but I... I... can't."

"Who's dead?"

"Nobody's dead. I'm just scared."

I cup the back of her head with my hand, my protective instinct kicking in and overpowering the selfish fear that's controlled me until now. Well, almost.

"Me, too. Oh, man. I... I saw your face, and I almost pooped my pants. Er, towel."

Lifting her head, she presses her lips to my skin, trying—and failing—to stifle her laughter. Her breath warms my shoulder.

"It's not funny."

"The way you said it is."

"I'm serious, Betts. You almost literally scared me shitless." Her ability to laugh at me relaxes me a bit more. I close my eyes and put my arms around her, then suck in a deep, shuddering breath, feeling fully oxygenated for the first time in several minutes. "Nobody's hurt or dead or dying. You and the baby are okay."

"Yes. Yes."

I look down into her face. "Then tell me what's up. Why are you scared? And if it's about something stupid, make up something else, because I'm going to be pissed off you put me through this."

"It's not stupid." All traces of amusement leave her eyes, to be replaced by more tears, and her mouth turns downward again.

I hold my breath, reluctant to interrupt or distract her with so much as a whisper of air or a word of comfort from me.

She blinks furiously to stem the flow of water from her eyes and chokes, "He... He wants to meet me."

I DON'T NEED TO ASK WHO "HE" IS. NOT EVEN I AM THAT dumb. Only one "he" wanting to meet her could raise this response.

"Oh. Oh, Betts. I... I'm..."

What am I? Sorry? Not really. Dismayed? No. Surprised? A little. Worried? Definitely. But why? I have no clue, so I give up on my original statement and merely pull her to my goose-bumps-covered body.

She sobs, her back spasming against my palm. I rub help-lessly, trying to ignore how cold I am now that my brain and adrenal glands aren't flooding my system with stress hormones.

Eventually, she stops crying and says after a hiccup, "I don't know why it's so upsetting."

I shift my feet on the freezing ceramic tile underneath us and suggest, "Maybe because it's kind of out-of-the-blue. How'd you find out?"

She sniffles and backs away. "That's the worst part. And you're going to be so mad. *I'm* so mad." She seems to notice for the first time that I'm mostly naked and leads me from the laundry room, waving her hand as if to tell me to follow her. "C'mon. I'll tell you while you put on some dry clothes."

Upstairs, she plops onto the bed and sits cross-legged at the foot of the mattress while I pull underwear, pajama pants, and a long-sleeved t-shirt from the dresser. With a grimace, she presses her hand to her side.

I toss my clothes on the bed and reach out to her. "What's wrong? Are you cramping? Maybe you should lie down for a while."

"It's only the tendons pulling, Nathaniel," she snaps, slapping my hand down. "Stop fussing. You make me nervous and paranoid. And my nerves can't handle it right now, okay?"

Her nerves? Between all that food I ate today, plus my recent rescue attempt, then coming home to find her in such an emotional state, it's a miracle I haven't gone into cardiac arrest. Making it all about me *might* be construed as selfish, though, so I let it go. In any case, she has the air conditioner set to "cryogenics," so if I don't get dressed soon, my gonads are going to permanently re-ascend to prevent falling off altogether.

"Okay. Sorry." I kick the damp beach towel free of my feet and yank on the dry boxer briefs, rubbing my thighs to encourage circulation to return to my lower extremities. Then I quickly slide on my pants and tie the drawstring at my waist.

As I'm pulling the t-shirt over my head, she says, "I got an email. From Chris."

I pop my head through the collar but leave the arms dangling free, so my chest and abdomen are still bare. "Chris? Baby-daddy Chris?"

She narrows her eyes at me. "Yes."

"Wait a second. How did he— Are you sure you're starting at the beginning? I feel like I'm missing some important information." Poking my arms into the shirt, I pull it down over my torso and gently lower myself to the bed next to her. "I thought you haven't been in touch with him since... you know."

"I haven't. Not since he and I signed the final papers." She stares into space as if watching herself in that memory.

I picture it, too: young, scared, pale Betty, signing with a shaking hand, a faceless guy standing next to her, waiting his turn, eager to relinquish his parental rights and get on with his life.

Frankie's there too. From what little Betty's told me about it, Kitty didn't show up until a few weeks later, fresh from a Parisian business trip with Witt, and when she did arrive, she pretended like nothing had happened. Frankie was the only one who supported Betty in the aftermath of the birth, a fact that kept Betty in their toxic friendship long after she knew she should break it off.

"Frankie," Betty says now, as if she can read my mind.

Disoriented, I grunt, "Huh?" I blink hard.

"You asked how Chris knew how to get in touch with me. Frankie told him. Of course."

Oh, my poor ticker...

Betty rests her hand on my knee. "Okay, now. Take some deep breaths, because that vein in your neck is freaking me out."

I jump to my feet. "I'm going to kill her."

"She's not worth it."

"Let me kill her first, and then *I'll* decide if it was worth it."

"Please. Sit." Betty pats the bed as if she's worried I'm going to leave right now to do the deed.

I comply with her request but only because my knees feel too wobbly to navigate the stairs.

"If you promise not to blow up, I'll let you read the email for yourself. It'll save me from having to tell you the whole story, because... I don't know if I can. I'm so tired." After she hands me her phone, she leans her head on my shoulder.

I gesture toward the pillows. "Rest your eyes for a minute, huh? This stress isn't good for you."

"Fussing..."

"Too bad. It's true. I promise to keep my cool if you'll lie down."

Yes, that's it. Because you shouldn't watch me or my throbbing vein while I read this email.

She must feel truly awful, because she agrees to my terms. When she's settled, and I'm sure her eyes are closed, I turn my back to her and press the button to wake up her phone, then swipe the screen to return to the open email. It takes everything I have not to audibly react to each part of the message from Chris.Haussman420. But I grind my teeth to headache-inducing psi levels and read:

HEY, Betty Boop. I hope this email addy still works and that you're happy, healthy, and all those things.

I'll get right to the point. Our son has been in touch with me, and he wants to meet you, too. The letter the adoption agency sent to you was returned to them. I guess you moved? I called Frankie and she gave me this address and said if my message bounces back, she might be able to have her lawyer contact yours to get the message to you.

I'd love to hear from you, but if you don't want to talk to me, at least contact the adoption agency to let them know your new address so Trevor (that's our son's name) can get in touch with you through the proper channels. He's a great kid, and you'll be glad you met him.

Pressing send now and hoping it doesn't bounce back!

Chris

. . .

P.S. IT SEEMS crazy you and Frankie aren't friends anymore, but I guess I understand why. I did a Google search of her pen name and... wow. Then I read the book she wrote about us. She made me sound like a real asshole, but whatever. So you married the Frank Lipton dude? That's double-crazy. Like something from a movie. Anyway, maybe I'll get the full story straight from you soon. Or not. Just seeing you would be great. XO

I READ the email three or four times, trying to desensitize myself to its overflowing presumption. First of all, "Betty Boop"? Seriously? After fifteen years, you contact a woman you impregnated and essentially abandoned in college and call her your old pet name for her? Gross. Then you drop a huge bomb on her like it's nothing and proceed to try to get the inside scoop on what basically amounts to a tabloid story? And you end the whole thing with a virtual hug and kiss?

"Well, this guy's a piece of work," I mutter, tossing her phone on the bed behind me and half-turning so I can see her.

My voice startles her. She opens her eyes and looks at me like she's not sure who I am or how I got to be in the same room. I smile as encouragingly as I can, waiting patiently for her to mentally return from wherever she was.

Looking down the length of her body at me, she says, "Yeah. Same old Chris. Acts like nothing's happened, like we talk all the time."

"One of those over-familiar types, huh?"

She nods distractedly then says, "I have a son named Trevor. I—" Her voice breaks and this time, there's no holding back the tears. She covers her eyes with her shaky hand and cries noiselessly until I crawl across the mattress, stretch my body behind hers, and gather her in my arms.

"Come on. That's enough for now."

"No! I need to talk this through with you. I need you to tell me it's going to be okay."

"It *is* going to be okay. And if you don't want to meet this kid, you don't have to."

"It's not that I *don't* want to. He has the right to know who I am and ask me all those uncomfortable questions I'm sure he has. But I just thought that part of my life was over." She waves her right arm at the room around us. "How do I explain all *this*? This new life I have, with a husband and a child and another on the way? His adoption seems so personal, like I specifically didn't want *him*. When really, I had fantasies all the time about keeping him. But I knew they were just that: stupid, childish, selfish fantasies. He needed a mother, not someone who could barely make sound decisions for herself most days."

"Then that's what you tell him."

"I dunno. Because that's the other thing: he's fifteen. So, like, how much *do* I tell him? It's not my place to give him a lesson in the ways of the world. I'm not his mother."

"But you are."

"No, I'm not. The woman who will accompany him to this terrifying meeting is his mother. I'm just the vessel that brought him into this world."

"Trevor's mom has probably been waiting a long time to thank 'the vessel.'"

She shakes her head, a series of squeaks escaping from her throat as she fights back more tears. Finally, she whispers, "I don't think I can do this."

"You don't have to."

"I can't not do it, though, right? I mean, isn't this the least I owe him? How can I possibly reject him twice? What would that make me?"

I squeeze her shoulder, too heartbroken on her behalf to respond.

"And what if he hates me? What if he's a miserable person, and the whole point of meeting me is to spit in my face and curse me for choosing to have him?"

"C'mon. He wouldn't go to the trouble of finding you if that's all he wanted to do."

"If it meant enough to him, he would. What if his life has been awful? What if he's one of those angry young males we see on the news all the time, collecting guns and waiting for the right moment to take out his frustrations on an unsuspecting crowd?"

I shake off the picture of a skinhead in a leather jacket with the Confederate flag pasted to the back of it. "I'm sure he's not. And even if he is, that's not your fault."

"How is it not my fault? I started it all. I set it in motion."

I grab her flailing hand and press it firmly to my lips. "Hey. Can we—" I sigh and look into her anguished face. "Let's start by answering one question: are you going to agree to meet with him?"

"Yes."

"That's all you need to know right now."

She stares into space for a few seconds, then asks, "You don't think he's sick, do you? Like, he needs an organ or bone marrow or something like that?"

"Chris would have mentioned it, right?"

Her shoulder lifts and falls. "Not if he thought it would scare me off."

"That's something you can ask about when you contact the adoption agency."

She sighs and nods. "Yeah. True."

Draping my arm over her side, I press the side of my face to hers and say, "You know what I think? He's at an age where he wants or needs to understand more about who he is. And he doesn't feel he can do that without hearing the full story. And you're the beginning of the story. He wants to hear the 'Once upon a time' so he can get to the 'happily ever after'... eventually."

"Yeah?"

"Maybe. It's as good a theory as any other. But there's only one way to find out for sure."

"Meet him."

"Yep."

"And you'll be there with me?"

That there was ever any question for her makes me want to weep. "Absolutely. C'mere." I roll to my back and gather her to me when she turns and rests her head on my chest. Then I hold her as tightly as I can without restricting her breathing. "Whatever you want to do, I'm with you. You don't have to worry for a second about that, okay?"

"Thank you. I love you so much, Nathaniel. You know that, right?"

"I do."

"And you think Georgia knows how much I love her, too?"

"No, but only because she doesn't have the capacity to understand."

"I don't ever want her to wonder."

"She won't. And neither will the next one." I kiss her hair. "Now, why don't you call it a night?"

"Will you come to bed, too?"

I glance at the clock over her shoulder and cringe when I see it's not yet eight o'clock. I'll be up in the middle of the night, wide awake, staring at the ceiling, if I go to bed now. But...

"Sure. I'm not going anywhere."

"I don't want to be alone."

She'll never be alone again, as long as I can help it. But that might sound more creepy than comforting if I say it out loud. Therefore, I simply adjust my chin so it's not digging into her skull, and I stroke her shoulder blades with my thumbs. Then I mentally run through the list of all the things I'm thankful for, starting with her. Always. No matter what's about to happen.

11

IN SICKNESS AND IN ENVY

Sick. Horribly sick. Contagiously sick.

When I return home from the nearest Urgent Care (which isn't near at all), after spending my entire Saturday morning there, I shuffle into the living room and hold aloft the white paper bag containing my prescription remedies. "Strep."

Betty covers her nose and mouth with her hand. "Oh, no!"

"Yep." I pop open the bottle of antibiotics and down one without any water. Which hurts like a mo-fo, I realize too late.

She punches the couch cushion next to her thigh. "Dang it, Nate! We were supposed to go shopping today."

"It's not my fault!" I shudder from another fever-induced shiver as I put the cap back on my drugs and pocket the white-capped plastic bottle.

I blame Jackson Andretti. More accurately, I blame his wolf-crying mother. Because when she brought him in Thursday, suspecting he had strep throat, I didn't take her seriously. I didn't even glove up when I told him to open wide and let me look down his throat. As soon as I saw the white patches there, however, I jumped back, washed my hands, and put on both a mask and gloves, but it was too late.

Actually, it's not that easy to contract it, so it probably wasn't from him but from Betty, who likely picked it up but never exhibited symptoms. Then we did what married people do, and *voilà*. I honestly don't have enough energy to explain the "carrier" phenomenon right now, though. Nor do I want to make her feel bad, after the week she's had, so I'm still blaming Jackson Andretti. (Plus who wants to admit that having sex with his wife could result in feeling this horrible? It's enough to turn a guy off for a whole week, or something.)

Anyway, it's not surprising I got sick. Neither of us has slept a full night in days.

One of my patients told me I looked like 'Jake from *Adventure Time*.' When I sought a second opinion from Betty and showed her the picture of my cartoon yellow doggy doppelganger with dark rings under his eyes, she laughed and said, "More like Lurch from *The Addams Family*, but your patient was too young to make that connection."

"Gee, thanks."

As for Betty, her insomnia seems to have invited morning sickness back to the party. I've been toeing the line between "nurturing" and "fussing" all week, trying to ensure her nervous stomach doesn't prevent her from getting enough nutrition. She's been about as receptive to my ministrations as a wild animal with an open wound. Same goes for any attention I try to give her current situation with Trevor and Chris. She'd rather hunker in the corner over her bloody paw and nurse it herself. And I get that. I guess.

So we lurched through the week like two extras in one of those zombie flicks that stress me right the hell out. By last night, I chalked up my malaise to lack of sleep catching up to me, but I worried Betty was equally if not more tired, so I dragged my butt through Georgia's bedtime routine, then fell asleep on the couch like an old fart.

Only when Betty shook me awake to ask me if I was going to go to bed did I notice a slight rawness in the back of my throat and an aching behind my ears. Again, though, I dismissed it as exhaustion and stress and crawled to bed.

When my burning throat woke me from a sound sleep around two o'clock, I knew I was in trouble. And I saw every hour on the clock from then on, despite eating as much ibuprofen as I felt I could safely handle at one time. Six o'clock was still several minutes away when I shot out the door in an effort to beat the weekend Urgent Care rush.

Of all people, I should have known better. There was a line at the locked entrance, and I wasn't even close to the front. I debated heading for the nearest emergency room but figured the wait time there wouldn't be any shorter; plus, I would have felt ridiculous going to the hospital for what I knew from my own mirror-and-flashlight inspection was a routine case of strep throat. So I stuck it out, and when they opened the doors, I checked in and slumped over in a vinyl chair to wait as patiently as possible through my chills for them to call my name.

Finally, they did. In the exam room, I rattled off my symptoms to the nurse and ordered my own strep test (yeah, I'm *that* guy when I'm sick), and she humored me but went through her usual routine (as I would have done in her place), then left me to wait for the doctor.

When the doctor came in, I gave her the same spiel I gave the nurse. Again, she nodded and hmmm'ed, but my self-diagnosis didn't speed her up at all. She looked down my throat, grimaced, ordered the strep test, and bid me good day.

Another twenty minutes ticked off the clock before the nurse came back with the swab. She said it would be at least ten minutes before the quick culture was finished, and if it came back negative, they'd have to wait up to seventy-two hours for a definitive result, but I'd be allowed to go home, at least.

"Yeah, yeah, I know the drill," I said less than graciously. "But it's going to be positive. So if you could get the doctor started on writing that 'script, that would be great. I'm allergic to anything in the cephalosporin family, and I don't want to take any of your super-antibiotics, either, so good old-fashioned penicillin would be great."

She stripped off her gloves and tapped the tube containing the swab against her palm. "Well, bless your heart! You hang tight now, and the *doctor* will decide *after* your culture results come in what the best course is."

It was my first experience with the *Screw you* "Bless your heart," and if I hadn't felt so horrible, I would have laughed, because I deserved it. Since my sense of humor was nowhere to be found, however, I merely collapsed onto my back on the paper-covered exam table, tucked my hands into my armpits, and shivered in the blasting air conditioning for the next thirty minutes. I'm sure they purposely made me wait longer for being such a jerkwad. I know *that* drill, too.

An hour later, I left the on-site pharmacy with my requested penicillin prescription plus one for a lidocaine rinse I'm supposed to gargle and swish every couple of hours. I almost didn't have that one filled but reconsidered at the last second, because you never know how desperate you'll be in the middle of the night. (I've found that out the hard way in many facets of life.)

"Now what?" Betty asks.

I inspect the instructions on the rinse. Twisting off the bottle's lid, I take an experimental sniff of the syrup. "Oh, gosh. I'd rather suffer through the pain, thanks." I toss it back in the bag with a loud crunch and limp toward the stairs. When I realize Betty asked me something, to which I never responded, I stop with my foot on the bottom step. "I'm going to bed. You do whatever you want to do. Go shopping with Laurel."

"I can't leave you here, all sick and alone!"

"I give you my blessing."

She tosses a throw pillow at me. "Stop trying to get out of going."

"I'm sick! And I'll be contagious for at least another twenty-four hours, so it'd be smart if you and Georgia steered clear of me. Getting out of the house altogether as much as you can would be even better."

She says nothing until I'm about halfway up the staircase, then calls after me, "I hope you're serious. Speak now if you want me to stay here and take care of you."

"I'm as serious as this case of strep throat, Betts. You guys have a good time." At the top of the stairs, I hear Georgia singing in her room, where she's supposed to be napping. "Someone's still awake up here," I say over the railing that looks down on the entryway.

Betty grumbles something back at me, but I can't hear it, and I don't care. I'm going to pretend she told me to go to bed. Because that's what I'm going to do.

In our bedroom, I toss the white paper bag containing the disgusting lidocaine in the direction of our bathroom, where it lands with a loud thump and crackle on the floor. I strip out of my cargo (a.k.a., "dad") shorts and the t-shirt I wore to UC but leave them in a heap on the floor next to the bed after I fish my drugs from the shorts pocket.

In the bathroom, I step over the prescription bag, shove four ibuprofen into my mouth from the bottle already waiting on the counter from the night before, and cup my hands under the faucet to get enough water to coax them down. Then I dodder to the bed, where I collapse on my stomach, my face buried in my pillows. With a thick slurp, I turn my head sideways so I can breathe. I moan but quickly cut myself off when the vibrating vocal chords trigger more pain. I'd pull the covers back and get under them, but that's too much effort.

Time to sleep.

* * *

BETTY'S VOICE in the distance wakes me. A blinky glance at the clock next to the bed sends my foggy head into a game of logic ping-pong that almost knocks me back out from the cognitive strain.

Is that 4:52 a.m. or p.m.?

If it's a.m., who's Betty talking to, and why isn't she in bed? And did I sleep more than twelve hours without moving?

If it's p.m., why is Betty still here? She's supposed to be shopping with Laurel, keeping Georgia away from the house and my germs.

Wait. Is it still Saturday, or is it Sunday?

Did I sleep more than twenty-four hours?

Did I sleep more than twenty-four hours?!

I kick at the covers, panicked at the thought. Immediately, my bladder clues me in that I haven't been lying here that long. I grab my phone from the bedside table and look at the date. And the "p.m." next to the time. Scratching my head, I perform a few tight, painful swallows.

OW!

Ow!

Ow.

Once I can concentrate on anything other than the burning sword of fire through my throat, I listen harder to Betty's lighthearted side of what's obviously a telephone conversation downstairs and try to determine who the other party is. She sounds way too happy to be talking to her mom. Someone in my family? Not likely.

"Oh, come on! It can't be that bad." She giggles. "No! Stop! ... Because he's your dad. *You* should be thankful you have one.... Who, mine? Ha! No. I've still never met him. Thank goodness. Please, don't tell me *he's* going to come out of the woodwork now, too. I can't handle it.... Huh?... No, that was Witt, my stepdad. He's a whole other story, but you're right; at least he was *present*... most of the time. I'm telling you, you dodged a major bullet by not being part of my family. You're welcome...."

What the...?

I drag myself from bed, staggering to the bathroom, where I shift over-the-counter bottles around on the medicine cabinet shelves, looking for the acetaminophen to alternate with that elephant's dose of ibuprofen I took earlier. When I find it, I toss back four caplets with the cup next to the sink, then curse under my breath when I remember Betty uses that cup to take her prenatal vitamin every day.

Heaving a huge sigh, I shuffle downstairs in my boxer briefs (yeah, I don't care) with the cup, glaring at Betty on my way through the living room as she shriek-laughs some more at the ceiling.

"Daddy!" Georgia greets me from the floor, where she's surrounded by toys. She scrambles to her feet and runs toward me.

"No, no, no. Stay away from Daddy," I croak, speed-walking into the kitchen to evade her.

She ignores my command and follows as fast as she can, laughing at what she perceives to be an impromptu game of chase. I temporarily block her entrance to the room with the open dishwasher door, but she tries to climb over it.

Gently pushing her away with my foot, I nestle the contaminated bathroom cup in the upper rack. "Ew! No. That's nasty. Stop. Stop. I'll hold you in a second."

No, I won't.

"Betty!" I rasp as loudly as I can without passing out from the pain. I press my hand to my throat when it's obvious she didn't hear me over her loud conversation with Jerry Seinfeld. Finally managing to nudge the toddler away from the dirty dishwasher, I close the appliance and cross the tiles to the refrigerator, where I seek out orange juice.

As I'm staring into the pitifully empty cold-storage unit, willing the jug to appear on the lonely shelf at eye level, where it usually squats, Georgia latches onto me, sitting on my foot and wrapping her arms and legs around my leg.

She pets my hairy limb. "'Raffe."

Normally, I'd laugh and give her a ride around the kitchen, but it's all I can do to lift my feet high enough to walk with my own weight, so I merely chuckle-groan, still hanging onto the handle of the fridge while its cold air swirls around my feverish face. "George," I whine, "I can't. The giraffe is sick. The giraffe needs your mommy to rescue it from the poacher. And go buy some friggin' orange juice."

"Friggin'?" she asks, sweetly tilting her head back and looking up the length of my body at me.

"Oh, that's a new one for you, huh? Great. Well, it's a relatively mild one, so it won't get you the reaction you normally enjoy."

The fridge beeps at me for having it open too long, as if to say, *"Are you in or are you out, pal? It's either here or it's not. Make up your mind and move on."*

"Yeah, yeah," I mutter at it, still not moving. Unable to move. Stuck here, with a kid on my foot and what feels like a wasabi-coated wire brush in my throat.

"'Raffe, 'raffe, 'raffe!" Georgia chants in time with the beeping refrigerator.

I close my eyes, contemplating the possibility of sleeping here, like this. I could totally do it.

Suddenly, Betty says right next to me (but still not *at* me), "Oh, geez. I have to go.... No, Nate's sick, and he's stuck in the refrigerator." She laughs, because that's hilarious, apparently. "No! He's hypnotized by it, or something. Plus, Georgia wants him to give her a ride.... She *is* cute... when she's not attacking people. Or cursing. Anyway. Gotta go. I'll let you know how it goes with Trevor.... No, that's not a good idea.... NO.... No, I'm not going to trash-talk you, but I'd prefer to meet him by myself. It's going to be awkward enough." She sighs. "Listen, I *really* have to go. We can talk about it more some other time.... Yeah.... Yeah.... Okay, bye."

My foot and leg become lighter and cooler as Betty lifts Georgia from them. Of course, the child doesn't go easily, taking two handfuls of hair with her and screaming, "Friggin' 'raffe!!" the whole way, followed by, "Daddy!"

Betty's fingers pry mine from the handle, and the light in front of me dims as the door thumps to a close. The beeping ceases. "What the heck are you doing?"

"What are *you* doing?" I demand in return, my words carrying a slur brought on by all the saliva I don't want to swallow. I sound drunk. I wish I were. Alcohol would be good right now. Not beer. Too much carbonation. But whiskey. Or brandy. Cooking sherry might deaden the burn, too.

I blink at Betty. "Do we have any liquor?"

"No. Well, we have some old margarita mix from back when I could still drink, but you're not drinking right now. Where's that stuff you're supposed to gargle?"

"I'd rather die."

"That's hardly your only other option." Shifting a still-wailing Georgia to her other hip, she disappears into the pantry and comes back with a giant can of chicken noodle soup.

I wrinkle my nose.

"I'll strain out the 'gross pink chunks and rubbery noodles' and bring you a big mug of broth. The hot saltiness will feel good."

"Who were you talking to? Where's the orange juice?"

"Uhh... I drank the last of it this morning. I'll run out and get some more in a few minutes, after you have your soup." She pats my face on her way past me. "And I was talking to Chris. He called."

She says it like it's no big deal. *"Oh, you know, Chris? That guy who almost ruined my life? Yeah, we're buds now. Just shootin' the breeze, talking about old times... like the time he knocked me up in college. Memories..."*

Somehow I manage to locate a non-irate response and ask, "How did he get your cell phone number?"

She focuses on popping the top on the soup while holding a wriggling kid. After dumping the contents of the can into a strainer placed over a gigantic mug, she transfers the noodles and "chicken" (that stuff's nasty) to the sink and puts the broth in the microwave, setting it for two minutes. Finally, she turns back to me and says, "We exchanged phone numbers in an email, just in case."

"In case of what?" Without waiting for her to answer, I add, "You woke me up."

"Sorry! I thought you had the bedroom door closed."

"Why would I have the bedroom door closed? You're supposed to be out of the house, shopping with Laurel. Why aren't you, anyway?"

She shrugs. "I felt weird and guilty, going without you. Plus what if I'm sick and just don't know it yet? I don't want to get anyone else sick."

"Do you feel sick? Does your throat hurt? Do you have chills? Or a headache?"

"I'm getting one, with all your nurse-y questions."

"Daddy!" Georgia screeches.

Betty clamps her hand over our daughter's mouth. "Oh, my gosh," she mutters through clenched teeth. "Will you please go upstairs and get back in bed, so she'll stop screaming in my ear for you?"

I lean to get a look at the microwave timer around her arm. "I'll wait for my soup."

She continues to muffle our daughter's cries with her hand and purses her lips.

"What did you and Chris need to talk about?" I ask, as if I didn't listen to most of her side of the conversation.

"The packet from the adoption agency came today, and I wanted to hear from him how it's all going to go down, since he's already been through this."

I nod. "Yeah, okay. But it didn't sound like that's what you were talking about."

The microwave beeps behind her. We both ignore it for the time being as she stares me down, and I return her defiant gaze.

"We were catching each other up, that's all," she finally answers. "I told him about you and Georgia and the new baby, and he—"

"He's married and has kids of his own, too?"

"No. Never married. No other kids." She retrieves my broth and hands it carefully to me. "It's hot. Use the handle, and be careful not to slosh it on your hands on your way up the stairs."

I accept her advice about the handle but don't perform a

single step away from the kitchen. If she thinks I'm leaving this conversation now, she's more delirious than I am.

"Sounds like he's a funny guy." I blow on my broth and watch her through my lashes.

"Always was. I guess that hasn't changed."

"And you guys are buddy-buddy now? After everything?"

"There's no need to make things ugly. What happened was a long time ago. It's in the past."

I stop blowing. "It's not in the past, though, now, is it?"

"I'm just trying to be civil."

"That sounded more than civil."

She waves me off with her free hand. "Go. Georgia's about to pop a vein. Or bite me. Which, come to think of it, you can, too."

Defying her seems like a viable option for a nanosecond (drugs make you entertain crazy thoughts), but I eventually come to my senses and do what I'm told, shuffling back to bed like a good little patient.

This conversation can wait until I'm coherent and the toddler's not present. We wouldn't want her learning any new words, now, would we?

12

INVASION OF PRIVACY

WHEN THE CELL PHONE NEXT TO MY ELBOW CHIMES WHILE I'm covering the front desk for Betty, who's using the bathroom for the millionth time today, I reflexively pick it up and swipe the screen to wake up the device. I *was* perusing Betty's (much more elaborate and getting-out-of-control) plans for the Christmas open house, but what I see in the email notification preview is much more interesting (but possibly more stressful).

"Nate sounds hilarious. I can't wait to meet him. Speaking of..."

I glance toward the bathroom, where I heard the toilet flush.

In fractions of a second, I reason:

This isn't your phone, and you know it.

But it looks like my phone—same make and model—so it could be mistaken for my phone, if I wasn't paying close attention.

No, it couldn't. The notification chime is different, the wallpaper on the home screen is a picture of you and Georgia at the beach, not the sonogram of Georgia that's been on yours for years... Need I go on?

Okay, so I'm fully aware it's not mine, but that incoming message could be from Laurel about Georgia. I'm just checking.

You know full well it's not from Laurel; it's from Chris.

Yeah, and he's saying my name in vain. I want to see what he's saying about me. I have that right. Right?

Wrong.

Well, I don't have time for an ethics lesson, complete with flow chart, so here goes.

I swipe to unlock the phone and click into Chris's full message.

NATE SOUNDS HILARIOUS. *I can't wait to meet him. Speaking of, have you had a chance to talk to him yet about the meeting? I know you wanted to do this alone with Trevor and his parents, but Trevor really wants me there. And we can do it on your turf, if that makes you feel more comfortable. Or somewhere neutral. That's your call, Boop. We just need to know where and when. Of course, let the agency and the Newsomes know. Trevor will keep me in the loop. I told him I'd light a fire under you. He's anxious to do this soon. Maybe it can be our Christmas present to him? LOL. Listen to me, sounding like a dad. Weird. Hope you're okay and didn't get whatever Nate had.*

XO

C

THE HINGES on the bathroom door down the hallway squeak. With no time to process the message, I mark it as "unread," close out of Betty's email, lock the screen, and slide the phone back in the general location where I found it. Grabbing the open house agenda is my final touch on attempting to look innocent before she arrives at the desk.

"Well?" she asks, nodding to the printout in my hands. "What do you think? Too much? The massage chairs are an addition since the last time we talked, but Pat likes the idea, and it's important to have something for the grownups, too."

Gesturing to the empty waiting room, she adds, "We need *something*."

I slap the paper on the desk and stand, unable to concentrate on anything but that email (except, possibly, the grating sound of the doctor's first name). "As long as you don't feel like you're getting in over your head."

The blinking blue light on her otherwise dark mobile phone grabs her attention. She lifts the device and snorts while swiping at the screen. "Please. I could organize something like this in my sleep."

"If you're sure."

"I'm sure."

I wait while she reads her "new" email, her cocky smile fading.

"What's the matter?"

Does it annoy you as much as it annoys me that he insists on calling you "Boop" and ends every email by kissing and hugging you, like he has that right? Or are you bothered by his high-pressure tactics, like Trevor's a used car he's trying to sell you? You want me to tell him to buzz off? I'll gladly do it.

After a three-second pause, she hits the button on the side to darken the phone, sets it aside, and says, "Huh? Oh. Nothing."

So that's how we're going to play this?

I set my jaw. When she blinks and smiles uncertainly at me, then says, "I'm going to call some food trucks in Columbia, see how far they're willing to travel for events," I pivot and retreat to my office.

"You do that," I say. "I'll be in my office doing some research, if you need to talk."

Thumbs already working furiously over the keyboard on her phone and tongue poking from the corner of her mouth, she mumbles, "M'kay."

As I close my door, I watch for a few seconds through the crack. That's an awfully intense face for someone researching food trucks. It looks more like the face of someone emailing her (presumably) hot ex-boyfriend behind her husband's back.

When I felt well enough to look through the adoption agency packet, I read through the profile form Trevor filled out, noting how normal and well-adjusted the kid seemed. He's a typical fifteen-year-old middle-class kid living in an Ohio suburb of Cincinnati. He's an Honor Roll student who's active in his high school's choir and drama programs. He's learning how to drive. He helps out part-time at the bookstore his parents own. His favorite movie is *Jurassic World*. He doesn't have a favorite type of music, but he did specify, "anything but country... no offense," on the form. His hobbies include video gaming, going to the movies, and hanging with friends, and he's interested in U.S. history.

Then I stared at the photo paper-clipped to the inside of the manila folder. It was a typical school picture: cerulean background, cheesy grin, post-P.E.-sweat-spiked hair. Betty's smile. And her cheekbones and nose. Otherwise... I assume he looks like Chris. Since that's his dad. And since Betty's white. And Trevor isn't.

Hey, at least those white supremacist, skinhead fears of mine have been completely put to rest.

I asked Betty, "Are you sure this is the right kid?"

She looked over my shoulder and smiled. "Yeah. I mean, barring a DNA test. Why?"

"Uh, no reason." I paused. "Well, a tiny reason. I didn't realize— You never told me Chris was not white."

Snorting, she said, "I told you he was from Hawaii."

"And?"

She laughed at herself. "I guess I assumed... Does it matter?"

"Of course not. I just... I... I always pictured some blond, tanned surfer dude."

"You got the 'tanned' part right."

"This kid also looks tall. Is Chris a big guy?"

Shrugging, she replied, "Yeah. He's above average."

"So he's Samoan?"

"Not Samoan. Geez, stereotype much? He's Pacific Islander, tall, dark-skinned, and broad."

"Like overweight-broad? Or muscular-broad?"

"In college, he was built. Who knows now? Do you look the same as you did in college?"

"Uh, yeah. Not that it's anything to brag about, in my case."

"What do you want me to say, Nathaniel?" she asked with a smirk. "You want me to lie to you and say Chris was flabby, ugly, and short, so you can feel superior to someone I used to know?"

"You used to *know* know him."

"Yeah, like you used to *know* know Heidi, someone who's a member of our family. And I don't make a big deal about that."

She had a point.

Still...

"Did he walk around shirtless all the time, showing off his chiseled physique?" I'll admit it, I was picturing a fire-twirling Hula dancer, complete with grass skirt and lei.

After she was physically able to talk again, she wiped her eyes and answered, "No. We went to college in Wisconsin, remember?"

"Why did he go to that school, anyway?"

"Because UW is a kick-ass school? Duh."

"Yeah, that goes without saying, but I'm sure Hawaii has kick-ass schools, too. In paradise."

Fed up with my interrogation, she stepped away from me

and lowered herself to the floor to play with Georgia. "I don't know. Why don't you email him and ask him?"

It wasn't *that* important.

And honestly, I don't care about his reasoning for college selection. Right now, I'm more interested in his email correspondence with my wife. Specifically, what I've missed up to this point. Chris's message today is clearly the continuation of a conversation.

"Nate sounds hilarious."

Oh, do I? In what ways? Has Betty presented me to Chris as a funny guy, like him? Because I'm not. Not intentionally, anyway. Or does he mean that I sound like a ridiculous buffoon, clueless while he chats up his ex-girlfriend/baby-mama in emails? I wouldn't know, because I didn't have time to scroll down and read the rest of the chain. You better believe I will later, though, the next time Betty has to empty her bladder.

In the meantime, I'll be making good on my claim that I'm in here doing research. Betty doesn't need to know it has nothing to do with medicine.

I'm interested in what this Chris guy brings to the table. *Not* because I fear she's interested. *Not* because I'm threatened by him. But because I'm a guy. A guy with a beautiful, smart, funny, way-out-of-my-league wife. And to be crass and caveman about it, I want to see who belongs to the swimmers that also made it across the finish line at one time. Okay?

Sue me for being primitive.

Checking the time and estimating I have about a half hour before my next appointment, I log on to my long-dormant account on that site that always has Betty's panties in a bunch about something—politics, former classmates' humble-bragging, or Frankie's (a.k.a., "Francesca Pembroke - Author's") latest status update. I type, "Chris Haussman" into the search box. Good news: only one person pops up. Bad news: his profile picture is an ocean sunset (*Real original, dude*), his cover photo is Iron Man (*Buh-rother*), and I'm not "friends" with him (and don't ever plan to be), so I can't see anything more. Damn.

My only consolation is that my privacy settings are such that he can't spy or stalk me on here, either. Not that he'd want to.

Or need to. He's probably "friends" with Betty, who posts plenty of pictures of you and Georgia and frequent status updates about your lives. Trust me; he already knows exactly who and what you are. And he's not impressed.

I navigate to her account and see that yes, Betty recently accepted a friend request from Mr. Mauna Loa. Also, she identifies herself as a Packers fan. (And you think you know someone...)

The only posts I can see from Tall, Tan, and Hawaiian are the ones he's posted to mutual friends' pages, and since the only mutual "friend" we have is my wife, the "Thanks for accepting my friend request" post, complete with silly, tongue-lolling emoji, is all I can glean from here. Unauthorized email access is much more informative. Unfortunately.

Like only this time-sucking site can do, though, it pulls me into a black hole of mindless scrolling, liking, and friend-requesting, including that of my neighbor and good friend, who smiles cheesily back at me from the deck of his boat. As soon as he accepts my request, I type in a private message to him, *Hey. What ya doin'?*

Well, I'm *not* watching porn in the middle of the day, I can tell you that much

I trust you're NOT "not watching porn" with my daughter nearby

What kind of sicko do you take me for?

No comment. I'll let you get back to it, then

Thank you kindly, sir. Everything okay?

Immediately, without considering the truth as a possible reply, I type, *Yep. Dandy. See you later*

Having heard Betty greet my next patient on the other side of my closed door, I log off and push away from my desk.

Focus, Bingham.

13

GRUMPY AND GIMPY

Imagine my surprise when the "Blub, blub, blub" of an underwater fart greets my ears from the general direction of my posterior. During a patient exam.

My eyes widen at the noise. My patient giggles. Her dad snorts. I blush and scramble to silence the phone through my pocket. "Sorry about that," I mumble, then laugh at the sheer delight the noise has evoked from my previously solemn companions. While I tap Brooklyn Forrester's reflexes, I ask, "Do you know anyone who likes to play jokes on you?"

She nods and points to her dad, Lyle, who laughs harder at being outed.

"Well, I have a friend named Winn who likes to play jokes on me. He must have downloaded that sound on my phone when I wasn't looking."

"Winn Baker?" Lyle asks.

"Yeah. You know him?"

He scoffs. "Everyone knows Winn. But yeah. Graduated high school with him. And that sounds exactly like somethin' he would do. For our senior prank, he and a buncha other guys dismantled a tractor and reassembled it in the entryway of the school. They almost got charged with breakin' and entering. But the school district let it go. I think they were secretly impressed. Kids have been tryin' to outdo that stunt ever since. How do you know Winn?"

"We're neighbors. And friends. And he loves to play jokes on me. Some of them aren't funny. But that ring tone is pretty funny." Smiling at Brooklyn, I say, "Open wide and stick out your tongue, please."

She does as she's told and holds still while I hold down her tongue with the wooden depressor and peer into her mouth with my light. "Lookin' good. I'm mighty jealous of those tonsils. Lost mine, oh"—I back up, squint one eye and do the math—"'bout twenty-five years ago. No, more than that. Oh, man. I'm old."

She giggles.

I switch off my light and toss the depressor and the light guard in the trash, then wash my hands and say, "Your dad tells me you sometimes get a sore tummy. Tell me about that."

Twenty minutes later, after ruling out a blockage and narrowing Brooklyn's problem to her new secret addiction to sugar-coated, sour gummy candies, provided by her dealer (her older brother, Kevin), I send father and daughter on their way.

Lyle leans close to her ear and whispers furiously, "Why didn't you just tell me? I have half a mind to tan your hide and make you pay for this visit with your allowance."

Betty and I exchange a glance at the desk, and as soon as the two of them clear the door, I say, "Umm, that's going to be an uncomfortable car ride home."

She laughs. "Right? Geez."

I smile down at her before remembering I'm mad at us. Clearing my throat, I look at the empty waiting room. "Anyway." Then I high-tail it to my office.

"Nate." She stops me two steps from my destination. To my back, she asks, "Are you okay? Do you still feel sick?"

After two days of obsessively checking her email every time she leaves her phone unattended, it's no lie when I answer, "Yeah. I do."

I hate myself for the cell phone spying, but now I can't stop. It's my only way to stay in the loop. Every cycle of message and response fuels my fury, though, to the point that I can barely look at her, much less talk to her.

It doesn't help that I'm still *not* one-hundred percent, health-wise. Losing sleep is only exacerbating the problem. I'm taking the antibiotics (three days to go), and I'm no longer contagious or in pain, but I'm worn down. My body's working hard to fight this off. At the end of the day, I'm exhausted from maintaining the minimum *bonhomie* required from someone who pokes, prods, and jabs kids all day long.

"Maybe you should have Pat take a look at your throat, check that those antibiotics are working."

I close my eyes, take a deep breath, and count as far as I can before my pause becomes too conspicuous. When I can trust myself to speak, I say, "They're fine. I'm fine. Just tired," and step into my office, closing the door gently behind me. Then I kick my desk as hard as I can.

Wait for it...

"Son of a bitch!" I limp to the couch and remove my shoe, squeezing and rubbing my violated foot. "Idiot!" I hiss at myself, then shout, "I'm okay!" hoping to prevent Betty from coming in here to check on me.

Fail.

The door opens enough for her to poke her head through. "What the heck's going on in here?"

I gingerly slide off my sock. "I stubbed my toe."

"On what?"

"My desk." I clench my teeth and continue massaging.

"That looks like more than your toe."

"Toe, foot, whatever. I'm fine."

"How did you accidentally hit your foot so hard against your desk that you hurt yourself through your shoe? Do you need some ice?"

"No. I need you to leave me alone."

She raises an eyebrow at me. "Excuse me?"

"You heard me. I don't need your help or your sympathy right now."

Tucking her chin closer to her body, she says, "Fine!" Before she closes the door, I hear her mutter, "Baby."

"I'm not a baby," I grumble to myself while inspecting my red instep, which provides plenty of evidence to the contrary.

Dr. Reitman emerges from her office and asks Betty, "What's his deal?"

"Heck if I know!" my wife replies, purposely raising her voice so I can hear them through my door. "Acts like he's the first person in the world to ever get sick. I guess we're all supposed to be so thankful he's 'powering through,' even though he's being a complete doo-doo head!"

I flip the bird at my door but quickly pull my hand down when she says, "And don't you dare flip me off, Nathaniel."

How the heck?

She and Dr. Reitman—or should I say, *Pat*—laugh like a couple of teenagers.

I hobble to the door, swing it open, and ask, "Do you have a hidden camera in here?"

Inspecting her fingernails, Betty answers, "Nope. But now I know you *were* flipping me off."

Dr. Reitman shakes her head. "Nate, Nate, Nate. Not nice." She looks down at my mismatched feet. "What's going on there? You have a boo-boo?"

"Need me to kiss it better?" Betty baby-talks, complete with pouty lower lip.

I return to my couch, walking as normally as possible, although it hurts like a mother, until I'm no longer in view of either of them. "You two are really mature."

"Simply trying to match the maturity level coming from that office," Betty says. "Show of solidarity, and all that." When I'm too busy wincing and cringing to reply as I stuff my foot back into my shoe, she adds, "And your next appointment just pulled up, so shape up. And no more potty finger."

That brings on more giggles from the ladies.

I double-knot my laces, stand, and give my foot an exploratory bounce, mouthing, *"Ha ha ha. You're so funny!"*

"I saw that!" Betty sing-songs.

All I can do is stare incredulously at the wall between us. How the hell is she doing that?

In all the foot-throbbing frustration of the afternoon, I forget about the wet fart in my pocket until it happens again, this time while I'm alone in my office, dreading the hour when I'm expected to go home and suffer through another evening of pretending I don't know my wife's emailing another man several times a day.

When I finally free the device from my pants and put it to my ear, I say, "Yo. Thanks for the awesome ringtone."

"You somewhere public right now? Because that would be hilarious!"

"No. I was with a patient the first time you called, though."

"Were you bent over?"

"No! Why would I be— Anyway! Is there a reason for your call?"

"Do I need a reason to call you? I thought we were past that stage in our relationship." When I don't answer, he says, "Your wife just left here with your sweet baby girl, and seein' her reminded me that you never called me back. Are we in a fight?"

"What? No. I'm at work."

"What are you thinkin' right now?"

"That I'm about to hang up on you," I say, smiling in spite of myself.

"Oh, you! Don't play hard to get, Yank."

I lean back in my chair and prop my feet on the corner of my desk. "Wouldn't dream of it."

"I'm callin' to check on you. Betty says you've been under the weather, and I haven't seen you doin' your dog doo rounds in the backyard. I'm startin' to worry."

"Me, too. There's going to be so much crap to shovel."

"Not about the poop! I'm worried about you!"

"Me? You never need to worry about me. I'm solid. Which is more than I can say for the dog piles in my yard after all the rain we've been having. So, this is what winter's like down here? Never-ending rain?"

"Pretty much. Hey, why don't you come on over tonight, and we'll shoot some pool in the man cave?"

"I'm not in the mood for—"

"C'mon! I need some guy time. And you do, too."

I sit up and slap my feet on the floor, only flinching slightly when my bruised one hits too hard. "Why? What have you heard? Did Betty say something to Laurel when she came to pick up Georgia? She's been gone from here for almost two hours, and you say she's just now leaving your place?"

"Whoa, whoa, whoa, Whistlebritches. She didn't say anything I wouldn't automatically assume, considerin' you've been cooped up in that house for a week, then spendin' even more time together at work."

"But she did say things?"

He laughs. "Yeah. She told Laurel you've been a grump for the past couple of days."

"I have good reasons for that."

"She also said she's worried you're mad at her about somethin', but she can't figure out what... blah, blah, blah, overthinkin' woman stuff... You haven't had sex in weeks..."

"Hey! I've been sick! And why the heck is she telling the whole world that, anyway?"

"Women talk about that stuff. And I wasn't, *technically*, part of the conversation."

"You were eavesdropping?"

The irony of judging him for such a petty infraction, in light of my recent activities, isn't lost on me. Still. I have to at least pretend to be shocked.

"They weren't talkin' quietly. Anyway, they got to have their little gripe session; let's have our own!"

I rub my face. "Can we go farther away than your den? What's that one place we passed on the way back from the movies? Remember, I thought it was a Chinese place?"

"General Lee's?"

"Yeah! That place. It's a bar, right?"

He laughs. "I've told you, I don't hang out in bars. If we're gonna drink, it's gotta be at your place or mine."

"Not mine!"

"Mine it is, then. You bring the beer."

I snort.

"What? I don't keep it in the house. Laurel doesn't like it. She tolerates wine."

"And the hard stuff, apparently."

"That was supposed to be for medicinal purposes."

I sigh. "Fine."

"Great. Give me until about seven. I promised Kirby I'd help him with his math homework. Truth be told, I'm always lost and have to Google the answers."

"It's tragic that you can't do fifth-grade math."

"Just you wait, smart guy. This new way they do it makes no sense. No sense at all."

"All right. You pay your dues by doing your elementary-level math homework; I'll pay mine by sitting through a tense dinner. I'll be over after I put Georgia to bed."

"Don't forget the beer."

"Yeah, yeah. I'm beginning to wonder if that's the only reason you hang out with me."

"'Insecure' doesn't look good on you, Yank."

Tell me about it.

14
ATTITUDE ADJUSTMENT

As I'm retrieving from the beer fridge my offering to my favorite closet drinker, Betty says from the top of the garage steps leading into the house, "Where you goin'?"

"Next door," I answer shortly.

She folds her arms under her breasts and shuffles her feet. "Oh."

My tone seeks no permission when I ask, "Is that okay?"

She either doesn't notice or doesn't care. "Yeah. I mean, I wanted to talk to you about something, now that's Georgia's in bed, but..."

A day ago, I would have dropped my precious beer on the concrete floor and raced her inside to have the conversation I suspect she wants to have, but stewing in your own resentment and anger for any length of time transforms your priorities. Suddenly, revenge is more important than anything. She wants to talk now? Well, good for her. My desire to talk—however secret it's been for the past two days—hasn't meant a darn. Now, I'm not feeling as accommodating.

Immature? Yes. Spiteful? Definitely. But now that she's

willing to let me in, I don't feel that sense of urgency from even a few hours ago.

"I guess it can wait," she concedes, when I don't offer to cancel my original plans.

The normal me would say, "Are you sure?" so it's telling when I don't double-check her sincerity before holding my cardboard six-pack aloft and hitting the button on the wall to raise the overhead door. Its squeaks and groans nearly drown out my sullen, "See you in a few, then."

Let her sit with her thoughts while I unwind with my buddy.

No fewer than four times, I almost turn back before I arrive at the Bakers'. But I stay strong (and stubborn and asshole-ish). Before I knock, Winn slides open the glass door to his den.

"Enter," he says, relieving me of my burden. He carries the beer behind his fancy wooden bar and sticks it in a fridge stuffed with soda cans and bottles.

"You have a huge bar for someone who supposedly doesn't drink," I remark while straddling the stool at the far end.

"Came with the house."

"Any way we could gently dismantle it and transfer it to my house, where it could get some proper use?"

He glides a bottle down the counter toward my waiting hand. I catch it, savoring the cold wetness against my palm and anticipating that first refreshing gulp while I await his answer.

"Your house doesn't have room for it."

"Yet. I'd build an addition for this thing. I'd build an entire house around it." I run my hand along the dark wood and the brass rail, then swig my beer.

"Thou shalt not covet thy neighbor's bar."

I swallow and say with my lips still against the bottle, "I'm coveting more about your life lately than your swanky man cave."

He chuckles and smirks. "You know what this sounds like to me? Sounds to me like things are gettin' claustrophobic for you at work, now that the old hide is there."

I pause as I decode this new term and translate it. Then I say, "It's one thing for you to call me Yank—I've been called worse—but I draw the line at having my wife referred to as the 'old hide.' C'mon, now."

He snorts. "Aw, don't get all prissy. It's an affectionate term."

"Doesn't sound affectionate. Or respectful."

"You prefer 'ball and chain'?"

"How about 'better half'?"

"If you're ever gonna fit in down here, Yankee Doodle, you're gonna have to stop wrinklin' your nose at all our colorful sayin's."

"Some of this area's colorful sayin's are mighty offensive, so I'll continue to pick and choose, thanks. If it makes you feel better, I'm a big fan of 'dadburned' and 'my lands.'" I grin over at him as a form of truce.

He waves me off. "Awright. Anyway, you're dodgin' the question."

"Which was?"

"How are things goin' now that you and Betty spend so much more time together?"

"Fine."

"You're not gettin' a little sick of each other? Too much of a good thing, and all that?"

"Everything's great."

"A second ago, things were just 'fine.' Now, they're 'great'?"

I nod at his sweatshirt. "Hey, how about those... demonic

roosters this season? I hear they're big contenders for that one... thing."

"They're the Gamecocks, and yes, we're in the running for the National Championship, like always. Well, not always. But recently. And I thought you didn't give a crap about football."

"I don't."

"So?"

"Listen, there's nothing to talk about. Betty works at the clinic now, and she does a great job—"

"There's that word again."

"—and we're all getting along fine, especially her and Dr. Reitman, and she's not only getting out of the house and doing something she enjoys, but she's contributing to our household income again, so what's there to say?"

He muses about that for a second and seems to be willing to drop it, so I relax. Then he says, "I just know if I didn't have a place to go that was my own, that if Laurel and I were together *that* many hours a week, both at home and in a professional capacity, it wouldn't be pretty."

"I love Betty."

"That's not the issue at all, and you know it."

"And she does a great job."

"You already said that."

"And the patients and parents like her."

"Well, duh. She's a friendly, funny, warm person. But?"

I inhale deeply and blow forcefully through my lips, flapping them together. "I can't put my finger on it, so I can't explain it."

He waits while I dig deeper in my brain for the information I don't necessarily want to divulge but am desperate to isolate for myself, if nothing else. When I do locate it, I'm too excited to filter, so I blurt, "It's like trying to pee when someone's watching you!"

Beer sprays from my friend's lips—and nose. As he mops up the mess with a towel he grabs from under the bar, he sputters, "What?"

I nod. "Yes. Having her there while I'm doing my job, something that's always been separate from her, is... It's unnerving. I don't feel like I can be myself. Or the version of myself that exists there."

"What the Sam Hill does that have to do with takin' a leak?"

"Stage fright. Pressure to perform."

"Oh, boy. This sounds like somethin' other than peein'," he mutters. "Sorry I asked."

"No! Not like that!" I laugh at how horribly I'm expressing myself. Organizing my thoughts, I try again. "Okay, forget the urination comparison. It's like... when I'm with the kids at work, I'm Nurse Nate. Sometimes I'm silly and sometimes I'm serious, and while it's similar to the way I am at home with Georgia, it's not exactly the same. When they're not your kids, it's different."

He nods. "Awright. I guess I get that. But what are you saying, then? Betty never knew this other side of you? She doesn't approve of it now that she's seen it?"

I shake my head. "No. I don't know. But I don't do it for her benefit. It's not about her."

"Then why do you care?"

Since I don't have a satisfactory answer for him or myself, I rub my thumb along my bottom lip and keep quiet.

"Do your thing, man. After a while, it won't feel weird anymore. You'll be able to compartmentalize and be—what'd you call yourself? Nurse Nate?—at work and the guy who fetches more ice cream and changes dirty diapers at home. Because that's the real problem, isn't it?"

"What?"

"She's the boss at home, and you're the boss at work."

"No!"

"Oh. She's the boss in both places?"

I pout into my bottle. "Screw you, man. We're a team, no matter where we are."

"Riiight... So, at the office, you don't say, 'Hey, move that appointment from one to three and call to let them know,' and 'Order more t.p., please,' and, I don't know... 'Hold this kid while I squeeze pus from this cyst'?"

"She's never had to assist with a patient."

"Yet. There'll come a time, right? Because the doctor will be with someone else or out to lunch or sneakin' in a quickie with Rob Jacobson—that sly old devil—and you'll be wrastlin' some rascal whose mama can't bear to witness the torture of her precious angel gettin' his booster shots, and you only have two hands, both of which you need for your part of the job, so you'll call her back there and have to bark orders to get 'er done. How well's that gonna go over?"

I gulp. "I won't *bark* orders. That's not me."

"Mmm. You may not describe it that way, but chances are, she will."

"Anyway, work isn't the problem. Like you said, I'll get used to my two lives mixing."

"What is it, then?"

I shrug morosely while I try to decide what—if anything— I'm going to tell Winn. After all, Betty and I haven't discussed how private we're going to keep all this stuff with Trevor and Chris, and truth be told, it's not my story to tell. But I have to confess to someone about my email reading, and I can't exactly disclose that without giving him the background. In the end, I say, "Screw it," and as briefly and matter-of-factly as possible, I update him on the stomach-churning drama in my life, including my despicable addiction to electronic espionage.

I conclude with, "See? I'm seriously jealous of your uncomplicated life right now."

Unimpressed, he sucks down his second beer. "Well, I don't have any studly ex-boyfriends, but I was kinda crazy in high school and college, so surprise teenagers are always a possibility. Maybe they haven't found me yet."

I want to laugh at his joke, but I can't muster it through my self-pity. So I keep drinking.

He lets me wallow for a few seconds, then says, "Do you think Betty still has feelin's for this guy? This Chris dude?"

"No!"

"And do you trust her?"

"Yes, for the most part." When he lowers his chin and looks at me through the tops of his eyes, I explain, "I trust her in the way that you mean, but I don't know that I trust her to do the right thing with this whole meet-the-kid scenario. Because I'm not even sure what the right thing is."

"But you'll recognize the wrong thing as soon as she does it."

"Exactly."

He says nothing to that, and I squirm under the implied criticism of his silence. Belligerence bubbles from my belly to my chest, finally erupting in a belch I follow up with, "I've waited a long time for this so-called American dream. The wife, the kid, the house, the dog... And now I have it, and I'm not allowed to enjoy it."

He laughs, but the noise quickly transforms into a groan. "Oh, man. You late-in-lifers are the worst."

I glare down the bar at him.

He throws up his hands. "You are! You build up being a husband and a dad into this epic adventure or this awesome club you've been tryin' to get into for years; then the bouncer lets you in, and you're madder than a hornet that it's just a leaky tent in the backyard that smells like farts."

"I didn't expect it to be perfect. Or always a good time. Or easy. All I asked was that I be allowed to muddle through in peace."

"Who's taking that away from you?"

I shrug, not wanting to say the scapegoats' names out loud.

"*You* are," he answers for me.

When I roll my eyes at him, he sighs. "I haven't known you all that long, Yank, so I may be way off-base, but I speak from experience when I say that nobody has the power to take away what you have—a love and happiness for your beautiful family and life—if you don't give them that power. And in your case, I can't believe you're going to let a fifteen-year-old who's just trying to figure out who he is or an overgrown frat boy have that power. Instead of supportin' your wife through this, you're gonna pout that it's makin' your life messier than you'd like?"

"You're right; you don't know me well enough to say any of that."

"I'm sorry. If I'm wrong, just say so."

"It's not about Trevor. Or Chris. This whole experience is changing my marriage."

"Boo-hoo. Marriages constantly change and evolve. Nobody has a perfect marriage."

"I get that. But I'm reading my wife's emails without her permission, and she's discussing with someone else plans that definitely affect me while at the same time not consulting me about them. And I'm constantly questioning her judgment, worried that she *can't* make a decision without me. And hating that I feel that way, knowing she'd hate it, too. And waiting for it all to go to pot, leaving me to clean it up. Like I always do." I drain the last of my first beer and nod. "That's what I'm most pissed off about. I'm tired of being the cleanup man. For everyone. At home, at work, with my extended family..."

Winn replaces my empty bottle with a full one. "That's who you are. It's always gonna be somethin'. If Trevor wasn't the focus right now, you'd be free to concentrate on how hard pregnancy is. And how guilty you feel that it seems like such a pain in the butt when you should be viewin' it as a one-hundred-percent blessin', because ain't hormones grand?"

I laugh. "True."

"Maybe you should have a conference call with Trev and Chris and thank them for takin' your mind off the hormone roller coaster every once in a while."

"I wouldn't go that far." But he's right that without this distraction, I'd have spent more time worrying about Betty and the baby, wondering if we're going to experience complications—or worse, given our history.

"Take each problem as you go and try to keep things in perspective. In five years, is this gonna matter all that much?"

"Maybe not. But maybe."

"It won't. In five years, this kid'll be in college, and you guys will just be some people he remembers fondly, because you treated him nice when he came to you. *That's* all you're gonna be to him: some nice folks in South Carolina who send him a Christmas card. And Baby-Daddy will be back livin' the swingin' single's life, doing— What does he do, anyway?"

"I have no idea," I admit.

"Whatever. Doesn't matter. He'll go back to doing that, and you'll never have to deal with him again. Meanwhile, you'll be doin' elementary school math homework with the help of Internet searches, puttin' aside money for family vacations and college and retirement, and spendin' your spare time scoopin' dog crap, drinkin' beer with your best bud—that'd be me, right?—and readin' those froufrou books you like so much.

And all that with a clear conscience, because you weren't a selfish butthead durin' a difficult time for your wife that wasn't even about you to begin with."

Oh gosh... he's right.

I set my half-empty beer aside. Suddenly, I have no desire to finish my drink or sit around here talking about hypothetical problems. I have a real issue waiting for me at home, and if I hang out here too long, Betty will go to bed without me. "Listen, I should head home."

"Don't get all mad at me now. Do you want me to tell you what you want to hear or what you *need* to hear?"

"It's not that. It's been a long week, and I shouldn't be drinking, anyway. My poor liver's crying, 'Uncle!'"

"If you're gonna let your liver call the shots..."

"I try to respect the wishes of my internal organs. They're kind of important." Despite everything worrying me, I force a smile. "And hey, uh... I'm sorry I monopolized the conversation tonight with my problems. That's embarrassing."

He walks me to the door. "Who said we were only talkin' about *your* problems?" Shaking my hand, he winks. "It's funny how you can be givin' someone advice and realize it's exactly what you need to hear, too."

* * *

I FIND Betty drowsing on the couch and watching *White Christmas*. As soon as I enter the living room, she sits up and turns off the television, as if I've caught her watching porn... or emailing another man (for example).

"You're back earlier than I thought you'd be."

I shrug. "Yeah. You wanted to talk?"

She pats the cushion next to her. "Sit with me?"

I do, despite feeling like a lap dog by complying so readily.

The urge to refuse, however, originates from an insecurity I feel equally obligated to reject. When I'm settled next to her, she immediately grabs my hand and threads her fingers through mine.

I stare down at our linked digits as she begins, "I'm sorry I teased you at work today about being crabby. If you're still feeling run-down, I should be figuring out how to help, not mocking you."

"I'm fine. It's— I don't need to be babied."

"Good. I'm not offering to baby you. But I do want to be more sympathetic. It sucks to be sick. And how's your foot?"

"It's fine. I bruised it, that's all."

"So everything's fine?"

"Is this what you wanted to talk to me about? My bad mood and what you can do to snap me out of it?"

She pauses, poised at the edge of the trap I'm setting. "Partly. There's something else I've been wanting to discuss with you, but you've been so..." Trailing off, she smiles nervously at my glower while I wait for the colorful adjective that never comes. "Anyway. I haven't been able to find the right time. You haven't been exactly approachable."

"Geez. I'm sorry. I didn't realize it was my responsibility to make it easier for you to do the right thing, *Boop*. Sorry I haven't been as 'hilarious' lately as you've billed me to be to your ex."

She drops my hand as if I've delivered an electric shock to her palm. "W-what?"

Righteous indignation chases away all the sense Winn talked into me mere minutes ago. I vault from the couch. "Oh, come off it! Stop insulting me further with the innocent act. I know Hawaiian Punch is all up in our business, trying to weasel his way back into your life."

Her nostrils widen, but otherwise, she's the picture of

placidity, leaned back on the couch with her hands resting on her midriff, her feet flat on the floor in front of her, knees spread several inches apart. "How do you know this?"

Lifting my chin, I answer, "I've read the emails. All of them."

"Why would you do that?"

Freaked out by her deadly calm and not nearly as defiant anymore, I palm the back of my neck. "It was an accident."

"An accident? How do you accidentally read an entire chain of emails about something?"

"Reading the first one was an accident. Kind of. Then I purposely kept up with the others. And before you get all self-righteous, I know what I did wasn't right, but was I ever going to find out otherwise?"

"Yes! Of course."

"When? When he showed up at the front door with the kid?"

She pops up faster than I thought she'd be physically able to do right now.

Must stay on the balls of my feet and prepare to run, if need be.

Standing in front of me, she pokes me in the chest with her index finger. "When I could tell you the whole story without you doing *this*—overreacting and making things worse with your stupid insecurities!"

"Oh, I see. When you felt threatened by another woman—which turned out to be completely baseless, I'd like to remind you—your worries were legit. But when I see with my own eyes the back-and-forth flirting you don't realize I'm seeing, I'm overreacting and being insecure?"

"Flirting? What flirting? If anything, I've been cold and non-committal with him."

"You weren't cold and non-committal on the phone."

"It was the first time we'd talked in *years*. I forgot how

much he made me laugh. Something *you* haven't done in weeks."

"Why don't you invite Chuckles over here to do something else to you I haven't done in weeks too, while we're at it?"

"That's not fair."

"Is it fair that you talk about our sex life to our next door neighbors?"

She blinks but recovers well to my knowing that, too. "Laurel's my friend. I was just adding that small detail to the evidence backing up my worries about you."

"You haven't seemed... interested since you found out about Trevor. And I've been sick."

"But it's more than that. Obviously. You've been spying on me!"

"Only for the past couple of days. And you've given me good reason to. If you'd sucked it up and had the hard conversation with me to begin with, kept me informed, like I deserve—"

"I was keeping you out of it so you didn't have to be the bad guy, okay?"

I blink down at her.

"Yeah, genius," she says. "I'm glad it's not obvious in the emails how hard I've been stalling, but that's exactly what I'm doing. I'm hoping Chris will do what Chris does best and lose interest in this whole thing. Then I can schedule a meeting with Trevor and his parents that doesn't include that guy."

"Why didn't you just tell me that?"

"Because I don't want any of this to be your problem."

"Uh, too late. And I didn't define it as a problem until you started keeping things from me. I thought it was something we'd get through together—like we always have. I'd rather know what I'm up against than be clueless, any day."

"Then ask!"

"I didn't realize I needed to!"

Her chest heaves, and she looks like she's about to continue the argument. Then her shoulders slump. "Okay. Fine. I'm sorry." She looks at me through her lashes. "I really am."

Weakening, weakening.

Why does she look at me like that? Oh, that's right; because it works. Every. Flippin'. Time. I'm such a sucker. Beats being an angry victim, though.

Taking a second to swallow my pride, I close my eyes, then say, "I'm sorry, too. I have been since I read that first stupid email. This has been horrible."

"That's why you've been so irritable, because you're sorry?"

"Yes. That, and... Do you understand how terrible it is to feel like a third wheel in your own marriage, like you're being replaced as your spouse's best friend?"

"Actually, I do. And it sucks. And you never have to worry about that."

"I don't like this guy."

"I'm starting to get that impression, yes."

"He gives me the creeps, all right? He's over-familiar in his emails, and yeah, he makes you laugh, but it's because he's working an angle. He's worming his way into our lives, and... and... I seriously want to strangle him every time I imagine him prancing around, fire dancing to impress you."

She laughs. "Oh, Nathaniel."

"I'm serious."

"That's what makes it even funnier."

In spite of myself, I smile sheepishly. "See? I can still make you laugh."

Kissing my chin, she says, "Tell you what. I'll shoot straighter with Chris next time he pressures me about a meeting date."

I hold her close so her warm core presses against mine. "Thank you."

"You're welcome. But you need to promise not to snoop around on my phone anymore. That's not cool."

"Fine. As long as *you* promise to keep me informed. All the time."

"Done." She stands on her tiptoes and puckers her lips.

I lower my face to hers, but right before our mouths touch, I ask, "Why does Chris think I'm 'hilarious'?"

"Because you are."

"You mean 'ridiculous'?"

"No. Hilarious. Nobody makes me laugh like you do. Sometimes unintentionally, but still."

"Great. That's just—"

She silences me with an eye-popping kiss that—if I still had my tonsils—would double as a thorough examination. As it is, I'm glad I'm no longer contagious and can match her passion with no worries.

"You taste like beer," she says, pulling back slightly.

"Sorry. I'll go brush my teeth."

She grips me tighter. "I wasn't complaining."

"Oh. Yeah. Right." I give her another extended "drink," during which she moans into my mouth, which almost springs a leak in my tap. Reluctantly separating from her, I pull her by the hand toward the stairs. "Let's put an end to that pesky sobriety of yours right now."

"No arguments from the horny pregnant chick."

I am the luckiest man in the world.

15

HIJACKED WEEKEND

As I was dozing off last night, I was informed of a slight change in my lounging-around-the-house-with-a-pink-covered-novel Saturday plans. Funny, at the time, I didn't care. When Betty's draped over me like a sexy surgical sheet, and I'm half-asleep on a brain cocktail of norepinephrine, serotonin, oxytocin, vasopressin, nitric oxide, and prolactin, I'll agree to anything. And she knows it. Maybe not all those particulars, but she gets the gist.

I guess I should consider myself lucky she's never asked me for anything super-important after sex... yet. I should keep my guard up, though. Not that it would matter. I'd still say yes.

Now I just want to get this over with.

When I arrive at the clinic shortly after noon, Rob's already started, reaching too far to loop the long strand of Christmas lights on the gutter clips. I run to the bottom of the ladder and grab its sides right before it topples sideways.

"Whoa!" I say, my pulse pounding at the close call.

He holds fast to the gutter in front of him, looking down between his body and the rungs at me. "Nate! You saved me from a humiliating accident."

"Humiliation may have been the least of your worries. What the heck are you doing, trying to kill yourself?"

"I'm trying to get this done as quickly as possible so I can get on with my weekend."

"You almost got on with eternity."

He laughs and backs down the ladder. "I guess I did." On firm ground once more, he shakes my hand. "Thanks for getting here when you did."

"Would have been here sooner but had to deal with a major diaper blowout—Georgia's, not mine—before I left the house."

"I wasn't expecting you at all. Otherwise, I would have waited. How'd you get roped into this?" He wipes sweat from his forehead and moves the ladder a few feet to our right.

I close one eye as if trying to recall the conversation word-for-word, then give him the "clean" version. "I believe it went down like this: 'Oh, and you'll be helping Rob put up the Christmas lights at the clinic tomorrow.' End of discussion."

He laughs. "Was that your wife's directive or Pat's?"

"My wife's! I mean..." I clear my throat, remembering he's probably picturing the conversation taking place at work, not in my bed. "Uh, Betty informed me right before I fell asleep last night." True story.

"Ouch. Bummer about the short notice. I've been doing this myself for years. When I sold this place, I figured I'd never have to do it again, but here I am."

"It's a miracle you're still alive."

He ensures the un-strung section of lights hangs clear of the rungs before ascending again. On his way up, he calls down to me, "Didn't rush it as much in years past. Had nothing else to do and nobody else to be with when the job was done, ya know?"

"I see. Well, you're no good to her dead, so let's take our

time and do this right."

Forty-five minutes later, the Victorian dazzles in the overcast afternoon. I pat Rob on the shoulder on my way past him with the ladder. "Good job, Doc. And you lived to be rewarded."

He wiggles his eyebrows. "Better yet. Can I buy you a beer for your trouble? You saved my life, you know."

It takes me a nanosecond to accept his offer, and after I stow the ladder in the shed behind the clinic, we walk down the street to the nearest bar and grill.

Inside the cool, dim chain restaurant, we scoot up to the bar and give our orders. While the bartender pulls our drinks, Rob nods down to my bare legs. "You do realize it's December, right?"

"Someone needs to tell the weather around here that."

"Ah, you Yankees are all the same. Give it a couple of years, and you'll wonder how you ever survived up there with that ice, snow, and arctic air."

"Talked to my brother the other day, and they'd had thirteen inches dumped on them. He didn't appreciate my laughing at him. Said, 'We'll see who's laughing in July, bro, when you're making your own gravy.'"

Rob laughs as our beers arrive in front of us. He lifts his bubbling amber glass to me. "To mild weather, ladder safety, and new friends."

"Hear, hear."

I take a few sips, then hold up my glass and consider the dark winter grind in front of me. It's no coffee stout, but it'll do. Not that I'm a beer connoisseur, by any stretch, but I did take for granted the wide selection in Wisconsin.

An uncharacteristic homesickness that has nothing—well, maybe a little—to do with beer overtakes me. While Betty still regularly refers to Green Bay as "home," I've seemingly left our hometown behind with barely a backward glance. I like it here in Jasper, despite feeling like quite the alien most of the time. It's not as if I fit in all that well in Packerland, anyway.

And I definitely don't miss the polar temperatures they experience up North at this time of year. Having said that, I still expect freezing weather and snow for certain things... like Christmas. I can't seem to get into the spirit of the season with warm winds and driving rain the way I could with a blanketing shower of fluffy flakes. This time of year is made for ugly sweaters and hot drinks and roaring fires. But none of those things have a place here. It's going to be surreal, celebrating the holiday with family at the beach. Maybe we can fool ourselves into believing the sand is snow. Can you sled down dunes?

"Anyway," I say, shaking myself from my maudlin musings, "I hope the weather holds for another week, at least. The open house includes a ton of outdoor activities for the kids."

"How extravagant is this thing going to be, anyway?"

After one more drink, I set down my glass and wrap my hands around it, slumping over the bar. "Betty and... Pat... have big plans."

Ew. Dr. Reitman's first name tastes so wrong! Why did I agree to try harder to use it? Sex, that's why. Another promise made in a post-coital moment of weakness.

Rob has no clue how awkward it is for me to say Dr. Reitman's first name, so he's a good person to practice on.

I clear my throat and try again. "Pat's going along with everything Betty envisions. Which is a lot."

"Your wife's a persuasive person."

"Tell me about it," I mutter, finishing my drink.

He nods at my glass. "Another?"

"Nah."

"You sure?"

I laugh. "I see my reputation precedes me."

"There's no reputation. Although I did hear something about you being a bad influence on Winn Baker, of all people. Something about you two splashin' around in his pool on Thanksgiving with all of your clothes on."

I blush. "Oh. That. I didn't realize anyone had—" I sigh. "Anyway. Better than no clothes, right? And I wouldn't call that being a 'bad influence.' Winn doesn't need anyone's help being eccentric."

"Everyone's used to *his* eccentricities, though. Folks around here don't cotton to 'new.'"

I sniff, then ask, "Is this open house going to work? You know, since 'folks around here don't cotton to new'?"

Contemplating my question and the bar, he pauses for long enough that I figure he's trying to decide how to break the bad news to me, but finally, he says, "We might be preoccupied with tradition in these parts, but there's something else we're equally good at, and that's making folks feel welcome. It's a weird combination of two things you'd figure would be at odds with each other, but somehow it works."

My leg hairs stand up in the mostly empty, air-conditioned building. Cupping my knees in my palms, I say quietly, "Yeah. But making people feel welcome and accepting them into the community are two different things. That first one is temporary. You can tolerate anyone for a short period of time. To tell those same people they belong goes a bit further."

"Belonging requires work on both sides."

I nod.

He pats my shoulder. "But y'all are doing better than I thought you would."

"We are?"

"Absolutely! I was worried at first that you wouldn't have any patients."

"You were?!"

He laughs at the horror in my voice. "Then I remembered one of the other local pedes is about a hundred years old and can't hear worth a darn, and the other one had an affair with one of his patients—"

"What?!"

"*After* she was of legal, consenting age, mind you."

"Still!"

"That's exactly what several parents said. For good reason. So, in comparison, a couple of Northerners aren't a bad option, even if one of them *is* a woman." He smiles wryly. "And it helps that you're married and have a family. A single male nurse around here would have raised a few eyebrows, let me tell you."

I shake my head and blow a huge breath through slack lips. "Wow." Then I remember it wasn't too long ago my own extended family was whispering behind my back at Nick's wedding, wondering when I'd be coming out. "Well, *y'all* don't have the monopoly on prejudice down here," I inform him, sliding off my bar stool.

Rob tosses a few bills on the bar and nods to the bartender across the way, who's watching a sports show's analysis of a college bowl match-up while wiping glasses with a white towel. "Aw, man! And here we thought we were unique."

"Nope. Just louder."

He rolls his eyes. "Yes." On a mutter, he adds, "Let's hope that's changing. I hear there are some new folks in town who might shift a few perceptions."

"Hey, no pressure, right?"

* * *

RUBBER TOTES of Christmas decorations litter the living room.

One box in particular holds a most adorable angel, draped in itchy green garland and giggling as her mom continues to heap and hook more ornaments on her limbs and clothing. It's one of those Norman Rockwell moments that sneaks up on me once in a while and leaves me breathless and sweaty with the everyday enormity of it.

To mask my emotions, I ask in a booming voice, "What's the meaning of this?"

Really, I already know: life. The true meaning of it.

Betty provides a less sentimental answer. "I thought I'd go through some of our stuff and select a few things to take with us to the beach, to decorate the place and make it feel more Christmas-y."

Kneeling next to her on the floor, I peer into the large tub that contains our daughter and spy boxes of knickknacks and a small wooden crate that holds the nativity set. "Okay..." I tuck a sagging strand of garland behind Georgia's ear. "I thought part of the draw of staying at the beach was not having to drag out all this stuff."

"It won't feel right without *something*. I promise to keep it to this one box. And the tree."

"We're going to take the tree? How?"

She shrugs and smiles sheepishly. "Borrow Winn's truck?"

I scrub my face and hide my eyes, but she pulls on my wrist and forces me to look at her. "Please?" she begs, complete with fluttering lashes.

One of these days, that's not going to work. Today is not that day. I sigh. "Fine. I'll ask Winn. But if he already has plans for his truck that week—which is highly likely—what's plan B?"

"We can get a live one at a roadside stand once your brother arrives with his SUV. Or I'll use one of the tabletop trees I bought for the clinic open house."

"*One* of the— How many did you buy?"

"One for each exam room."

"Four?!"

She nods, then continues to pull plush toys from other boxes and toss them at Georgia, who giggles with each one that hits her. "Hold this one. No, this one. Wait, this one. Okay, this is the last one."

I sit back on my heels and survey the room more critically. "You dragged all this from the garage by yourself?"

Head buried in a tub, she muffles back at me, "Georgia and Reba helped."

I'm sure. By being major tripping hazards. "Why didn't you wait for me?"

"I wasn't sure how long you were going to be, and I wanted to get this done while it was on my mind. Now, where the heck are the stockings? It's not Christmas without stockings."

She hands back to me a wreath with a few wonky pinecones stuck to it. This *is making the cut? I don't think so.* I toss it into another nearby box, hoping it gets lost... permanently.

When she comes up for air, holding our stockings victoriously aloft, I grin innocently at her. "You found them. Great. Now, let's put the rest of this stuff away, so we can all take naps."

"Naps? Who has time for naps?"

"Babies and me."

"Not me. I need to message your mom and Heidi about stockings." She pulls out her phone and clicks the most convenient social media app where she can be sure both women will see her missive. Before she can draft one, however, she says, "Whoaaaa... What the— Nathaniel, you were quite the busy boy on here this week. What gives?"

My cheeks warm, but I avert my face while collecting

Christmas paraphernalia and returning it to its storage containers. "I was bored at work."

"I thought you deactivated your account forever ago."

"Every once in a while, when I have nothing else to do, I lurk and see what everyone's up to. You posted some cute pics of George at Halloween."

"The photos turned out great."

"Chris liked them."

"Everyone liked them." She taps her thumbs against her phone's screen, ostensibly firing off that message to Heidi and Mom. When she's finished, she looks up and smiles. "Well, not everyone. Your brother said she looked more like Hitler than Charlie Chaplin, but everyone else liked them."

"Yeah, I responded to his comment and said, 'Your kids *act* like Hitler.'"

Betty cracks up. "I guess it's a good thing you don't go on there often. And maybe you should avoid the site when you're tired... or drunk."

"I was at work! I wasn't drinking."

"We're going to say you were, though, if the topic comes up at Christmas."

"It won't. Nick will think it's funny. Because it's true."

She crawls across the floor on her knees and grasps my upper arm. "Seriously, though. Why were you on there? Were you cyber-stalking Chris?"

"No. Maybe I tried, but his privacy settings are too tight, and I don't care enough to friend-request him."

When she clicks her tongue, I insist, "Really. I *am* mildly curious about the guy, though. What does he do? Where does he live? You can tell a lot about a person by the pictures he shares of himself online."

"You mean, like the ones you posted of Nick's bachelor party however many years ago that are still out there?"

I chuckle. "Uh, yeah. Like those. I want to make sure he's not some weirdo. How well do you know him, anyway?"

"Well enough, wouldn't you say?"

"Not like *that*. You haven't been in contact with him in fifteen years. You've never known the adult version of this guy. It... it makes me nervous." I clear my throat. "You guys are too important to take a chance on a stranger."

"Did you ever consider he's changed for the *better* in the past decade and a half?"

"Honestly? No. It rarely works that way."

Georgia lobs a glass ball ornament at us. It hits me in the face and bounces into the bubble wrap-filled box in front of me. "Hey! Nice shot." I'm too thankful for the diversion to scold her for her aggression.

She climbs over the side of the tub and runs toward us, knocking into us at full speed. "My mommy!"

Betty and I grunt melodramatically at the collision. Then I say, "Nobody's debating that, George. But you do need to learn how to share." I pat Betty's tummy. "Baby."

"*I* da baby!" Georgia says.

"Are you?" I wrinkle my nose. "I thought you were a big girl."

She looks uncertain, then smiles. "Yes! I da big girl... and da baby."

Betty grabs hold of our daughter's hand and rests it against her bump. "Feel that? Baby's in here."

Georgia looks down at their hands. Suddenly, her head snaps up, and she pulls her hand away. "Sish! Sish in Mommy's tummy! Daddy's turn!"

I laugh and let her pull my palm to rest over Betty's belly button. When the tiny flutter meets my fingertips, I gasp as if I can't believe it. Georgia grins. "See? Sish!"

"It's not a fish, George. It's a baby."

She cocks her eyebrow and lifts one side of her mouth. "Babies not in tummies!"

"Yes, they are," Betty says.

"Actually, George, you're right; they're *not* in tummies. The baby is in Mommy's uterus."

Betty scoffs at my anatomy lesson.

I ignore her and focus on the toddler instead. "Can you say, 'uterus'?"

"You-fuss."

"Close enough. That's where babies live until they get big enough to come out and meet us."

"I yaunt a you-fuss."

Betty laughs, but I somehow manage to keep a straight face. "Well, you're in luck, because you have one."

Georgia drops her chin to her chest and pulls her shirt up to bare her belly, one almost as round as her mom's. "With a baby?"

"Nope." *Oh, dear God. What have I done?* "Not now. Maybe when you're a big girl, though." *Really big. Like 80.*

"I *am* da big girl." She points to Betty's abdomen. "Baby." Then to her own chest. "Big girl." Then to her chubby gut. "You-fuss."

I gather her in my arms and squeeze, kissing her where her neck meets her shoulder. "You're too smart, Georgia Lou." Loosening my grip, I cradle her like a newborn and say down into her face as I rock her, "How about you stay my baby a bit longer? Aw, look at my sweet baby!"

"Goo-goo-gah-gah. Dada-dada!" She sticks her thumb in her mouth and flutters her eyes closed.

Yeah, just like that. Perfect.

16

OPEN HOUSE

"OPEN HOUSE" MAY NOT BE THE MOST PRECISE TERM FOR what this event has evolved into. For one thing, activities have spilled from the clinic into the yard and beyond. From the outside, it looks more like a street fair, complete with food trucks, face painting stalls, a photo booth, crafts table, bounce house, and a tented throne area for Santa (a.k.a., "Winn").

Inside the clinic, Christmas threw up. As Betty promised, a table-top tree with a different theme (fishing, gaming, music, and sports) graces each of the four exam rooms. A full-sized fir festooned with the more traditional balls, baubles, tinsel, garland, and lights looms over the waiting area. The usual seats in that room have been moved out to make way for massage chairs, all currently occupied the last time I walked through. Garland and strings of popcorn and cranberries climb the banister leading upstairs to Dr. Reitman's locked private quarters. We've wrapped our office doors to look like presents, complete with ribbons and bows. A gingerbread Christmas village sprawls across the front desk. Both inside and outside, Christmas music plays.

And the people... so many people! The whole town is here.

Right now, half of them want to know when Santa will be back from his break.

I snag Betty around her waist as she bustles past me, moving toward the street with a towel bunched in her hands. She giggles as she spins into my arms. With her back to my chest, I lean down and rest my chin on her shoulder, placing my mouth close to her ear. "Hey there, Santa's helper. Any idea where your boss is?"

"He's giving our daughter a private audience while cooling off in your office. Said he'd be out in a few."

"The natives are restless."

She presses her fists against my hands, which I've palmed against her belly in the hopes I'll feel the baby stir. But all's quiet. "Then maybe you should go get him. It might be hard to budge him from the air conditioning vent he was standing over." Turning to face me and holding up the towel, she says, "I have to go clean up a punch spill in the photo booth."

We back away from each other, grinning. "This is crazy," I declare after a group of people walks between us, laughing and discussing what to do next.

"But awesome! Let's hope it works."

"It will," I say more confidently than I feel. She doesn't need a reality check right now. She needs someone to tell her, "You did a great job, Betts."

"Thanks!" She blows me a kiss. "Go find Santa."

I'd rather hang out with her, even if it means mopping up sticky spills, but I head for the clinic on my mission to keep Jolly Old St. Nicholas on task.

On my way, I wave at Dr. Reitman, who pulls me toward the crafts table to introduce me to the kids and parents creating ornaments there. Before one of the moms can get too in-depth with me about my stance on vaccines, I say, "I like immunizations. They're important. And I hate to rush away, but I've been told to find the big guy before there's an uprising. It was good to meet you all. Come in to the clinic or give me a call, and we'll talk longer."

I trot up the porch steps and escape into the building, nodding and smiling at the folks in the massage chairs, who barely glance at me as they savor their relaxation time. My smile fades as I slip into my office and close the door behind me. I lean against it as if I'm worried someone's going to try to force their way in.

A hatless, beardless, fat-suited Winn looks up from his plate of food on my desk and freezes mid-chew, his eyes wide and panicked. He relaxes when he sees it's me.

"Oh. Yank. You scared me. I thought I was about to scar a kid for life while he was lookin' for the commode."

"Just me." I gesture to Georgia, who's playing on the floor at his feet. "I guess you don't care about my daughter's childhood illusions?"

He shrugs and goes back to his hot wings. "As soon as she saw me in full costume earlier, she pulled my beard down and called me by my first name. Too smart for her own good."

I laugh. "Yeah. We have some fun years ahead of us." I pick her up from the floor and kiss her cheek. "Anyway... Everyone's wondering where Santa went."

Mouth full, he replies, "I'm eating as fast as I can! Laurel took forever to bring this to me."

"Thanks for doing this, by the way."

"No problem. It's good for continuity, ya know? I'm Santa at the store, Santa in the parade, Santa at my parents' party... I wear this dadburned suit more in December than I do my real clothes."

"Well, you're a saint for it in this heat."

He washes down a mouthful of barbecued beans with some lemonade. "I gotta say, this is hot for December, even for us.

And the sun! You guys lucked out and got a gorgeous day for this, but whoo-hee! Santa coulda done with more cloud cover. Mrs. Claus could bake cookies in that tent."

"Why Mrs. Claus? You can't mix ingredients and drop them on a cookie sheet?"

"I'm the toy guy; she's the baker."

"Just get your sexist butt back out there. It's only a couple more hours."

Standing, he grabs his hat, wig, and facial hair from the other end of the desk. As he adjusts his costume pieces, he says, "Keep the bottled water comin'. I'm sweatin' like a whore in church."

I wince and glance at Georgia, who's luckily more interested in my Adam's apple than anything we're saying. "I'll make sure you stay hydrated," I say while she chases the knot up and down my neck. "It would be bad for business if Santa died on our watch."

* * *

BACK OUTSIDE, after a cursory inspection of the bathrooms and a reloading of toilet paper and hand soap, Georgia and I work the front yard. We're exiting the face painting booth, where Georgia's had a simple rainbow drawn onto her round cheek, when Rob approaches us, accompanied by a tiny blonde woman who looks like she hasn't stopped smiling since she was a cheerleader in high school.

After the initial niceties, Smiley, who I'm told to call "Derva," asks, "So what church are y'all goin' to?"

When I sputter and fail to come up with an answer to what seems like a highly personal question to ask someone you've so recently met, she rushes on, "We'd love to have y'all at

Gateway as our special guests. Just make sure you tell an elder I invited you. That's Derva Pilkington."

"Uhh... Okay, but we're not looking for a place to go to church right now."

"Oh, you silly thing! You're funny!"

"I am?"

"Listen here, now. Our big Christmas show is comin' up tomorrow night. It's amazin'. The folks in charge keep outdoin' themselves every year." She tweaks Georgia's unpainted cheek and manages to come away with all her fingers still attached. "This little angel would love it! Music and lights and all kinds of fun!"

"Right. Well..."

"I won't take no for an answer, you big goober. Tell ya what... If I see you there, I'll be sure to call up here on Monday mornin' and transfer my whole family from Dr. Trist to that doctor lady I saw walkin' around here."

"Dr. Reitman. And... that would be great, even if I can't make it to your Christmas pageant... thing. Because Dr. Reitman is a phenomenal physician. How many children do you have?"

"Seven and another on the way." She leans closer. "But don't spread it around. We're keepin' this one hush-hush for a while longer."

"Oh. Congratu—"

"But I just *know* you'll be at the show tomorrow, because fair's fair. And remember, you have to tell anyone who asks that Derva Pilkington invited you. I wanna get credit for ya!" She laughs like she's kidding, but something tells me she's dead serious. "When you're saved, you will feel..." She folds her hands and presses them to her chest, looking rapturously toward the sky. "...so free. So unburdened."

"Oh, I was baptized a long time ago. Don't remember it,

but I was." I chuckle nervously, glancing at Rob, who shakes his head nearly imperceptibly then closes his eyes and sighs when my revelation receives a finger wag from Derva.

"If you're talkin' about that infant-baptism-head-sprinklin'-thing some churches do, that's not the same."

"Actually, it—"

"No, no. To be saved, you have to go down to the river, where you're fully submerged as you decide to accept the Lord into your heart. And a baby can't do that!" She slaps my arm like we're joking around about newborn potty training, not discussing eternal salvation.

"My daddy!" Georgia protests the stranger's touch.

"Oh, now darlin'," Derva coos, "nobody's tryin' to steal your daddy. I'm tryin' to save him!" She has that crazed look in her eye that tells me I'm not getting out of this conversation unless I forfeit any right to being right.

I smile down at the pregnant proselytizer. "Derva, it's been great meeting you, but if I don't find my wife and offer to help out around here, *nothing*'s going to save me."

Her eyes widen at my joke, but before she can object to my blasphemy, I shift Georgia in my arms and side-step both Derva and Rob, hoping he won't hate me for abandoning him. It's a risk I'm willing to take, though.

As soon as we're out of earshot, I mutter, "Whew, George. That was a close one. Eight new patients would be nice, but... at what cost?"

"Shit!" she agrees cheerfully.

"Hey, hey, now. Don't let Derva hear you say that. She'll stage an exorcism... down by the river."

I quick-step toward the last place I saw a glimpse of Betty, near the bounce house. She's not there or at any of the food carts (surprisingly), but I'd recognize that sweet bottom anywhere when I see it sticking out of the photo booth. Sure enough, she's on her hands and knees with a towel and some multi-purpose cleaner, scrubbing at the textured metal kick plate.

I nudge her butt with my shoe. "Hey. You're *still* cleaning this up?"

"Not 'still'; 'again.' Slurpee this time." She holds up the now-blue towel for me to see.

After setting down Georgia, I offer Betty a hand up. She staggers to her feet, then immediately sits on the patent leather seat in the booth and pulls Georgia onto her lap. She pats the cushion next to her. I gladly accept her invitation and pull the black curtain to shut us off from the rest of the party.

She presses the button to get the camera going, and we make kooky faces through several of the clicks, but then our eyes meet over Georgia's head, and I chuckle. "I love you."

"I love you, too, Nathaniel."

I lean over and kiss her, wrapping my hand around her far shoulder to keep her firmly in place. The way she kisses me back would result in a full make-out session... if Georgia weren't there... and we weren't surrounded by the population of the entire town. I pull away first, but not because I want to. She licks her lips, and it's all I can do not to reach for her again, but I look away, clear my throat, and pat down my hair.

The booth plays a tune to notify us our "session" is over and spits a strip of photos from a slot next to the curtain. I grab them and laugh. Handing them over to Betty so she can see and show Georgia how "silly" we are, I say, "I'm glad we finally had some real portraits made at the beach this summer. We don't take enough pictures."

"We're too busy *living* life to look at each other through lenses."

"We need to document it, too, though. Because someday,

all this will be memories. Unreliable, puff-of-smoke memories..."

Betty raises her eyebrow at me. "Have you been drinking?"

"No!"

She laughs at her accusation and my vehement response to it. "Sometimes you get sappy when you've had too much to drink."

"I'm not being sappy!"

"Rambling on about puffs of smoke..."

I playfully push her shoulder, clenching my teeth. "I love you and want to remember everything. And since I have trouble remembering why I walked into a room sometimes, it's a good idea to use any memory aids at our disposal, like family portraits, to help me out in my old age, which has just about arrived."

Rolling her eyes, she glides along the bench, nudging me with her hip. "Well, those were expensive. And you griped to the photographer the whole time about how hot it was."

"That's my role. I gripe; you apologize to the people with us. It works."

"Speaking of, we have a party to finish hosting, then teardown and cleanup, then I have a date with our bed. I may sleep all day tomorrow."

"Who's going to do my cooking and cleaning if you sleep all day?" Unfortunately, I can't say the line without cracking up, so my joke isn't even worth a fake glare from her.

Instead, she pushes the spot between my shoulder blades, propelling me from the booth onto the grass, where I barely keep my footing. Georgia giggles behind me. Half-turning, I say toward them, "Hey! Careful. Someone could get hur—"

Bam! I stagger backward after hitting a wall of man, then struggle to stay on my feet for the second time in less than a minute.

"Hey, Pal," he barks. "Watch where you're goin'! Oh. Man. I'm sorry."

After regaining my equilibrium, I look more closely at the guy who's nearly killed me, then yelled at me for it, then apologized. I blink into the sun, sure I'm imagining things. Because no... it can't be.

From behind me, Betty croaks, "Chris? What are you doing here?"

17

CHRIS MISS

AFTER RECOVERING FROM THE SHOCK OF COMING FACE-TO-face with Chris, Betty introduced us.

I was prepared for the physique, which is every bit as impressive as I imagined (I'm sure he'd look amazing in a grass skirt, if he's into that kind of thing), but I thought people this beautiful only existed on movie sets. Betty's told me Trevor looks just like his dad, and since that kid smiles at me every day from the side of my refrigerator, I figured there'd be no surprises in the looks department if and when I finally did meet Chris.Haussman420 in person. I was wrong. This guy doesn't exhibit any of the teenage gawkiness seen in that school picture on my fridge.

It's as if a maharajah got it on with a Roman goddess and produced some human super-species with perfect everything. Sparkling teeth. Cheekbones, nose, and a chin you could use to cut diamonds. Dimples—in cheeks and chin. Dark, almost black, eyes surrounded by lashes so thick they look like eye liner. Even his hair is hanging in there. Damn it. I thought, if nothing else, maybe he was thinning on top. But no. Well, I can't see that high, so maybe he is. Doesn't look like it from here, though. His black mop hangs in relaxed curls that fall level with his perfect earlobes (yes, earlobes can be perfect, because his sure are). The only imperfection—if you can call it that—is a tiny chickenpox scar on his otherwise smooth forehead. But that merely seems to add character.

Good God. If he looked anything like this in college, it's a wonder he doesn't have thirty more kids running around. I bet women were throwing themselves at him on a regular basis... and most of them didn't have to be drunk. Hell, if this guy propositioned *me*, I'd consider myself downright flattered.

During the introductions, Chris was all grins, like it was a crazy—but pleasant—surprise to run into us. In Jasper, South Carolina. Population: 3,874 (and change).

Now, in response to Betty's original question, he says, "I was checking into my hotel down the street and saw all this going on. Figured I'd scope it out, grab some boiled peanuts, and get my bearings. What are the chances that you guys are responsible for this spectacle? Wow. Huge turnout for such a tiny town! This your clinic, Nate?"

On cue, Dr. Reitman approaches us. Happy to oblige Georgia's reaching arms, she takes hold of the toddler and bounces her gently on her hip. More awkward introductions of Betty's "college friend" ensue, and I say, "This is Dr. Rei— Pat's practice. I'm just the FNP."

"Nate's my business partner," she corrects. "Isn't that right, Georgia?"

"Yes!" Georgia squeals, squirming as the doctor tickles her ribs.

Betty blinks rapidly at Chris. "You still haven't said why you're here."

He smiles down at her. "Look at you! You look *exactly* the

same! It's like you've been stuck in a time capsule for the past fifteen years. Not fair! The rest of us are getting older. Older-*looking*, anyway. I still feel like a college kid. Act like it, too, most days."

Nobody says a word to that. I don't have a clue what I'm supposed to do or say here, and Betty looks like everything she wants to say would create a scene, so we kick at the grass and chuckle nervously until Dr. Reitman edges away and says, "Well, it was nice to meet you, Chris. Nate, can I take Georgia with me to make my final rounds? She's a great icebreaker."

"Yeah. Just, uh, try not to make her mad, or she'll spew obscenities."

With a salute, the doctor moves off in the direction of the crafts tent, and I turn back to Betty and Chris, the latter of whom points to me with both index fingers and says, "This guy! You're hilarious, man!"

I smile weakly. "O-okay..."

"I can't imagine that sweet mini-Boop being anything but an angel. She's gorgeous, you two. And when's this little one due?" He pats Betty's belly, but she quickly moves away from his reach while I try to locate the eyeballs that have popped from my sockets and landed in the turf at my feet.

Teeth clenched, fists balled, and eyes narrowed, Betty growls, "Why. Are. You. Here?"

Gotta tell you; *my* asshole's tight, and I'm not on the receiving end of that look or question.

Finally, Chris drops the jovial class reunion act and leans forward, lowering his voice. "Can we talk privately somewhere?"

I'm about to object when Betty says, "You have ten minutes," and points toward the clinic's front door. Walking closely behind him, she tosses back to me, "We're going to use your office. I'll be back out in time to clean up."

"Um. Okay? Are you sure?"

Her answer is a double-thumbs-up over her head as she trots to catch up with our unexpected guest. I watch after her, weighing the pros and cons of following them.

Pro: keeping an eye on this untrustworthy stranger and hearing firsthand why he's here. Cons: dying by Betty's hand when I suggest by my presence that I don't trust her to a) take care of herself and b) fill me in later with all the facts; abandoning Dr. Reitman to host the last few minutes of this crazy Christmas party by herself; losing my poo the next time that guy touches any part of my wife's person, especially the part carrying our unborn child; being beaten to a bloody pulp by someone who's built similarly to Kocoum from Disney's *Pocahontas* after said losing of poo.

In other words, in no way does joining them in my office end well for me.

Cursing under my breath, I watch the front door close, obscuring my view of the reunited pair. And still I stand here, impotent.

A clearing throat to my left and slightly behind me draws my attention. I glance back to find Lyle Forrester. "Uh, Nate?"

With a quick, fortifying inhale and a long blink, I paste on a smile and fully turn to face him. "Yeah. Lyle. What's up? How's Brooklyn's stomach?"

"Fine. It's amazing how good you feel when you stop stuffin' your face with candy all the time. I was so embarrassed that's all it was. Here I thought she had some horrible disease, and I bring her to the doctor, like a hysterical moron."

Locating Georgia across the yard, getting her other cheek painted while sitting on Dr. Reitman's lap, I say, "They have a way of making us push the panic button. It's always better to be safe, though."

"I shoulda just asked her what she'd been eatin'. That's

what her mom—my wife—would have done." His swallow reaches my ears, above the music. "But anyway. I still have a lot to learn, I guess. And I need to stop worryin' every pain and sniffle is cancer. It's hard, though..."

I tear my eyes from Georgia and clap my hand on his shoulder. "Man, I'm sorry. I— I didn't know."

The only disadvantage to no longer having Velma around is that we don't get the backstory on patients like we used to. She would have been all-too-eager to tell me Lyle was a widower, raising his two kids alone, and I would have been much more understanding about his gruff reaction to the candy overdose diagnosis.

He sniffs, looks away, and gently shrugs off my touch. "Whatever. It happens."

"Yeah, but—"

"It's okay. I have to go. I just wanted to say thanks for doin' this today. The kids had a great time. They even got me to make this ornament." He holds up the Popsicle-stick Rudolph face by its yarn loop. "I hate glitter."

"Me too, man. But good job."

He laughs. "Thanks. Guess this means I'll have to put up the tree this year."

"Looks like it. I'm glad the whole family had fun. And don't hesitate to call if you have any concerns about the kids... or just need to talk."

He ducks his head but nods at his shoes. "Thanks. That's... real nice." Chin higher, he holds out his (sparkly) hand. I grasp and shake it. "You're a good guy."

I laugh at the surprise in his tone. "Thanks. I... try to be."

Backing up to join Brooklyn and Kevin, who are waiting for him by the curb, he says, "Oh, and tell your wife we said, 'bye.'"

As he turns his back to me and strides toward his kids, I look at the emptying yard and mutter at the blowing trash, "Yeah. Will do."

* * *

BACK IN HIS STREET CLOTHES, Winn follows me around the clinic's filthy front yard, holding a trash bag while I repeatedly bend and stoop to collect the three billion pieces of garbage scattered across the lawn. "And this guy is alone with Betty right now? In your office? And you're okay with that?"

"I trust her."

"Of course, you trust *her*. But what about *him*? He could be a psycho, making this whole thing up about the kid to get closer to the woman he never stopped loving."

I consider it for a second but dismiss it when I recall all the official correspondence we've received from the adoption agency and the Newsome family. When my heartbeat returns to normal, I say, "You need to stop watching *Lifetime* with Laurel."

He shakes the bag to settle its contents and opens it wider for me to toss in my latest handful. "Seriously, though. I couldn't stand to be cut out of the loop."

I clench and unclench my teeth, then say, "I'm not being cut out of the loop. As soon as I'm done out here, I'll go inside and check on them to make sure everything's okay. Frankly, he should be more afraid of her."

"Yeah, I wouldn't want to get on Betty's bad side."

"I've been there. It's a scary place. Which is why I'm respecting their space and staying out here."

"They've been in there a long time, though, huh?"

I have to admit, that's true. The original ten minutes has

expired threefold. But I've texted her a couple of times to see if she wanted me to come get her, and the last time, she replied, *Everything's fine. Sorry it's taking so long. Almost done.* Querying her again would be overkill.

"They have a lot to talk about, I guess."

And I really *don't* want to talk, so I take the bag from my friend and say, "Hey, you've done enough today, man. And now Laurel's watching Georgia while we clean up. Why don't you go salvage what you can of the evening?"

He laughs. "I got nothing better to do."

"I can't believe that. Surely, there's a project in your wood shop you've been working on. Or you have some Christmas shopping to do."

"You trying to get rid of me, Yank?"

Busted, I smile and shrug, then return to trash-collecting. "Maybe. I'm tired, and something tells me my evening is not going to go as I'd planned."

"Which was?"

"Soaking in the tub, reading a book, then falling asleep like an old man on the couch."

"You're gonna have to up your game, my man, if you're gonna compete with that Chris guy. From a hundred feet away, I could see he's all that. Looks like Betty's taste in men has *drastically* changed since college. Lucky for you."

"I'm not competing with anyone."

He snorts. "If you say so."

"I'm not." I thrust the trash bag back at him. "I'm going inside to put the waiting room back together."

And eavesdrop, if possible.

Or exclusively eavesdrop, I decide when I close the front door behind me with a soft click and find the waiting room already restored to order and deserted.

I creep to my office door and lean against the frame, tilting my head as close to the paneled wood as possible without brushing my hair against it. Their voices murmur from the other side, but after a few seconds of straining, my ears adjust to the low volume and start to make out words, starting with Betty's.

"...satisfied by what you see?"

"...not like that."

"...bullshit... ...it like, then?..."

I focus on moderating my heart rate and breathing to prevent drowning out what little I can hear, but adrenaline doesn't want to cooperate. Finally, I resort to holding my breath altogether and taking tiny sips of air only when I absolutely have to.

"They're nervous, that's all," Chris says. "And I'm sort of the mediator. They trust me."

"Shows how much they know. Well, now you can report back to them that Nate and I are who we say we are, and everything is as I said it is: we're busy with a billion things right now, but we're looking forward to meeting the three of them after the holidays. Okay?"

"Yeah. Absolutely. Only I talked to Nate for, like, three seconds out there. I'd like the chance to get to know him better."

Oh, barf.

"Why?"

There's a grin in his voice when he replies, "To make sure he deserves you, for one thing."

Betty mutters something I can't quite hear, but I can easily fill in the blank with several of my own retorts (one of which is, "He doesn't").

His loud burst of laughter gives a hint as to her real answer, followed by, "Kidding, kidding! No, but seriously. One of the things the Newsomes are most nervous about is how all this is going to affect your family. They don't want to disrupt things or cause problems between you and Nate. With me, there were no worries on that front. I don't have a wife or kids, so it's been an uncomplicated reunion. But it's different for you."

"Nate's fine with all this."

Not quite *fine with the jack-in-the-box ex-boyfriend, actually.*

"Good. Great. I can't wait to talk to him more and see how fine he is."

I jump back from the door when Betty's voice suddenly booms at me, mere inches away. "You don't get to take charge of this whole thing and play the hero now, after all these years."

"That's not what I'm trying to do. I'm trying to make things easier for them. It's the least I can do."

"And make me look uncooperative in the process."

Now his voice is just as close as Betty's, and something knocks against the wood near my ear. "That's not my intent. At all. But what can I say? I'm a hopeless charmer. I seem to remember you used to like that about me."

I rest my hand on the shiny brass lever, ready to bust in, but resisting that urge with every single synapse and nerve from my brain to my fingertips.

C'mon, Betts. You've got this. Don't make me go all Neanderthal on this guy's ass. I'll wind up hurting myself.

"Back then, it was romantic. Now it just makes you seem sleazy."

Yes! Atta girl!

The handle rattles. I leap toward the front desk and roll over the top of the counter, *almost* landing on my feet but off a tad on the angle, the rubber soles of my casual shoes squeaking on the wooden waiting room floor before my feet fly out from under me altogether, landing me squarely on one butt cheek. But not for long. I roll to my knees and spring to my feet, grabbing the back of the nearest chair, which I pick straight up and put exactly where it was, hoping it looks like I was moving it from a great distance, minding my own business while rearranging the waiting area.

One glance over my shoulder at the emerging couple (*not* a couple) tells me I've failed miserably.

Betty cocks an eyebrow at me. "Interpretive chair dancing again?"

I attempt a laugh at myself, hoping they only saw the finale to my fancy foot- and butt-work. "Just making sure it's exactly where it needs to be."

"He's a little high-strung," Betty says to Chris, "but we love him anyway."

"Can I buy you two dinner?"

Noooooooooooooooooooo!

"We should finish up here and get Georgia," Betty says smoothly, almost sounding sorry.

"Oh, she's invited, too, of course. I figured she was still around here somewhere. You sent her home alone?" He winks at me. I barely manage to keep my eyeballs from rolling toward the ceiling.

"She's with a neighbor while we clean up here," Betty says. "That reminds me; I need to settle up with the vendors."

"Pat's already done that," I say, impressed with myself that I said the doctor's name so casually and without stuttering. If we're "partners" now, then why not spew her first name all over the place? Better yet, I should come up with a sweet pet name for her. Perhaps... Chicken Patty.

Before that nauseating thought distracts me too much, I continue, "The tent rental companies will be by tomorrow to get their stuff; we only have to fold up tables and chairs and store the arts and crafts stuff."

"I'll help," Mr. Can't-Take-A-Hint says.

Betty waves him off. "Don't be silly."

"No, I mean it. I'll help you out, then we can get your little girl and grab some dinner. Everyone has to eat. Might as well let me pay for it."

I'd like to make this guy pay for several things; my dinner isn't one of them.

18

BASED ON A TRUE STORY

COOL AS CAN BE, CHRIS LOUNGES ON HIS SIDE OF THE BOOTH at Cracker Barrel (we wanted to show him a classy time) and sizes me up after Betty departs with Georgia.

When our daughter said, "Potty, potty!" for the third time, I said, "Not it." Normally, I don't mind being the one to take her (that way, I can ensure she's learning proper hand-washing technique), but I've left this joker alone with my wife plenty today; we're overdue for some quality one-on-one time.

So far, I'm sure he's had no trouble comparing himself to me and coming out ahead. After all, I spent the majority of the day in the sun and wind, shook about a thousand hands, found out my baptism "didn't count," handled roughly a ton of trash, met the father of my wife's first child, and fell on my ass.

Now I'm sitting across a table from this stranger-but-not-a-stranger in a tacky chain restaurant, wondering what he and Betty talked about for a half hour before I overheard (ahem) the rest of their conversation. And he's giving *me* the stink-eye.

Okay, not really. He's looking more at his phone than at me, which is rude but fine. I don't want to be the subject of his scrutiny. Plus, the more he stares at that device, the more I can openly study him.

Determined not to be the one to break our stubborn silence, I examine him, desperate to find some flaw other than that chickenpox scar, since we all have one of those somewhere. His nose is a tad large, come to think of it. Maybe I wouldn't have sex with him, after all. (I'm shallow like that.)

Finally, eyes still on his phone, he says, "I've spent a fair amount of time trying to imagine Betty's life over the years, and I have to say, this is not one of the scenarios I envisioned."

"Married with kids?"

He laughs. "That. And living in a town like this, holding down a front desk at a private medical practice."

"That's temporary. And we like it here."

"You do? You guys don't fit in at all. Which is a compliment, by the way."

He sets down his phone and smiles at me, as if he's presented me with a gift—the gift of his approval.

Before I can defend Jasper any further (that's not easy to do on the best of days, honestly), he continues, "She was something else in college."

I push the broken paper ring from my napkin and silverware bundle around the table with my index finger. "Still is."

"Yeah, I'm sure, but... I mean... That's why when she got pregnant and didn't want to keep the baby, I totally got it. It hurt when she turned down my marriage proposal, but she was going places, and the last thing I wanted was to stand in her way. Turns out, she was going... here?"

My shoulders tense at more than one detail he's dropped in that loaded monologue, but I choose to focus on the last part. "We have a good life."

He waves away my umbrage. "Oh, I'm sure you do."

"You say you're sure, but you don't seem convinced."

"Well... You know..." He raises his hands to gesture to the room around us.

Although it's a Saturday night, the place is only half-full. Still, it's the busiest I've ever seen it. Even the after-church crowd on Sundays doesn't challenge its seating capacity. But Jasper's draw isn't its hopping night scene for swinging singles. It's a quiet area where people settle down to raise kids. Or retire. Do I wish its population were more culturally diverse? Absolutely. But it's not like Green Bay was some great melting pot, either.

Refusing to make it easy for him, I shake my head. "You'll have to spell it out for me. I'm just a stupid hick nurse in a stupid hick town."

"Don't be like that, man. I'm only saying..." He blows out a large breath and starts over. "I've lived all over the place..."

"Good for you."

"...so towns like this... They're quaint but claustrophobic. And Betty always struck me as too adventurous to be happy in a place like this."

"It's been a fairly big adventure, moving more than a thousand miles away from everyone we know."

"I guess that's one way to look at it."

"That's been our experience." I gulp the rest of my water and, ice held between my back molars, ask, "What do you do, anyway, that has you crisscrossing the globe so much?"

"This and that. I get bored with things quickly."

You don't say.

"And what, specifically, made you decide to go to UW, of all places?"

With a smirk and a wink, he translates, "You mean, what twist of fate sent me colliding with Betty?"

"Something like that."

He shrugs. "I wanted a mainstream American experience.

Where better to get one than the upper Midwest? You don't get more mainstream than that. Coming from Hawaii, that was exotic. I was amazed by the amount of snow I saw my first winter there. I'd never seen snow before, period. So it was wild. And while island life is more laid-back, I liked how friendly and calm—in their own ways—the people of Wisconsin were."

"What did you study?"

He bounces his leg under the table and flexes the muscles in his neck while rolling his head. "I didn't declare a major until they made me."

Shocking.

"And when I did, I went for something versatile: business. Figured it would come in handy someday, no matter what."

"Has it?"

His eyes shift sideways. He looks over his shoulder as if searching for someone—probably Betty—to rescue him from this conversation. "A time or two."

I laugh at yet another of his evasive answers. "Are you a drug dealer?"

His head snaps back around. "What? No!"

"Figured I should check. Since you're elbowing your way into my family." I smile and chuckle to soften the statement, but I also punctuate the end of the sentence with a tiny nod that says, *"I'm not kidding."*

His earnest head shake tells me my message has been received. "I recently wrote a screenplay, and I'm trying to get it optioned. It's a waiting game, though, so I have a lot of time between phases of the project."

"Perfect time to reconnect with Trevor, then."

And stir the pot in other people's lives.

"Exactly."

Betty returns to the table, huffing and puffing with Georgia in her arms. "Good grief. I thought this kid would never go."

"She did, though?" I pull our daughter into my lap and finger-comb her wild hair away from her face.

"Yes. Finally. And then some."

I squeeze the pooper and kiss her head. "Good girl! Wow! That's so... big."

"But she was more interested in giving a concert at first."

"She has a ton of personality," Chris declares. "Reminds me of someone I know." He taps his lips as if trying to place who, then points to Betty, who blushes as she settles next to me.

"She's much more stubborn than I am."

Chris and I both laugh at that as the server approaches our table and asks if any of us want dessert. Betty nudges me with her hip while perusing the pictures of sweet treats. "Shut up." To our server, she says, "I'll take the apple pie."

"With ice cream?"

"Of course."

I stifle a sigh. Normally, I wouldn't care, but I want this dinner to be over, so we can go home and put Georgia to bed, and I can download from Betty the information I desperately want. The only download Betty seems interested in, however, involves a few hundred calories.

The thing is, I want to hate this guy. I want to tell him to get out of our lives—permanently. I want to tell him to go to Hell. I want to rewind and have Betty delete the email account through which he was able to contact her. Or further, go to a different college. But life doesn't work that way. Meeting Chris and having Trevor made her the person she is today, and I freaking love that person. A lot. Maybe too much. No, that's not possible. But enough that I want to make all of this go away.

Unfortunately, Chris has the time and the means to have

found her no matter how many obstacles were thrown in his way. His screenplay is merely a diversion; his true current project is bringing Trevor, Betty, and himself back together. Maybe not as a permanent family unit, because he doesn't strike me as the type to do "long-term," but getting the three of them into the same room together seems to be challenge enough, and it's a mission he's chosen to accept.

Conversation becomes stilted as we watch Betty eat her dessert. There are a million dead-end topics between these two, and Chris seems determined to try to explore every one of them. Betty is equally determined to throw up roadblocks. He asks about Frankie/Francesca, but Betty hides behind the court order that prohibits us from speaking publicly about it.

"This"—Chris jabs his finger against the table—"isn't publicly."

When Betty's only reply to that is to spear another soft apple and pop it into her mouth, I say, "We can't take the chance that someone overhears us or that you repeat it to someone—however innocently—and that person repeats it, and on and on. Anyway, it's not our favorite subject."

He seems to respect that, but his next attempt nudges a related land mine, *Girl Noir*, and his small—but dastardly—role in the story.

"It's fiction," Betty says firmly when he protests his innocence.

"Damn right, it is! That's not how it went down, and you know it."

She shrugs. "Yeah, but whatever."

What?

Let's review, shall we? In Frankie's book, loosely based on Chris and Betty's experience with young love, surprise pregnancy, adoption, and—ultimately—a birth mother and son's reunion, the most fictional part, as I understand it, is the kid tracking down his biological mom, followed by the romance that develops between the adoptive father and the protagonist. Everything else is fairly close to real life. Supposedly. That's what Betty's told me—or led me to believe—the entire time I've known her.

Now, Chris says "that's not how it went down"? And Betty agrees without argument?

Before I can question this development, she says, "Let it go. It's not like anyone knows it's you."

"It's *not* me. It's some white, male, privileged jerkhole who abandoned someone he supposedly loved during one of the most difficult times in her life. I have my faults, but I would have never done that."

"She got the male privileged jerkhole part right," Betty mutters, then laughs at his outraged reaction. "I'm kidding! Listen. That other stuff made for a better story, that's all. Poetic license, I guess. I'm not the author. Take it up with her."

He leans back in his side of the booth and sulks at his water glass. "I might."

Despite my sudden nausea, I steal the last bite of pie from Betty's plate, amid her and Georgia's loud protestations, and gently push against my wife's side by scooting down the booth. "C'mon. It's been a long day. For everyone."

Betty reaches for the check, but Chris, emerging from his pout, slaps his hand on top of it. "I said this was on me."

Thing is, I thought most things were on him. It's starting to sound like that's not the case. At all.

* * *

I FIGURED AS SOON as we were finally alone, all my questions would burst from me, but hours have passed, and I've been as silent as a mute librarian (yeah, *that* silent). If Betty's noticed, she hasn't mentioned it. She's kept to herself, as well—probably talked out, thanks to You-Know-Who.

Now, as we lock up the house for the night and prepare for bed, I realize I'm too tired for any more talking today. Tired in general. Tired of Chris. Tired of surprises. Tired of thinking. Tired of wondering. Tired of worrying. Just... tired. I'd rather sleep than try to reconcile the version of Betty's history I've been led to believe with reality.

After all, I'm sure there's a perfectly logical explanation for everything. She didn't seem eager at dinner to refute Chris's claims, nor did she seem panicked that what he was saying might conflict with what she's told me or be brand new altogether. We may as well have been talking about a movie we'd all seen that each of us interpreted differently. Unfortunately, I saw an edited-for-TV, censored version and didn't even get the whole story. I definitely need to watch the director's cut.

But if you're me, you don't start a movie at ten o'clock. Not that there's any risk of my falling asleep during this particular feature. On the contrary, I'm afraid it will keep me awake all night.

So I brush and floss, strip down to a t-shirt and my boxer-briefs, and plump my pillows like nothing out of the ordinary happened today. Nope. I meet my wife's former lovers all the time. We regularly hang out at family eateries and stuff ourselves with Southern food. We trade barbs and dance around awkward topics every day. What's weird about that? Nothing.

When Betty slides into bed behind me and snuggles up to my back, I close my eyes and try to relax. Relaxing isn't the easiest thing to do, however, when someone grabs a big handful of Old Faithful. My eyes fly open, I gasp, and my whole body—every part of it—goes rigid.

Betty laughs against my back. "Sorry. Didn't realize I'd be taking you by surprise."

I bring up my leg to nudge her hand aside. More testily than I intend, I say, "Do you mind? I'm trying to sleep."

Rising up on her elbow, she slaps me between my shoulder blades. "I knew it! You're mad."

"I'm not."

"You never turn down sex."

"Yes, I do. You're not *that* irresistible. Don't flatter yourself."

I get another slap for that.

"Stop hitting me!"

"The only times you've ever said no to sex was after walking in on your mom and dad..."

"Oh, dear God. Please. Do you have to keep reminding me?"

"...when you're sick..."

"Yeah, I'm not a big fan of spreading disease."

"...and when you're miffed. Your parents aren't here..."

"Thank goodness."

"...you're perfectly healthy at the moment..."

"How do you know? That fried okra isn't sitting well with me. And what's with the gravy on everything? Did I not say 'Hold the gravy'? I might as well not be talking when I order food around here. 'No, I don't like grits—it's like eating baby barf—and not everything has to be smothered in gravy.' What's so difficult to understand there? Also, they're deaf to the 'un-' in 'un-sweetened tea.' If I wanted to drink sugar water, I'd go in the backyard and tip the hummingbird feeder into my mouth."

"...which leaves one possibility: you're pissed off."

"I'm more complicated than you give me credit for."

"No, you're not."

I flounce onto my back. "Yes. I am. I may not have some romantic, tragic love affair in my past, and there will be no exotic billionaire playboys popping up to regale you with stories from my crazy college days..."

"I should hope not."

"But that doesn't mean I'm not capable of complex feelings."

"Nobody's saying it does."

"It also doesn't mean I can't relate to or understand the truth. As in, what *actually* happened, not what you suppose I can handle. And not what you assume I *want* to hear. Or what you need me to believe, so that I see you as vulnerable. I don't get off on playing the big, macho hero, so you don't have to spare me the gritty details."

She pulls back her chin and drops her jaw. "Where the heck is this coming from? Who says I've done any of those things?"

"It seems to me like you, Frankie, and Chris have completely different stories about what happened back then. And you have an extra-special version just for me. I guess I should feel flattered, but..."

"First of all, I can't believe how many times in one day I've had to explain to two grown-ass men the difference between fiction—which is what Frankie's version is—and real life."

"I understand the difference well enough to know that what little you've told me over the years has its own truth-bendiness."

"'Truth-bendiness'?"

"You know what I mean."

"No, I really don't. Please, tell me what I've told you that isn't true, according to you."

"You said you were basically charmed by some rich frat boy, got careless with your fun, crazy, college-kid sex, and got pregnant. Then when you decided to put the baby up for adoption, he disappeared. Now, I'm finding out, 'Well, he stuck around a while, long enough to sign the adoption papers, anyway.' And tonight, Chris dropped the nugget that he asked you to marry him, but that didn't fit in with your big career plans."

"My 'big career plans'? You mean, like growing up? And finishing college? Those 'big career plans'?"

"To hear him tell it, you were the next big thing."

"In what? Spending my step-dad's money? When he knew me, I was a stupid, spoiled, fucked-up little girl with daddy issues."

"He didn't see you that way."

"That's because he had all the same issues times a thousand. All he saw in me was a willing piece of ass, trust me. Now, through the magic of hindsight, I was a real diamond in the rough, huh? Puh-lease."

"It sounds like he was in love with you."

"Oh, I'm sure. He was in love with the idea of being in love. Us against the world. But it would have never worked. Which is what I told him when he proposed. If you count, 'Hey, if we get married, my dad will build us a house, and we can get a nanny to take care of the baby' as a proposal. Which I didn't."

"So you told him to leave?"

She mulls that over for a second. "Effectively, yes."

"That's *not* what I've thought happened."

"I'm sorry if I wasn't more explicit, but I never lied to you, not even by omission. You've obviously filled in a few blanks yourself, when you were always welcome to ask me. Maybe *you* needed me to be the victim; *you* needed me to seem vulnerable."

"No. That's not it."

Her eyes flash in the dark. "You saved me from Frankie;

maybe you needed to feel like you saved me from Chris, too. Or at least the memory of being abandoned by him, which I never said happened."

"What? Who said I saved you from Frankie? *I've* never said that. If anything, it was the opposite!"

"I've always liked to think we saved each other."

"Okay, fine. Whatever. We're not talking about her, though. We're talking about Chris, who you've always said 'left.'"

"He did!"

"And abandonment is implied when you say that in the context of a guy with a pregnant girlfriend."

"That's another incorrect assumption you're blaming me for, then?"

"No, I've used the word 'abandoned' in conversations about this, and you've never corrected me. And I'm sure you told me he 'ran away.'"

"He did. He took my out and ran with it. Which is fine. That's what I needed him to do."

"But he says he wanted to stay."

"You've known this guy for less than twenty-four hours, and you believe his version of things more than mine, the woman you're married to?"

"I didn't say I believed him *more*. But I've been taken by surprise by the additional information he's provided. Plus, there are contradictions in *your* story."

"My 'story.' See, every time you call it that, you imply it's not true."

I pinch the bridge of my nose. "I specifically remember a conversation in an Atlanta hotel room where you said he ran away with no explanation."

"If I said that during an emotional moment, it was an exaggeration. The bottom line is, he's a flake. He would have gotten bored with being a father and a husband in less than a year. And then I would have been screwed, because if you think his dad would have let us get married without an iron-clad prenup..."

I say nothing to that. What can I say?

"And the real shame of all this is that Chris will get bored with Trevor, too. Soon. And suddenly. One day, he'll just be done with it. He'll stop communicating with the kid, and the rest of us will have to figure out what to do about that. All because he was 'at loose ends' and couldn't leave well enough alone."

I close my eyes and imagine the mess that's going to be... eventually.

"The one decent life choice I've made was breaking up with him."

Ouch.

At that telling declaration, I return to my side, away from her. "Well, I'm glad you're happy with that *one* decision in your life."

She sighs. "That's not what I meant."

When she tries to nestle against my back again, I throw off the covers, swing my legs over the side of the bed, grab my pillow, and stomp toward the door.

"Nate!" She tries to scramble to a sitting position but never makes it, finally giving up and resting on her elbows as she watches my exit.

"If you're not going to leave me alone, I'm going to another room. Good night."

19

FACT VS. FICTION

THE CLINK OF CERAMIC ON WOOD, FOLLOWED BY THE nutty, pleasantly skunky scent of coffee wakes me up way before I'm ready the next morning. A dip in the mattress pulls me toward the edge of the guest bed's mattress. Betty rubs my shoulder, then kisses my lips and nestles her head high on my chest, under my chin. "I'm sorry, Nathaniel."

Still half-asleep, I grunt in reply, taking a minute to remember why I was sleeping alone and what she could possibly be apologizing for. When I do recall the events from the day before and our bedtime conversation, the twinge of resentment tries to take hold, but tenderness wins out.

I wrap my arms around her torso and say into her hair, "You're forgiven."

"Really? Or do you just not want to sleep in this bed anymore?"

"It *is* terrible. How many guests have we tortured with this thing?"

"Not too many. It prevents people from overstaying their welcome, though. I say we keep it. But you're not allowed to sleep in it anymore."

"Deal."

She tries to lift herself off me, but I tighten my embrace.

"Your coffee's getting cold."

"Don't care."

Against my hip, a tiny tremor pings, similar to a ringing cell phone on vibrate. It's not quite the same as a forceful, third-trimester kick, but it's still as sweet. Maybe sweeter.

Before I can comment on it, Betty says, "I really thought you knew everything. I realize you got the story kind of piece-meal, and your introduction to the facts was that stupid book, but I figured by now all the pieces of the puzzle were firmly in place in your mind, because they are in mine. I've forgotten you can't feel what I felt. Those emotions and memories aren't there for you, to help you keep it all straight. I've been selfish, dropping details here and there and leaving you to figure it out, because I'm uncomfortable talking about it. And that's wrong."

This time, she pushes hard enough against my chest to break my hold. I open my eyes so she can see I'm awake and listening. After I stroke my thumb against her wrist for encouragement, she settles on the side of the bed and angles toward me. "So, here's what happened. From the beginning. You deserve that."

"All right. Only if you want to talk about it."

"Wanting you to know outweighs not wanting to talk about it."

"I'm listening." Something tells me I'm going to need coffee for this, so I prop myself against the headboard and reach for my mug. That first hot sip reassures me I can handle this.

"I met Chris in a marketing class. We happened to sit next to each other the first day of the lecture, and he made me laugh by making smart-ass comments about the professor during the lecture. That was the extent of our interaction for a whole semester, but he asked me out right before the teacher handed out the final. Considering it was the first course in which I'd ever had perfect attendance, I said yes.

"Things got serious between us fast. I spent more nights at the apartment he shared with a couple of his fraternity brothers than I did in my own dorm room. I—" She looks down at the bed. "He was the first guy I really fell for. But by some miracle, I didn't ditch all my other interests and focus all my attention on him. I was proud of myself for keeping at my studies and going to class. Figured that made me a real grownup. And I still pictured myself working in a big city someday, pitching ideas in boardrooms, or whatever. At that point, I had no idea what my skills and interests would translate into in the real world. That was one of the best parts of college, though: anything was possible. I still believed I could do and be whatever I wanted to be, once I figured out what that was. And I felt like I had all the time in the world to figure it out." She rolls her eyes at herself and chuckles.

"We all feel that way at that age."

"Yeah. Well, one thing I was sure I *didn't* want to be—then or possibly ever—was a mom." She pauses and smiles sadly. "Which proves how ignorant I was. I had no clue it could be like what I have with Georgia. I thought kids kept you from doing the things you *really* wanted to do. That's how my mom made it seem, anyway."

"Kitty wasn't a good spokesperson for the role."

She laughs. "No. Not at all. So when I missed my period two months in row, I knew I was in trouble. All my plans, all my dreams... they seemed completely out of reach when I pictured myself trying to do it all with another person relying on me for everything. Mom wanted me to get an abortion—

offered to pay for it but not take me and be there with me; Chris wanted us to get married. Neither of those seemed right. Frankie was the one who gave me the information about the adoption agency."

"Wow."

"Right? She was a good friend... sometimes. Not that adoption was a perfect solution, either, but it seemed a whole lot better than my other options. Of course, I made sure Chris was okay with it. If he wanted to be a dad and raise a kid, I offered to sign over my parental rights and let him do it. But he only wanted to do it if I was part of the deal. Which spoke volumes to me. It meant he didn't want to be a parent any more than I did; the kid would have been an afterthought. And not having any concept of maternal instinct or unconditional love at that time, I was terrified I'd resent that baby for ruining my life."

She winces and covers her face with her hands. "Gosh. I was such a horrible, selfish, terrible—"

I set down my coffee and pull her hands away. "Hey. You were a kid."

"No. I was an adult. Old enough to vote, old enough to get myself in that predicament, old enough to believe I knew everything."

"Barely. And you were terrified. You weren't as selfish as you think. You didn't want to place all that baggage on that baby before he was even born. Ultimately, you were thinking of what was best for him."

"And for me."

"So what? Sounds like nobody else ever considered your interests. You had to."

Unwilling to cut herself any slack, she shrugs.

"It's just... I don't mean to interrupt, and I'm sorry if you're about to get to this, but... I get that you guys didn't feel ready to be parents, responsible for a helpless infant, but if you and Chris were so in love, why didn't you two stay together anyway, after the adoption?"

She chortles. "We were over long before Trevor was born. The experience changed us. And not for the better. All we did was fight. He started every conversation with more pressure about getting married and keeping the baby. After a while, it became a habit. And a challenge. He wanted to win. He wanted to wear me down until I gave him his way. And it wasn't even what he truly wanted. Most of his arguments revolved around how he—meaning his dad—could afford for us to have a nanny. And I thought, I will *not* be like my mother, leaving my kid to be raised by someone else so I can flit around doing whatever I want. Sure, I was too old for a nanny by the time Witt came along, but if it hadn't been for Frankie's parents, I would have dropped out of high school, because nobody else was ever around to make sure I went. I was *not* okay with continuing that cycle of indifference. And I was sure I'd be exactly like my mom. After all, I didn't want to keep my own baby."

"You never considered accepting Chris's proposal?"

She swallows loudly. "Oh, I considered it plenty. It would have been the easiest thing, in the short-term. Would have made for a lot less uncertainty. One day, I'd cry that I had to give up the baby; the next, I'd cry that time was moving too slowly, and I wished it was just over already. I was a mess. I had no idea what I wanted, so it was best to give him to people who knew for *sure* they wanted a child and would never take him for granted. Anyway, we'd already been paired with a couple, and while I could legally back out at any time and change my mind before we signed the papers, I couldn't do it to those people, even if I didn't know them by name."

"So you broke up with Chris. How far along were you by then?"

I wait while she remembers and does the math. "Five, six months?"

"Wow. Things went downhill fast."

"Yeah. And being around him was torture. Not just because of the non-stop arguing, either. His presence was yet another reminder of what a screwup I was and how everything that used to make me happy made me miserable. So I told him if he didn't transfer to another school for the next semester, I would. He did. Said he always wanted to check out Colorado and heard they had some good party schools.

"He came back to sign the adoption papers, and he gave me a quick hug, but we didn't talk to each other. And that's the last I saw him or heard from him until he emailed me last month."

She picks at the comforter, and I wait a few more seconds to make sure she's finished, then say, "Thank you."

Her chin lifts. "Huh?"

"Thank you for telling me that. All at once. From start to finish."

"It's not finished, though, is it?" she asks, her eyes filling and her lips trembling. "It's never going to be finished."

I open my arms. "C'mere."

She crawls into my lap, and I make a conscious effort not to grunt or groan, no matter how unprepared I am for her weight. When she's finally comfortable (at least one of us is) and still, I kiss the top of her head and say, "It's one of those things that has far-reaching, long-lasting consequences."

"As it should. I get that. And if I'd truly wanted to be left alone, I could have made that happen, legally. But I always thought, 'What if something comes up, like he needs a kidney or something, and I'm their last hope at a transplant?' I wanted him to have the option to find me someday, if he wanted—or needed—to. I never imagined Chris would be part of the deal, though. And I didn't realize it would be this hard. I didn't realize how much I hate the person I used to be and how much it hurts to have to remember her and acknowledge that I was like that." Unable to go on, she sobs against my chest.

I pat her back, letting her get it out for a few minutes while I consider everything she's told me and imagine going through that, myself (with a few biological modifications, of course). Finally, when only the occasional sniffle escapes her, I say, "It sucks. Most people get to grow up and leave their worst parts behind, having learned from their past bad behavior, with little or no record of those things. But because you chose the hardest way—and I do think it was the hardest choice of the three you felt you had—there's living, breathing, walking proof of something you feel deep shame about. But Betts?"

"What?"

"That's pretty cool." When she snorts, I explain, "It's cool because he's also proof of that incredibly hard thing you did. He's part of your legacy. And from what I've read and from what Chris has said, Trevor's a good kid."

"I can't take credit for that, though. Only half of the biological stuff is thanks to me. His personality is a credit to his parents. The ones who raised him."

I tap the top of her head. "You want to argue nature versus nurture with the psychiatrists' son?"

She chuckles. "Maybe."

"Because we Binghams regularly discussed stuff like this at the dinner table and considered it 'relaxing discourse.'"

"Oh, to be a fly on the wall. You guys were such nerds!"

"'Were'? The point is, when you meet Trevor, you're going

to be surprised at all the little things he does that remind you of Chris and you, things that are part of his DNA, things he couldn't possibly have *learned*, because he's never met you."

"That's going to be weird."

"And emotional. And overwhelming."

"Maybe I should wait until after the baby's born."

"It'll be okay."

"I'm a mess right now."

"Be a mess, then. You're allowed."

"Because I'm pregnant right now, everything feels so similar to the way it did then. So the memories are even more intense, because..."

"Hormones."

"Stupid hormones." She rolls off me, wedging herself between my legs and the wall. Looking up at me, she says, "And I can't stand for you to be mad at me, on top of everything else."

"I'm worried, that's all. This is strange. *Chris* is strange. We don't know this guy, but he's running the show. I'm not mad at you, Betts."

"You were last night. And you had every right to be. But I'm trying." Her chin puckers. "This is just so hard."

"Hey, hey, hey. Please, don't cry."

"You said I could be a mess!" She dabs her eyes.

"Okay, yeah. You're right. Have at it."

"No, I'm okay." She takes a deep breath. "I'm much better now."

"MOMMY? DADDY?" comes from the room next door.

Before I can move, Betty lumbers to her feet, resting a hand on my knee to keep me in place. "Finish your coffee. I've got this."

For once, I don't argue. Something tells me she needs to

prove that statement to herself, fast-forward to the present in her mind and remind herself she's not that scared, incapable college kid anymore.

I take up my lukewarm coffee and gulp it. "I'll be there in a minute. Don't have any fun without me."

FITTING IN

I LOVE HER, AND I RESPECT THE HELL OUT OF HER FOR telling me the whole truth, which didn't paint her in the most favorable light, but that doesn't mean every one of our problems is magically solved. In fact, one of our biggest problems has been in *my* house for the past hour, sitting on *my* couch, petting *my* dog. And I'm not happy about it.

But Betty convinced me that having Chris over to hammer out a final plan for her big reunion with Trevor was the easiest, fastest, most painless way to get him out of town for good.

"Why does he have to be involved at all?" I practically whined when she proposed the meeting.

"Because that's what Trevor wants, for some reason. And resisting it is only prolonging the agony. Let's get this over with."

"Does he have to come here? Why don't we meet at the clinic?"

"I don't want to chase Georgia around the office. He can come over while she's napping, and we won't have to deal with any of that. Or ask Laurel or Pat to watch her *again*."

"Fine," I said, sulk heavy in my tone. "Whatever. But we

get right to the point. No weird detours down Memory Lane, no 'Let's be friends' nonsense. We talk dates, venues, and agenda, and then he leaves. I have half a mind to contact the adoption agency and complain about this harassment."

"No!" Her eyes widened with a panic that seemed dispro-portionate to my statement. "I don't want the Newsomes to get in trouble for circumventing the system. They went through the proper channels initially. Their having to do some extra digging was my fault for not keeping my information up-to-date with the agency."

"Using the birth father as their private detective is inappro-priate, though."

"He volunteered, I'm sure. This is unfamiliar territory, and we're all trying to figure it out as we go along. Let's not make it messy and contentious. That will only make the eventual meeting with them more awkward and stressful." She absently rubbed her abdomen, reminding me the last thing I want is for her to be more stressed out about this.

"Okay. But I mean it. He's not staying for dinner or taking us out for drinks or any of that nonsense. If you can't be firm with him, let me handle it. I don't mind being a jerk."

"No. Obviously," she muttered, then quickly smiled. "Joke!"

Yeah. Whatever. I'm over it. No more Mr. Nice Nurse.

So I've been curt to the point of rude throughout the reunion planning session, playing the part of timekeeper, ensuring we stay on-topic and on-task. It hasn't been easy, either. The guy's all over the place, going off on weird tangents and laughing at his own jokes. At one point, I almost asked him, "Dude, are you on drugs?" but I figured it would come off as me being a jealous turd. And what if he'd answered, "Yes"? Then I'd have to do something about it, and... can we just get through this?

Chris had his list of possible dates from the Newsomes,

and by process of elimination, we chose a weekend in late May. It's way closer to our baby's due date than I'd prefer, but they wanted to wait until the first weekend in Trevor's summer vacation, which was reasonable.

Venue was a bigger sticking point. There's no way Betty's getting on a plane to travel to Cincinnati that far into her third trimester. At the same time, I don't want to play host to these strangers—or Chris. Since we still have five months, we've decided to table that decision and each consider a list of possible neutral, yet private, locations that would serve our purposes.

That leaves agenda, for which Betty is prepared. "Let's keep it simple," she says. "That way, we can allow for hiccups. Introductions and Q&A to start, then play it by ear from there, depending on how that goes."

Her "play-it-by-ear" suggestion surprises me, considered how much she deplores that concept, but then again, planning for spontaneity totally fits her personality.

Chris laughs. "'Q&A'? Once a PR junkie, always a PR junkie. This isn't a press conference."

"There's no point making a bunch of plans for relationship-building activities and outings if we don't hit it off. We should all have the option of a quick departure, if that's what ends up being most comfortable."

"It's not going to be like that. You'll see."

"Well, I need that escape hatch," she says bluntly. "If we schedule meals and trips to amusement parks"—she nods to the tablet on Chris's lap that lists several such ideas—"I'll feel obligated to participate. Plus, I'll be as big as a house by then, so I don't envision myself traipsing around a three-thousand-acre blacktop theme park."

"Fair enough." Chris closes the document and turns off the device. "I guess that's it for now, then. I'll go back to the hotel and call the Newsomes, brainstorm with them some venues, and we can reconvene for dinner. What time works for you two?"

Before I can object, Betty stands and says, "This is good for now. We can figure out everything else through email. Make sure you copy Nate on the messages, so we're all in the loop."

And, looking like he has no idea how it's happening, Chris finds himself on the front porch, staring at our door, then backing out of our driveway in his luxury rental car.

Betty rubs her hands together, as if dusting them off. "I need a nap. And when I wake up, dinner should be ready."

I stare at her backside as she ascends the stairs. Finally, before she disappears into our bedroom, I say, "Uh, okay. Yeah. I'll work on that."

But that's still hours away, so after staring at a sleeping Reba for a few seconds, I decide to dig out my running shoes and go for a jog.

Which has turned into a walk. Because neither the dog nor I are built for running right now. And Reba stood so resolutely at the front door when I tried to leave that I knew she'd whine there and disturb Georgia and Betty if I left her. So here we are.

The fall-like temperatures—in the middle of December—and sun are perfect for a Sunday, head-clearing stroll. Or so I thought.

After the third person to slow and stare at me actually brings their vehicle to a stop, rolls down their window, and asks, "You okay there, Hoss? You need a lift somewheres?" I realize the previous passersby weren't gaping at my legs as they drove past us in their pickup trucks; they were wondering what in tarnation—to use the local vernacular—my problem was. (Out of gas? Dead battery? Escaped from nearby prison or mental institution?)

Several more drivers stop to check on us after that initial contact. Each time, I patiently explain I'm merely taking a walk, which earns me more skeptical expressions. Apparently, Reba and I are the only beings in this town who think locomotion via legs is an appropriate mode of transportation. By the time I get to Main Street, I'm ready to duck inside somewhere —anywhere—to escape the open gawks and obnoxious horn-honking. Fortunately, I've arrived at Baker's Hardware. Unfortunately, there's a large "No Pets Allowed" sign on the front door.

"Shit," I hiss, smiling apologetically at the glaring couple in their Sunday best who skirt past me to enter the store.

Stepping away from the door, I say down to Reba, "Well, Shortwad, now what?"

She pants up at me, looking slightly more derpy than usual as she tries to catch her breath.

"I pushed you to your max distance, didn't I? And we still have to get home. Let's—"

"Yank!"

My head snaps up at the sound of my friend's voice.

Winn leans out the front door of the store, then exits completely, looking me up and down. "What in the Sam Hill are you wearin', boy?"

I glance down at my Badgers sweatshirt and athletic shorts. "Clothes?"

He laughs, blowing into his hands. "Aren't you cold?"

"No. I'm quite comfortable in the sun."

"Hm. Well, I got a complaint from a coupla customers that some weirdo with a dog was loiterin' by the front door, swearin' to himself. Would that be you?"

"What? No. Maybe. But cripes! What's wrong with people?"

Instead of providing an answer he doesn't have, he kneels down to scratch Reba behind her ears. She immediately flops to the sidewalk and presents her belly to him.

"Make him work for it, Rebes. Sheesh."

"So, what's got you mutterin' cuss words out here, scarin' away my customers?"

I nod to the sign on his door. "I wanted to duck in here for a second, but I realized I couldn't bring Reba inside."

He squints up at me. "Yeah. Sorry. I'd make an exception for you, but Burke would throw a hissy. Plus, that would open up a whole canna worms I never want to open up. Reba's one thing, but Grady Jemes's basset hound leaves a trail of pee and poop behind it everywhere it goes. And if I let you guys in, he'd be one of the first ones to cry, 'Foul!'" He rises to his feet and places his hands on his hips.

"I don't want special treatment. I just wanted to give her a place to rest. Preferably away from all the staring."

"Put some real pants on, and you wouldn't have that problem. Although I must say, you have some fine legs... for a guy."

I point my toe to flex my calf. "That's because I occasionally do this thing called 'walking.' Especially on nice, sunny days like this one. Maybe some other people around here should try it."

"Baby steps, Yank. You're not gonna come in here and revolutionize everyone's thinking."

"Walking is a revolutionary idea?"

"Around these parts? Yeah. Lots of people live miles outside of town."

"Rob Jacobson offered to drive us less than a block when we went for a beer after putting up Christmas lights. And he's a doctor. Well, was."

"You drank beer with another man? How could you?"

"Rob lets us drink in public. He's not ashamed of our love... of hops."

"That's cuz he's an Episcopalian. Anything goes with those guys."

"Are you going to help me with my original problem, or what?"

He blinks at me. "I didn't realize you'd asked for my counsel."

"Where can I take Reba to let her rest before tackling the walk home?"

"You walked all the way here from *home*?"

I roll my eyes. "It's, like, two miles. Tops."

"Still! I thought you drove here and were strollin' up and down the street."

"Who drives somewhere to walk their dog?"

He shrugs. "I dunno. I don't have a dog. Or particularly enjoy walkin' or joggin'. So I wouldn't know about that. But there's a place called The Barkery down the way, where they sell homemade dog treats and such." He jabs his thumb over his shoulder in the direction of the other side of the street. "I'm surprised you've never been."

"Betty and I haven't explored Main Street that much yet. It's on our to-do list."

"They might not be open, since it's Sunday, and all. You know, that day of rest, when people go to church? Maybe you've read about it in National Geographic?"

I stick out my tongue at him. "Yeah, whatever." Nodding at his apron-covered front, I say, "Looks like you're working today, so I don't want to hear it."

"Burke had someone call in sick at the last minute. I'm fillin' in 'til he can find someone to cover the rest of the shift, knucklehead."

Laughing, I clap him on the shoulder and tug on Reba's leash to coax her back to her feet. "Thanks for the tip about the dog shop. I'll walk down there and check it out."

"You do that. I'll catch you later, Yank."

* * *

THE BARKERY WASN'T OPEN, but some wrought-iron chairs and a table provided a sufficient rest area outside the closed business. We kicked back with our faces tilted toward the sun for about fifteen minutes before reluctantly making our much-watched walk home.

Now, having delivered my coerced promise of dinner, I sit on the couch with Betty on the floor in front of me, where she's receiving a post-meal shoulder massage. Because eating is hard work. While I knead, she moans, her head lolling and falling forward.

Georgia comes running. "You hut her!" she says, fists raised as she rushes toward us.

I stick out my foot to block her impact and say, "You hit me, and you're going in time out. I've about had it with that shi—nonsense."

Betty laughs and raises her head. "Baby doll, you have to stop hitting."

"My mommy!" She pushes my leg aside and cozies up to Betty's side.

Wrapping her arm around our daughter, Betty says, "That's right. I am. Always. You don't have to be mean about it, though."

Georgia points up at me. "He mean!"

"I am not!"

"You hut Mommy."

"I'm not hurting your mommy." I lean forward and pick up

Georgia, then set her in my lap and arrange her legs on either side of Betty's head. "Here. I'll show you." I rest her hands underneath mine on Betty's shoulders. Gently squeezing, I say, "See? Like that."

Betty groans. "Ah. Feels great. Thank you."

Georgia shakes off my hands. "I do it."

Gladly letting her take over, I sit back and oversee for quality control and assurance purposes. After less than a minute, though, Georgia scrambles down from my lap and returns to her toys, tossing over her shoulder, "Daddy's turn."

Gee, thanks.

Betty drops her head back between my knees. "Well, that was an improvement. Nobody got hurt and nobody cursed."

"It *can* be done," I intone. "Now, I feel invincible. Like I'm almost ready to take on my whole family in less than a week."

She rests her temple against my knee. "It'll be fun. I'm looking forward to seeing everyone. And getting away for a few days. Looking out over the ocean... sitting on the beach... reading a book... sleeping late... Maybe even spending some time alone with you."

I snort. "Good luck with that."

"I bet your mom and dad would keep an eye on Georgia for a couple of hours for us."

"And leave Nick and Heidi with my parents and all the kids?"

"They can have an evening alone, too. We can watch the boys for them."

"That doesn't sound like fun at all."

"They deserve some quiet time."

"Yeah, yeah," I mutter. "Fine. Does this mean we don't have to get them anything for Christmas? Because that's still on my to-do list. A night of babysitting those kids surely exceeds the monetary value of anything we'd give them."

She pinches my big toe through my sock. "I already got them something."

"Oh. One less thing for me to do, I guess. What'd we get them?"

"'We' got them a nice bottle of wine..."

"Good start."

"...and a framed copy of our family portrait."

My hands freeze on her shoulders. "And?"

"That's it."

Oh, Lord. We've become those people. *"Merry Christmas; here's the best gift in the world: a picture of us." Gross. Could we be more narcissistic?*

"You don't approve?" she asks when I merely continue massaging.

"It's fine."

"No, it's not. I can tell by the way you're pinching me. Ow." She shrugs her shoulders from my grip and rubs one of them while half-turning to look at me. "You think we should add something to it? The frame's nice. And the wine wasn't cheap, either."

"No. I'm sure they'll love it."

"But?"

I pause, then plunge. "But... You know how they are. Last year, they got us that!" I flap my hand toward the flat-screen TV mounted to the wall across the room from us.

"We can't begin to match them in extravagance."

"Yeah, but..."

"That's why it's best to keep it classy and simple, so it doesn't look like we're trying."

"A portrait and a bottle of wine definitely says, 'We're not trying.'"

"Not trying to *compete*," she clarifies with a scowl. "Plus, even if we did have the means to buy them expensive gifts, they already have everything!"

It's true; my brother's favorite hobby is seeking out new trends—in electronics, cars, home improvement... you name it —and he *loves* to be the first one at work, on his block, in his group of friends, and in our family to have something. Then when someone else raves about it, he can say, "Oh, yeah, I've been using (insert fad gadget here) for a few months now. We love it. The only problem is..." He especially likes that last part, crapping on the person's joy by pointing out a flaw they haven't had the chance to discover. Why? Because he's Nick.

He's been like that our whole lives. *"Oh, you like that block-sorting toy? Yeah, that was one of my favorites when I was your age. Except the star is small enough to fit through the circle and the square holes, so you don't have to be one-hundred percent accurate. Takes some of the challenge out of it. Come talk to me when you're ready to upgrade to the See-n-Say. Now that thing'll change your life."*

"The portrait is more than fine. Is that what Mom and Dad are getting, too?"

"That's one of the things, yes. But they're also getting some Christmas ornaments from Georgia. Plus, we got your mom a pendant from us and your dad that crap-ton of golf balls he specifically asked for."

"Oh, yeah."

She crawls to all fours and uses the coffee table to stand. "Now I'm going to be self-conscious about your brother's gift. But it's all we can afford."

"Don't sweat it. I'm sorry I said anything."

"Yeah, well, you did. And with the new baby, we do need to be more judicious. I have major buyers' remorse about those portraits—they were more expensive than I expected."

"They turned out great, though."

"They're already outdated."

"We get a repeat customer discount on our next session. And we can always order a smaller set of the ones with the baby."

"Yeah, but we'll have to get newborn portraits, too."

"Who says?"

"I do! We got them for Georgia. We should do the same for this one. Otherwise, he or she looks back at photos and says, 'Wow. Mom and Dad loved my sister more than me.'"

I can't help but laugh at her already worrying about sibling rivalry, attributing these thoughts and feelings to a child who can't even blink yet.

"You, of all people, get how tricky it is!" she says, obviously offended by my amusement.

I stand and cross the room, trying to placate her with a hug. She allows me to touch her but doesn't return my embrace.

"I don't want to screw this up, Nathaniel."

Cupping the back of her neck in my palm, I murmur close to her ear, "You won't, Betts. Because you care."

"That's not always enough."

"You'll back it up with actions, and it *will* be enough. Just don't get so uptight about these things, okay? You want newborn portraits? We'll get newborn portraits."

She relaxes against me, resting her head on my shoulder. "Things are tighter—financially—than I thought they'd be. You're making more, but I'm bringing in less than half what I did back home. Pat paid our moving expenses, but that's only part of the expense of relocating. Getting settled here has been spendy."

I smile at a term I haven't heard since moving away from Cheeseland. "Okay, but we still have more than enough."

"And now, we have travel arrangements to make for May, and depending on where we decide to meet up with the

Newsomes, that could be a big chunk of change. Then just a couple of weeks later, this baby will be here, and—"

"It'll be amazing." I push back and look down into her worried, flooding eyes. "Hey." A quick glance tells me Georgia's still occupied with her toys on the floor and isn't about to jump to her mother's rescue like some deranged toddler Rambo, but just in case, I turn the two of us so Betty's back is to our daughter. "Are you going to be okay?"

She rolls her eyes, then swipes the tears that escape when she does. "I don't know. Yes. I mean, probably. Everything's so overwhelming."

"What can I do to help?"

"Nothing. You're perfect."

My snort makes her smile.

"I always find something to worry about, no matter what."

"That's just who you are. You can't help it."

"Well, it's annoying."

I kiss the tip of her nose. "Minus a couple of memorable meltdowns, you were calm and collected while you were pregnant with George."

She ponders that. "Yeah, well, I had to be, because *you* were a nervous wreck."

"I was waiting for you to come to your senses and change your mind about being with me," I half-joke.

Recognizing the seriousness in my statement, she tilts her head, cradles my cheek in her hand, and clicks her tongue. "Aw, Nathaniel."

"Pathetic, right?"

"Anyway, who says you're in the clear now? Every bite into one of those nasty radish sandwiches brings you one step closer to singledom."

"That's not even a little bit funny."

She shrugs. "It's a bluff. I don't work without you." Before I can react to that declaration, she steps away and turns to address the other person in the room. "Georgia Lou. Let's go. Bath time."

"Noooooooooooooooooooooooo! I no yaunt a bath!"

To head off a major tantrum, I pluck her from the floor, tuck her under my arm, and tote her up the stairs ahead of Betty, jostling her more than necessary until her whines turn to giggles.

No more tears.

21

TINSEL AND TENSION

Nobody told me being a dad means staying up half the night before Christmas Day assembling toys. And I never envisioned the possibility on my own, because this hasn't been part of my experience so far with Georgia, nor did my dad ever do this. But Nick insists it's necessary.

"You're such an amateur, Bro. You put the toys together the night before; otherwise, you'll have the worst Christmas ever, with kids hanging on you and whining about how long it's taking."

"Yeah, but... Tearing off the wrapping paper and seeing the box underneath is most of the fun for kids."

He snorts. "Screw that. You put a red bow on it and call it good. When they run into the room at whatever ungodly hour they get up, they see everything at a glance and are too freakin' excited to care about wrapping paper. Then they go play, and you're left to a peaceful Christmas morning with your coffee and your wife. If you're lucky, you might get something extra in your stocking."

I roll my eyes at his one-track mind.

"I thought you'd be all over this, anyway. Less waste. Saves the planet. Blah, blah, blah."

Unfortunately, I've already wrapped the three boxes containing Georgia's unassembled gifts. But I unwrap them, careful to save the bows, and get to work on the floor in the middle of the living room with Nick, who has about six times the number of toys to put together. Heidi, Betty, Mom, and Dad provide important (ahem) oversight while contributing zero sweat equity, but they tap out around eleven o'clock, leaving Nick and me to labor alone.

Now, approaching one a.m., I'm less sure about this plan. I've been finished with Georgia's toys—a medium-sized plastic doll house, a battery-operated push mower (which I'm sure we'll regret after listening to it for a few hours), and a small picnic basket, complete with fake food—for a while, and the things we got Nick's kids didn't require much more than adding a few decals. But my brother still has a ton to do. Abandoning him and going to bed feels wrong. So I grab the nearest box—a tricycle for his oldest, Massimo—and dive right in. Unfortunately, the instructions keep going blurry. I finally set them aside and pinch my eyes.

"This is stupid," I say.

"Go to bed then, pussy," Nick mutters around the mouthful of screws he's using to put together an all-wood tool bench.

"I don't get why you got them all these big things that required so much assembly, knowing you'd have to transport everything home."

"Why do you think we drove, numb nuts? Because we wanted to see Appalachia from the ground?"

"A more logical approach would have been to buy them plush toys and other small, easy-to-pack things, ship them ahead of time, pre-wrapped, to Betty and me, and bring an additional large suitcase to stuff them in and check for the flight back."

"Three kids, three and under, on a plane? Four planes, total, since there are no direct flights here? You're joking, right?"

"Okay, but still. How are you going to get all this stuff back to Green Bay?"

"It'll fit. I measured the back of the SUV. Don't worry your little head about it. Anyway, the kids didn't ask for plush toys; they asked for these things. Have you ever experienced a Christmas where three kids don't get what they asked for?"

"No."

"Neither have I. And I don't plan to."

"Stop acting like you're so much more seasoned than I am. Massimo's only a few months older than Georgia, so we've been dads for about the same amount of time."

"Yeah, but you've had one, and I've had three."

"It's not a contest!"

"That's not what I'm saying. I've had a trial by fire, Bro. When you have more than one, they'll eat you alive if you don't learn fast."

"Whatever." I pick up the instructions that were definitely not written by someone whose first language is English and continue work on the trike. "Maybe if you'd tell your kids 'no' once in a while, they wouldn't be so difficult."

"And maybe if *you* did more yoga, you'd be flexible enough to go fuck yourself."

Without looking, I toss a piece of foam packaging at him and hit him in the shoulder. It bounces off and skids across the rug.

When we stop laughing, he says, "Anyway, looks like your little princess got everything *she* wanted, even if it meant you had to borrow your neighbor's truck to get it here and back."

"The truck was for the tree and ten tons of decorations we hauled here—which, you're welcome. And Georgia didn't ask for anything specific. So stuff it."

"You think your kid's always going to be perfect, especially once this new one arrives, you have a rude awakening ahead of you."

"Georgia's not perfect."

"Oh? Does she sometimes refuse to eat her vegetables? Gasp."

"Yes, now that you mention it. But she also has a mouth like a sailor right now."

He grimaces as he tightens the screws to hold two wooden panels together. "Yeah, Massi went through that, too. It'll pass. Try not to make a big deal about it."

"And she's so protective and possessive of Betty, it's ridiculous. She attacks anyone who looks sideways at her mother."

"Hm. Wonder where she learned that."

"No idea."

He snorts. "Bro, *you* are so protective of Betty."

"What? No, I'm not. She can take care of herself."

"You wouldn't know it, the way you act. 'Is it too hot in here? Too cold?' 'Do you need more water while I'm up?' 'Need a snack?' 'How are those ankles?' 'Can I follow you to the bathroom and help you wipe, my love?'"

"Shut up! I am not like that."

"Close."

"There's nothing wrong with being thoughtful and attending to someone else's needs once in a while. You should try it."

"You smother."

"I don't!"

"You're probably annoying the crap out of her with your

hovering. Trust me, I've been there. That first pregnancy after a miscarriage is scary but—"

"It's not that, okay? She has a lot on her mind. And if I want to give her a little extra TLC, that's my business."

"I'm just saying, Georgia's taking her cues from you."

"I'm not physically attacking anyone who comes near my wife."

"Yet."

"Why don't you just drop it? You don't know what you're talking about."

"Like you don't have a clue what it's like to live my life, but you have no qualms spewing your holier-than-thou parenting advice."

With extra precision, I set down the instructions and the screwdriver and rise to my feet. "Good luck assembling your spoiled kids' shit," I say on my way up the stairs. "See you in a few hours."

"Merry Christmas, dick."

Man, it's good to be back together.

* * *

THE NEXT DAY begins way too early, as most Christmases that involve children do. I wake up to the unsettling sensation of being watched and find that Georgia has climbed from her portable crib and is standing with her face inches from mine. As soon as my eyes open, she shouts, "Santa Winn comed!"

"What?"

I rub my face, but she grabs my hand and pulls on it. "Hoowy! Santa Winn comed!"

"She thinks Santa is Winn," Betty translates in a raspy voice behind me. "I couldn't convince her otherwise last night, and I was tired, so I finally said, 'Yes, Santa Winn will bring your presents, but you have to sleep first.'"

I groan. "Great. A lie in a lie. Parenting at its finest."

Sitting on the side of the bed, I stretch while Georgia climbs the trailing sheets and plops her full weight into my lap. I subtly shift her to the side, where she straddles my thigh and bounces on it.

"Hoowy!"

"I *am* hurrying," I say, moving her off my lap altogether and onto the mattress beside me.

She pulls on Betty's leg. "Mommy! I sleeped!"

"Yes, you did. Good girl." She sits up. "Give Mommy and Daddy two seconds to wake up like you."

I grab my phone on the bedside table. The device tells me it's not even six o'clock.

"Daddy's hair's siwwy!"

Patting it down, I mutter, "Yeah. *Everything's* sticking up this morning." I stand and bounce on my feet, trying to get the blood flow to redirect to other parts of my body. My brain would be a good start. By the time I put on some flannel pajama pants and brush my teeth and hair, I'm no longer a walking eye-poke hazard, so I open my arms to Georgia, who launches herself at me from the foot of the bed.

She plants a kiss on my minty lips. "Mmm, candy canes! Santa Winn bringed candy canes?"

The answer is, "Hell no," but still I hedge, "Maybe. Let's go down and see."

"Wait for me," Betty says, scooting down and dismounting the mattress, pulling her cami over her peek-a-boo belly button and shrugging into a fluffy robe hanging on the bathroom door. "Okay. Let's do this thing."

"I doubt anyone else is up yet," I say, stepping into the hallway. Finger to my lips, I place the tip of my nose against Georgia's. "Shhh... Let's be quiet, okay, George? Gamma and Pop-Pop and Uncle Nick and Aunt Heidi and all your cousins are still sleeping."

"WAKE UP!!" she bellows over my shoulder, toward the other bedrooms.

Betty covers her own mouth to stifle her laughter, and I drop my chin to my chest.

When her first command doesn't get immediate results, Georgia yells again, this time louder, adding, "IT'S CHWISSMAS!"

That brings them running. Or running as far as they can respectively make it. Banging and excited yelling comes from behind the door to the room shared by Massimo and Cruz. A crying baby is the only sound from Nick and Heidi's room, although I'm sure Nick feels like crying, too. Dad opens his and Mom's door, and I involuntarily flinch and look away—just in case. But they're both decent, obviously, and clearly delighted by their wake-up call.

Mom's eyes sparkle on her way past us, and she pauses long enough to kiss her only granddaughter on the cheek and say, "That's right, sweetie. Assert yourself."

Dad snags Georgia as he passes. "Hey, there. Let's go see what Santa brought you."

Before I turn to follow them down the stairs, Nick's door opens, and he glares down the hall at me.

"*Sorry,*" I mouth.

He rolls his eyes and steps across the way to release his two oldest sons from their room. Massimo and Cruz run full-speed at my knees, but I manage to catch them before they send all of us down the curved staircase. I set Massi on his feet and remind him to go down the steps on his bottom, like he does at home, but I keep a grip on Cruz, figuring it'll be faster and easier to carry him than try to supervise his descent.

"Pwesents!" he squeals next to my ear hole.

Heavy footsteps close on my heels signify my older brother's grumpy presence. I ignore the muttered cursing behind me as his youngest suddenly quiets, most likely sucking hungrily at his mother's breast.

Pretending we didn't go to bed angry and that my daughter didn't wake the entire house before dawn is going to be a tall order today.

I focus my attention on the nephew in my arms. "What did you ask Santa to bring you?"

"Cars!"

Not recalling any cars in the pile of toys last night, I say, "What else?"

"Tools!"

Whew. "Well, let's see what we've got." As soon as I arrive on the first floor, I set him down and let him run in the direction of the formal living room, where the fireplace, tree, and majority of the Christmas decorations are.

Before we turn the corner, Nick snags my elbow.

Anticipating his annoyed rant, I say, "I'm so sorry. I told her to be quiet, but she—"

He waves off my apology. "I'm sure mine would have been up soon anyway."

"Oh. Yeah. Well, thanks for understanding. Do you want to wait for Heidi to finish feeding Blaze?"

"Nah, she'll catch up to us in a few."

When delighted gasps and giggles and claps sound from the living room, I glance anxiously that way, worried we're missing the kids' reactions. The toy lawn mower fires up, and Georgia yells, "Cut gwass!" I hope Betty remembered to grab her phone and is getting good pictures and video.

Nick lets go of my arm. "Go on. I just wanted to say sorry about last night, but it can wait."

"Consider it done," I reply with a pat to his shoulder. "And I'm sorry, too. I love your kids. And... I... I love you, too."

He wraps his arm around my shoulders and traps my neck in the crook of his elbow. "Oh, for crying out loud. Don't be such a puss," he says, dragging me toward the living room.

* * *

IT'S NOT until a couple of hours later, when Nick and I are making three tons of French toast in an efficient assembly line, that we have a chance to catch our breath. It's been chaos in the house as the kids bounce from one toy—and one wall—to another, too excited about the newness of everything to focus on one activity for long.

For all his tough-talking about obnoxious kids and hoping to get "an extra something" in his stocking, my brother was one of the most engaged adults in the room as his two oldest boys explored their gifts from Santa. He crawled around on the floor, showing each of them how everything worked and demonstrating some of the more complicated features. He laughed when Massi's first attempt at pedaling the trike nearly took out the tool bench it had taken him forever to assemble. His coffee went cold as he lay on his side on the floor next to Blaze, setting off the lights and sounds as he showed the nine-month-old how to play his new piano. And he couldn't be bothered to look at his stocking or open the gifts under the tree for himself until Betty and Heidi took the children upstairs to get them dressed.

Now, everyone else is walking on the chilly beach while he and I figure out how to feed everyone. He dunks triangles of bread into an egg-and-milk mixture while I supervise two electric skillets—one holding the toasting bread, the other frying the first of what seems like five pounds of bacon.

I remove the finished meat slices and place them on a paper-towel-covered stretch of counter, then pat the grease from them with another paper towel. As I'm adding the next round of meat to the skillet, Nick says, concentrating on sprinkling cinnamon on the toast wedges, "I felt horrible last night after you left, and I thought more about what you said."

"C'mon. Don't dwell on it. I was a jerk, too."

"No, I... I totally forgot about this whole adopted kid thing you and Betty are dealing with."

"Oh. That. Yeah. She's... This is difficult for her."

"You never talk to me about it."

"What's there to talk about?"

He snorts and waits for me to move some fully cooked toast to a plate so he can place the soaked pieces he's prepared. "Uh, bro... Have you ever uttered that question in your life?"

"I guess I just did." After tending to the toast, I poke at the bacon and step back when it sputters indignantly at my interference.

"Mom told me the kid's dad is a pain in the ass. Except, she used the term 'inappropriately involved.'"

"Sounds like Mom."

"So, is he? What's going on with that?"

I shrug. "Chris? He's gotten close to Trevor and his parents. They trust him. So he's kind of the go-between."

"Isn't that awkward for Betty? And you?"

"She wants to cooperate and make this as easy as possible for everyone."

"What about you?"

I turn down the heat on the bacon, then meet his eyes. "I want to rip the guy's throat out."

"I bet."

"But it's not my place. I've already overstepped a couple of times."

"Like how?"

"I was a jerk when we were trying to figure out a good weekend for everyone to meet up. I went all über-nurse on everyone, saying Betty couldn't fly after a certain date, and the venue would have to be close to a hospital with a state-of-the-art maternity ward, in case she does go into labor."

He laughs.

"It's the only part about this I feel I have a say in."

"I can't imagine Betty's been sitting back letting a couple of dudes argue back and forth over her. That doesn't sound like her at all. Doesn't she have her own list of demands?"

"No." I wipe my hands on a towel. "It's kind of scary how passive she's been. I keep waiting for her to tell me to shut up, but she doesn't. Sometimes she stares into space, like what we're talking about doesn't involve her."

He winces. "That's weird. Bro, your bacon's burning."

"Huh?" I look down and flinch when I see he's right. "Shoot." Removing it from the skillet as fast as I can, I inspect the ten or so pieces against the paper towel. "They're not that bad. I'll eat this stuff."

"Me, too. I like it crispy."

More raw food goes onto the hot surfaces.

I sigh. "The thing is, I'm in a horrible position. I just want this whole thing to be over. But if I make it too obvious how I feel, I look like a heartless jerk, like anything and anyone who came before my life with her is insignificant and should be forgotten. And that's not my stance at all. But damn if I can verbalize my feelings."

"You're scared."

"No, that's not it."

"Not as in, 'frightened'; you're worried she's going to get hurt."

I stare at him for a while, then bite the inside of my cheek, look down at the bacon, and nod. "Hell, yes."

He claps a hand on my shoulder. "Listen, bro. When it comes to protecting the ones we love, we're all just a fart away from crapping our pants."

I snort at his disgustingly colorful point, then take a deep breath as he pats me on the back with the handle of the spatula.

"I mean, what do you really know about this Chris dude, anyway? It's totally natural for you to feel protective. He could be a druggie—or worse, a science denier. You don't want to expose your family to that, Bro!"

"So true, man."

"Well, whatever you do, don't give into the urge to get physical with the guy. Sounds like you can leave that up to Georgia, anyway. And it's more socially acceptable for a two-year-old to punch a dude in the balls. Stand back and let it happen."

That may be the best advice my brother's ever given me.

22

GUARDIAN ANGEL

THAT NIGHT, AFTER THE KIDS HAVE BEEN TUCKED INTO BED, after the adults have exhausted themselves talking and laughing at memories from Christmases past, after much alcohol has been imbibed by five-sixths of our drinking-age party, and after the clock has struck midnight, drawing to an official close an incredibly long, loud, but fun day, Betty and I slide between the cool sheets in the still-unfamiliar room and settle down for the night.

Without preamble, I whisper so as not to wake Georgia in her portable crib next to our bed, "I'm horny as hell."

"You really know how to woo a girl, Nathaniel."

I laugh at myself. "You know me—the King of Romance."

"Almost as romantic as when you offered to give me an enema last week."

"Hey, that offer still stands, if you need it."

"Gross."

"Anything to help the cause."

"I'm not constipated, but I also don't want to have sex with our daughter mere feet away from us. I can't believe you do."

"Normally, it would be an absolute deal-breaker for me, but

tonight... C'mon, Betts. It's Christmas."

"You're drunk."

"No, I'm not. I'm just a little loose."

"Uh-huh."

"If I were drunk, would I be able to do this?" I press her hand between my legs.

"Oh, dear. You *are* in a bad way."

"You can fix it."

"We'll wake her up."

I crane my neck and look into the portable crib. "Psst. George."

The toddler doesn't so much as twitch an eyelash.

I turn toward Betty and pull her against me. "She's out of it. We'll just have to be super-silent. I can do it; can you?"

"No sex worth having is *that* silent. And it would be humiliating if *anyone* heard us."

"They won't. Don't worry."

She pulls her hand from my crotch and scoots away from me. "That's rich, coming from the King of Worry."

"It's the King of Romance." I pursue her across the mattress and whisper near her ear, "And right now, I'm the King of Horny."

She adjusts her head on her pillow. "Well, I'm the Queen of Tired."

With a kiss to her neck, then her shoulder, I laugh, then say with my lips pressed on her, "Fine. Cuddling, it is."

The smile is strong in her voice when she relaxes her back more fully against my front and laces her fingers through mine. "Thank you. That would be nice."

"That's because I'm also the King of Nice."

"Ruling all those kingdoms must be exhausting. Good night."

I assume that's the end of it, and I'm dozing with my forehead pressed at the base of her neck when she suddenly—well, as "suddenly" as she's physically able, which isn't very—flips to face me.

"Huh? What's the matter? You want to sleep on your left side? Wait. That *was* your left side," I say, my rambling words slurring from both near-sleep and those last two hot toddies that were probably a mistake.

"You got me all worked up, Your Majesty."

My smugness returns, like I knew all along she'd come around before I passed out. "I see."

"Go turn up the volume on the noise thingy."

I gladly comply, cranking up the "ocean" sounds on the white noise machine to its highest level. As I creep back to bed, I keep an eye on Georgia, whose only response to the added ambiance is to put her thumb in her mouth and suck loudly. Normally, I'd remove it, but sacrifices to orthodontia must be made so I can get laid.

Under the sheets once more, I quickly dispense with Betty's nightgown, despite her objections that we should keep as much of our clothing on as possible, just in case.

"In case what?"

"I don't know. One of the kids comes down the hall looking for the bathroom and stumbles in here?"

"That's not going to happen."

"Lock the door."

Sighing, I get up once more. On my way back to bed, I strip off my own clothes, placing them in a pile on the floor between my side of the bed and Georgia's crib, so I can quickly dress again afterward.

Skin to skin with Betty, I kiss her neck, then her chest, then her breasts.

She moans, so I press my lips to hers and, smiling, say, "Shhh... No noise, remember?"

Several minutes later, I'm afraid neither of us is being as quiet as we swore we would be, but there's still no stirring in the crib next to us, so I stop worrying about it. Afterward, I move my mouth from her lips to her breasts and torso, stopping with a firm, lengthy kiss right next to her navel. I turn my head and rest my ear against the spot I've kissed and plan to lie like this for several minutes, until I get my breath back.

That's when something sharp and heavy crashes into my skull. At the same time, Georgia yells, "My mommy!" and Betty gasps in a way that has nothing to do with sexual satisfaction.

The assaulted spot on my head burns, then immediately feels both hot and wet. I scramble to my knees and clamp my hand to the injury. Blood dampens my palm.

"Fuuuuuudge, I'm bleeding!" I hiss.

Betty quickly yanks her nightgown on and flicks the lamp switch on the bedside table, which does a nice job of spotlighting my full frontal nudity. She's too busy admonishing Georgia for her latest violent attack to notice or care. "You hurt your daddy! We don't hit. How many times have we said it?"

Georgia takes one look at me and screams, "Hairy monstuh!" and frantically tries to climb from the farthest side of her crib.

"What the heck did she hit me *with*?" I ask, pulling the bloodied comforter around me as best I can with one hand while trying to keep pressure on what feels like a massive head wound.

As the covers shift, something falls to the floor with a thunk. It's the heavy, ceramic angel figurine Mom and Dad gave her. (Thanks, Mom and Dad!) "Oh, my gosh! She could have brained me with that! I thought you took it out of her crib before we came to bed."

Betty lifts our hysterical child from the crib before she hurts herself. "I thought *you* did."

"Never mind. Can you grab some towels from the bathroom? I'm bleeding all over the damn place."

"There's no need to curse," she scolds on her way past me with Georgia. "I'm sorry I lost my temper with you, sweetie, but you scared Mommy and hurt Daddy, and that's not okay."

"He hut you! You cwied."

"What? No! Daddy wasn't hurting me." She tosses a hand towel into my lap. "Daddy was... loving Mommy."

Pressing the towel to the crown of my head while simultaneously trying to wipe the blood from my fingers, I groan. "Oh, please. Can we *not* try to explain to her what was going on?"

A knock sounds at the door. "Is everything okay in there?"

Before I can object, Betty rushes to the door, unlocks it, and swings it open to reveal Mom and Dad, who are standing in the hallway, blinking sleepily through the overhead light. "Georgia hit Nate over the head, and he's bleeding... a lot. He might need stitches."

Dad looks past both women, takes in my naked shoulders and comforter-wrapped body, and says, "I see... Uh, is that the ocean? It's not that loud in our room."

Betty thrusts Georgia at my mom and turns off the white noise machine.

"Goodness," Mom says. "Do you always have that thing on so loud?"

I try to cover more of myself while not dripping various bodily fluids. "Mom, Dad, thanks for your help. If you'll, uh, take Georgia to your room now, that would be great."

As they reverse into the hallway, Georgia howls, "Nooooooo! I yaunt Mommy! Daddy hut Mommy! Mommy cwied!"

"I wasn't crying," Betty mutters to the floor, her cheeks blazing.

Nick's face appears behind Mom and Dad. "What the? Holy crap." He pushes past our parents, and Betty steps aside to let him into the room.

"I'm fine," I say, rolling my eyes at his *"I'm not a gynecologist, but I'd be happy to take a look"* t-shirt. "Just a nick."

My brother ignores my claims and pulls my head into the light where he can see it better. "What happened? Dang. Head wounds bleed so much." After a few extremely painful, not-at-all gentle dabs at my scalp, he says, "Bro, you have a major gash there."

"Ya think? Someone lobbed a three-pound ceramic angel figurine at my melon."

Nick gives me control of the towel once more and bends over to pick up the assault weapon. "Yep. Looks like the tip of this wing is what got you."

"Is it broken?" Mom wonders, bouncing Georgia in an attempt to soothe her.

"My head or the angel?"

"The angel's fine. That blood will come right off, I'm sure," Nick says, winding it up and handing it to Dad as it starts to play the opening chords to "You Are My Sunshine."

Betty thrusts my clothes at me. "Come on. Get dressed."

"I'd love to, but it's kinda busy in here right now."

Finally, Mom and Dad take a more permanent leave, with Georgia protesting her exile all the way down the hall.

Nick stays in the room with us, holding a clean towel to my head while I dress in the clothes discarded next to the bed only a few blissful minutes ago.

"I hope it was worth it, you two," he says with a smirk, his chest puffed out.

"You're hilarious," I reply, pulling up my underwear and pajama pants.

"What were you thinking?"

I set my jaw and bite back a number of retorts. "Betty and I can take it from here."

"You're not going to the hospital for this. I'll sew you up."

"Thanks for the offer, but..."

"C'mon! My doctor's bag's out in the car. I always keep one in there, in case I come up on an emergency."

"Aren't you the Boy Scout?"

"Do you want my help, or do you want to be one of *those* people, the ones we all laugh at, who show up in the ER in the middle of the night with crazy sex injuries?"

"This isn't a sex injury."

"Guys!" Betty says. "Please. Can you stop bickering for one second?" She lowers herself to the side of the bed then flinches when her palm lands on a tiny red puddle on the sheet.

"Watch the wet spot," Nick says with a snort.

"Oh, gosh. So much blood." With that, all the color drains from her face as she slumps to her side on the mattress.

"Geez," I grumble, still holding the towel to my head with one hand and in no condition to do much more than keep her in position with my other hand so she doesn't slide to the floor.

Nick pushes the comforter completely off the bed and settles her on her left side in the middle of the mattress. "Hang on." Less than a minute later, he returns with Heidi, who pulls out a pair of foam earplugs while taking in what looks like a murder scene and an unconscious Betty.

"Oh, my gosh. What's happened?"

"She passed out." I fan my wife's face with my free hand but don't achieve much air movement.

Nick rolls his eyes at my inadequate explanation. "From

what I've gathered thus far, Nate and Betty were gettin' it on, and they woke up Georgia, who then brained Nate with an angel figurine when she thought he was hurting Betty."

Heidi pushes her fist against her lips and giggles. "For real?"

I glare at both of them. "You forgot the part where I flashed my daughter and scarred her for life."

"Bah! She's too young to remember the 'hairy monster,'" Nick says. "Or so you hope."

Heidi stares at my head. "Gosh, that towel's really bloody. You probably need stitches."

Nick springs into action. "Oh, yeah. That's right. I was about to go get my bag so I could sew him up. You have an extra disposable razor in your suitcase, babe? I'm gonna need to shave around the wound."

"Yeah. Front zipper compartment of the large roller." When he leaves, she nudges me aside and sits on the bed next to Betty. She taps her sister-in-law's cheek. "Hon?" Betty's eyelids flutter open. "You all right, sweetie?"

Betty tries to sit up, but Heidi places a firm hand on her shoulder. Cupping her hand to her forehead, Betty remains lying on her side. "Oh, no. Did I pass out? How embarrassing."

"It's not a big deal. You got a little woozy from all this blood. Not that I blame you. Yikes." She turns to look at me. "Nate, you okay? You look pale, too."

"I've had better nights." I plop down next to her. "I've had worse ones, too."

She smiles indulgently at my lame attempts at both humor and optimism. "Sit tight, now. I'm sure Nick will want to do your little surgery in the bathroom, but it may be a while until he gets back with all his stuff." She grasps one of Betty's hands and one of mine in each of hers, then surveys the room one more time and shakes her head. "Something tells me we're not getting back our security deposit."

DATE IN THE DUNES

OUR LAST NIGHT IN MYRTLE BEACH IS SUPPOSED TO BE OUR date night, but going somewhere nice with a patch of hair missing is out of the question, so Betty and I plan to stick close to the house, taking a picnic down past the dunes. She stuffs the quilt and other blankets in an open-topped canvas tote; I lug the tapas, sparkling grape juice, and reusable plastic place settings and cutlery in the insulated picnic basket we received as part of our gift from Nick and Heidi for Christmas.

"Now remember, kids," Nick says, blocking our exit. "Public indecency will land you in jail. You can't expose yourself to *other* people's children. So control yourselves on the beach and try to keep your pants on."

Betty blushes and laughs. I push past him with a glare, understanding this is only the beginning of a lifetime of harassment from him on this topic.

"Hey, is that any way to treat the person who saved your life?" he calls after us.

I knit my fingers through Betty's as we set off down the long boardwalk that leads to the sand.

"You have to learn to laugh at it," she says. "Otherwise, he'll keep teasing you."

"Maybe by the time my hair regrows, I'll think it's funny."

She leans back and cranes her neck to try to see it. "It's not that bad. He did a good job. Very precise."

"I don't care about my hair."

"Liar."

"Okay. I care a little. It looks dumb. But it'll grow back. What sucks the most is, well, everything else. We woke up the whole house! And I could handle the shame, but—"

"There's no shame. We were doing what people who love each other do."

"Yeah. Privately. What kind of degenerate sicko can't control himself when his daughter's in the same room?"

"She's a baby."

"Well, she got an early lesson in adult male anatomy... from me. Which is so wrong. I did to her what my parents did to me—"

"Your parents didn't *do* anything to you. You happened upon them in a private moment. So did Georgia. And she's already over it."

"Is she? I overheard her say to Massi earlier today, 'Daddy tickuhs Mommy wiff his mouf.'"

Betty laughs so hard she stumbles. I steady her elbow and can't help chuckling, myself, at her response.

"What did you say?" she asks.

"I stayed out of it, hoping Massi would have a similar story about Nick and Heidi, but he just said, 'Awkward!'"

Betty snorts. "That's his new favorite word. He doesn't even know what it means. And Georgia won't remember what happened. Especially if we all pretend it didn't happen. If you keep going on and on about it and acting all shy around her or insist she talk to a counselor, the memory will take hold."

"You've been talking to my parents."

"Your mom."

"Her advice was to drop it?"

"Yes."

"I wish that had been her strategy when *I* saw *them*."

Having arrived at the beach, I descend the steps one ahead of Betty and offer her more firm support as she navigates the slippery sand-covered wood in her flip-flops. "It's different when you're an adult and understand what you're seeing and have the capacity to make long-term memories."

Once on the ground, she threads her arm through mine, and we survey the area for a good landing spot.

"You want to walk for a while first? Get farther from the house?" she asks.

I glance at the looming structure in the distance behind us. "Nah. This is good. Unless you want to walk."

"Maybe after we eat. I'm starving." She points to a semi-shady spot close to us but far enough from the boardwalk, which is shared by several other houses along this stretch, to separate us from people entering and exiting the beach. "That looks good."

We spread out the quilt and unpack the food. Wrapped in a blanket, Betty leans back on her elbow, her feet crossed at her ankles, and raises her plastic wineglass. "To still being enough in lust that we can do stupid things to embarrass ourselves."

I roll my eyes at her toast but smile and drink to it, anyway. Then, after contemplating the bubbles in my chalice between sips, I say, "To all love. Romantic, platonic, parental, brotherly... unconditional."

"Hear, hear." Betty gulps the rest of her juice and secures her now-empty cup by burying its stem a few inches into the sand. Then she sits up and leans toward me. I try to kiss her, but she looks down at the last second, so my lips hit her forehead.

"Hey!" I protest.

She laughs. "Sorry. I was going in for some food." She gestures to the small containers between us.

"Yeah, I get that now. I should have known you'd only go to the trouble of moving to eat."

My passive-aggressive challenge works as planned and results in a long, lazy kiss that makes me wish I could snap my fingers and transport us somewhere more private. After several seconds, Betty pulls just enough away to whisper against my mouth, "I'm really, really horngry."

I open my eyes and laugh. "Then you should take care of half that problem and eat." I hand a plate to her and gesture to the olives, hummus, cheese, bread, and fruit around us.

As soon as her plate is full, I drape her blanket around her back and shoulders, and she pulls the front closed around her plate to protect it from the blowing sand. I take up a position with my right knee touching her left and arrange my own blanket, then stare out at the rough, churning water. The wind buffets, kicking sand onto the quilt and occasionally into our eyes. Still, it's one of the best dates I can remember.

After several minutes of companionable and silent chewing, she says, "This is lovely, but I miss home."

I pause to evaluate my own feelings. "I don't. Snow and ice and—"

"Not *that* home. *Home*. In Jasper."

My shoulders relax. I grin over at her. "Me too."

She sets our empty plates in the hamper, refills our cups, and settles herself between my legs with her back against my chest. I wrap my blanket more securely around both of us, then rest my chin on her shoulder and both hands flat on either side of her tummy.

"Couple more weeks and we find out what this little thing is," I say, tapping my fingers.

"Yep. A boy sish or a girl sish?"

"Do you think Georgia's going to try to kill him or her?"

"Yes."

I laugh at her immediate, too-honest answer, then turn my head slightly and kiss her cheek. "Nah. It'll be okay."

"You're sporting a sizable injury that suggests otherwise."

"The baby's not a big, hairy monster that will tickle you with its mouth."

She tilts her head back and cackles. "Not big, no. But it's your kid, so it'll be hairy. And wait until Georgia sees me breastfeeding."

"If we keep her informed every step of the way, it'll be okay. I have some ideas. I'll work with her."

"Can I be in on the plan, too, since I'll be the one holding the baby to my breast?"

"Of course."

"Thank you."

"Betts?"

"Hmm?"

"It's going to be great."

"I can't wait."

RISING WATERS

Hoping I don't sound too rushed or impatient, I say goodbye to yet another new patient and duck back into the room as quickly as possible to disinfect it and prepare it for the next child-parent pair, who have been waiting out front for at least fifteen minutes past their appointment time. They'll sit in this room for a while, too, while I attend to another patient, already in Exam Room #3.

After wiping down the table, I take a peek at the schedule on my phone and curse when I realize the patient in that room has another unfamiliar name but is only down for a half-hour time slot. That means, starting now, I supposedly have fifteen minutes with her if I'm going to be on time for the following appointment. Not only is that impossible, it would be rude to attempt. It's equally rude to keep people waiting, though, especially if they're here with a sick, miserable child.

I toss the spray bottle of antibacterial soap and vinegar under the sink, scrub my hands, and rush to the room next door, grabbing the chart from the plastic pocket on the wall and giving it a cursory glance before performing my courtesy knock-and-enter.

"Hey, there! Verity? I'm Nate. I'll be taking care of you today. What's up?"

Repeat six more times, and by the end of the day, collapsing on the waiting room floor is a real possibility. After locking the front door behind the last patient, I sag against the wood and glass and roll slowly across it to face Betty.

She laughs at me as she slides her arms into her jacket. "You gonna be okay?"

"No. I mean, yes. I mean, wow. When is Dr. Reitman back from vacation, again?"

Betty smirks. "Next week. Looks like the open house worked. The rest of the week is jam-packed, too."

That news should delight me, but it only exhausts me. And introduces the topic I've been dreading all afternoon. I pause for a second and watch Betty shut down her computer, leaning over from a standing position, her tongue poking from the corner of her mouth.

"Hey, Betts?"

"Yeah?" She straightens, then grabs her purse from the coat tree behind her.

I fight through my fatigue to strike the right tone: *laissez faire*. Avoiding eye contact is good, too. Despite an aching back and building headache, I push away from the door and straighten the already-tidy waiting area, rearranging magazines on the tables and tossing a couple of rogue die-cast cars at the toy chest.

"Uh, remember how we agreed that new patients should get longer appointment times, because we have to give parents time to fill out forms, then we have to ask them all those questions to get patient and family history, blah, blah, blah?"

"Yep," she answers distractedly, then gasps. "Oh, no! Did I forget? I did, didn't I? How many times?"

I wince and pinch one eye closed. "Every time?"

"No!"

Collapsing into the closest chair, I nod as I deliver the unfortunate diagnosis. "Yeah."

"Dang it! I'm sorry!" She glances helplessly at her dark computer, then bends over and turns it on again. "I've gotten so used to there being enough time between appointments that it doesn't matter, and we only decided on Monday to start using the longer slots..."

"It's not a big deal. Well, it sort of is."

"No wonder you were so behind all day!"

The machine whirs and beeps to life. She drums her fingers on her desk while she waits. Her purse drops to the floor at her feet. As soon as she pulls up the scheduling software, and I see the multicolored grids reflected in her eyes, I can tell all my days for the foreseeable future are going to be like today was. My only consolation will be that Dr. Reitman will be back, so I'll have someone to share the load with. I might even get a lunch break at some point.

Betty groans. "Oh, man! I spaced out hardcore. I'm so sorry." She looks up at me and laughs, I'm assuming at the way I've slid so far down the chair that my butt hangs in midair. My back rests on the seat, and I'm only supported by my legs, bent at ninety-degree angles.

I'm sure I do look ridiculous, but her amusement pushes my dangling temper over the edge. "Easy for you to laugh; you're not the one running your ass off all day."

"I'm not laughing at my mistake. Well, yeah I am. Stupid pregnancy brain! I almost forgot to turn off the coffeemaker this morning before I left the house."

"Don't tell me stuff like that."

"You want me to lie about it?"

"No, but I'd rather not be told at all. You need to pay more attention to what you're doing."

"I *am* paying attention to what I'm doing."

"Apparently not. You're on the verge of burning down our house, and you can't remember something as simple as giving new patients longer appointments."

"The house wouldn't have burned down. The coffeemaker shuts off automatically after a couple of hours. We would have had a burnt-up pot, that's all. Big whoop. And I said I was sorry about the scheduling snafus. It's an adjustment. The other appointments are still categorized correctly, so it's not like I've been giving you fifteen minutes with each kid, regardless of the reason for their visit."

"In effect you have, though, because I'm falling so far behind."

"Go faster, then."

"I'm going as fast as I can without being perfunctory."

"Pshh. You don't have to tell every patient a story about when you were a kid. Or show them your head stitches, which considering how you got that injury, is a little creepy to be showing off to juveniles."

"I don't give them the background info! But it's a fairly obvious wound that lends itself to questions from curious kids. It's easier for me to address it on *my* terms. Anyway, why don't you spend less time eavesdropping and more time making sure you're doing *your* job correctly?"

She pushes back from her computer and glares across the desk at me. I straighten in my chair, partly because this posture is killing my back, partly because the set of her jaw tells me I should arrange myself in a less vulnerable position. Her hard blinks soften, then quicken. She bites her lower lip, possibly to keep it from trembling. Her chin puckers.

Oh, no. Nonononono. Mad is okay. Scary, but okay. But this…?

I jump to my feet and round the end of the counter.

"Betts, I'm sorry. Don't cry."

Of course, that only hastens the arrival of the tears. She covers her face. "I don't understand why you're yelling at me about this."

"Was I yelling? I didn't mean to yell."

"Well, you were. And I said I was sorry. What more can I say? What do you want me to do? I can't go back in time and be less stupid."

"For crying out. You're not stupid."

"Apparently, I am! I can't do something as simple as schedule appointments on a calendar."

I try to pull her hands away from her face, but my fingers slide off her jacket sleeves, so I swivel her chair and crouch in front of her, cupping her knees in my palms. "Come on. It was an honest mistake. Any time you alter the way you do things out of habit, there are bound to be hiccups."

"But now you're tired and crabby and yelling at me about it."

"You've got to be kidding me," I accidentally mutter out loud.

She drops her hands and looks down at me. "You are!"

"Okay, okay! I'm not denying that I was a jerk!"

"You're yelling at me again!"

"Because this is ridiculous, and I don't know how to fix it!"

Extending her leg, she pushes her foot against my shoulder and rolls away from me, knocking me to my butt. Resigned, I wrap my arms around my knees and lock hands, watching helplessly as she rushes from the reception area, down the hall. The bathroom door slams.

I sit motionless for several minutes, staring at my office door while I listen to her sob. "Damn hormones," I grumble, hoping if I say it, it will be the whole truth, and I won't have to take responsibility for my part in this mess.

She makes it sound like I'm sitting there, shootin' the shit with patients, reminiscing about the good old days. In fact, I'm talking to them while I look in their ears and mouths and throats. I'm distracting them while I stick them with needles, injecting them with vaccines or extracting blood for evaluation. I'm getting to know them so that next time they come to see me, they're not petrified to the point of puking. I'm multitasking!

I close my eyes and rest my forehead against my knees, because what just happened has little to do with how I interact with patients. Unless she's standing right outside the door, she can't hear what we're saying, anyway. She's inferring (correctly). And she doesn't want me to change the way I do what I do, even if I could. All she wanted was to feel less foolish, to have me share some of the blame. Instead of giving that to her, I got needlessly defensive. In hindsight, all I needed to do was say, "It's okay," and work with her to troubleshoot a fail-safe.

We have the technology, Bingham.

Rising to my knees, I walk on them to her desk and kneel in front of her computer. With a few clicks, I set up a pop-up reminder that triggers every time someone ticks the "new patient" box and defaults to a one-hour appointment. It should have been set up like that all along, but like Betty said, it's been so slow around here since we started that it seemed unnecessary—and counterproductive—to limit the number of people we could see each day.

I'm looking at tomorrow's schedule, trying to predict where the biggest trouble spots will be, when I hear the toilet flush, the water run in the bathroom sink, and the flip-top metal trash can lid bang against the wall, followed by the squeaky door hinge. Betty re-enters her desk area and drapes her jacket over the back of her chair, then pushes the chair closer to me, nudging my foot with one of its casters. "Move over," she says.

I stand and step aside.

She bellies up to the computer. Hand on her desk phone, she averts her red, puffy face. "Can you get Georgia from Laurel's?"

"Uh, yes. But what are you doing?"

"I'm going to stay here and call to reschedule some of these appointments."

I sigh. "You don't have to do that."

"Yes, I do. I messed up; I'm going to make it right."

"Betts—"

"That's what professionals do. I'm sorry I got upset. You were only pointing out an error in my work, and—as a co-worker and supervisor—you were right to do that." She clicks open one of the new patients' appointments, which immediately flashes an error message to inform her its duration is too short. After a couple of blinks, she dismisses the dialogue box with a precise mouse click. "Oh, good. You idiot-proofed it for me."

"That's not—"

"No. That's good. I was wondering if there was a setting. You beat me to it, that's all."

I squeeze her shoulders. "Come on. Let's go home. I'm more than capable of handling tomorrow's patient load, and we can get the rest of the week straightened out after we've both had some rest. There's no need for you to work overtime on this tonight."

"I won't ask to be paid for it."

I laugh. "That's the least of my worries."

She shrugs me off. "Please. I want to fix this. And I want to be alone. We're already late getting Georgia. Go."

Dropping my hands to my sides with a soft slap against my thighs, I sigh. "Fine. There's no convincing you..."

"Nope."

"...so I'll leave you alone. Call me as you're about to head out."

"I'll try to remember, but no promises. I won't stay late, though." Picking up her phone and dialing the first number serves as my dismissal. I edge behind her and drop a kiss on top of her head on my way out.

In the parking lot, I squint up at the ominous sky. I slow on my way past Betty's car when I notice her open sunroof. It only takes a second to close it for her before hopping into my own car for the quick trip home. It's the least I can do.

* * *

AT THE BAKERS', Winn greets me at the door with Georgia in his arms. She hides her face in his neck and mutters something about Santa.

"Welcome back, neighbor!" Winn says, holding the door open with his back and standing aside to let me in. "I was about to call you to make sure you weren't hoofin' it from work in the dark. People drive crazy around the curves. Plus, it's about to storm somethin' fierce."

One look at my serious face stops his public service announcement/weather report. "Whoa. Everything okay there, Yank? You look about as cloudy as the sky."

I attempt a weak smile that gains power when Georgia finally decides to acknowledge my arrival and reaches for me. I gather her to me and kiss her forehead. "I'm fine. Just tired. It was a long day. Sorry I'm so late."

"Are you?" He winks. "Where's the old— I mean, better half?"

"Still at work, finishing up some stuff. Where's yours?"

"Took the boys to basketball practice. It's just me and the little ladies."

For the first time since walking through the door, I notice Rumer on the floor in front of the TV.

"Oh, hey, Rumer. Whatcha watchin'?"

Without turning to look at me, she replies, "Teen Titans."

"What was that, Miss Thing?" Winn says, tossing a throw pillow at her back. "Stop mumblin' and look at people when you're spoken to."

She does as she's told and smiles sweetly at me. "Teen Titans, sir."

For about the thousandth time, I resist the urge to contradict Winn and tell her she doesn't have to be so formal with me. His kids, his rules. But I'm much more comfortable as a buddy, not an authority figure. I grin back at her. "Awesome." We discuss favorite characters for about thirty seconds, then I let her get back to her show.

Georgia pats my chest and rests her head on my shoulder. "My daddy."

"Boy howdy. You gotta get outta here with her. She does stuff like that, and both Laurel and I start talkin' crazy, like how much we miss that age and 'Aren't babies the best?' and... and..." He reaches for the door and holds it open.

I laugh. "I'll bring her over here next time she throws a tantrum, and you'll be magically cured."

"She doesn't throw tantrums here. Must be somethin' you're doin' wrong." Again, he winks, then something behind me grabs his attention. "Say, what the heck happened to your head, Yank? That's the weirdest hair loss pattern I've ever seen."

I clap a hand over the spot, immediately regretting it when my fingers nudge my stitches. "Oh. That. Well..." I debate telling him the whole story—it would be great for a laugh—but decide I'm too tired. "Family vacations get wild sometimes."

"Aw, c'mon. You gotta give me more than that."

Pushing the storm door open, I step onto his porch and inhale the rain-scented air. "Some other time. I better get movin' before the storm hits."

"Hungwy!" Georgia says.

"That, too. Thanks, again, for keeping her later than usual."

"Hey, it gives us our baby fix, so you work late whenever you want."

"I not da baby! I da big girl!"

Winn and I laugh at that as I jog across both of our front yards to dodge the first drops that have started to fall from the sky. From the safety of our own porch, Georgia and I watch the clouds let loose what looks like solid sheets of water.

"Wain!"

"You can say that again."

"Wain!"

I set her down on the porch, and she runs to the rail, hanging onto the spindles and sticking her face through the gaps. We stare, transfixed, for a few minutes, then I say, "Let's go, George. Time to eat."

She follows me into the house, calling, "Mommy? Mommy! It's wain!"

Reba's the only one to greet us, stretching and yawning.

Georgia hugs the dog around her neck. "Weba, it's wain!"

Reba shoots me a long-suffering look while she submits to the handling.

"Sorry, Rebes. I tried to get home faster. I hope you can hold it."

As soon as Georgia lets her go, the dog waddles to the back door and whines.

"Or not. Hang on." I catch up to her and let her out, observing as she trots to the edge of the patio, does her business while blinking through the downpour, and returns to the door.

While I'm scrubbing the dog dry in the laundry room, Georgia appears in the doorway.

"Where da mommy?"

"The mommy is at work."

"I yaunt him."

"Her. You want *her*."

"Huhr."

"That's nice, but you're stuck with me tonight."

She stomps her foot. "Nooooo. I yaunt my mommy!"

It's going to be a long night.

* * *

PART of the long night includes a thunderstorm that knocks out the power during Georgia's bath. Both child and dog fuh-reak out, of course, so I spend the next half-hour trying to convince the two trembling beings in my lap how much fun it is to live without lights. Or TV. Or the noise machine.

Georgia's finally warming up to the adventure of illumination by candlelight and flashlight when the electricity comes back on, almost scaring Reba as much as the outage originally had. The dog scampers from room to room, cowering in doorways, sniffing the air, as if she can smell the danger left behind by the darkness.

I reset the clocks on the appliances, then carry Georgia to bed. As I tuck her in, she pushes the covers away, saying, "Da dark. Da dark."

"The dark went away."

"Where da mommy?"

"She'll be home soon," I blindly promise.

"Da dark got Mommy?"

"The dark didn't get anyone. See? We're still here."

She glances nervously at the window but finally lets me cover her for good. "I no yaunt da dark."

"We'll note that in your chart. Now, go to sleep, George."

Reba appears in the doorway, sniffing and whining.

"Weba no yaunt da dark."

"Reba's a scaredy-dog. You're a brave, big girl." I lean down for one more kiss. "Good night."

"Da door!" she yells when I try to close it.

Sighing, I say, "Fine. I'll leave the door open and the hall light on. Good. Night."

Back downstairs, I put away the snuffed-out candles and superfluous flashlight, then tidy the few toys Georgia pulled out while I made dinner. After that, I'm not sure what to do with myself that doesn't involve self-destructive fretting. I try watching TV, but I lose track of plot lines during my frequent phone checks. Eventually, physical exhaustion takes over, and an extended contemplation of the ceiling beams segues into a deep, dreamless, coma-like sleep while sitting up on the couch.

My ringing cell phone wakes me.

Trying to sound as alert as possible, I answer, wishing I'd thought to look at the time before bringing the phone to the side of my head. "Hey-lo."

"Hi," Betty says. "Don't be mad that I haven't called before now."

Since I don't want to admit I have no idea when "now" is, I simply reply while trying to blink moisture into my eyes, "I'm not mad. What's up?"

"I tried to leave here, but every route I took, including some convoluted ones, courtesy of the GPS, was flooded."

I sit up straighter on the couch. "What? You're kidding." Listening more closely to the still-pouring rain hitting the roof, though, I'm not surprised. "Did you lose power there, too?"

"No! Did you guys?"

"Yep. Only for the longest half hour of my life."

She laughs. "Who was worse, Georgia or Reba?"

"Considering I could somewhat reason with Georgia, and she wasn't panting in my face, I'd have to give that award to Reba. By the way, we need to get her teeth cleaned. Her breath is unbelievable."

"Write it down, so we don't forget."

"What are you telling me, then? You're stuck there? And where's 'there'? Are you back at the clinic?"

"Yeah. I called Pat, and she told me where I could find the spare key to her apartment, so that's where I am now. I'm going to sleep in the guest room."

"Or Winn and I can come rescue you in his boat."

"The guest room is fine. Sorry to leave you alone with Georgia... and Reba... in the storms."

"I've got this. I'm just glad you're okay, and you're not going to try to get home. Flash floods are scary."

"Yeah. They are. As I was heading back here to regroup, a wall of water came at me on Main Street, when I was stopped at the light, and it physically pushed my car backward a good five feet when it hit me."

My heart races. "Oh, my gosh."

"It was wild. But nobody was behind me—I guess I was the only one stupid enough to be out—and the water receded after that, so I high-tailed it back to the office and decided not to try anymore."

"Good plan. I'd be pissed at you if you died."

"Can't have that, then. So, it's settled. I'll stay here, and hopefully the rain will stop, and I'll see you in the morning. If you can't get here, call me as soon as possible, so I can reschedule appointments."

"Right. Of course. But I heard it's supposed to stop."

"Be careful."

"I will." I pause. "This is horrible timing."

"Are flash floods ever well-timed?"

"I was referring to your being stranded at work tonight."

"Oh. That. I guess it's not that big of a deal. Pat's bachelorette pad is pret-ty nice."

"Don't get too used to it."

"What are you talking about?"

"Being married to an idiot like me isn't ideal, especially when you also have to work with me, but I'll always try harder after I realize how stupid I've been. Unfortunately, I have to be stupid first. And realize it. And sometimes that takes a while."

She laughs. "You're not a stupid idiot."

"Lots of evidence to the contrary."

"I'm extra-sensitive right now, which is annoying. And shouldn't be your problem."

"Uh... I caused the problem."

"Not all by yourself."

"True. You were there. I remember vividly."

"I'd hope so, considering it was just a couple of hours ago."

"More like four or five months ago."

"What?" She laughs. "Oh, you're talking about— I don't mean because of the baby."

"Yeah, I know. I was joking to make up for being such a jerk today."

"Can we just forget about that?"

"If it's not being pregnant, and it's not being married to a big jerk like me, then what has you so on edge?"

"Promise you won't get mad?"

"No, but you should probably tell me, anyway," I say when I deduce what else could be upsetting her right now.

She sighs. "Chris is driving me nuts, pressuring me about where we're all going to meet in May, and I get that everyone needs to make travel arrangements and plans, but I can't decide, which is so unlike me, and I don't know how to handle that. There are so many moving parts and factors to consider, and... and... every suggestion he makes seems wrong, but I don't have any legitimate counter-offers, so..."

Reining in my building rage, I pick at the sofa cushion next to me and say, "Breathe, all right?"

I hear her follow my instructions, then I continue, "We'll sit down tomorrow and figure it out."

"When? I fixed your schedule—where I could—but it's still ridicu—"

"Don't worry about it. We'll find time. And by the end of the day, we'll have a list of places to send back to Chris. In fact, I'll send him the list."

"No, I—"

"Betty, I want to."

"Yeah, but this is my thing. You don't have to be bothered with it."

"It's no bother." I roll my head on my neck to try to relax, then I smile so she can hear it in my voice. "Chris and I need to get better acquainted, anyway."

"It *would* be nice not to have to deal with him anymore this week. He's been so persistent..."

"I'm glad to take over."

Her voice is a mix of wistful, weary, and relieved when she says, "I wish I were home right now."

"I wish you were, too."

"I could use a Nathaniel super-hug. And maybe a few other things."

I chuckle at her naughty tone. "I see. Hijacking Winn's boat is starting to sound like a much more attractive option."

"Absence makes the heart grow fonder, though. I'll see you in the morning."

"Should I get there early? And meet you upstairs? We can talk about stuff then. Or... not talk."

"You probably *shouldn't*, but if you do, I wouldn't have a problem with it."

As soon as we say our "I love you"s and hang up, I set the morning wake-up alarm on my phone for thirty minutes earlier than usual, then reconsider and ratchet it back to fifteen. I won't need *that* much time.

25

NURSING LESSON

Dr. Reitman's back, Betty and I are back, my hair is back, and neither Betty nor I have heard from the Big Kahuna in months, not since the Newsomes accepted our proposed meeting place.

"I don't know what you said to Chris—and maybe I don't want to know—but thank you," Betty said to me this morning at breakfast.

To avoid lying, I merely grinned across the table at her, sipped my coffee, and replied, "You're welcome."

Actually, I *don't* think she'd be thanking me if she knew what I said, verbatim. And what he said back. And what I said back. And so on. It's probably best if she doesn't delve too far into the details.

The official email correspondence was civil and involved all parties. To explain why I was the one initiating contact, I mentioned something about Betty being a bit worn out from all the back-and-forth. Then I gave everyone a bulleted list of possible meeting places that included Myrtle Beach, Charleston, Edisto Island, and some other nearby tourist towns that wouldn't require us to travel too far and could double as decent vacation spots while we're all there. We can enjoy the sights together... or not... depending on how things go. The Newsomes accepted Charleston, and that was the end of the email chain.

As soon as the venue was settled, however, I fired off a text message to Chris only.

Now back off.

He quickly responded, *What's your problem, man?*

You. Stop emailing Betty. You need to talk to us about anything, you email or call me.

Whatever. Does she know you're going all macho-man on her?

Nope. And you're not going to tell her, either. You're going to shut up and go away for a while.

Or what?

I had to consider that one for a while. Because as usual, I hadn't thought it through. And she wouldn't be okay with me going rogue. I should have lied and told him that yes, she knew I was sending these texts, and they were her idea. But since the decision to be honest had already been poorly made (integrity will get you every time), I had to figure out some way to ensure Chris never tattles on me. It had to be a consequence worth his compliance, a bluff he'd never risk calling.

With shaking hands, I finally replied, *Or we're out. And I'll be glad to explain to the Newsomes that it was because you wouldn't stop harassing us*

They won't believe you

I have the emails to prove it

A few hours later, he wrote back, *Fine. See you in May*

Sounds great. Oh, and you might want to delete these texts, since your lack of denial is, effectively, an admission

You're a dick. I'm just trying to do right by Trevor

Then leave Betty alone.

He let me have the last word, which was highly gratifying,

I'll admit. But also worrying. And I did feel slightly guilty when I spent a clandestine hour in my office the next Saturday printing out all of Betty's emails to and from Chris for the past four months. But I said I had proof. And now I do. Resting safely in my bottom left desk drawer.

Four and a half months later, business is booming at the clinic, the weather's amazing, and Betty's third trimester has been a pleasure cruise with nary a hiccup—other than the hilarious in utero ones occasionally witnessed from us on the outside. It's easy to delude ourselves that life has returned to the status quo.

Never mind the status quo frequently includes a sweet-one-second, psycho-the-next toddler and a baby on the way who's already shown us his or her stubborn side by keeping his or her legs firmly crossed in ultrasounds but whom we'd like to keep alive when he or she arrives, nonetheless.

The months have flown, and the big meet-up with the Newsomes is a week away. With such a nerve-wracking event on the horizon, it would be nice if we didn't have to worry about Georgia attacking anyone for touching Betty. We considered leaving Betty's bodyguard with the Bakers or having my parents come here to stay with her, but Betty wants us all together, so it's time to get serious about curbing this unsavory behavior.

Armed with Georgia's doll that looks like a real newborn (yeah, it's creepy), a receiving blanket, the time-out chair, a nursing pillow, and a book my parents recommended to me on this issue, I stride into the living room on a late Saturday morning, hoping I exude more confidence than I possess. This is the one time I wish I were more into sports. Maybe then I'd have a helmet somewhere I could wear during this exercise.

Betty looks up from the book she's reading (*Ooh, I loved that one. A bit of a departure from Rainbow Rowell's first published works but still great)* and smiles as I hand her the pillow and set my book on the coffee table and the time-out chair in the corner, facing the wall. "Uh-oh. This looks serious."

Georgia remains engrossed in playing with her fake food, using her "Mommy" voice as she tosses a fish, an apple, and a loaf of bread into a pan and stirs it all together.

On the couch cushion next to Betty, I spread out the blanket and center the doll in it, then swaddle it.

"That thing's eyes..." Betty mutters.

"Nick and Heidi's hearts were in the right place, but wow. I wouldn't play with this thing, either, if I were a kid. It's perfect for what we're about to do, though."

"Which is?"

"You're going to hold it and feed it and snuggle it, and we're going to see how George reacts."

"Oh, boy."

"She needs to learn."

"It's such a nice day outside. Maybe we could do this some other—"

"We've put it off long enough. Sish will be here in a couple of weeks, and Georgia's going to have to share you with complete strangers next weekend." I cradle the swaddled doll in my right arm. "Whip out the milk jug, and let's go."

She narrows her eyes at me. "For real?"

"We have to make this as authentic as possible, so she knows what to expect." I roll my hand in a "hurry-up" motion.

Betty hesitates but eventually unpacks her left breast from her bra and shirt, muttering the whole time that she's not dressed for nursing, real or otherwise.

While she grouses and prepares, I clear my throat and say, "Hey, George. C'mere a second. We're gonna pretend something."

She spins on her bottom, away from her apple-fish-bread stew, her face alight, "Pwetend?"

"Yeah!" I pat the doll in my arm. "Look. Let's pretend the new baby is here, and we have to take care of it."

The sparkle in her eyes dims, but she approaches me anyway with a wary, "Otay."

"Great!" I kneel down to her level so she can look at the doll. "See the sweet baby?"

She wrinkles her nose.

Before she can protest, I rush on, "Let's *pretend* this is our new baby."

"Is it da boy or da guhl?"

"Uhh..." I look helplessly at Betty, who shrugs, then points to her bare boob and mouths, *"Get on with it!"*

"Uhh... I don't— What do you want it to be? You can pick this time."

"Not wike Bwaze. He cwies all da time."

As I often have to do now that she's more verbal, I stifle my laughter at her Elmer Fudd-like observation. After all, this is serious stuff we're about to do. "A girl, then?"

She nods. "A guhl. Like me."

Trying not to show my excitement that without too much prompting, she's allowing herself to identify with the doll— and therefore, as they said in the book, less likely to "hurt" it— I say casually, "All right. A girl just like you. Isn't she beautiful?"

"Not weelly."

Betty snickers from the couch, which draws Georgia's attention that way. She runs to her mom, flings aside the nursing pillow, and climbs on her lap—or what's left of it. "What's wong?" She points to Betty's breast. "What's dat?"

"I'm going to feed the baby... if your daddy ever brings it —*her*—over here."

As if I'm truly carrying a newborn, I slowly and carefully

lower myself to the sofa on my wife's left and pat my lap. "Georgia, come sit with me so Mommy can feed the baby."

"No!" She wraps her arms around Betty's neck and buries her face there, too. "My mommy!" she muffles.

Betty rolls her eyes but pats Georgia's back a couple of times while saying, "It's okay. I'm still your mommy. But I have to feed the baby now. She's hungry." She pries herself from her daughter's grip and deposits the toddler into my lap, none-too-gracefully.

"Hey, be careful of the baby!" I admonish, shielding the doll from being crushed. Before Georgia can scramble back into Betty's lap, Betty grabs the nursing pillow and wraps it around her waist, then takes the doll, pressing its face against her exposed boob. I adjust it so the back of its head is exposed and vulnerable to the rest of the room. Getting more into the act, Betty caresses the baby's back and rump through the security blanket and looks adoringly down at it.

It's only a doll—a fugly one at that—but for a second, watching her, I have a hard time catching my breath. Then my eyeballs sweat. Just a little. Then I have to tell myself to do normally involuntary things, like swallowing and breathing.

A chubby hand intrudes on the peaceful vision and clamps down on the doll's shoulder. Ripping the baby away from Betty's breast, Georgia booms, "My mommy!!!" Before Betty or I can react, the doll rolls onto the floor at our feet, its head clunking on the bottom shelf of the coffee table when it lands. Doll out of the way, Georgia directs her ire to the other conspicuous and vulnerable object in the room, smacking the top of Betty's breast with a sick slap.

Too late, Betty shields herself with both hands. "Georgia!"

I lift our daughter by her upper arms, near her shoulders, and plunk her onto the time-out chair, facing away from us. Crying and screaming, she tries to swivel, but I persistently hold her in place until she gives up turning but kicks the wall repeatedly, then flattens her body like a board to slide off the seat that way. More dogged than she is (barely), I repeatedly readjust her so that her bottom rests in the chair. Eventually, between her sobs and struggles, she tires and ceases resisting. I keep my hands on her shoulders, just in case.

Crossing her arms over her chest, she yells, "I hate you!"

Like it doesn't bother me at all, I choose not to reply to that. Instead, when she's quiet enough that I can be heard, I say, "You don't hit. Ever. Never, never, never."

Her response is blowing raspberries forcefully enough to spatter the wall in front of her.

"You stay right here and don't move." I let go of her shoulders, which she takes as her immediate cue to try to get up. I push her gently onto the chair again. "Georgia Louise, I mean it. You sit there and look at the wall."

"No!"

I glance over my shoulder at Betty, who's examining what appears to be a bright red hand-shaped welt on her chest, right above her nipple.

"Are you okay?"

"Yes. Wondering how the heck the kid on your lap was able to do that while you just sat there, but..."

Rather than admit to my woolgathering, I say, "It happened so fast! After she knocked the doll away, why didn't you protect yourself?"

"I never dreamed in a thousand years she'd smack *me*."

"Neither did I, obviously."

She winces and hisses as she repositions her bra.

"Hey, what are you doing?"

"Getting dressed."

"No! We have to try again."

Leveling an incredulous look at me, she says, "You're out of your mind. My boob can't take anymore."

"Aw, c'mon. You can switch to the other side."

"Why don't I slap your boobs around and see if you'd like to be the stand-in? I'm done with this today, Nathaniel."

"I don't have boobs," I mutter, re-seating Georgia for the hundredth time. Through clenched teeth, I tell my offspring, "You're not getting up until you've been still, so I suggest you sit nice, or I'm putting you to bed."

"Nooooo! No, no, no, no, no!"

Did I stutter and say, *"I'm taking you to the torture chamber"*? Judging from her reaction, I did. I hold her fast to the chair, then circle in front of her, careful to guard my junk from her flailing feet.

"Hey," I say quietly getting as close to her red, mottled, spittle-spewing face as I dare. Is that brimstone I smell? "Georgia Lou, calm down."

"You mean! I hate da baby! It eats Mommy."

From the couch, Betty says, "No, it doesn't, sweetie. The baby drinks milk. And the milk comes from my breasts." She rises and opens the cabinet under the bookshelves, where she keeps Georgia's baby book. Flipping to one of the first pages, she opens it fully and brings it over to us, kneeling down so Georgia can see the picture of herself getting her first feeding in the hospital. "See? You did it, too. That's how some babies eat. It doesn't hurt the mommy... much," she mutters at the end, quickly smiling to cover her unfiltered aside. "And sometimes you can help, too." She turns the page and points to a photo of me feeding Georgia from a bottle and grinning at the camera. "You can give her a bottle, like Daddy's doing here for you. Because that's what big sisters do."

"You are going to be a great big sister." I add, hoping I'm not lying.

"I not da sister!"

"Yes, you are. Whether you like it or not. And your brother or sister is going to love you so much. They're going to want to be just like you."

This I can say with absolute certainty. No matter how often Nick blamed me for broken items or bad behavior, no matter how many times he sat on my head and farted, no matter how much he mocked me in front of his friends to make himself look cool, I hero-worshiped that guy. Maybe that's pathetic (Maybe? Definitely!), but it's true.

To this day, I catch myself using him as a measuring stick for personal and professional achievement. And as much as I try to deny it, I crave his approval and feel great those rare times I get it. That sibling bond is incredibly strong. I only hope my kids have a slightly less adversarial relationship than I've had with my brother.

Georgia grabs the page and flips it back to the hospital pictures, slapping her palm against the one of her and Betty. "My mommy!"

"You have to share your mommy," I say. "That's all there is to it."

"No!"

I sigh, look down at her chubby knees, and puzzle through how to reason with such an illogical being. Since she's no longer trying to escape, I let go of her shoulders and stroke her dimpled knuckles with my thumbs. "What about your buddies, Kirby, Titus, and Rumer? They have to share a mommy with each other, but that works out, right?"

She nods grudgingly.

"And they share their mommy with *you* every day when we go to work. They don't hit you or slap their mom. That's not nice! They're nice, right?"

Again the teary nod. I step away for a second to grab a

tissue from a box on the bookshelf, and I return to wipe Georgia's face. Next, while tidying her disheveled pigtails, I ask, "How do your friends share their mommy with you? What do they do when you're at their house?"

Her tiny shoulder comes up toward her ear, but she says, "Dey pway wiff me."

"Yep. They play with you."

Lifting her hopeful eyes, made bluer by her recent crying, she asks, "I pway wiff da baby?"

"Uhhh... maybe. Yes. Later. Not at first, because babies are fragile. And they're not good at playing."

"But you get to teach the baby how to do everything," Betty says, rescuing me from my bumbling response. She tries to close the baby book, but Georgia holds tight. "Do you want to keep looking at the pictures?"

"Yes. I do."

"Come on, then." Betty carries the album to the couch and waits for us to catch up to her. "Let's look at the cutest baby in the world."

"Me?"

"Yeah, you!"

Betty and I sit side-by-side, and Georgia climbs onto my lap. Those two study each picture like it's the first time they've seen it, but I hardly look at the book at all. I'm too busy watching them. And marveling at how much things have changed in all of our lives in such a short amount of time. Georgia's gone from helpless newborn to headstrong toddler with a definite personality of her own—for better or worse. Betty's gone from happily single, corporate marketing professional to married mom and medical office manager. And I've gone from the saddest excuse of a man to the luckiest, happiest dad, husband, murse, and business partner.

I sniff through my stinging sinuses, blink my eyes, and clear my throat.

Georgia stops mid-commentary on a photo of herself covered in cake on her first birthday. Turning in my lap to face me, she rises on her knees and strokes my face. "Sorry, Daddy. Don't cwy. No more hits."

I laugh and hug her. "Oh, George. I'm not crying about—"

Betty nudges me, then widens her eyes when I glance her way.

"Uh, I mean... You promise?"

With a solemn nod, she pats my hand. "Pwomise."

"Okay. Thanks. That makes me feel better."

"Good. Wook at dat birfday cake I ated!" she says, returning to her original position with a rough plop against my legs.

"You were an animal," I concur. "Best cake-eater I've ever seen."

"Da baby eats cake. No eating Mommy! I teach da baby."

Oh, Lord.

I'll take it, though. Teaching is a huge improvement over beating.

26

REUNION

Everything about this situation is strange. I'm in a strange hotel room, putting on new clothes, getting ready to meet strangers. Much about it brings on a sickening sense of déjà vu, hearkening back to weekends parading in front of readers, pretending to be someone I wasn't. Only today, I'm wearing a comfortable pair of chinos, not binding skinny jeans, and a blue dress shirt with its sleeves rolled to mid-forearm, not some pretentious vintage tee paired with a man-scarf (an oxymoron, if I've ever heard one).

On the other hand, it also feels like a group job interview. What position am I even applying for, anyway? Stepfather? Not really. I'm more like the boring replacement dude Betty chose instead when she decided it wouldn't be all that great to play house for the rest of her life—or however long it lasted— with a spoiled frat boy.

And then again, it also feels like a nerve-wracking first day at a brand new school. I have the never-worn clothes and the fresh haircut. Will my classmates like me? Am I about to meet people who will be lifelong friends, or is this the beginning of a long, toxic relationship? Chris sure seems like a bully in this scenario, the cool kid who everyone appeases to stay on his good side, because nobody wants to be shoved in a locker or given a swirly on a daily basis. But what about the Newsomes? What does it say about them that they've allowed him to so fully take over this show?

And he's fully taken over. That's why we're staying in this opulent historic hotel in the heart of downtown Charleston. A Marriot or Best Western on the beach wouldn't do. No, it had to be *this* place, with its valets and concierges. Where you can hear the clip-clop of horses' hooves from the carriages on the thoroughfare below. Where you can have a massage or a five-course meal—or both at the same time—delivered to your room. Where you don't have to take a single step outside to satisfy your addiction to overpriced and over-roasted, sugary coffee. Where a pianist plimpers in the lobby (no canned Muzak for this place).

Upon check-in last night, I almost said, "No," and took Betty and Georgia elsewhere. And it's not because these two nights are going to cost more than what we spend to eat for two months. It's because this place isn't us. And I couldn't imagine feeling *more* uneasy about this weekend until we walked through that revolving glass door into the marble foyer that glittered under the numerous crystal chandeliers.

Only two things held my feet to that shiny floor in front of the reception desk: exhaustion after a full day of work, then a two-hour-plus drive—thanks to construction and Memorial Day traffic—to our destination, and an irrational refusal to be the first one to blink. Oh, and a third thing: the chance of finding another room within a hundred mile radius of this place was nil. We likely would have ended up back in Jasper.

So here I stand, surrounded by celery green glass tile and white crown molding, leaning against the perfectly restored trough sink with spindly legs. I check the time, then my nose hairs, once more when I see I still have a good ten minutes before I agreed to meet Betty downstairs in the hotel lobby. She said the walls of our room were closing in on her and that she preferred to wait under the palm trees in the courtyard with Georgia while I finished shaving and dressing.

Nose hair inspection leads to sideburn measuring (I could have sworn the right one was longer than the left, but nope; an optical illusion, I guess), which leads to a familiar fretting about my eyebrows, which always seem so woolly and out-of-control when I stare at them too long and don't take into account the rest of my face. Context is everything. They're thick, but they don't join in the middle, and there are no stray wackadoo strands that veer from the rest of the crowd. Anyway, I don't have time to do anything about them, because—

A clicking at the door, followed by it swinging open and Betty bursting through it startles me from my shallow obsessing. I emerge from the bathroom, adjusting my collar, pretending that's the last thing I had to do, and I was about to join her downstairs.

She doesn't give me a second glance, though, as she flings her dress and Georgia equally carelessly onto the four-poster bed and race-waddles to the wardrobe in the corner.

"Uhh," I grunt. Georgia giggles and continues to bounce on the satin comforter, not at all mindful of the mattress's edge, which comes closer with every slippery hop. I rush to grab her before she tumbles.

In only her bra, panties, and ballet flats, Betty turns from the wardrobe to face me and nibbles her thumbnail. "That dress makes me look pregnant."

"Okay. Because you are? Very much so?"

"I don't need to be so in-your-face about it, though, do I?

'Hey, Trevor. I gave you up, but I'm ready for *these* kids now. Aren't they lucky?'"

"That's your mom talking. Lots of people who give up kids for adoption when they're young—too young to be parents—go on to have families later on in life."

She returns her attention to the mirror on the closet door, turning sideways and hefting one breast in each hand. "What about this bra? It feels like my sweet chariots are swinging low."

I laugh at her description. "They're swinging just fine. You need to put some clothes on. The Newsomes and Chris are expecting us any second."

"Exactly. And you're up here, leaving me alone down there to keep Georgia entertained and... and... to speculate and over-analyze stupid things. Like what I'm wearing. And if my tits are sagging. And how much this weekend is costing. And how we're going to start the conversation that's about to happen."

Ignoring the probing Georgia's doing in my ear with her nimble fingers (and rather sharp fingernails), I circumnavigate the bed, snatching Betty's dress on the way. I drape it over her shoulder. "You looked nice in this. And your tits are fine."

"Tits!" Georgia parrots, making me sigh and Betty groan.

"Oh, great. Let's hope she breaks out every curse word in her repertoire this weekend. Show these people what great members of society we are."

"We're perfectly normal. And it's also normal to be para-noid about every little detail and obsess over what everything about us says to an outsider looking in."

"Now *your* mom's talking."

"Yes, she told me this last time I spoke to her on the phone about the meeting and how nervous we are," I admit. "But she's right. For once. We should give her credit for it."

Georgia grabs my face in both of her clammy hands and

squishes my cheeks as she forcibly turns my head. "Daddy, wook at *me*!"

"Hang on, George," I say, trying to wrest control of my head from her to continue my conversation with Betty, who's still staring at her abdomen in the mirror, her eyes narrowed critically.

"Stop giving the baby the stink eye, all right? It's not their fault the timing worked out this way."

"Daddy!"

"By the end of the weekend, all this will be over."

"And then what?" she asks, whirling on me.

I blink against the itsy-bitsy spider crawling up my face and over my eyes. "Then we move on with our lives, I guess. Georgia, stop!"

For once, she listens, resting her head on my shoulder. I pat her back and kiss the top of her head to reward her for leaving my face alone. She pats my chest and murmurs, "Daddy."

Betty watches us for a few seconds, then blinks and looks away, at the floor. "This isn't an isolated thing for me to get through, though. I can't even picture what 'moving on with my life' means after this. Is Trevor going to be part of that life—physically, that is? Because he never stopped being a part of my life. Only now I have a name. And an updated picture."

"And in a few minutes, you'll have more."

"I was okay with what I already had."

"But he wasn't. He needs this."

"He's fifteen. He has no idea what he needs."

"I'm sure his parents talked to him about it extensively before they got in touch with the agency. It'll be okay."

Betty looks up. "You don't know that, Nathaniel."

I take a deep breath and hug Georgia tighter to me.

"I have so much explaining to do," Betty says, her shoulders drooping, her eyes closing. "It's draining."

I step to her side and wrap my free arm around her, gripping her upper arm in my hand. Her head lolls against my shoulder. "Hey. Take it one question at a time. Don't feel like you need to tell him everything at once. Maybe he *doesn't* want to know everything. Maybe he just wants to know *you*."

She nods against me.

Georgia raises her head and looks around me at her mom. "You otay?" she asks.

Betty laughs and puts her arms around my waist, turning inward and smiling at Georgia. "Yeah, sweet girl. I am."

Georgia reaches for Betty. "*My* mommy."

I pull her away, though, saying, "Mommy needs to put her clothes on. Down you go." I set Georgia on the floor and pat my hair to make sure I'm not about to walk around with the baby-mussed look. My phone chimes with an incoming text. I glance and see it's from Chris, who's wondering, *"Where are you? I'm waiting in the lobby."*

I tap back, *"On our way down now,"* then say, "Let's go."

Betty sighs and pulls the dress over her head once more, then follows me to the door. "Yeah, yeah. I don't have anything else to wear, anyway."

27

THE NEWSOMES

OUTSIDE THE DOOR TO THE SPECIAL MEETING ROOM reserved for this momentous occasion, Chris pauses with his back to us, as if giving us a moment to collect ourselves. Betty grabs my hand. I squeeze her fingers and smile over at her. She smiles back and seems subdued, although I'm sure she's a jangle of nerves on the inside. Georgia pulls on my other hand, trying to drag me back toward the piano in the lobby. "Panno, Daddy!"

I'm about to address her demand and promise her we'll check it out later, when Chris unexpectedly spins, pressing his back against the meeting room door, and faces us with a solemn expression aimed directly at Betty.

How does he get his eyebrows to do that, with one so far up and the other nearly touching his eyelashes? I give it a go but quickly realize I must look like I'm in the beginning stages of a grand mal seizure and stop before anyone notices and shoves a bite guard into my mouth.

"You ready for this, Betty Boop?"

She wrinkles her nose, says, "Yes," and tries to reach for the door handle, but he blocks her way.

"I know this is overwhelming..."

"What a coincidence. That's exactly how I would describe your aftershave. Now move."

I laugh in spite of my own nerves, then lift Georgia so she'll stop yanking on my arm.

Chris smirks. "Okay. I get it. You always did ramp up the snark when you were nervous or scared."

"Yeah, you know me so well. Can we just get this over with?"

"This isn't something to 'get over with,' though. This is the beginning of something huge, something great, something beautiful. Take it from someone who's already experienced it; it's something you're going to want to savor and remember."

"If you don't open the door and get out of the way, you're going to experience being body-slammed by a hugely pregnant woman. It'll be something *you* remember for the rest of your life."

He continues to hesitate, so Betty starts counting. "One..."

"If I were you, I'd do what she says," I finally intercede. However awesome it would be to witness her take off his head, it wouldn't make for the best first impression with the Newsomes, who are still waiting for us on the other side of the door.

Chris shrugs and depresses the handle. "Fine. I was only trying to—"

"Be a drama whore?" Betty says. "That's always been your specialty. This isn't a scene in your stupid screenplay."

I snicker and scratch my eyebrow.

"What are you laughing at?" she snaps.

"Uh, nothing. Just enjoying the show."

"Well, this isn't a good time for me."

Before I can apologize or defend myself, Chris pushes the door open with his shoulder and steps aside to allow us entry.

More of a suite than a traditional meeting room, the plush-carpeted, open-plan grouping of rooms features a long table typically associated with business meetings, plus a kitchenette and sitting area, complete with television. The windows in the sitting area overlook the stone-paved courtyard. The table holds muffins, pastries, fruit, a coffee urn, and pitchers of orange juice and water, plus plates, cups, and cutlery.

As with everything Chris has organized this weekend, it's overkill. We could have just as easily done this in one of our rooms, or a separate room if he was so hell-bent on a private, yet neutral, setting. Heck, we could have reserved a small study room at the local library. But no. *This* has to be the stage for our introductions. Of course. Maximum drama *and* a way for him to show off his "no expenses spared" approach.

Two adults and a gangly teenager rise from the sofas in the sitting area. Betty and I skirt the food-filled conference table to arrive within hand-shaking distance of the trio and say our awkward, stilted hellos while Chris takes over the introductions that are hardly necessary.

Trevor shakes Betty's hand then impulsively hugs her. She chuckles nervously but returns his hug, albeit stiffly, her posture rigid and bottom sticking out as she tries to avoid pressing her belly against him. Trevor's parents, Marcus and Donna, smile on. Chris snaps some pictures with his phone. I perfectly impersonate the immovable lump in my throat.

"My mommy!" Georgia predictably says when the hug goes on longer than she deems appropriate.

I'm so used to hearing Georgia say that by now that it takes a while for me to register what it could mean in *this* context. Then I kind of want to puke.

Everyone freezes except Trevor, who shrugs. "She's right, guys." His joke falls flat with the grownups, so he grins and says, "Oh c'mon, everyone! Relax! She's a baby. It's not like she's actually being a jerk about it. Plus, I have an awesome mommy, too, so... No worries."

Donna smiles at him. "Thanks, Tubby."

"Mom!" He covers his face. "You promised not to call me that."

She winces. "Sorry. Old habits." She turns to Betty. "When he was a baby, he was so chubby, his rolls had rolls. He could out-eat Marcus. I brought pictures, if you're interested."

Betty clears her throat and fidgets. "Oh. Well. That's... Yes. I'd like that. Later."

The Newsomes retake their seats on the couch. Betty chooses the chair closest to Trevor's end of the sofa. Chris plunks himself in the chair next to hers, but separated by an end table. I claim the last available seat on the edge of the room, nearly straddling the threshold to the conference table area. I don't get to settle for long, though, because as soon as I put Georgia down on her feet, she runs for the table.

"Hungwy!"

Getting her something to eat is as good a diversion as any, so I follow her, keeping an ear on the conversation in the adjoining room while I peel a banana and pour her a small portion of orange juice.

"Trevor," Chris says like the earnest moderator of a town hall meeting, "do you have anything you specifically want to ask Betty? That might be the easiest place to start."

Oh, yeah, easy as pie. What a moron.

Fortunately, the teenager has a ready answer, so we don't have to sit in more awkward silence. He scoots to the edge of his seat and angles himself toward Betty. "Well, I've already asked Chris a bunch of stuff, and he's been really nice about answering my questions."

I'm sure. No doubt coming out looking like a prince, too.

"I just wanted to meet you. And, yeah, I'm curious about

some things, but I mostly wanted to see who you are now, make sure you're okay. Make sure you know *I'm* okay."

Betty's eyelids flutter, and she pulls a tissue from the box on the table next to her. "Okay. Wow. That's... Are you sure you're only fifteen years old?"

"You could answer that better than anyone," he quips.

She laughs. "I'm pretty sure, then."

Georgia runs back into the sitting area with her banana clutched in one hand. Betty pulls her into her lap and straightens her skewed plastic barrettes.

Glancing at me first, Donna smiles nervously at Betty. "Chris tells us you and your husband work together at a pediatric practice? Is that how you met?"

Since Donna's looking at Betty, I defer to her to answer more completely. "No, we met through a mutual friend."

"Good old Frankie," Chris says. "You know, Donna, the woman who was nice enough to give me Betty's email address when the agency's letter was undeliverable?"

Donna nods. "Oh, yes! The author." She tilts her head at me. "Were you friends with her and Betty and Chris in college, too?"

Swallowing loudly, I lick my lips. "Uh, no. I met Frankie much later. A few years ago."

"So, Trevor!" Betty says brightly. "Summer vacation. Besides *this*... any big plans?"

Chris rolls right over that desperate attempt at a subject change. "Wait, wait, wait! How you two got together is a great story. You should tell it."

Betty releases a suddenly squirmy Georgia, who crosses the room and drops her half-mangled banana into my lap. I lift it from my pants with two fingers and hold it away from myself. Having unburdened herself of the unwanted fruit, Georgia goes to the window, where she slaps her slimy hands against the glass, leaving gooey smudge marks.

"Maybe some other time," Betty says to Chris's prompt. "I'd rather talk more about Trevor. You just finished your sophomore year, huh? How'd you do?"

"Not bad." Pointing back and forth between his biological parents, he asks, "But which one of you can I blame for being so bad at math?"

Chris immediately points to Betty. "That would be her."

"I'm not bad at math!"

"Well, you were never the best. I remember helping you study a few times."

"That was statistics."

"Technically math."

She turns her back on Chris and says to Trevor with a tight smile, "Anyway. I'm sorry math is a struggle for you."

Marcus rolls his eyes. "If you call getting straight A's a struggle."

Betty laughs. "Hang on. Is this true? You're getting A's in math but still don't consider yourself good at it? Don't be that guy."

"I have to study. And I turn in extra credit to make up for the lower grades I get on practice work."

Since Georgia's performance is starting to garner stares from people out in the courtyard, I jump up and pull her away from the greasy glass. In the nearby kitchenette, I grab a napkin and plunk the toddler on the counter, where I wipe her hands, wrap the banana in the napkin, and toss it in the trash.

In the other room, Betty says, "You'll be fine. Not everything comes naturally, but that doesn't mean you're bad at something. Plus, sometimes it's good to have to work hard for grades. It teaches you how to study, which you'll definitely need to figure out before college. If you plan to go, anyway."

"I do."

"Trevor's a gifted singer," Donna tells us, which makes him blush. I wink through the archway at him and mouth, *"Moms,"* which cracks him up.

Chris turns around to see what I'm doing. "What did I miss?"

"Nothing," I answer.

Betty sits farther on the edge of her seat. "A singer, huh? You definitely didn't get that from me."

"Really? Because Chris can't sing, either. And he said he remembers you had a pretty voice."

"He must be confusing me with one of his other girlfriends."

I snort as I intercept Georgia from another run at the windows. Holding her on my hip, I stand with my back to the room and look with her at the fountain in the courtyard. "Birds," I whisper, then help her count them.

"Ha, ha," Chris says. "Very funny."

"I thought it was," Trevor replies. "So, singing comes from some distant, unknown part of my DNA, but now I can definitely tell where I get my sense of humor."

"Yes, thanks for that." Marcus's dry tone makes us laugh. All of us but Chris, that is.

"Hey, I'm funny!"

"Funny-*looking*," Betty mutters, eliciting more chuckles from the room.

My eyes widen, but I reveal no reaction to the others, merely start over counting birds when they flutter and resettle.

The rest of us seem to realize that what makes Betty's joke funnier is the irony behind it, but the pout is strong in Chris's tone when he says, "I've said nothing but nice things about *you*. And this is how you repay me?"

I turn to see Betty's reaction to that. With barely a glance at her ex, she replies, "Lighten up, Christopher. And anyway, nobody asked you to lie and say how wonderful I am."

"I never lied!"

"My pretty singing voice was just an exaggeration, then? Because you used to make fun of me all the time. Said I sounded like Kermit the Frog."

Oh, hell! She does! I've been trying to place it for years…

"But for these guys, I have the voice of an angel? What, were you afraid they wouldn't want to meet me if I wasn't perfect?"

"Betts…"

She ignores me and taps Trevor's knee. "What else did he tell you about me?"

"Uh, I don't know. Stuff. Nothing bad, though. And stuff that I can already tell is true."

"Like?"

"Well, like that you're funny and beautiful and… and… smart."

She slouches back into her chair. "Ah. I see."

"Otherwise, he hasn't told us much," Donna says quietly. "We all agreed it would be better for us to learn for ourselves who you are now, not who you *were* when you…"

I'm not sure whether to be relieved or dismayed when she trails off.

Betty stares at her knees.

Chris kneels next to her chair and grabs her hand. "I didn't badmouth you *or* try to make you out to be an angel, Boop. I swear."

She nods, then whispers, "I'm sorry." When she looks up, tears drip from her lower lids. With an embarrassed smile, she says to the three Newsomes on the couch, "I'm… I'm so sorry."

I slide between the wall and the back of Betty's chair and

rest a hand on her shoulder. She lets go of Chris's hand to grasp my fingers. Chris returns to his chair.

"Nate can confirm I'm a little... unpredictable right now."

Not willing to do any such thing, I merely squeeze her shoulder and adjust my grip on Georgia.

Betty clears her throat. "Anyway. I promised myself I'd say this before the end of the weekend. And maybe sooner is better. Let's get the mushy stuff out of the way." She shoots a wobbly grin at Trevor, who nods encouragingly.

"You should totally say whatever you want."

On a shaky inhale, she says, "Okay," and takes a second to steady herself. "I'll try not to ramble, but here goes. I don't have any lame excuses for you. I don't even want to try to defend the person I was back then. She was stupid and scared and selfish." She holds up a hand when Trevor opens his mouth to object. "No, let me finish. I was only a few years older than you are right now. And it probably seems like you already have a decent grip on life, but you're way more mature than I was at your age, and I wasn't much more mature than you are now when I had you. I knew nothing but thought I knew everything. And part of what I thought I knew was that I was going to be the worst mom in the world. I was certain of it. Nobody could convince me otherwise. Chris tried to. Every day, he said it would be fine. That the three of us would have a great life. And meeting you now... maybe we would have. But at the time, it was too important to risk. You know?" She drags her hand across her lips. I hand her another tissue. "Thanks, Nathaniel."

After a dainty sinus clearing, she continues, "I figured you'd be better with *anyone* besides me, but when the adoption counselor told me about your mom and dad, it was like I was able to take a deep breath for the first time in months. They were going to fix everything. And they did. They have. I can see that. You're happy and healthy and funny and smart..." She stops and nods down at her knees for several seconds.

The worst thing for any of us to do would be to interject and try to fill the silence or rush her, especially to say, "It's okay. You don't have to keep going."

But Chris is an idiot. And his main mission so far this weekend seems to be to prove how disastrous a marriage between him and Betty would have been. So of course, he says exactly that.

She slowly lifts her head and turns it to focus the full force of her acidic glare on him.

"Shit," I mutter involuntarily.

"Shiiiit," Georgia echoes.

I'm too busy bracing myself for the confrontation that's about to happen to chastise my daughter. My muscles tense. My testicles ascend. My breathing ceases.

Finally Betty says in a near-growl, "Yes. I. Do. Did you not hear me earlier? I said if I did nothing else this weekend, I would say this. And I don't need or want your condescending help. So if you don't mind..."

Through his tan, Chris blushes. "Fine. I just thought..."

"Yeah, well thinking was never your strong suit, so shut it."

He chuckles indignantly. "You don't have to be a bitch about it."

"Bitch!" the parrot on my arm squawks.

This time, I do react. But not to my daughter. No, there's another potty mouth in this room who's much more deserving of my immediate attention.

I plop Georgia into her mother's lap and, pointing to the suite's door, say to Chris, "Out."

"Excuse me?"

"Out. Side. Now."

"I'm not leaving."

"Oh, yes you are. We both are."

Nobody says a word. Chris appeals to the Newsomes with a nervous laugh, but they all find their laps suddenly more interesting than his face.

"You either walk out with me, or I drag you," I say, still not raising my voice. I may as well be discussing the weather (warm and muggy, in case you were wondering).

That gets him to his feet, although why I'm not sure. He and I—and everyone else in this room—are fully aware there's no way murse-y me could drag a person his size anywhere. But he saves us both the embarrassment of confirming it.

Out in the hallway, he smirks at me. "What's the goal here, pal?"

"I'm not your pal. But you and I are going to pretend like we are for a while so Betty can say what she needs to say without your constant interruptions."

"We're going to stand out here in the hall?"

"Nope. Let's go." I stride in the direction of the lobby. It's time for another morning drinking session.

28

TOXIC MASCULINITY

AT THE BAR, CHRIS ORDERS A RUM AND COKE. I'D KILL FOR a simple beer, but this seems to call for something stronger, so I ask for a scotch on the rocks.

Great. I'm turning into my father.

Before our drinks arrive, Chris says, "There's no need for you to feel threatened by me. I'm not out to win back Betty. I'm just trying to get everyone through this. You know, finish what I started."

"I'm not threatened by you."

He chortles. "Yeah. Whatever."

I focus on the cut crystal tumbler arriving in front of me and take a bracing drink to resist punching him in the throat.

Although I cease protesting his assessment of the situation, he says, "C'mon. Those texts... Classic jealous behavior. But you don't have to worry."

"I'm not worried about you."

"Okay. Let's assume that's true."

"Because it is."

"What are you worried about, then? Why this hostility

toward me, man? I'm a nice, peaceful guy. Otherwise, you would have been in trouble a long time ago."

I roll my eyes then return them to a close study of my amber beverage. "This whole thing has been a bad idea. Especially at this time."

"Getting in the way of your happily-ever-after life?"

Since I'd rather die than reveal anything more personal to him than what I had for breakfast, I don't consider for a nanosecond confiding in him about the miscarriage last year. Instead, I simply say, "No. But you've introduced a brand of needless drama into our lives that I work hard to avoid."

"Ah, yes. Well, you're so sensitive like that."

"What's that supposed to mean?"

He chuckles. "Nothing. Except what I said. You're very... evolved. Not at all who I expected Betty to marry."

Don't take the bait. Don't take the bait.

"Who'd you expect her to marry?"

Idiot!

"Besides me? Nobody, honestly. When she rejected me, she made it sound like marriage wasn't for her."

"Probably to soften the blow."

He stares straight ahead. "But I figured if she ever changed her mind and did take the plunge, it would be with someone... stronger. Driven. No-nonsense. Someone with balls. Manly."

He turns his head to watch that last word land, and for the thousandth time, I marvel at how black his eyes are. Freaky black. Like they're all pupil. It crosses my mind that his drink may not be the first mind-altering substance he's put in his body today, but I shrug off the suspicion I recognize as possible wishful thinking to justify my jealousy and resentment.

Instead, I merely grin and shake my head once. "Well. Shows how much you knew her, I guess."

"I guess. Because I got it totally wrong."

"Dude, if you're trying to goad me, it's not going to work. We'd be better off whipping out our dicks right here on the bar"—the bartender glances nervously our way—"measuring up, and getting on with our lives."

"It's not about—"

"Isn't it?" I set down my drink, dig my wallet from my back pocket, and toss some money next to my glass, then swivel on my seat so my elbow is on the bar, and I'm facing him more fully. "Or is it about *that*?" I jut my chin toward the bills. "Because if so, let me log in to my bank on my phone, and you can take a gander at my account balances and feel great about yourself."

"That's not—"

"The bottom line is that she's moved on."

"With you. Her hero."

"Uh, no. She saved herself long before she ever met me. But I do try to be the partner she wants and needs. One who cares about who she is and how she feels and doesn't get off on controlling her. Because I'm 'manly' enough not to be intimidated by someone who thinks for herself."

"What can I say? You've got it all figured out."

I snort and pick at the tiny blister at the base of my finger, under my wedding ring. "Most days, I don't know anything. But that's why this works. Because she's okay with that. I don't have to pretend I have a clue. Maybe if you'd figured that out about her, we wouldn't even be here right now." The mere thought makes me shiver, but I keep my tone light, raising my eyes and smiling. "Thanks for being such a heavy-handed jerk. You guys make it so much easier for wimps like me."

I hop down from my bar stool and pocket my wallet. "I'm going to rejoin the others. I suggest you stay here and enjoy the bartender's company for a while longer. The door will be locked."

As I'm leaving the bar, he yells after me, "You have some stones, man! I paid for that room!"

Ignoring the rheumy stares of the other morning drinkers, I pause at the threshold to the lobby, turn, and say to him, "That's what you get for calling my wife a bitch. I'm not *that* evolved."

* * *

BETTY EVENTUALLY UNLOCKED THE DOOR, after Chris promised he'd do more observing and less talking. Seems like she and the Newsomes got the rest of the serious stuff out of the way, anyway, while he and I were supposedly male bonding (a.k.a., "marking our territory") at the bar. By the time I returned to the room after a quick detour upstairs to brush the liquor from my breath, they were looking at the baby pictures Donna had brought and laughing at butterball baby Trev.

I kept out of the way and tried to keep Georgia occupied, but after lunch, she'd had her fill of being cooped up in those rooms, so I took her for a short walk for some fresh air, then whisked her away for a nap. Reading for those two hours was my original objective, but with Georgia snuggled against me like a baby-shampoo-scented teddy bear, I didn't have a chance. I dozed off and fell into one of those mid-day comas that requires several attempts at waking and results in long-term grogginess.

By the time I surfaced from that nap, Betty had returned to our room, having separated from Chris, Donna, Marcus, and Trevor, who were planning to spend their evening at a nearby aquarium. While we waited for Georgia to come around, we made our own plans. "Outdoors" was the final consensus, so we ate dinner on the patio of a casual bistro, then drove twenty minutes to Folly Beach for a leisurely wade and seashell hunt.

While Georgia ran drunken circles around us, filling the plastic bucket with only the most worthless detritus brought in by the tide, Betty filled me in on the rest of the day's conversations. The talks centered mostly around Trevor, but every now and then, things veered toward Betty's life between college and now. Eventually, after skirting the topic several times, she told them how she and I met, without getting too far into the legal weeds of the Frank Lipton debacle.

After catching me up, she fell silent. And I understood. She'd been talking all day. We strolled hand-in-hand on the hard-packed sand, turning our full attention to Georgia's unbridled joy over her discovered "tweasures."

On the return walk, both of my companions were less enthusiastic. There wasn't much I could do for Betty's fatigue, but I looped the bucket of shells onto one of my wrists and carried Georgia on my shoulders to the parking area, where we hosed the sand from our feet. Whistling snores from both the front and back seats provided the soundtrack to our drive back to the hotel.

Now, all three of us scrubbed and pink, we lounge in our matching hotel robes and eat strawberries while watching cartoons in bed. Georgia's finally coming down from her second wind and has fallen silent between the two of us. Occasional checks tell me she's still awake... but barely and not for long. Similarly, Betty's been holding the same strawberry for at least ten minutes while she stares vacantly at the screen on the dresser a few feet from the foot of the bed.

I gently take the fruit from her fingers before she drops it onto the pristine white sheet. Despite my care, she startles when she feels the berry slipping from her grasp. "Oh!"

I chuckle at her. "Just trying to prevent a mess."

She grins sheepishly, then glances at the equally dozy toddler between us. "As if policing a two-year-old wasn't bad enough."

"I'm okay with it." I drop the fruit in the silver bowl with the few other remainders and reach behind me to set the container on the bedside table. Settling against the headboards and adjusting the pillows for cushion, I say, "Sorry I abandoned you for a while this morning. I hope she behaved herself while I was gone."

Betty runs her fingers through Georgia's thick, still-damp hair. "She was fine. I'm glad you remembered to bring some toys and books with you when you came back. I was so nervous and distracted when we first went down..."

"Me, too."

"Anyway, thanks for babysitting Chris for a while, too. What'd you guys talk about, anyway? Did you give him a talkin' to?" She winks.

While I consider my answer, I watch Georgia's blinks lengthen until they're no longer blinks.

Betty pokes me in the upper arm with her index finger. "Well?"

Pulling myself from my stare, I look over at her. "Nothing."

"Liar."

"He drank a rum and Coke; I drank a Scotch..."

"At ten a.m.?"

"Yep. It was gross."

"And you two just sat there drinking, without saying anything?"

"We may have said a few things."

"You looked furious when you left. I almost wanted to follow you to see what happened."

"It wasn't that exciting."

"Did you guys talk about me?"

"Nope."

"Nathaniel! Stop lying to me!"

"Shhh... You'll wake up George," I say through my chuckles.

"You're such a jerk. I told you everything *we* talked about while *you* were gone. It's only fair you share, too." She rolls to her feet and bends over the bed to pick up Georgia, but I beat her to it, gathering our daughter in my arms before Betty can put more strain on her back than she already has.

After tucking the child into her portable crib, I turn to my wife and pull her to me. "It was just a bunch of stupid guy stuff. Chris thinks I'm jealous of him..."

"Are you? You shouldn't be! Ugh. I look at him and wonder what I ever saw in that."

I kiss her nose, then stiffly rock her back and forth, like a pre-teen slow dancer. "I can understand exactly what you saw in him. But you do make an odd pair. You come up to his bellybutton."

She slaps my chest. "Do not."

"Okay, not quite that high."

"Are you going to be serious?"

"Nah. We've had enough seriousness today."

After a sigh, she rests her ear against my chest. "Fine. Then make me laugh."

No pressure.

I caress her shoulder blades with my thumbs as we continue swaying, more fluidly now. Finally, my scattered thoughts land on a nugget that may satisfy both her need for information *and* amusement. "At one point, I did offer to compare dicks with him."

"What?!"

"I thought it might get him to back off."

"How would that—"

"Guys are weird. Just go with it."

Her belly quakes mirthfully against mine. "You guys are idiots."

"Well, we didn't actually do it!" I pause. "But if we had... Which one of us would have come out ahead?"

She pulls away from me and retreats to the bathroom. "I'm *not* answering that."

I follow her, groaning. "Oh, man, I knew it. He's massive, isn't he? Ten, eleven inches?"

"I never measured it, and I'm not good with spatial estimates. Anyway, it was a long time ago."

"Oh, man. It's worse than I thought."

Busying herself with brushing and flossing, she remains resolutely silent.

When we reconvene in bed and turn off the lights, I say into the dark, "Really. Now that you don't have to look at me when you say it, how much bigger is he?"

"This conversation is crass."

"Exactly how you like it," I tease, curling around her and resting my hand on her belly.

She slaps blindly at my face and lands a lucky blow.

I laugh. "Ow!"

"You're not going to drop it, are you?"

"Probably not."

"If you must know, he's not all that. Okay?"

"Whoa-ho! Do tell!"

"There's nothing to tell. He's average. But because he's such a big guy everywhere else, he actually looks small-ish."

My gleeful grin fades. "Whatever. You're only saying that to make me feel better and so I'll shut up about it."

"Yes, I want you to stop talking about it—I can't believe we're having this conversation—but I'm not lying."

"Why didn't you say so to begin with, then?"

She shrugs, her shoulder knocking against my chin. "It seemed mean to talk about him like that, about something so superficial and dumb. Like I'm making fun of him or trash-talking him. And I'm not. I'm better than that."

"Yeah, yeah."

"I am! I'm classy. Now, shut up and go to sleep. It's late, and I told the Newsomes we'd meet them for breakfast before we head home."

"We're not spending the whole day with them tomorrow?"

Her hair rustles against her pillow as she continues to try to get comfortable. "I just want to get out of here. It's been nice meeting the three of them, and it has eased my mind about things, so in that regard, it's been good."

"But?"

Her pause is so long, I begin to wonder if she nodded off while formulating her answer. I lift up on my elbow and look down at her face. Her eyes are wide open, staring ahead.

"You okay?"

She blinks. "Yeah. I'm trying to figure out how to say this without sounding like the worst person in the world."

I brush her hair from her cheek. "You don't have to weigh your words with me, Betts."

Her chin wrinkles, and the cords in her throat stand out as she swallows furiously.

"Hey... It's okay."

After a long, quavery breath, she says, "I gave him up for a reason. And when I did it, it was a permanent arrangement. I don't fault him for wanting to know where he comes from. His motivations are so selfless, too—he wants to make sure *I'm* okay and that I know *he's* okay. I mean, that's..." She closes her eyes and bites her lower lip. "Anyway. He's a good kid. And Donna and Marcus are good people. It could have had a much different outcome, which is one thing I've always been afraid of finding out. But now I *know* I did the right thing."

"You did."

"That's all I need to know. More than I needed to know. But nice. And now, we all need to keep going on our separate paths. But Chris keeps trying to pick us up and put us on the same path again, and I don't want to be there."

"Then you don't have to be."

"But how do I say that without seeming like I'm rejecting Trevor *again*?"

"You deal directly with the Newsomes. It's okay to tell Chris to go away. You have as much say in this as anyone else does."

"I guess."

With a final kiss on her cheek, I return to my pillows and nestle her back into my chest. "It'll all work out. Get some rest. It's been a long day."

"You're right. I'm wiped out. I love you."

"I love you, too."

I squeeze her more tightly and rub my thumb back and forth on her warm, twitching bump, her steady breathing helping me tick off the seconds as I lie awake, worrying.

FAMILY BREAKFAST

A COOL FRONT PASSES THROUGH OVERNIGHT, SO THE DAY dawns bright, crisp, and light. The sun is still freakishly warm for this time of year, but for once it's not steam cooking us through a layer of suffocating humidity.

After quadruple-checking that Betty and I have all seven tons of paraphernalia we had to pack for a simple two-night stay, we set off for our last hurdle of the weekend before returning to Jasper and some semblance of normalcy.

I inhale deeply while carrying Georgia across the parking lot of the restaurant where Chris and the Newsomes are already waiting. "Ah! I can breathe!" I say to my daughter, laughing when she imitates me with a drawn-out "Ahhhh!" followed by a sloppy kiss on my cheek that makes up for the low humidity in the air.

"My daddy."

"Yes. I am. Always. Nothing will ever change that."

Well, except death. But now may not be the best time to have a conversation about mortality.

Betty catches up to us and walks through the door I hold open for her. "We're late," she mutters, her brow furrowed.

"It's hardly a big deal."

She walks faster, nodding past the hostess to indicate the rest of our party is waiting for us.

We arrive at the table and greet our fellow diners. Betty may still be a nervous, tense wreck, but the Newsomes flash smiles all around. Marcus stands to shake our hands. Donna and Trevor distribute less inhibited hugs. Chris barely glances up from his phone.

Trevor gestures to the empty chair next to him. "You can sit here, Betty."

She blushes and pats his shoulder on the way into her seat, then fidgets with her napkin-wrapped silverware. "Hope you guys haven't been waiting long."

"A bit," Chris mumbles from Trevor's other side.

Donna holds the wooden high chair steady so I can slide Georgia's legs through the holes and get her settled. "We just got here."

"Thanks," I say with a smile. I sit between Betty and Georgia and drop the diaper bag on the floor under the high chair.

"You're still talking to me today, huh?" Betty says to Trevor.

"Yeah! Why wouldn't I be?"

She shrugs, lifting the large menu from the table in front of her and opening it, keeping her eyes trained on the laminated pages containing colorful photos of food she'd normally be ready to inhale but judging by her pallor doesn't appeal this morning. "I dumped a lot of information on you yesterday and wouldn't blame you for thinking less of me."

"It could have been worse."

"We're grateful to you, Betty," Donna says with a quick, nervous glance at Chris. "To both of you. Maybe we haven't done a good enough job of expressing that, but we are."

In a choked voice, Betty replies, "After seeing what a great kid Trevor is, I should be thanking you."

"Why don't we agree we all have a lot to be thankful for and order some food?" Chris interjects with a mighty sniff that has more to do with impatience than emotion as he flags down the server.

I lean forward and stare down the table at him. His eyes flicker toward me for less than a second, but he continues to pretend I'm not here. Which is fine by me, as long as he behaves himself.

Returning my attention to my menu, I sit back and quickly scan the choices for both Georgia and me, so by the time the server arrives at my side, I'm ready to recite our orders.

When it's her turn, Betty hands her over her menu and says, "Just water for me, thanks."

"You okay?" I whisper when the server moves on to Trevor.

She nods but it's the terse head-bob of someone dismissing a question more than answering it.

"You don't seem okay."

"My stomach's uneasy, that's all." She sips her water.

"You want me to ask if they have ginger ale?"

"No. I can order for myself, Nathaniel, but thanks. I'll be okay once we're on the road. I'll rest my eyes."

"Okay. You should probably try to eat something, though. Toast?"

A spoon sails into view and clatters on the table in front of me. Georgia yells, "Fwying spoon!"

Betty groans and arches her back as if to stretch it. "Georgia. Please. Don't throw things."

I pick up the utensil and place it out of the toddler's reach, then grab a plush toy and her sippy cup from the diaper bag to distract her from her loss.

"Everything okay down there?" Chris asks with a smirk.

I look up and notice the server has gone, and our companions are staring at us. "Uh, yes. Fine. So. Amusement park is on the agenda today, huh?"

Trevor sits higher in his chair. "Yeah! I wish you'd come with us. I'd ride all the kiddie rides with Georgia."

Chris clears his throat. "The place we're going doesn't have a bunch of kiddie rides."

Betty winces. "It's just as well. We need to get back to the dog. Plus, I'm pretty tired. Sorry."

"No need to apologize," Donna says. "I'm the one who feels terrible. In all the excitement yesterday, I didn't get a chance to ask you anything about your impending arrival. Like *when* you're due."

Betty gulps more water, then sets down her glass. "Any day now, I guess. Our due date is the week after next."

"Oh, gosh. You're almost there!"

"Yeah. I'm sure that's obvious, though. I can't get much bigger."

"You carry it well."

She grimaces as she readjusts in her chair. "Thanks. It hasn't been too bad, until now. I'm heading into those truly uncomfortable weeks, you know?"

Donna mildly replies, "Actually, I wouldn't. Never had that experience. I can imagine, though."

Betty's face whitens further, then floods with color. "Oh, my gosh. I'm sorry. I—"

Donna waves off her chagrin. "Please. I didn't mean to make you feel bad, but I didn't want to pretend to fully understand, either. Being pregnant is one thing I do wish I could have experienced. Maybe not the discomfort—I'm not a fan of that. But the rest of it seems so amazing."

Betty ducks her head and pats her bulge. "It *is* miraculous."

Before another awkward silence can overtake us, Marcus asks, "Georgia, are you excited to be a big sister?"

Georgia merely stares at him, then hides her face against my upper arm.

The Newsomes laugh.

"She, uh, thinks we're having a fish," I say.

"Sish!" she muffles against me.

I rub her back. "We're a little nervous, too, about how she's going to react. Our efforts to explain things haven't gone well so far. But she'll be fine." I turn to Betty. "Right, Hon?"

She smiles wanly. "Yeah. It'll be an adjustment... for all of us, but..."

Trevor asks, "Are you having a boy or a girl?"

When Betty simply looks at me, as if she's as curious about the answer as everyone else, I chuckle. "Our little 'fish' is shy about showing us what's going on down below."

"Sish, sish, sish!"

"What about names? Trevor's a pretty awesome name..."

Betty's too busy laughing and nudging the joker to reply, so I quip, "Trevor was our first choice, but since it was already taken..." I wink. "We like Henry Nathan for a boy and Madeline Grace for a girl."

"Such nice names," Donna approves with a gentle smile across the table at us. "And maybe it's fun that you'll be surprised on delivery day. Although... when it's hard to tell, I've heard that usually means you're having a girl."

"Guhl sish!"

Chris slides his phone onto the table and yawns. "Or maybe you can't see the little guy's equipment because he's a bit on the small side."

Betty's head swivels his way, but before she can say anything, Chris continues, "We knew right away that Trevor was all boy, didn't we, Boop?"

I scrape my lip on my bottom teeth and look up at the ceiling, digging deep for serenity and self-control. *I will not use any private information to my advantage here. I'm a grownup. Dick size is not an appropriate breakfast topic. It's also considered bad manners to crawl down a table and throttle someone. Keep calm, Bingham.*

Trevor hides his eyes. "I hope I wasn't doing anything embarrassing."

"Nope. But it was out there."

"Really, Chris?" Betty says through clenched teeth. "Enough."

"What? I'm not allowed to contribute to the conversation?"

"It's not what you're saying; it's how you're saying it."

"Oh, I'm sorry." He sounds anything but. "I didn't realize we had an etiquette expert at the table this morning."

Marcus smiles tightly at me. "Nate, do you have a preference? Would you like a son to round out the set?" He winks.

"Nate's not the type to go in for all that macho stuff!" Chris answers for me. "Right, Nate? You're too—oh, what's the word I'm looking for?" He snaps his fingers repeatedly.

"'Mature'?" I supply.

As if I've said nothing, he points to me. "...*perfect*. You're too perfect for gender preferences."

"It's sex, not gender. Gender is a social construct, something you choose to identify with. Sex is chromosomal and manifests itself physically."

He rolls his eyes and jerks his thumb toward Betty. "And she had objections to *my* contribution to the conversation. At least I didn't put everyone to sleep with a boring lecture."

"Didn't mean to lecture. I was merely pointing out an important distinction."

"Which was? That you're a pedantic know-it-all?"

Marcus taps his finger on the table in front of him, as if

he's trying to get the attention of a recalcitrant pet. "Hey," he says softly to Chris. "What's the deal?"

"It's okay." I return my attention to Georgia, who would probably agree with Chris that the conversation is boring, considering how determined she suddenly is to reach the salt and pepper shakers. "I'll shut up and gladly perpetuate his ignorance."

Chris scoots his chair back loudly on the tile floor to get a better look at me. "Excuse me, but I can hear you!"

"I'm not trying to prevent it."

"You have something you want to say to me, you say it to my face, all right?"

By now, other diners are craning their necks and turning around to see what the commotion is.

"Keep your voice down," Betty hisses at Chris behind Trevor's back.

He grabs his phone and stands. "I don't need this."

She looks up at him and says with more exasperation than concern, "Where are you going?"

"To get some air." With a pointed look on his way past me, he adds, "*Someone* is sucking all of it from the room."

I press my hand to my chest. "Me? I—"

But he's gone, weaving his way through the crowded dining room, jostling a few chairs and earning some glares in his wake.

Trevor makes a move to follow, but Donna freezes him by quietly saying his name and giving him a subtle head-shake. After a conversation between the elder Newsomes held entirely through pointed looks, Marcus rises and, with a sigh, says, "I'll, uh, be right back."

After he leaves and everyone else in the restaurant goes back to their food and conversations, I pour myself some more coffee from the carafe in the center of the table. "Sorry about that. I didn't mean to provoke him."

Betty grabs my hand in my lap. "That was *not* your fault."

"He's been weird all weekend." Trevor rolls his eyes. "All tense-like. And hyper. Like he can't sit still. Like I am before a solo."

Donna pulls the paper ring from her napkin-and-cutlery bundle and folds it as small as she can. "He put a lot into this weekend. He wanted it to go well. And it has, for the most part. Anyway. Let's talk about something else."

None of us has another topic on standby, though, so we entertain ourselves by seeing who can get Georgia to giggle the hardest (Trevor's the best) while we wait for our food to arrive and for Chris and Marcus to return.

During one of Georgia's prolonged giggling fits, Trevor abruptly turns sideways in his chair and faces Betty. "Would it be okay if I emailed you now and then to… keep in touch?"

Betty consults Donna, who nods and smiles.

"I promise not to be a pest."

"I'm not worried one bit about that," she says as she neatly prints her email address on the back of a receipt I've fished from the diaper bag. "I'd love to hear from you. Any time."

"We can be… friends."

"Absolutely. It'll be nice to know what's—"

Before she can finish, our server arrives with our food on one of those mega trays that always makes me feel like a glutton. At the same time, another person in a white shirt and black pants rushes into the dining area, looking wild-eyed and sweaty.

"Excuse me. Is there a Nate Bingham in here? Nate Bingham?"

I'm almost afraid to claim the name, but the panicked expression on the host's face tells me this is no time to play coy.

I stand and half-raise my hand. "That's me."

"A guy outside named Marcus needs you. He's in the parking lot with another guy who collapsed."

Betty and Donna gasp. The host waves me forward and starts to leave without me, so I throw my napkin on the table and rush to catch up with him, glancing back at Betty. "Stay here," I say, strongly suspecting there would be a better chance of winning the lottery than her honoring that request but feeling the need to try, anyway. You can't win if you don't play, right?

When I push through the restaurant's front doors, it's obvious where Chris and Marcus must be, but there's a crowd, too, so I can't see them. "Call 911," I say to the host, trotting ahead of him.

"Already done," he replies. "We have protocol."

I forge through the bodies, repeatedly shouting, "Excuse me!" Finally, I arrive at the patch of blacktop Chris is currently occupying, in the throes of a seizure. The ligaments in his neck, arms, and legs stand out as they flex without ceasing. His normally healthy complexion is gray, his skin shiny with sweat.

My heart pounds. Witnessing a seizure is something I'll never get used to, but my medical training kicks in as I kneel next to Marcus. Staying clear of flailing limbs, I perform a quick visual assessment for any serious injuries. Finding none, I ask, "What happened?"

Marcus's voice shakes when he answers, "I don't know. We were just talking—not even arguing, really—when his eyes rolled back in his head, and he made this awful, demonic noise, and crumpled to the ground, then started doing this." He motions toward our convulsing acquaintance.

Repositioning myself near Chris's flopping shoulders, I gently push him more onto his side than his back, but I act as more of a prop, not gripping any part of him, to avoid causing him—or myself—any inadvertent injury. I keep watch on his face and study the saliva that trickles from his mouth onto the tarmac, examining it for blood or vomit. It's clear, which is a good sign that he didn't bite his tongue, and we don't have to worry that he aspirated any of his stomach contents into his lungs while on his back.

"How long's he been doing this?"

Marcus clambers to his feet and runs his hand over his short scrub of hair. "Forever? It feels like an eternity."

"Longer than three minutes?"

"About that, by now. I'm glad you're here, man. I didn't have any idea what to do. I always heard you should have them bite down on something, but his jaw might as well be wired shut, it's clamped so tight."

"No, you did the right thing by staying out of his way. You could have hurt him—or yourself—by putting anything in his mouth."

Marcus mutters a curse.

"Don't worry. Help is on the way. We'll make sure he doesn't hurt himself, in the meantime."

"Oh, Lord."

I hear Donna's voice, and my head snaps up. Her face pokes through the unfamiliar throng that's still too close.

"Can everyone please back up?" I shout, my adrenaline giving way to annoyance. "Where are the others?" I ask Donna at a normal volume.

She waves ambiguously behind her. "Outside but back there. Betty didn't want to fight through the people with Georgia. Trevor stayed with her."

"You might want to keep Trevor back."

She nods and retreats to the parking lot's perimeter. Marcus goes with her.

When Chris's tremors subside, the crowd wanders off, as if his medical emergency is no longer entertaining enough, which allows me to see the rest of my party. The three Newsomes huddle together, Donna and Marcus consoling a distraught Trevor.

I wave limply at Betty and try to convey a sense of reassuring calm with a slight smile. When her brow remains furrowed and her eyes troubled, I motion her over, and she slowly approaches, gripping tightly to Georgia's hand.

While I wait for them to arrive, I lean over Chris's side and check his pupils for equal reactivity. I also feel around on his torso and limbs for less obvious injuries. Other than some scrapes and bruising, he seems fine. No bumps or other worrisome wounds that would indicate he hit his head or broke anything during his fall. Now if only he'd wake up (although that could take up to an hour) and the paramedics would arrive...

When the girls finally make it to within talking distance, Betty, breathless, releases Georgia, braces her hands against her lower back, and sticks her belly farther forward. "What's up?" she asks, like this is a typical Sunday morning for us.

"Daddy!" Georgia claps her hands, as if I'm down here giving a great performance.

"Hey, baby girl."

"Whatsa madda him?"

"He'll be okay," I say for convenience's sake, taking more liberty with the facts than I would if I were talking to someone old enough to drink from a lidless cup. More for Betty's benefit, I add, "It's just a seizure."

Just a seizure. Right.

But why? I'm definitely more concerned about what brought it on than by the event itself.

"Does Chris have epilepsy?" I ask.

Her nostrils flare as she ponders my question and catches her breath. "Not that he ever told me."

I shake my head and stare at a line of tar patching in the blacktop next to my knee. "Damn. I wonder what the heck...?"

Normal, healthy guys his age don't seize out of the blue. There has to be an impetus, a cause. Sure, he was upset when he left the table, but he wasn't enraged to the point of stroking out or whatever. And stress doesn't bring on seizures unless you're predisposed to them for some reason, as with epileptics. Of course, some prescription—and recreational—drugs can bring on seizures...

On that note, I ask Betty while keeping my eyes on the patient, "Did Chris ever do drugs when you knew him?"

"No! Wait a second... Is that why he's seizing?"

"Maybe. I honestly don't know."

I'd try to reach in his shorts pockets, but one of them is wedged against the ground, and the other is so full of his phone that I can't get my hand in there to check for anything else. I don't want to move him. Plus, it's not the smartest thing in the world to go rooting around in someone's pockets when you're not wearing gloves. If this *is* a drug issue, that's a sure way to get a needle stick. And who knows what this guy's carrying?

I sit back on my heels. "Where the hell's the ambulance? Slowest response time ever," I grumble, then hear the siren in the distance. "Ah. There it is. Finally." I look up at Betty to joke about frequently finding myself on the ground with other guys in her presence, but my grin dies as soon as I see her sweaty, worried face.

It wouldn't be right to abandon the unconscious guy; otherwise, I'd jump up and give her a great, big hug. "Oh, Betts. It's okay. I promise. I didn't mean to scare you with the drug question. He could very well be an epileptic. Just because you aren't aware of that part of his medical history doesn't mean he doesn't have it. He could have developed it in adulthood, even. They'll check him out at the hospital—"

She shakes her head. "It's not that."

"What's wrong? Georgia? She's fine. She doesn't get it. And Trevor... he's a tough, smart kid. As soon as Chris wakes up, and they get a chance to talk, Trevor will be okay."

"No, it's..." She stares down at Chris.

I follow her gaze, searching for anything amiss—other than the fact that he's passed out in a parking lot. "Oh. That. People often urinate during seizures. It's not a big deal. Sure, he'll be embarrassed when he wakes up, but we won't mention it, right?"

"Nate."

"Yeah." I squint up at her, making a visor with my free hand.

"Now's probably not the best time to tell you this, but you should probably know... I'm in labor."

RARELY IN MY LIFE HAVE I EVER EXPERIENCED SUCH A CRAZY mix of emotions. Starting with petrified. Then helpless. Then a whole jumble of stuff like elation, impatience, and worry prompt me to abandon (not-so-gently, I'm afraid) the unconscious man on the pavement, pick up Georgia, and stand in front of my shaking, sweating wife.

After a few seconds, logic and practicality sink in once more, and I ask her, "Are you sure?"

She nods, and a miserable laugh bubbles from her.

I bob my head toward the ambulance screaming into the parking lot. "Well, that one's already reserved for someone else, but maybe you can be his ride-a-long."

It takes only a few seconds to explain the situation to the paramedics, who tell us they can only take one patient at a time, but we'll get to the hospital faster by following them, rather than calling another ambulance. So that's what we do. They load a now-stirring Chris into the back of their rig, I tuck Betty into the front seat and strap Georgia into the back seat of mine, and we scream through the streets, with the Newsomes not far behind.

At the hospital, we split up. Chris and the Newsomes stay in emergency while a nurse escorts us Binghams to maternity. Calling Winn is one of my highest priorities. Without looking at the time or considering what day it is, I step into the hallway, pull him up on my phone and do exactly that while Betty changes into a hospital gown and gets settled.

Playing keep-away with Georgia and the phone, I tell him what's happening but don't have to make any specific requests before he says, "I'll be there in less than two hours. I'm not going to have to listen to the *Frozen* soundtrack all the way home, am I?"

Flooded with relief, I tell him we'll hang onto that for our own return drive, and we disconnect.

I press my forehead to Georgia's, close my eyes, and take a deep breath. "Santa Winn is coming to town."

"Santa Winn?" Georgia parrots. When I nod, she says, "Yay!"

A couple of hours later, as I transfer Georgia's stuff from our trunk to Laurel's minivan, I'm too preoccupied with getting back upstairs to Betty, and Georgia's too excited to go on an adventure that ends at one of her favorite places, the Bakers' house, for us to perform the usual separation anxiety routine.

I kiss her on the head after buckling her into her newly installed seat in the van and slide the door closed. Turning to Winn, I say, "Thanks for doing this. I—" I chuckle. "It's been a helluva morning."

"I'll say. And don't mention it, Yank. You pulled me away from one of the reverend's longest-winded sermons in recent memory."

"Aw, man. You were in church?"

"Every Sunday."

"Is that what today is?"

"Yep. It's also your kid's birthday."

I grin, the joy expanding in my chest again. "Yeah. Well, here's hoping. You remember how labor can drag out."

"I don't envy you the next few hours. Speakin' of, you better get back to your better half."

I stick out my hand for him to shake, but he pulls me to him for a hug, instead. Without hesitation, I return his back-thumping embrace, not caring that my eyes are suddenly juicier than a stifling Carolina summer day. When we part, his eyes are no Vegas desert, either.

Clearing his throat, he rounds the back of the van. "Give Betty our love, ya hear?"

"Absolutely." I follow him to the driver's side and blow one more kiss into the back seat from his open window as he turns the key in the ignition.

"Don't you worry about your two-footer, either. She's in good hands with us."

"That's why I called you." I sniff and dash the last of the moisture from my eyes with the heels of my hands. "Okey dokey, then. See you in a couple of days. Oh, shit! Reba..."

"We got 'er. You focus on what's goin' on here. Keep us posted. We want pictures! And y'all be careful comin' home."

He takes off, and I move my car into long-term parking, calling Mom and Dad in the process to get them up to speed. Mom gushes about what a great story this will be for the little guy or gal someday and promises to call Nick to spread the word.

On the way back to maternity, I take a detour to the bathroom to scrub the parking lot grime more fully from my arms and legs and splash some water on my face. My final stop is the cafeteria, where I grab a cup of coffee and a banana, which I scarf in the elevator. Betty won't be able to eat, and it would be cruel to eat in front of her. But I also don't want to pass out during delivery because my blood sugar's all out of whack, and I haven't eaten since those strawberries last night.

By the time I return, I've been gone about forty minutes. Tops.

Apparently, a lot can happen in forty minutes.

"There he is!" one of the seemingly three hundred people packed into the delivery suite says when I come to a gobs-macked halt in the open doorway.

Betty, her feet in stirrups, her knees to her chest, and her hands braced behind her knees, glances over at me and says, "Is that coffee for me?"

Oh, good. She's still joking. I'm not a dead man.

I toss the nearly full cup in the nearest trash can and pass through the parting sea of surgical smocked strangers to get to the head of her bed, immediately defending myself. "When I left, you were at, like, a seven, and they told us we had hours still!"

She winces as a contraction builds. "Hang on. A little busy here," she says in a pinched voice while the unfamiliar man between her legs tells her to push.

"Yeah," I say faintly. Watching this makes me feel more impotent than a seventy-year-old before his bedtime dose of Viagra.

A nurse appears at my side. "You okay there, Dad? You're not a fainter, are you?"

I shake my head.

"If you are, speak up now so we can get a chair over here."

"I'm fine," I snap. "I just— I stopped to use the bathroom and eat a banana."

She pats my arm. "Well, bless your heart, Sugar. It's okay. You made it in time. Barely."

Betty collapses against the pillows and turns her head toward me, smiling tiredly. "Anyway," she says, picking up right where we left off, "You left to take Georgia to Winn, and I felt fine. Well, not *fine*, but as good as could be expected. The epidural was finally kicking in, and... Yeah."

"You still look uncomfortable."

"There's a ton of pressure. So much. Like, eye-bulging."

I nod and transfer a strand of sweaty hair from the side of her face to behind her ear.

"But you weren't gone twenty minutes, and I felt like I needed to push. Big-time. Like, if I could move my legs, I would have crossed them. I called the nurse in here, and she checked and said, 'Oh, Lawsy. Well, hello there, little one.'"

In spite of the overall vicarious horror I'm experiencing, I laugh. "Oh, no."

"Oh, yes. The head was right there. Things have happened fast since then."

I kiss the top of her hair. "I'm so sorry. I was talking to Winn, and then I—"

"It's not a big deal. I mean, now that you're here. I was freaking out for a bit, though, knowing how disappointed you'd be if you missed this—" Her veins stand out in her neck, and blood floods her face. "OhhhhhhIhavetopushagain!"

The doctor nods at us, so I say, "Go, then," and count her up to ten.

When we get there, she says, purple-faced, "Not done," and after a quick breath, continues for a few more beats.

"Okay, okay. Stop!" The doctor says, grabbing the bulb syringe being pressed against his shoulder by the nurse behind him. I step down the bed a few feet and crane my neck to watch him suction the baby's nose and mouth.

Betty pants behind me.

"Oh, Betts..."

"What? What's wrong?"

"Nothing. Nothing. She... he... whatever... This Fish is a keeper."

She laughs, and the doctor says, "Whoa, whoa, whoa. Careful now. The shoulders are next, and I don't want you to tear, so no laughing, sneezing, coughing, or pushing too hard while we work 'em out. Got that?"

I return to Betty's head and kiss her nose while she pants and waits for the doctor to give her the final go-ahead. When he does, I say, "Ready?"

She sets her jaw. "Let's do this."

31

DAD TO DAD TO DAD

IT'S NOT UNTIL A FEW HOURS LATER, WHEN BETTY WONDERS aloud how Chris is doing, that I remember other people exist in this world outside of this room. For a while now, I've been all about Betty and my new son, Henry. And occasionally whoever else wanders through here and interrupts our bonding session.

And now she has to mention *him*.

She holds out her arms toward the baby and me and wiggles her fingers. "Maybe you should give me a turn holding my own child and go see if you can find out anything."

I groan. "Awwww, Betts. I don't wanna."

She laughs. "C'mon. I'm worried about him! And you were, too, until I told you I was in labor."

"I'm over it now."

"Liar."

I sigh. Truth is, I am still curious about what caused Chris's seizure. But if it's a choice between leaving this room to satisfy that curiosity and staying here with my wife and new son, there's no contest.

She clears her throat impatiently. "Hand him over, baby

hog." When I don't budge, she clenches her teeth. "Don't make me come over there, Nathaniel."

"Can you feel your legs yet?"

"Not really."

"Then I'm not worried." Still, I rise from the glider rocker and carry the warm, fragrant bundle to her. Before depositing him in her arms, though, I pull him back a few inches. "This is only temporary. I'll be right back."

"I *will* get my legs back eventually, and if you don't start sharing, I'll use them to kick you in an extremely sensitive place. Making masterpieces like this little guy will be a distant memory."

"Not nice." With a final kiss against Henry's long fingers, I relinquish him to his mother. "But I love you anyway." I drop a peck on her forehead, too.

"Mmm-hmm. Call Chris."

"Okay, okay. I'm going!"

I step into the hall but backtrack at the last second to get one more glimpse of the two of them. My reward is the heart-melting sight of Betty, eyes closed, pressing her nose, then her cheek, to the top of Henry's knit-hat-covered head. It takes everything I have to back away then turn toward the plush family waiting room at the end of the hall to make my calls. I could stand there and watch them all day.

But I promised. And the sooner I do this, the sooner I can get back to them.

The waiting room is empty, so I have my choice of any of the chairs or sofas, but I prefer to stand by the windows, looking down on the resort-like hospital grounds. This place is incredible. I hope our insurance covers our impromptu stay. That slightly petty worry niggles at the corner of my mind as I mentally compose a text to Chris. Finally, after much deliberation, I tap into my phone, *An update for an update?* hoping to get some response. And soon.

Ten long minutes later, when I'm starting to worry I'll have to take my chances with sweet-talking someone at the guest services desk downstairs, the device dings in my hand.

Marcus here. Is this Nate?

A bit puzzled by that response (Who else would it be? Surely, I'm saved as a contact in Chris's phone, as much as we've communicated via text), I chuckle and type back, *Yes...*

Just checking. Wasn't sure you were Mr. Barfity Barf Barf Wonderful.

Nice. Suddenly, I'm not as interested in this guy's wellbeing. Then again, that's not as bad as some of the things I've privately called Chris, so I guess we're even.

Ha! That fits. How's Chris?

There's a long pause, then I receive, *You go first. How's Betty?*

Great! It's a healthy boy fish.

Congrats! You somewhere you can talk? I'll call you. Or we can meet up.

This does not bode well. Thing is, though, I still haven't eaten. I held Henry so Betty could eat a hot meal (yeah, that's why I volunteered to hold him) and told her I'd go down to the cafeteria and grab something as soon as she was done, but that never happened. Basic needs like hunger haven't seemed all that pressing. But now that I've stepped away, I've broken the appetite suppressing spell of euphoria and could murder something substantial. Plus, Marcus would need special clearance to come up to this floor with its fancy-schmancy security measures for new moms and babies, so I reply, *I'll meet you down in the cafeteria in 10 minutes*

Sure? I don't want to pull you away

Guy's gotta eat. See you in a few

I tuck my phone in my back pocket, and on my way past

our room to the elevators, I poke my head in to tell Betty where I'm going. She's sound asleep, head back, mouth gaping. Henry blinks up at her from her arms, like he's trying to figure out what's going on.

"Oh, geez." I hurry into the room and gently lift him.

Betty jerks. "I'm awake!"

"No, you're not," I say with a chuckle. "And I should be mad at you, but you two are too cute."

"It's still my turn!"

When I place him in the bassinet, she kicks up more of a fuss, mostly for show, before relaxing against her pillows.

"I'm going downstairs to talk to Marcus about Chris. He didn't want to text the update to 'Mr. Barfity Barf Barf Wonderful.'"

"What?"

"Apparently, that's what I'm called in Chris's phone. Asshole."

She snickers. "I'd love to hear your ringtone."

"I can only imagine. Anyway... Figured I'd get something to eat while Marcus gives me the latest."

"I was hoping Chris had been discharged by now. Is it a bad sign that he hasn't?"

I don't want her to worry, so I smile and shrug. "Ah. I'm sure everything's fine. Probably a precautionary measure, especially if this is the first time he's ever had a seizure. Tests take time."

Her raised eyebrow tells me she's not buying any of this malarkey. I rush on, "Anyway, as long as Henry's content, you should get some rest. Any minute now, he's going to figure out how to use that voice of his to make us do whatever he wants. Until then, sleep."

She nods. "Okay. Don't be long, though. I'm really worried."

"Don't worry."

"You telling me not to worry never makes me worry less. In fact, that's when I worry more."

"I'll be back soon." I point to her. "Don't hold that baby while you sleep."

She pulls the starchy sheets higher on her chest and sticks her tongue out at me. "You're not the boss of me, Nathaniel."

Duh. Everyone knows that.

* * *

LIMITING portion control during dinner is easy with Marcus sitting across the table from me in the hospital cafeteria, updating me on Chris's condition. When he tells me the seizure was a result of cocaine use, my appetite flees as suddenly as it had returned.

"He says he's an addict, and the only thing that's going to fix it is another stint in rehab."

I set down my fork and wipe my mouth on my napkin, then throw it on my plate. Marcus apologizes, but I wave him off. After all, it isn't *his* fault. And my gut told me it had to be something like that. In my heart, though, I was still harboring the hope that Chris had a legitimate medical condition none of us knew about, because... well, we don't know him, period.

"How many stints have there been?" I ask Marcus.

So quietly, that I have to strain to hear him, he answers, "Several, apparently," while staring at his fingers woven together on the table in front of him.

"How's Trevor?"

"Shaken up. Donna took him back to the hotel. He wasn't happy about that. He wanted to stay with Chris and show his support."

I curse under my breath.

Marcus nods his concurrence. "Yeah. This day's been one long public service announcement, for all of us. On the one hand, I have this overwhelming desire to protect my son from witnessing such an ugly, horrible thing. On the other hand, I want to hold him there and make him watch, show him what happens when 'an occasional good time' turns into a lifestyle and hurts the people around you, destroying your life and your health."

"You're still here, though. What does that mean?"

"It means I didn't feel right leaving him all alone in an unfamiliar city during this crisis."

I run my thumb along my wedding ring and realize that even if Betty and I weren't stuck here because of our own situation, I'd still feel obligated, like Marcus, to see this through, too.

"Are they keeping him here? Do they have a rehab clinic on this campus?"

"Yes and no. There's an outpatient facility nearby affiliated with the hospital. His attorney is trying to convince him to check himself in there voluntarily when he's discharged. He wants to get out of here and make arrangements at the place he's gone to before, but there are some legal things slowing down the process. And because he seized, they want to keep him at least overnight for observation."

"Maybe that's for the best, anyway. Sounds like his designer rehab center isn't exactly working out for him."

Marcus laughs. "I thought the same thing. But it's not my place. I'm just glad he's doing *something.*" He pauses while I stare at the potted plant next to our table and scratch the rough stubble poking along my jaw. Then he says, "I also stayed, because I... I wanted to make sure Chris left you and Betty alone."

My head snaps up. "What do you mean?"

"I didn't want him texting you and generally intruding on your special day. That's why I still have his cell phone." He digs it from his pocket and holds it up. "And I only felt comfortable leaving him when we found out how tight security is on the maternity ward. Donna and Trevor tried to visit you guys before they left, with no luck."

"Oh. Yeah." I lift my arm with the computer chip bracelet around my wrist that syncs up with the bracelets on Betty and Henry. "They scan this thing every time I fart."

He laughs. "That's good. But I wanted to make doubly sure."

"Does he know you're down here talking to Mr. Barfity Barf Barf Wonderful?"

"Yes. And he wants to talk to you, too."

I say nothing at first while I picture that actually happening. I'm not particularly interested in listening to the excuses —and possibly more lies—of an addict.

Into my hesitation, Marcus says, "I told him that might not be the best idea, but I'd pass along the message."

I laugh but impulsively decide, "Why not?"

"Well, I can imagine a few reasons."

"Yeah, me too. But I'm feeling generous. You know, I've had a decent day, overall." I grin and stand for good. "Have him text or call me when he's ready. I need to get back upstairs. Betty's worried about that idiot. Which pisses me off, you know?"

"Me, too. This should be a happy day."

"I know he didn't orchestrate this health crisis of his, but he *did* cause it, directly, through his choices and behavior."

"Most health crises can be attributed to that, though. We still sympathize with someone who has a heart attack, no matter how many burgers we've seen them eat."

His gentle reminder makes me sigh. "People don't have to

break the law and put other people in danger to feed their burger addictions."

"Yet."

"Plus, he was a massive douche on more than one occasion this weekend. He'll probably blame that on the drugs, too, but it made an already-stressful meeting even more awkward."

"I'm so sorry about that. We had no idea—"

"None of us did! It's not your fault." I ruffle my hair and shake my head. "If anything, I'm kicking myself. I saw the warning signs. But I've had selfish reasons to believe the worst of this guy from Day One, so I didn't trust my gut. And I didn't know him well enough to recognize his behavior was uncharacteristic. It wasn't until Trevor mentioned something about it at breakfast... Even then, I figured the stress of the weekend was making him act out. Some medical professional I am."

He waves away my self-criticism. "You're a good guy, Nate. Good guys give people the benefit of the doubt, even when they don't deserve it."

I laugh, considering the not-so-nice thoughts I'm having about Chris right now.

As if reading my mind, Marcus says, "I'd be glad to be there when you talk to him."

"Nah. It's best if there are no witnesses." I wink when he looks worried. "I'll make sure he's okay, physically, hear what he has to say to me, and leave it at that. I just want him to go away, to be honest."

Marcus stands and shakes my hand. "You have our support with that. Donna and I will still keep in touch with him, for Trevor's sake, but as far as Betty's contact with us, it'll only be with Trevor, Donna, and me."

"I appreciate that."

"And congratulations on the new baby. That's the best take-away from today, for sure."

I grin. "He's amazing, to say the least." I clear my throat and lift my tray. "You mentioned that Trevor wanted to see Betty and Henry..."

"Yeah, well... Email us some pictures."

"I'll have to check with her, of course, but we *could* meet up somewhere on our way out of town. Should be sometime tomorrow afternoon or evening, I'd imagine, barring any complications."

"If it's not any trouble..."

"It's not. At all. It won't be a long visit, or anything, but the least we can do is ease Trevor's mind and let him know we're still... friends."

Marcus nods and follows me to put up my tray then walks with me from the cafeteria. "That would be nice. Give us a heads up when you're about to be discharged, and we'll figure it out."

"Sounds like a plan."

* * *

BETTY TOOK the news about Chris's ongoing addiction better than I thought she would, which is probably more appropriately than I am. For some reason, I'm taking it personally, like it was all part of a larger plan to disrupt my life. That makes no sense and is a rather narcissistic view on the situation, but that's where I am right now. We moved more than a thousand miles from family members who weren't the best for us to be around all the time; now this guy crashes into our lives and manages to insert himself into my son's birth story. Incredible.

Obviously, I'm well-versed in the medical facts regarding addiction. I'm also fluent in the psychology of it. That makes me highly sympathetic and diplomatic about the issue... in a theoretical sense. When the problem gets this close to my wife and kids, though, it's a whole other story. No, this guy has to go. And the sooner the better.

Betty agrees, with some stipulations. "It would be one thing if we were part of his support system, if he was relying on us to help get through this, but we're not. He's not. If he ever comes to me and says, 'Betty, I need you and Nate to help me,' I'm there. Otherwise, this is something he needs to get through with the help of his true friends and family."

Since we're on the same page there, I only feel slightly guilty when I conveniently neglect to tell her about my visit to Chris. She doesn't need to worry about that. Instead, she deserves to be relaxed and happy, nursing Henry, focused on positive things. Powder-nose Chris isn't going to intrude on another single second of this momentous day for her; not if I have anything to say about it.

I'm resolved to keep things polite and matter-of-fact at this bedside tête-à-tête. Any sign of escalation and I'm out of here. There's nobody available to bail me out of jail. Plus, the only thing this guy deserves from me is pity. I'm not willing to give him anything else.

Therefore, when he looks up at my knock on his door, sets aside his book, and leads with, "Thanks for agreeing to talk to me," I simply reply, "You're welcome," and wait for him to get on with it.

Careful not to tangle the wires of the monitoring devices attached to him, he rises and moves to a chair by the window, motioning for me to join him in the other one next to it. I'd rather not get too comfortable, but towering over him while he talks might be misconstrued as a power display, so I sit, bracing my elbows on my knees.

Shoulders slumped, he stares at his hands in his gown-covered lap. "I know it's been a long day, and you have more important things going on. Marcus told me you and Betty had a boy. Congratulations, man."

"Thanks. She did all the work, but I'm still proud of the outcome."

He looks over at me. "And they're both okay? You still had a couple of weeks to go, I thought."

"They're fine, thanks."

"Good. Good. Well, I won't keep you long. I just wanted to..." He swallows audibly. "Apologize, you know? For everything. And thank you for helping out when I— Anyway..."

I recall my part in the parking lot drama that seems more like a lifetime ago than a mere twelve hours in the past and shake my head. "Other than making sure you didn't hurt yourself, I didn't do much.

"That was plenty, though. And it's not easy to witness something like that, either."

"This isn't the first time it's happened, then?"

He picks at his cuticles. "No. When I started to come to in the back of the ambulance, I knew exactly what had happened."

"How are you feeling now?"

"Groggy." He smiles sadly. "And having some fierce withdrawals. Other than that, I'll be fine."

We speak at the same time.

"Betty's worried about you."

"Listen, Nate, I..."

I raise my eyebrows, waiting to see if he'll choose to finish his statement or respond to mine.

"Oh. I figured. She always did worry about me. And Frankie. And everyone around her. Tried to act like she didn't care much, but she did. Which is why it never made sense that she thought she'd be a bad mom. She was a mom to every friend—and boyfriend—she ever had. And that's why I want to say I'm glad she found someone to take care of her, for once."

"I try. When she lets me."

"That's the thing. I guess you've figured it out, how to be what she needs without making her admit she needs it. I could never strike that balance. Maybe because I always wanted to take credit for being the big hero, the big problem solver."

"She's not a huge fan of that."

"Nope. In fact, she has no idea you're here right now, does she?"

"Hell, no."

We grin at each other like idiots.

"What are you supposedly doing?"

"Getting some overnight stuff from our car. Oh, and running to the nearest open store to grab a simple outfit for the baby for tomorrow. But I'll get that from the hospital gift shop and save myself some time... and gas."

"You're good."

"I'm learning. More and more every day. Not that it's about manipulating her or lying or whatever."

"Nooooo..." He snorts.

"No, really! It's like you said: she *prefers* a more subtle approach."

Still laughing, Chris stands, and I jump to my feet, too. He holds out his hand, which I shake, surprised our talk is already over. "Well, Nate, it was... interesting—and advantageous, in my case—meeting you. I suppose it's too much to hope we'll wind up friends..."

"Not likely," I admit as lightly as possible.

"Fair enough. Tell Boop I said goodbye... for good, this time."

"I will." When I summon the nerve to tell her this conversation happened.

He lets go of my hand and sighs.

Feeling decidedly dismissed and anxious to run my errands so I can return to Betty, I stride to the door, a million things going through my mind in the few seconds it takes for me to travel the short distance.

At the door, I turn and say, "Hey."

He pauses while returning to the bed, as if he can't simultaneously move and listen.

"Get better... for good this time."

He shoots me a sloppy salute. "I'll try, Nurse."

Ah. There's the anger I've been expecting to join us this whole time. Fashionably late, I suppose.

I chuckle bitterly. "You'll try."

"Yep. That's the best I can do." He tucks his feet under the sheet and blanket and picks up his book, holding it open at his place.

Blinking at his weak promise, I scratch my head and debate whether it's worth my breath to even say what's on my mind. Probably not. But I'm going to, anyway. "This isn't just about you anymore."

He rests his book facedown on his lap but stares straight ahead at the clock on the wall.

"The minute you decided to meet with Trevor, you made this bigger than you. Do you get that?"

"Yeah. I get it, Ward Cleaver. And like I said, I'm going to try to beat this. But I've been here enough times before to understand it's not as simple as willpower."

"You owe it to that kid to make it that simple this time."

Finally, he turns his head to look at me. "Are you always this insufferably sanctimonious? Because seriously, if that's the case, I'm surprised Betty isn't still hittin' the bottle. Although maybe she is. I looked for the signs, but maybe she's gotten better at hiding it. It's pretty socially unacceptable to booze it up when you're pregnant or nursing."

I take several steps toward his bed but stop myself, clenching my fists at my side.

He laughs. "Oh, sure. Slug the guy in the dress who's attached to a bunch of machines."

Punching hurts. I was going to strangle him. Instead, I take a deep breath and blow it back out while looking up at the ceiling. Then I lower my chin and head for the door for good. "Well, uh, don't worry. Marcus, Donna, Betty, and I will be there for Trevor when you abandon him for real this time."

"Screw you, man! You don't know me."

How I wish that were true! "Good luck, dude," I toss over my shoulder. My hands shake as I hit the button to call the elevator, so I jam them in my pockets.

There are only two people in this place I actually care about, and neither of them are on this floor.

32

GOODBYE AND HELLO

FOR SOMEONE IN SUCH A HURRY TO ENTER THE WORLD, Henry has been relatively chill since then, taking in his surroundings like a wise old man who already realizes the only thing in life guaranteed to stay the same is the world's insistence upon regularly changing. He changes rooms, he changes clothes, he changes diapers. He moves from one breast to the other, from one feeding to the next. He falls asleep in one person's arms and wakes up in another's. Or in a car. And all with just enough complaint to let us know he's capable of it, if pressed.

I can't stop marveling at him. I might be worse about it this time than I was with Georgia. And I couldn't have fathomed that was possible. But with her, the amazement at being a new dad to someone so perfect was tinged by the constant terror I was going to screw it up. Maybe not that day or the next or the next, but eventually. And I was always on guard, waiting for that moment to arrive.

On the other hand, her arrival in our lives was so unplanned, so effortless. One minute, I was sad and single, the next I was content and married and paternal. She was a miracle, for sure, but one I didn't have to work for.

This guy... He almost never was. But now that he is, I can't remember when he wasn't. And when I contemplate how close we were to letting the fear of another heartbreak rob us of ever meeting him... Let's just say this kid's not wanting for kisses and cuddles. Or anything. He's loved beyond measure.

Not that the amount of love I feel for him is greater than what I feel for Georgia (you can't quantify "infinity"), nor is it a different love ("unconditional" has only one brand), but my reaction to the emotion has changed—toward both of my children. And Betty, too. I'm no longer afraid of feeling it to its full extent. Or showing it.

I don't give a damn what anyone outside of this love bubble thinks of me. They consider me over-the-top? Whatever. They suppose I should tone it down? Too bad. They think I'm "insufferably sanctimonious"? Don't care. They figure I'm setting myself—and my family—up for disappointment when this level of caring can't be sustained or matched outside of our home? Screw them. I'm sick of trying to anticipate what the rest of the world is going to throw at us and letting that dictate how *I* live.

This is my life. This. Mine. There is no, "Well, *eventually* I see myself (insert a bunch of theoretical bullshit that reads like a fifties sitcom script and ends with 'and they lived happily ever after')." This *is* the happily ever after. If I want it to be.

And I do. Man, I do. I am ready for it.

This is also the beginning, though. And the messy middle. I don't expect everything from here on out to be easy or perfect or untouched by outside influence. It's still life. But I'm owning it. And I have Henry to thank for it. He was born, and I held him, and it *hit* me: *This is it.*

I hope that's how Donna and Marcus felt the first time

they held Trevor. I hope my brother's felt it with at least one of his kids. I hope I gave my own parents that feeling at one time or another. My wish for every person on the planet is to experience it at some time. And not necessarily as a result of holding their child—not everyone is as lucky (or so inclined) to do so. But if everyone was filled with that sense of purpose, of belonging, at least once in their life, we'd have a much more satisfied world population.

Maybe that's not realistic, but it *is* possible. And those of us who have been blessed enough to feel it need to commit it to memory and recognize more often what a freaking gift it is. Don't focus on that hangnail or the piles of dog crap that need to be picked up in the yard. Don't treat life like something that needs to be endured, merely putting one foot in front of the other over and over until you reach your destination: death. Life is about life.

That might not sound like much of an epiphany for some (normal) folks, but it's been a game-changer for me.

I hate to admit it—and I never will to the man, himself (because I'm not *that* much of a Mr. Barfity-Barf-Barf Wonderful)—but meeting Chris opened my eyes to a few things, too. I try not to take Betty for granted, but I'm a guy, and I'm human, and while I'm more in love with my wife than ever, an all-consuming constant state of infatuation isn't something you can sustain in a long-term relationship. The fact that I'm in a position to take someone like her for granted, however, makes me feel like the luckiest guy in the world.

Chris could have been—almost was—that guy instead. Then who knows where I'd be? I can't contemplate it. The only Coke habit I can afford comes in red cans and rots your teeth.

"In two thousand feet, merge right to take the exit and arrive at your destination on the right."

"You can turn that off now," I say to Betty about the GPS on her phone. "I can figure out how to get there from here, considering I have the rest area in my sights."

"I like her voice. It's soothing."

"Arriving at your destination."

"See? Isn't it good to be validated? We made it!"

I peer through the windshield, searching for the Newsomes. When I spot their rental, I pull into the parking space beside it, and three people emerge from the vehicle. Before I push the button to put our car in park, three faces press against the back windows, and three simultaneous "Awww!"s come from those faces.

"I think they like him," I say, squeezing Betty's hand.

She opens her door. "Well, who wouldn't?"

One person immediately pops to mind, but we'll find out for sure in a couple of hours.

The Newsomes and Betty form a circle around me as I heft the infant carrier from its base and hold it in front of me at chest height somewhat like a human Lion King, presenting my new son to his adoring onlookers.

Donna whispers, "So tiny!"

Marcus chuckles. "That hair sure looks familiar."

Trevor nudges his index finger underneath Henry's open hand and grins when the baby reflexively makes a fist around it. "His hand feels so soft, like it's not even really skin but more like silk." He looks up at Betty and nods at her midriff. "I can't believe he was in *there* the last time I saw you. That's so weird to think about."

Betty laughs. "I guess it would be if you didn't see the transition from inside to outside."

"And I'm totally okay with that." He glances nervously at me. "If you have a video on your phone, I don't want to see it.

It was bad enough watching the one at school a couple of years ago."

"It happened too fast for us to take a video, anyway."

Donna says, "Georgia's going to love him."

"We'll see," Betty and I reply together, then laugh at our concurrence.

"She will," Marcus promises. "And she'll be his greatest protector throughout life, too. You watch."

It didn't work out that way with Nick and me, but it's not worth arguing the point. I merely smile and say, "Here's hoping."

While Betty gives Donna and Trevor hugs and reinforces her promises to stay in touch through email, I step aside with Marcus and say, "Chris?"

"Checked into rehab this morning. Medical tests from yesterday came back okay."

"I hope his treatment is successful, wherever it is."

"Me, too. For everyone's sake." Marcus smiles down at Henry when the baby stretches and yawns in his seat.

Betty notices the stirring infant. "We better get going so we can make some progress before he wants to eat again."

After one more round of hugs and goodbyes, we hit the road, headed back to our new normal, one that will be forever shaped by the events of this weekend.

* * *

KIDS ARE UNPREDICTABLE. But we already know that. We know it well. Still, unpredictable unpredictability can throw one for a loop.

Therefore, when Georgia doesn't even blink upon seeing Betty carrying Henry into the Bakers' house in a sling, but instead leads her mother to the couch and pats it, saying,

"Feed da baby," I'm unsure how to respond or react. It puts me on guard, definitely. What's her game? Do almost-three-year-olds play mind games? Not any I've ever met, but that doesn't mean it's not possible.

Betty and I exchange glances—mine nervous, hers bemused—before she takes Georgia up on her invitation and sits on the couch, saying, "He doesn't need to eat right now, but we can sit so you can get a better look at him."

"Yes!"

Laurel and Winn look on like proud parents, giving me the distinct impression I'm standing on the outside of an inside joke.

"What's going on?" I mutter to Winn from the side of my mouth.

His lips lift in a Mona Lisa smile. "Laurel and I have been workin' with her. We show her the pictures you sent from the hospital and tell her about her little brother and how she needs to be a big helper."

"Yeah?"

I keep my eye on the action on the couch, ready to spring at the first sign of violence. But Georgia's all cordiality, "helping" Betty adjust the nursing pillow, tossing the discarded sling so it's out of their way and so she can see every bit of her new sibling in the flesh. So she can kill him?

My innards bubble with barely contained anxiety.

Still not looking away, I say, "We worked with her—*a lot*—to prepare her, and... she beheaded one of her dolls during our last try."

Winn laughs. "Well, she gets it now."

"How can you be sure?"

"Because I told her that Santa Winn only visits nice little boys and girls." He raises an eyebrow at me and smirks.

"You threatened her with no Christmas?"

"Yes."

"Oh, geez. That's going to be a fun one to enforce."

"Yank, listen to me, buddy. You have to employ every trick if you're gonna get out of this thing alive."

"'This thing,' meaning?"

"Parenthood! When reasoning doesn't work—and it rarely does with toddlers—you have to pull out the big guns. Santa. Jesus. Grandma and Grandpa. Kids don't care what their moms and dads think. They know we'll always love 'em. Because we're idiots and show our hand on that right away."

I sigh.

"Which is only right, I agree," he continues. "But that doesn't leave us with much leverage when it comes to terrorist negotiations, now, does it?"

"'Terrorist negotiations'!"

"They're two-foot terrorists, admit it. Only difference is, they're cute, and they don't have the fine motor skills to operate weapons. But given the choice between eatin' their lima beans and suicide, most of them would gladly strap on that bomb vest on any given night."

I chuckle. "In summary, you showed her some pictures and threatened to cancel Christmas."

"*And* I told her you'd bring her a sucker from work every day, as long as she doesn't hurt her brother."

He nods and waves to Pat and Rob, who have just arrived and are skirting the couch as if witnessing and trying not to spook two wild animals that are sniffing each other out.

"Winn! That's..."

"Look!" He gestures toward the peaceful couch, where Betty and the baby are finally settled, and Georgia's leaning over to kiss—not kill—Henry. "Results. You can thank me later."

"I'll send you the dentist's bill, too."

"Those baby teeth gonna fall out, anyway."

He has a point there.

Betty, as vigilant as I am for impending disaster, asks without looking at me, "Nate, are you getting pictures of any of this?"

"Oh!" I spring into action, pulling my phone from my pocket. "Sorry. I was keeping my hands free for emergency toddler extraction duties."

Laurel laughs. "I got some good ones, don't worry. I'll send them to you later." She waves me toward the couch. "Now you get in there, so I can get some with all y'all."

After getting hugs and congratulations from Rob and Pat, I do as I'm told and sit next to Betty. Georgia immediately crawls over her mom's knees to get to my lap. "Daddy, wook! A new bwuvvuh."

"He's pretty cool, isn't he? But his head does *not* pop back on, so you have to be nicer to him than your dollies."

She wrinkles her nose and lifts her upper lip in a sneer. "He not a dolly; he da baby!"

"Right. That's what I'm—"

"Siwwy Daddy. Be nice, or nooooooo Santa Winn."

"Oh. Okay. Got it. I'll keep that in mind."

"Look up here!" Laurel says, waving toward herself.

Winn stands behind her, sticks out his tongue, and crosses his eyes, then shouts, "Daddy farted!" at the same time Laurel snaps the picture.

Our first official family photo features a startled newborn, a laughing father, a grinning mother, and a giggling girl. None of us has our eyes open.

It's perfect.

ACKNOWLEDGMENTS

I had to work hard to get into the mind of a man in *Let's Be Frank*. It was frighteningly easy and comfortable in the subsequent books. Therefore, it was difficult to say goodbye.

Many people made it easier, though, starting with loyal readers. You put your zeal for the continuation of the story before your dread of it ending. It may seem like a minor thing, but it's not. It was huge. It reminded me the story wasn't over yet, and I had a lot of fun, exciting, hard work left to do. Moreover, you let me know that people were waiting! That got me up at 4:30 a.m. more effectively than any alarm clock some days.

Those most excited were my beta readers. Erin Baker, Nicole Ford, Elizabeth Jenkins, Lynda G., Natasha Walsh, Hans Campbell, Karen Richmond, and Bethany Dodson, you poured hours into your diligent studies of the book and responded with insightful questions and suggestions. This feedback significantly impacted some parts of the story, resulting in the kind of send-off Nurse Nate (and the other characters in the trilogy) deserved. Thank you, betas!

Thanks to Maggie Sokolik, Dorothy Zemach, and the

entire Wayzgoose Press team for their enthusiastic refresh of the cover, back blurb, and overall presentation. Nurse Nate has never felt so appreciated or spiffy!

As usual, without the support, encouragement, and understanding of all of my friends and family, I'd be nothing. My husband picks up more slack—and dirty laundry—than any spouse should have to pick up. Not to mention, he makes me laugh and feeds me and tells me I'm smart. Thanks, Clint! My friends regularly remind me that real people are even more interesting than paper people, and that's saying something. Love you guys! And my family never lets me forget I'm just the nerdy second-youngest child in a large group of talented, funny, interesting people who love me, despite knowing every single embarrassing thing I've ever done or said. I love you all!

More specifically, my mom is my biggest fan, in writing and in life. Mom, you love me unconditionally (not an easy feat). When I feel like giving up, you always know the right thing to say, and you defend me from my biggest critic, myself. Your faith in me and, more importantly, in God, is an inspiration. Thank you! Love you more.

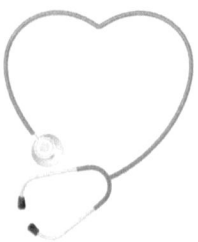